OUR
KIND *of*
PEOPLE

CAROL WALLACE

G. P. PUTNAM'S SONS ❖ NEW YORK

PUTNAM
— EST. 1838 —

G. P. PUTNAM'S SONS
Publishers Since 1838
An imprint of Penguin Random House LLC
penguinrandomhouse.com

Library of Congress Cataloging-in-Publication Data

Names: Wallace, Carol, 1955– author.
Title: Our kind of people / Carol Wallace.
Description: New York : G. P. Putnam's Sons, 2022. |
Identifiers: LCCN 2021040575 (print) | LCCN 2021040576 (ebook) |
ISBN 9780525540021 (trade paperback) | ISBN 9780525541684 (ebook)
Subjects: LCGFT: Novels.
Classification: LCC PS3573.A42563 O97 2022 (print) |
LCC PS3573.A42563 (ebook) | DDC 813/.54—dc23
LC record available at https://lccn.loc.gov/2021040575
LC ebook record available at https://lccn.loc.gov/2021040576

Printed in the United States of America
1st Printing

Book design by Lorie Pagnozzi

*In loving memory of the world's best
mother-in-law, Peggy Hamlin*

OUR KIND *of* PEOPLE

CHAPTER 1

---◆---

THE LADIES LUNCH

May 1874

Helen Wilcox peered from her motionless carriage at the clock on the steeple of Grace Church and took a deep breath. It was noon. Six ladies would be arriving at her house on West Twenty-Sixth Street in half an hour for a luncheon to meet her elder daughter, Jemima. Six powerful ladies—the women who would decide whether Jemima would be invited to attend the highly exclusive Dancing Classes in the fall. Helen came from a family with deep roots in New York society, but the committee was known to be quixotic, eager to pounce on slights and improprieties. And here Helen sat, trapped in the chaotic traffic of Fourth Avenue as it inched toward Union Square. No experienced New York City hostess chose to run an errand the morning before she entertained guests to luncheon. But to Cook's horror the rhubarb custard hadn't even begun to set, so after a hasty consultation Helen had set out in the carriage to the French pastry-cook's shop downtown. She now sat with a box of *mille-feuilles* on the seat beside her, counting down the minutes until her guests were due to arrive.

She rapped on the hatch in the roof of the carriage, which flipped open. The coachman, Morrison, peered down at her. "Yes, ma'am?"

"Don't you think Fifth Avenue would be better? I'd hate to be late for my own guests."

"Maybe so, ma'am," Morrison answered. "Never worry, I'll get you home in plenty of time for Miss Jemima's luncheon."

The hatch closed and the carriage turned westward on Eleventh Street. As they finally turned north and the horses eased into a trot, Helen heard a shout followed by a brief burst of invective from the carriage box as the vehicle came to a sudden stop. Morrison had originally been a groom in the Wilcox's Wagon stables and his salty language sometimes reflected it.

The hatch opened again. "Beg pardon, ma'am. Only a big dray cut in front of me all of a sudden. We'll be moving soon. Roadworks ahead, but traffic's moving beyond."

"Thank you, Morrison," Helen said before he had a chance to go on. In most well-managed households servants like Morrison were unobtrusive, but Joshua had never bothered about formality and Morrison had been one of her husband's first employees. Helen gazed out the window at an immense hole in the cobblestone roadway, from which a pickaxe emerged rhythmically while the carriage inched past. She should never have tried to go down to the Village to replace the ruined dessert . . . but she'd wanted every last detail to be just right. The streets of New York were always clogged with carriages and wagons and pedestrians and barefoot urchins. Joshua had grumbled so often about the traffic that Helen no longer heard his complaints, but she felt a new sympathy for him. After all, he ran a freight transport company. More traffic meant fewer deliveries, and thus had a direct effect on the Wilcox family's household budget.

But according to Joshua, the congested streets had also created an unexpected opportunity. Over a year earlier, he had turned to her at breakfast and proudly announced his purchase of an elevated railroad. Just like that, as if he'd bought a new horse! It turned out to be a single engine with one car, running on an iron track thirty feet above Ninth Avenue. According to Joshua it sped between Dey Street downtown all the way north to Twenty-Ninth Street (or vice versa) in a mere twenty minutes! If only she could travel a similar distance with such speed, Helen thought, she'd be at home with plenty of time to re-pin her hair, check the flowers on the table, and reassure Jemima, in whose honor the luncheon was to be given.

It was rare for Helen to think of the Elevated with such enthusiasm. In the past year it had exerted an endless drain on Joshua's attention and the family's finances. It seemed to drink money, Helen thought: new track, new cars, the absolute requirement to expand. Of course she wanted it to be successful, and not just for the money; she loved her husband and wished to see his ambition fulfilled. But the risk! He was attempting something that had never been done before in New York, and if it failed . . . Helen could never complete that sentence, even in her thoughts. The prospect was simply too frightening. Besides, Joshua had assured her that if the Elevated succeeded as he expected, Helen could stop worrying about money and instead enjoy what it could purchase.

But the rosy future her husband had sketched for Helen a year earlier had not yet materialized. Joshua now had three partners, each of whom had been obliged to pour thousands of dollars into the Elevated. There had been no accurate way to forecast the expense of extending and reinforcing the track above New York's streets, because it had never been done before. In the event, the process required not only vast sums of money but also engineers, architects, lawyers, permits, and cooperation from the city government. Like any groundbreaking enterprise, the project met with untold setbacks that Helen had heard about in detail. (Occasionally to well beyond the point of boredom.)

Yet as she sat fretting in her carriage, willing the brewery wagon in front of her to move forward, she thought of the little railroad in the sky with more respect; any alternative to crawling uptown at a snail's pace would have been more than welcome. She was tempted to get out and walk—but then she would appear at her own luncheon in an untidy state, out of breath and overheated. She simply should not have risked leaving the house on a morning when her guests were so important.

Even Helen, raised in the traditions of conservative old New York, had her skeptical moments. Why should a self-appointed committee judge a young girl's eligibility to join a series of dancing lessons that were really just a pretext for exclusion? Yet that was how New York society worked. The United States might be a democracy but some of its citizens still yearned for the ancient system of rank that had been abandoned by their forebears. In lieu of the clarity provided by titles, Americans were judged instead by vague and elastic concepts such as "background." Helen's family history was impeccable, but Joshua was an unconventional spouse for a woman in her world. So her daughters would be scrutinized with great care—not to say malice—before being invited to the Dancing Classes, which would in turn influence their success as debutantes. And here she sat, imprisoned in a carriage inching northward as the bells of the Church of the Ascension struck twelve.

Meanwhile, in the Wilcoxes' brownstone house on West Twenty-Sixth Street, preparations for the luncheon proceeded smoothly in the kitchen and the dining room; a luncheon for eight ladies was an entirely routine matter. The table was set with spotless starched linen and heavy silver cutlery. Savory aromas wafted from the kitchen and the parlor was spotless. Nick, age thirteen, was up in the schoolroom reluctantly writing out French verbs under the steely eye of Mademoiselle Cabrol, who knew a lost cause when she saw it but had to earn a living somehow.

One floor down, in the bedroom she shared with her sister, Alice, Jemima was seated in front of the dressing table, fretting. "But where do you suppose Mama is?" she asked plaintively, watching in the mirror as Alice gathered her curly light brown hair into a braid.

"She said she'd be back by noon," Alice soothed her. "Hold still, I'm almost at the end. Now pass me the ribbon."

"She must be caught in traffic," Jemima said, proffering a length of pink grosgrain. "I wish I weren't so pale," she added, pinching her cheeks to make them rosy.

Alice stepped back from the mirror. "But green eyes are so unusual," she answered. "I think your looks are quite distinguished."

Jemima sighed. Alice was a genuine beauty, with her big blue eyes and golden hair. Distinction wasn't much consolation to a girl of seventeen who only wished to be found pretty by potential dancing partners. She picked up the hand mirror to gaze at her tidy braid, then stood and spun around, feeling the hem of her rose-pink dress swirl behind her with a satisfying swish.

"Come," Alice said firmly. She led Jemima out into the upstairs hall and opened the door of the wardrobe, where a mirror hung. The hall was gloomy and the mirror cut her off below the knees, eliminating the thrilling novelty of her first full-length dress. But Jemima couldn't help smiling. She looked practically grown up, she thought with satisfaction.

"Still," she said. "I wish you were coming out first."

"Nonsense," answered Alice. "You'll be a great success."

"I won't, you know," Jemima countered. "I can never think what to say to boys."

"You expect too much from them," Alice said calmly. "You have to ask them question after question about their dogs and their schools, or whatever sport they play. Hold still now," she added, and nipped into her parents' bedroom. She came out rubbing her palms together.

"What's that?" Jemima asked, backing away as Alice started to smooth back the hair at her temples.

"Just a tiny bit of Mama's hair pomade," Alice answered with a satisfied smile. "It keeps those flyaway bits in place. *Tres soignée,* as Mademoiselle would say."

The sisters' eyes met and they giggled in a very un-grown-up way.

The grandfather clock in the front hall struck quarter past twelve, and Jemima turned to Alice. "But Mama still isn't here! What should I do?"

"The ladies are all quite fond of you. At any rate they will be very soon," she said in a bracing way.

"You wouldn't wait for Mama with me, would you? To keep me company?" Jemima asked.

"No," Alice answered cheerfully. "They're just ladies. They won't bite you."

So when the first guest rang the doorbell a little bit before twelve-thirty, Jemima was pacing up and down the parlor in her almost grown-up dress with her hands clasped behind her back so she couldn't fidget with the ribbon on her braid. She knew what was expected of her. She would speak when spoken to, answer politely and cheerfully, agree with restrained enthusiasm to chance remarks about the weather or any other inoffensive subject. But she would have given anything, in that moment, to switch places with Alice.

CHAPTER 2

❖

LOOKED RIGHT THROUGH HER

September 1874

Four months later, on a fine September afternoon, Jemima once again paced in the parlor waiting for her mother. She peered out the bay window: Morrison waited patiently on the box of the carriage with the reins slack in his hands. Jemima crossed to the big mirror set into the paneling of the front hall and untied the bow beneath her chin to seek a more flattering angle for her hat. She had been so eager to put up her hair, another of the marks of adulthood for a girl. But now her best straw bonnet perched oddly on the thick braid Moira, the Wilcoxes' housekeeper, had pinned to the back of her head. And the hairpins scratched, too. Mademoiselle was fond of a French saying, *Il faut souffrir pour être belle*—"One must suffer to be beautiful." Jemima knew she would never be beautiful, but it seemed women also had to suffer to be merely presentable—which was hardly fair. Neither her father nor her brother made any effort to achieve their own good looks. She turned and smoothed her dress over her newly corseted waist, which to her eye seemed delightfully slim but according to Mademoiselle verged on *maigre*—"scrawny." Thus, not a compliment. But generously proportioned women like Mama's friend Mrs. Burke must suffer terribly with their waists and ribs squeezed tight by whalebone and lacing. (Meanwhile gentlemen simply shrugged on their

{7}

frock coats, tied their cravats, and got on with life.) Overhead she could hear her mother's quick steps as she headed down from her bedroom. "We may stop at Mama's for tea," her mother was telling Moira. "But we'll certainly be home in plenty of time for dinner."

"And Mr. Wilcox?" Moira asked, peering over the balustrade. "He'll be dining at home this evening?"

"I haven't heard otherwise," Helen answered as she reached the first floor. "You look very nice, dear," she said. "But I think your hat might look more becoming this way." Deftly she untied the bow, re-settled the hat, and tied it again—all as if Jemima were only nine years old instead of seventeen. At least there was no one to watch besides Moira, gazing down from the landing.

"Enjoy yourself," she said to Jemima. "You already look like a very fine young lady."

"Thank you, Moira," Jemima answered, since fine young ladies had to be polite even when people told flattering fibs.

"Make sure Alice finishes her reading before she starts practicing the piano," Helen instructed Moira. "And Nick must not leave the house until he has done his sums. Tell Cook he's not to sneak out through the kitchen."

"Yes, ma'am," Moira said, though all three of them knew that Nick's movements were beyond their control. Boys, to Jemima's constant frustration, had a great deal of freedom and Nicholas Wilcox took advantage of it.

Once they were settled in the carriage, Jemima's mother patted her knee. "Your aunt Dora's going to join us at Stewart's," she said. "She wants to help choose your dress."

"Oh, Mama!" Jemima exclaimed. "Such a fuss! Couldn't you stop her?"

"No, dear. She's as excited about the Dancing Classes as you are."

"I don't doubt that," Jemima answered. "Since I can barely stand the idea of them."

"Surely it's a good thing to learn some of the steps and get to know your partners before you are officially out in society." Helen met Jemima's worried gaze. "Perhaps you could think of the classes as a rehearsal for your first season," she suggested.

Jemima glanced at the familiar storefronts on Sixth Avenue and took a deep breath before asking, "Must I come out into society? Papa says a debut is just a way for girls to find husbands, but that's not how you two met."

"No, but it's the way people like us . . ." Helen failed to complete the sentence and began again. "Traditionally young people from families like ours socialize at dances. It's just the way New York works. And I know you may feel a little bit apprehensive, but—"

"I never know what to say to boys," Jemima interrupted her mother.

"You don't seem to have trouble talking to Nick," Helen pointed out.

"But he's not someone I might meet at a party," Jemima protested. "And dance with, and maybe have to marry."

"You don't *have to* marry anyone," Helen put in swiftly. "Least of all at the age of eighteen."

Then the truth came out: "I know, but, Mama, what if I'm a wallflower?" Jemima asked. "Stuck on one of those little gilded chairs next to the chaperones, while all the other girls whirl around with handsome partners."

Helen sighed. Jemima's vivid imagination so often ran away with her. "Sweetheart, you will not be a wallflower, the chaperones will make sure you dance as much as you like. And as far as conversation goes, you only need to ask the very simplest questions like, 'Isn't it warm in here?' or 'Where will your family spend

Christmas?'" Jemima fiddled with one of her glove buttons and looked unconvinced. "Would it help to think of the boys you'll meet as simply older versions of Nick?" Helen went on.

Jemima's distaste was visible. "That wouldn't be appealing."

Helen took Jemima's gloved hand in her own. "Lots of us are nervous about meeting new people," she said, "but fretting never improved anything. So in a minute we're going to get out of the carriage and go into Stewart's. Remember that your grandmother has offered to pay for your dress, so be polite. She has excellent taste and you'll look very pretty."

Jemima answered, "I am always polite," but she was unconvinced about her looks.

Yet her mother was correct in one way; if a girl were to be transformed anywhere, that magic might occur at A. T. Stewart's. The store occupied an entire square block at Broadway and Ninth Street, with its six sales floors illuminated by a gigantic central skylight. Silks and woolens and velvets, ribbons and laces woven in dozens of patterns lay strewn on the counters behind which stood serious young women in black, ready to show and measure and cut. Ladies strolled in pairs or threesomes, murmuring to each other. Single women perched at counters, nodding earnestly to saleswomen as they fingered silk flowers or compared brocade patterns. The very air was perfumed.

Jemima had been to Stewart's, of course, but never as a budding young lady whose appearance was important enough to require the advice of experts like Aunt Dora and Grandmama. She spotted the two of them across the sales floor examining a bolt of lavender taffeta. "Mama," she said, and touched her mother's elbow, "look, they're at that counter over to the left." As they began to walk down the long aisle, the imposing figure of Annabelle van Ormskirk came gliding toward them.

Impeccably sheathed in slate blue merino, her rather small gray eyes flickering from face to face like a queen acknowledging her loyal subjects, New York's social leader cleaved a path between the cases of silk flowers and the bolts of ribbon in every imaginable color. Helen spotted her at the same moment as Jemima, and her heart sank. Annabelle had been a bully since they had played together in Washington Square Park as little girls, and marriage to one of the most significant landowners in New York City had given her legitimate social power to determine the limits of polite society. Individuals whom Mrs. Van Ormskirk acknowledged (or "knew," in New York's parlance) were invited everywhere that counted. Those whom she ignored might as well not exist. Time seemed to slow down as Annabelle paced toward Helen, who felt Jemima move closer as if to protect her. She tried to approximate a cheerful smile, and said clearly, "Good morning, Annabelle."

Did Annabelle's steps slow down? She certainly met Helen's gaze. She even, Helen thought, glanced at Jemima. Then, impassive and unspeaking, she averted her eyes and continued down the aisle.

Helen felt heat flood to her face and couldn't help glancing around. Had anyone seen? Were there witnesses to her humiliation? By her side, Jemima frowned. "Why didn't Mrs. Van Ormskirk answer you?" she asked.

Helen took a deep breath and wished that tears hadn't just welled up in her eyes—Jemima noticed everything. "I don't know," she answered, searching her reticule for a handkerchief. Silently, Jemima proffered her own. They had drifted to a halt near a display of silk camellias, while a few dozen feet away, Dora and her mother were frowning. "Sometimes Annabelle speaks to me and sometimes she doesn't," Helen answered flatly.

"How can she get away with that? It's so cruel!" Jemima slipped her hand into Helen's. "Let's go meet Grandmama."

"Of course," Helen answered. But before they could move, she heard her name called from another direction.

"That Annabelle van Ormskirk is a mean cat!" Sylvia Burke exclaimed from a yard away, then surged forward to kiss both Helen and Jemima. "I saw her cut you, Helen. I've never witnessed anything so rude in my life." It was too bad Mrs. Burke's voice was so loud, Jemima thought. She seemed to be attracting quite a bit of attention.

"Annabelle has always been a law unto herself," Helen murmured. "If you'll excuse me, Sylvia, my mother is waiting for me. We're choosing fabric for Jemima's first evening dress."

"Lucky girl!" Mrs. Burke said as she beamed at Jemima. "Helen, will you two come for tea sometime soon? I'd like to get to know this lovely young lady." She smiled warmly at Jemima, who couldn't help smiling back.

"Of course I will," Helen said. "I promise." Then there was more kissing and Mrs. Burke fluttered away, turning back to wave at them halfway down the aisle.

"Does Grandmama know Mrs. Burke?" Jemima asked.

"No, dear," Helen answered. "Mr. Burke made his money in plumbing. Far too indelicate for your grandmother, even if Sylvia weren't so effusive."

"*Plumbing*," Jemima repeated with a grin. "How plebeian."

"Don't mock your grandmother," Helen reproved her gently. "She grew up in a different time."

"Oh, I know, Mama, but it does seem a little silly. Papa's money comes from freight wagons and passenger cars. Though—is that why Mrs. Van Ormskirk was so rude?"

"Mostly," Helen answered. "You know Papa wasn't the kind of man my parents or their friends knew socially. Our wedding caused a great deal of chatter."

"And Grandmama doesn't really like Papa," Jemima murmured. It seemed odd to discuss this amid the displays at Stewart's, but she wanted to take advantage of her mother's momentary frankness. "Sometimes she looks at him and just sighs. Is it because he comes from upriver?" She could see her grandmother and aunt perched at their counter just out of earshot. "Did she want you to marry a lawyer like Uncle Noble?"

"Sweetheart, that is a story for another time," Helen protested. "Let's go see what Mama and your aunt Dora have found for you before they get tired of waiting for us."

"They look so much alike, sitting on those stools like china dolls," Jemima commented.

"Yes, they do," said her mother, "but don't say it to their faces."

In fact, Selina Maitland and Dora Latimer made a very pretty picture, poised next to a pile of silks on the mahogany counter. They shared the demure doll-like prettiness that had made Selina the most popular debutante in New York in 1838. She had relished presiding over a tea table on Washington Square in the 1840s and '50s, when New York was still a provincial city, untouched by industry or immigration. In those days some three hundred thousand people lived in roughly five square miles, but the ones who mattered to Selina's friends numbered in the hundreds. Many of the families were related by blood and many more by the kinds of discreet, profitable interlocking businesses that could be run by gentlemen. For scores of years they had managed each other's money and written each other's wills. They had backed each other's shipping ventures, bought each other's houses, and married each other's cousins. They did their work with pens and handshakes, buttoned into high-collared shirts and long snug coats as if to demonstrate their distance from manual labor.

Selina Maitland had reveled in this world. Some women might

have been bored by the strict routine of her life: the summers at the Maitland family's Spring House up the Hudson, the winters on Washington Square, the quiet dinners and select dances, and what passed for the peak of excitement—the opera season. But Selina raised her two daughters as she had been raised and looked for no further novelty than the pleasure of presenting them to society and steering them into marriages as satisfactory as her own.

It was a pity that Dora—as pretty and conventional as her mother—and her appropriate lawyer husband, Noble Latimer, had not had children. It would have been delightful, Selina had often thought, to bring out a granddaughter whose father's family roots went back to the Dutch settlers. Even a moderately pretty girl with that kind of background would be a successful debutante. In contrast, Joshua was a terribly unconventional son-in-law who had brought energy and ambition to his marriage—but no family money, no helpful relatives, no sense of how New York worked. Worse, Jemima was reserved, bookish, too tall, and too thin.

Yet there she was. And because Selina Maitland was not entirely hard-hearted, she kissed her granddaughter on the cheek and settled down to help her choose a becoming gown for these newfangled Dancing Classes. Jemima's looks presented a challenge but something could be made of her unusual coloring. After all, green eyes were not common and the girl had a certain natural elegance.

As Selina and Jemima studied a set of fashion plates, Dora drew her sister aside and whispered, "Did I just see Annabelle van Ormskirk cut you?"

"Yes," Helen answered. "Imagine explaining *that* to poor Jemima, who's already nervous about being in society."

"But what did you *do*?" Dora asked.

"What *could* I do?" Helen retorted. "I just explained—"

"No," Dora broke in. "What did you do to make her cut you?"

"Nothing! Sometimes she does speak to me. Once she even asked how 'Mr. Wilcox' was. I was astonished. Imagine me asking about 'Mr. Van Ormskirk'! Sometimes I think she's just playing with me, like a cat with a mouse."

"Oh, nonsense." Dora dismissed this. "Even Annabelle wouldn't be that cruel."

"Never mind, Dora, it's done," Helen said with irritation. "To change the subject, Joshua thought we should probably close the Spring House this coming weekend."

"So soon?" Dora protested. The Spring House was only two hours away by train, so the family often spent autumn weekends there well into October, if the weather stayed fair and warm.

"He thinks the storms will come early this year," Helen said. "I don't know whether to believe him, but we might as well do it sooner rather than later."

"I suppose you're right," Dora answered. "I'll persuade Mama that Noble suggested it. She's more likely to agree if she thinks the idea came from him. And I'll suggest Miles Latimer should come as well!" When Helen looked puzzled, Dora went on, "You remember, he's Noble's cousin, just returned from studying architecture in Paris? Mama will love that. He's very handsome."

Helen's face cleared. "What a good idea! He can distract her and we'll get all the work done twice as fast."

"Exactly," Dora agreed. "And Miles sings, too. Maybe he and Alice can perform for Mama."

"What a paragon, Dora!" Helen exclaimed. "I can't wait to meet him. Will he stay with you for long?"

"Until he finds work. Unfortunately, an architect with a degree from some Parisian academy might have some trouble in that re-gard," Dora answered with an edge of irony that was unlike her. "He wants to build grand houses, but . . ." They both shrugged. Nobody had money to build a grand house in New York after the Panic of 1873, the financial crash that had caused so much trouble a year earlier.

"Maybe Miles will be able to marry money," Helen suggested. "I know! One of the Van Ormskirk girls!"

"Imagine Annabelle as a mother-in-law," Dora whispered, and they both burst out laughing. Then their mother turned away from the fabrics on the counter before her and scolded them, as if they were no older than Jemima.

CHAPTER 3

◆

THE SPRING HOUSE

September 1874

Many well-off New York families possessed country residences that allowed them to escape the heat, odors, and disease of the crowded city. The Maitland house, two hours by train up the Hudson River in a little town called Tenders Landing, had originated as a farmhouse poised on a granite bluff overlooking the water. Over the years, as the Maitlands made their fortunes in finance, the first house was swallowed by successive additions. An octagonal tower housed a library on the first floor and Selina Maitland's airy bedroom on the second. A wing extended southward to provide formal spaces for entertaining and more bedrooms, with splendid river views, upstairs. The verandah wrapping three sides of the house served as an outdoor parlor in fine weather. No one knew quite how many rooms the house held if you counted the servants' quarters, the attics, and the cellars.

Everyone in the combined Latimer, Maitland, and Wilcox families enjoyed the semi-annual rituals of opening and closing the Spring House. Selina, in particular, relished making lists and issuing commands. The rest of the family wore their shabbiest clothes and carried out the tasks assigned to them, which sheer novelty made entertaining.

That fall, Miles Latimer accompanied the Wilcoxes to Tenders Landing, to Jemima's and Alice's delight. Miles combined good looks and sophistication, which gave Jemima a degree of hope for the future. Because at some point in the next few years, she and Alice would have to find husbands, and thus far, Jemima's limited experience with young gentlemen was discouraging. The sons of her parents' friends were just boys like Nick and anyway, they all preferred beautiful Alice. Her father's partner Robey Gregson seemed to enjoy Jemima's conversation, but he didn't really count because he wasn't in society. Actually she suspected that Robey was in some way scandalous, from the way her aunt Dora's voice dropped to a hush every time he was mentioned. Jemima suspected that Mr. Gregson flirted with the wrong kind of women; actresses, perhaps.

But now handsome, relatively young Miles Latimer sat next to Jemima on the train to Tenders Landing, reading a novel in French as they waited to depart. Mademoiselle had always warned the Wilcox girls that contemporary French novels were unsuitable, yet there was *Madame Bovary*, just feet away. Jemima felt worldly by mere proximity.

Just then the conductor standing on the train platform blew his whistle and shouted "All abooooard!" A moment later the door of their car opened with a bang and Aunt Dora flew in as if on a gust of wind, awkwardly clutching her pug, Trixie, to her chest. Jemima noticed that her usual ladylike composure had been shaken— possibly by the slender, elegantly turned-out man behind her, who was carrying her carpetbag.

In the resulting fuss—was there a seat for Dora? Could Miles take the dog, Trixie? So kind of you to help; oh, nothing at all— Jemima noticed that Dora didn't look the man in the eye. Which was odd, because he was extremely courteous. He settled her carpetbag on the rack and as he turned away from her, Jemima could have sworn he bowed. Just slightly, as if he were accustomed to bowing to ladies and hadn't quite lost the habit. Also, though his rather long hair was glossy black, a single white streak ran back from his temple. Jemima had never seen such a thing and was wondering how it came about (a sudden shock, perhaps?), when he looked directly at her and smiled. Jemima couldn't help smiling back, then flicked her eyes away. What was she doing, grinning at a strange man?

The train was already pulling out of the station by the time Aunt Dora was settled and all of her baggage stowed. Jemima ended up holding Trixie.

"Why is the dog in your lap?" Miles asked. "Shouldn't it stay with Dora?"

Jemima eyed him. "Probably. Does she bother you?" she suggested.

"No, but she's shedding all over your skirt." Hairs from Trixie's pale fur were all too visible on Jemima's dark traveling dress and also on Miles Latimer's sleeve. She tried to brush them off, unsuccessfully.

"Who was that man helping Aunt Dora?" she asked. "And why was she so rude to him?"

"Apparently he's rather scandalous," he replied.

"Why?"

"How old are you?"

"Seventeen. But I read lots of novels, and nobody tells girls anything. I could be leaping to conclusions about a perfectly nice gentleman," she added craftily.

"I doubt it. His name is Felix Castle . . ." He came to a halt. "Don't tell your mother I told you this. It's pure gossip." Jemima tried to erase the eagerness from her face. "He does something called stock speculation. Do you know what that is?"

Jemima shook her head silently.

After a moment's thought Miles explained, "Basically, he gambles in the stock market. Buys shares in businesses when he thinks the stock price will go up dramatically."

"Surely that's simply clever," Jemima said, faintly disappointed.

"Yes, well, he's devilishly successful," Miles went on. "Sometimes he borrows money to buy stock, drives the price up, and sells out just before the prices drop. There are fellows who make pretty good money just following Castle's lead."

"And what's wrong with that?" Jemima asked.

Miles thought for a moment. "You ask an excellent question," he conceded. "He's ruthless with his creditors and he takes risks most respectable New York money men wouldn't touch." Then he smiled. "All in all, people don't think Felix Castle is 'a gentleman' because he's so keen on making a profit. But I think his real offense isn't the way he makes money but how he spends it. He's built a remarkable house. It has a private theater attached. He stages opera performances there. He . . ." Miles paused, clearly groping for a way to express the next bit. Jemima stroked Trixie's silky ears and tried not to look curious. "He promotes the careers of some of the female singers," Miles concluded. "It's rumored that he pays for, um, voice lessons. And costumes, possibly." He looked uncomfortable, so Jemima knew he was telling the truth.

"And ladies like Mama and Aunt Dora would never know him," Jemima prompted, "because of his terrible reputation."

"So I'm told," Miles said. "One thing I can tell you with confidence is that there is a private ballroom in his house. With a fountain that can be filled with champagne for parties. I know someone who's seen it."

"Ohh!" Jemima answered with sudden enthusiasm. "That sounds marvelous!"

"How could you know?" Miles asked. "You've surely never had champagne!"

"No, but I know it has bubbles. A champagne fountain would be delightful, don't you think?"

He paused to consider. "No. I can't quite see how you would clean it. Aside from the blatant vulgarity of the thing."

"Blatant vulgarity?" repeated Jemima.

"Something that exists purely to demonstrate how much money you spent on it," Miles answered.

This was a new idea for Jemima and she fell silent, considering it. Some people were richer than others, that was obvious. The Van Ormskirk house on Fifth Avenue was immense, for instance. And Mama's friend Mrs. Burke had just been given a very large diamond brooch in the shape of a crescent moon, which she'd worn to tea at the Wilcoxes' house. That was probably "blatant vulgarity." Jemima's mind drifted to the elements of the dress she had chosen at Stewart's that day when they saw Mrs. Burke. She realized now how her grandmama had steered her toward something beautiful and demure—no chance of being vulgar. It was made of gleaming apricot-colored silk, with matching velvet ribbon trim. Aunt Dora and her grandmother had talked about her figure very frankly as she stood before them in her corset and petticoat. It would have been embarrassing except that Grandmama had said matter-of-factly, "We should make the most of Jemima's natural elegance"—as if Jemima were a doll.

The problem was that "natural elegance" wouldn't go far on a dance floor. Not when it was accompanied by natural shyness. Alice could talk to anyone; she said you simply had to keep asking questions, but Jemima had tried and somehow it didn't work. Once she had asked Thomas Lawrence what he was reading and he had just looked at her, silently opening and closing his mouth like a fish.

It was too bad Alice wasn't the elder daughter: She could have made friends of all the boys and then, when Jemima had to go to the Dancing Classes a year later, they would dance with Jemima as a way of currying favor with Alice. As it was, Jemima would just have to soldier on. Mrs. Van Ormskirk had started the classes as a way to give her eldest daughter, Caroline, experience in a ballroom, Mama said. Jemima suspected that no amount of experience would make some girls (like herself, or Caroline van Ormskirk for that matter) more appealing to a group of teenage boys. But Mama had been preoccupied lately, so Jemima did her best to hide her apprehension.

She thought perhaps the Elevated Railroad caused the friction she sensed between her parents. The railroad had turned out to be much more expensive to run than Papa had expected. Worse, it wasn't earning money fast enough; Jemima had overheard an angry late-night conversation between her parents in which Mama had called Papa stubborn and he had called her shortsighted.

Then Mama had asked—rather loudly—"Where will the money come from for the girls' debuts? We will have to entertain, Joshua." He had muttered something and then Mama had answered "Nonsense!" and slammed the wardrobe door. Jemima had described this episode to Alice the next day, but Alice didn't seem concerned. There were things you could change and things you just had to endure. To Alice, fretting in advance made no sense at all, but Jemima couldn't seem to help it. Alice often reassured Jemima; Jemima often enlightened Alice.

She seemed to understand people in a way that Alice didn't. She always sensed, for instance, when Moira's bunions hurt ("She walks like this," Jemima would say, imitating Moira's halting step). At family meals she spoke less than anyone but came away with more information. And Jemima read so perpetually, so indiscriminately, that she was a constant source of information about matters Alice barely knew existed.

Across the aisle of the train, as it rattled its way northward with the Hudson River unspooling in a broad blue ribbon below the Palisades, Helen glanced at her girls in the seats ahead of her. She was suddenly struck by a vivid memory of riding this very train heading back to the Spring House at the end of her first social season. She had not been a successful debutante. In those days the popular girls were engaged before everyone dispersed for the summer, and her mother had been very disappointed in her. For an instant Helen relived the combination of relief and apprehension she'd felt at the time. Relief that the ordeal of the season was over, certainly. But also—she remembered now, though it had not been so clear at the time—she had felt a sense of escape. The prospect of spending her life with one of those bland, polite, juvenile dancing partners had filled her with misgiving. How, she had wondered, did married people ever fill the decades together? Silence at the dinner table, silence in the carriage, pleasantries and temperate courtesy in between? She suddenly recaptured the moment the train pulled into the Tenders Landing station at the end of that trip, when she had breathed deeply as if for the first time in months.

And now, Alice sat gazing out the window with the glow of the afternoon sun gilding her hair. What young man in his early twenties would not want to marry a cheerful, uncomplicated beauty? Barnabas Silsbee, Thomas McCloud, Jonathan Weeks—all of the pleasant youths from prosperous families would flock to her side. Without question, Alice would be a belle.

But Jemima was a more complex case. Helen tried to imagine her elder daughter married to a stockbroker or a lawyer—even a university professor, though Helen didn't know how a girl might meet one of those. Possibly a painter? She considered the notion of an artist falling in love as he painted Jemima: Would they converse? Would the artist be well-read? Might he be foreign? (Jemima was good at languages.) Could an artist support a girl from a good family in the way she'd been raised? Would they have to go live in some remote neighborhood near the Central Park? Perhaps Joshua would be successful enough by then to buy a house for the newlyweds? It was at this point that Helen realized her imagination was running away from her, and furthermore that the train had begun to slow down as it approached Tenders Landing.

Yet in the bustle of the rest of the day, Helen's thoughts continued to wander. As she folded quilts into trunks and closed the shutters of the bedrooms, beat the summer's dust out of a hooked rug, or counted silver forks into the chest that Joshua would take to the bank, she was aware of handling her own heritage. Each of these objects had its own significance. Your dinner would taste the same eaten off a tin plate as off a china one, but the Maitland porcelain exported from China proclaimed that the family had inherited money and good taste. If Jemima married a college professor or a painter, would they have pretty dishes?

And what about the Elevated Railroad? Helen felt disloyal questioning Joshua's judgment—over the years he had provided well for her and the children. But she knew that he had been taken aback by certain elements of the business: huge sums owed to suppliers, the cost of coal to run the engines, and the exorbitant price to build new track. According to a brief and disturbing conversation with her husband, Helen knew that he envisioned a grand future for the

Elevated: tracks running uptown and downtown, all the way as far north as Sixtieth Street where the Central Park began. Larger engines, Joshua had told her, could pull more cars. They could even build stations atop the track, shelters for passengers to wait in on rainy days. "But what would that all cost?" Helen had asked.

"A fair penny," Joshua had conceded. "But we'll find investors. It's such an important project for the city. And for us," he'd added. "Eventually it could be hugely profitable. Do you know how many men travel more than twenty blocks to get to where they work?"

She had reminded him at that point that bringing out the girls would be expensive. She had even created a written estimate of the costs for Jemima's debut, including the new wardrobe their daughter would require. When she'd presented it to Joshua he had merely looked blankly at it and handed it back to her. "Is this really necessary?"

"Yes, Joshua," she had responded flatly. "I've been talking about the girls' debuts for years. This is how families like mine make appropriate matches, and if the girls aren't formally presented to society with a dance or a reception, if they don't go to their friends' parties, they won't meet the kind of young men we want them to marry."

"Dull young blockheads," he suggested, "working in Grandpapa's bank."

"You're oversimplifying. But we do want the girls to choose husbands from among the families we know, with reliable backgrounds."

"Can't all of that nonsense come out of the usual household budget?" he'd asked.

"Of course not!" Helen had replied with some heat. "Jemima will need quite a few new dresses. So, I'm sorry to say, will I. And in addition to her coming-out dance, we'll need to entertain quite frequently. It's a year away, but I want to be sure you know how expensive it will be."

He had gazed at her, frowning, but then shrugged and said, "All right. I'll take this into account. And the same the following year for Alice?"

Helen had nodded.

"I don't suppose either of them would elope with a dashing stranger and spare me this expense?" he had asked her with a raised eyebrow and the hint of a smile.

"Your daughters have been carefully raised," Helen had told him, smiling back. "There's no chance they'd do such a thing." At that point he'd pulled her into his lap and kissed her on the cheek, and they'd talked no more about it. But ever since then, she had listened very carefully to talk of the Elevated.

As it happened, there was plenty to hear that evening. Miles Latimer's presence provided an extra fizz of novelty. He had spent most of the day under Selina's supervision, rolling carpets and shrouding the fragile old Empire furniture in canvas covers. Then, while the family gathered in the central hall, he had seated himself at the piano and suggested that Dora sing with him. She hesitated but he played the opening bars of "The Last Rose of Summer," which even Joshua recognized, so she complied.

"We should make sure dear Miles hears Alice play," Selina murmured to Helen as they listened to Dora's still-girlish voice. "He might make a good husband for her, you know."

"Mama, Alice is only sixteen," Helen whispered. "No need to start matchmaking yet."

"I'm just keeping my eyes open," Selina replied, applauding gently as the song ended. "Your girls won't be easy to find husbands for, you know."

"What an unkind remark!" Helen retorted in shock. "Why would you say such a thing?"

"Oh, I mean no harm," Selina answered, "they're good girls." She turned to look Helen in the eye. "You've raised them well, dear, they're modest and well-mannered. But . . . there are other factors to think of. We can discuss those back in the city. I hope we can get through dinner without hearing more about Joshua's railroad," she added, as if that were part of the problem. Then she stood to lead the group into the dining room.

Helen felt a tide of heat rise on her cheeks as she followed. How dare her mother insult first her daughters and then her husband? So casually, as if she spoke of them always in a disparaging way! "Finding husbands for Helen's girls," she must say to her friends, "will be so difficult." Did she move on to Joshua next? Whisper behind her hand, "A kind man, despite his background," or some other condescending nonsense?

But little as Selina approved of her son-in-law, he was the center of attention at the dinner table because a reporter for *The New York Times* had ridden the Elevated and found it . . . "Exhilarating!" shouted Nick, who had snatched the newspaper off the central hall table where his father had left it. "Listen to this: 'The little train swoops above the street like a bird, so that the rider arrives at his destination almost before he has left it. If the Hudson Elevated Railroad can provide transportation as reliable as it is thrilling . . .'"

"I think that's enough," Selina interrupted, neatly plucking the newspaper from Nick's hand. "We may be dining informally this evening but we have not entirely abandoned civility. Miles, would you sit at my right? And Noble, no, Nick at my left. Where I can keep an eye on you."

"Happily, Grandmama," Nick said, and carefully held her chair while she seated herself. Helen exchanged glances with Jemima across the table—Nick would never have thought of such a thing at home. It was nice to think that he was learning good manners, even if he seldom exhibited them to his immediate family.

Conversation was general and noisy through the soup and the roast duck, then Noble stood up and tapped his glass with a knife as the kitchen maid removed the last plates. Miles, seated next to Helen, whispered, "Oh, dear. Is he going to speak?"

"Briefly," Helen answered. "Family tradition." Noble was actually a charming orator; in just a few minutes he recapitulated the family's season at the Spring House—Alice learning to drive the pony cart, Nick's bout with poison ivy, the sturgeon Dora accidentally caught when Noble momentarily handed her his fishing pole. Then, also following family tradition, Helen and Joshua took one last walk to the nearby waterfall in search of a few minutes of privacy.

The moon was full as they set out across the meadow surrounding the house, and Joshua tucked Helen's hand into the crook of his elbow. "Was it a busy day? I'm sorry I couldn't get here earlier. At least you had Miles to help shift the furniture."

"And Nick," Helen added. "He's stronger than he looks. Are you pleased about the article in the *Times*?"

"Oh, of course," he answered. "Should I go back for a lantern, or is the moonlight sufficient?"

"We know the path well enough to follow it in the dark," Helen answered. It meandered through the meadow and into the sparse woods to a spot where a bench looked out over a stream leaping down over a small granite cliff. "It's nice to have Miles with us. Mama's always pleased to have a new man to flirt with." She sighed heavily. "I wish she weren't so critical of poor Jemima."

"I think Jemima doesn't even notice most of the time," Joshua answered.

"She may fool you because she's not demonstrative, but I know she's worried about the Dancing Classes."

"Worried about Dancing Classes!" Joshua repeated. "Why, for heaven's sake?"

"That boys won't ask her to dance," Helen told him, pointing out the obvious.

He turned to her as they stepped into the shadow of the trees. "Why wouldn't they?"

"She's shy. And not pretty in the usual sense."

"Who says Jemima isn't pretty?" Joshua protested hotly. "She's . . . what is the word your mother uses? Something French."

"Mama says *belle laide*, which means 'beautiful/ugly,' and the girls speak enough French to understand it," Helen stated. "Jemima will be a distinguished-looking woman but for now . . ." Helen sighed.

"I suppose she might be rather formidable to a boy her age," Joshua conceded. "Maybe she shouldn't go to those Dancing Classes. She can learn to dance at home."

"With you?" Helen said somewhat pointedly. Joshua was enthusiastic but not elegant on the dance floor. "No, she needs to take part. It's not just the steps that are important. It will be helpful to know other young people when it comes to the real dances."

"And that's how New Yorkers pair up," Joshua commented dryly.

"This is the world we live in, Joshua."

They had reached the roughly carved stone bench overlooking the stream. "Let's sit for a moment," he suggested. "Will you be chilly?"

"Not really," Helen answered. But Joshua took off his coat and draped it over her shoulders all the same, then put his arm around her.

"Is there a boy you think would make a good husband for Jemima?" he asked.

"No," she answered quickly. "They all seem so terribly young, even the ones who are at college already."

"When I remember what I was like at twenty, I know I would have found Jemima alarming. She has that way of looking right through you . . ."

"I know just what you mean," Helen agreed. "Older than her age, by far."

"What would you want for her?" Joshua asked. "If you could conjure the perfect husband out of thin air?"

"Alice will be much easier," Helen said, avoiding the question at first. "She's so straightforward. And her looks help. The boys will flock to her and she'll have an endless supply of small talk for them. But Jemima is so easily bored. She would need a husband as clever as she is."

"Find her a librarian, then," Joshua said with a snicker.

"A husband who can support her comfortably," Helen retorted with an edge to her voice.

"A librarian with an independent fortune," he amended helpfully.

Helen sighed. "Tease all you like," she said, "but it's no laughing matter. One of the most important things a mother does for her daughters is guide them into appropriate marriages."

"But sometimes, sweetheart, the mothers have nothing to do with their daughters' choices. Look at us!"

"Oh, I do," Helen said soberly.

He turned to see if she was teasing him. "You aren't suggesting you regret marrying me?"

"Not that, no," she reassured him immediately, leaning against his shoulder. What she didn't say was that sometimes she wondered what her life would have been like if she'd married one of the boys from her world. Even more, she feared now that her daughters would pay for her unconventional romance with Joshua. Even if Joshua's bold predictions about the Elevated came true and it made a great deal of money, family backgrounds mattered. Would the girls have a harder time finding husbands because Joshua was their father?

CHAPTER 4

❖

A SWIFT COURTSHIP

1854–57

Helen Maitland had not been a pretty girl. She took after her big-boned father, and her hair was a strange golden-brown color with a rough texture. All of Selina's judgment had been required to find colors that flattered Helen's skin, but nothing could have made her fashionably delicate. In an era that favored the rosebud, Helen Maitland was a sunflower.

And—cruel fate for a debutante—the boys didn't admire her. She was tall at seventeen, even in the soft, flat slippers of the era. She waltzed stiffly and failed to make small talk. Some of her partners even suspected that they bored her. Young men wrote their names in her dance card, of course, but only for one dance. She spent agonizing spells perched by the chaperones at the edge of the dance floor, trying to school her face into a cheerful smile while her fellow debutantes whirled past, laughing. At home in front of the mirror, she practiced that gay, lighthearted manner but knew she was not convincing. By the spring of 1855, when New York's social season ended, it had to be admitted that Helen was not a success.

All the same, there were always wallflowers. Helen's lackluster season was unfortunate but unremarkable, especially in light of her father's mortal illness; everyone knew that Andrew Maitland had doted on his elder daughter. Some of New York's ladies wondered who would temper her mother's criticism, especially during the year of mourning after her father died. Nobody could have predicted that she would marry a *stable boy*, however!

Only he wasn't, not really. He came from one of the sturdy hardworking families in Tenders Landing. When the railroads had come up the Hudson a dozen years earlier, prosperous families like the Maitlands followed, building rambling mansions along the river to escape the heat and disease of urban summers. Joshua's father had sold them horses and trained local boys as grooms. His early death had put Joshua, at sixteen, in charge of the business and responsible for supporting his mother and sister. For the next seven years Wilcox Stables had provided well-trained horses to the gentry of the Hudson Valley. Young Joshua had branched out by starting a delivery service as well, driving a wagon up and down the River Road behind an immense gray stallion named Pete. Tenders Landing considered it outlandish that Joshua had bought this huge creature—imported from Europe, no less!—but the local horsemen appreciated his worth. Pete's progeny were soon prized as draft horses in the stables of working farms and summer estates alike. They practically served as walking advertisements for Wilcox's Wagon.

So Joshua Wilcox, while more impressive than your average groom, did spend a lot of time in stables, the Maitlands' among them. He had sold Andrew Maitland one of Pete's imposing offspring and several riding horses, including one for Helen. He liked the girl—admired her, even. She was an excellent horsewoman, far more graceful in the saddle than on the dance floor. (Though of course Joshua couldn't know that.)

After Andrew Maitland's death, Selina decided to spend the winter of 1855–56 in Tenders Landing rather than returning to a new widow's social seclusion in the city. This turned out to be her crucial error. It was a mild winter. Helen rode daily, drawing comfort from the steady temperament of her big bay mare. Sometimes she met Joshua Wilcox on the trails that threaded through the estates along the Hudson. They always stopped, country-fashion, to pass the time of day. Sometimes they met accidentally in town, where she was allowed to call at the post office for the mail. He helped her sell off most of her father's stable. One night her mare got colic and she sent a message to Joshua in a panic. He was already "Joshua" to her, which was all wrong by city standards.

Of course by the spring of 1856 she had fallen in love. He was so handsome, so much more manly than those sheepish youths in the parlors of New York. Tall, blue-eyed, blond, with a golden beard and a beautiful smile; what shy girl could have resisted him? Especially when, one day, he took her hand in his callused one and called her "Helen." She knew it was wrong, and she didn't care. He *saw* her, and in those days no one else did. Besides, he was cheerful and honest and made her laugh.

Was Joshua in love with Helen?

He didn't know. If she'd been little Mollie Nesbit, whose father ran the mill in Tenders Landing, he would have married her in a heartbeat. As it was, he knew no other woman would ever make him feel the way Helen did: smarter, braver, handsomer than he knew himself to be. He craved her company and longed to get his arms around her . . . just to begin with. But he knew his place, and it wasn't at a dinner table with Selina Maitland. So when the Maitlands prepared to return to New York at the beginning of September, he resigned himself to letting Helen go. She would return to what they both knew was her rightful setting. He told himself that the easy connection between them was just an accident.

Then, a few days before the Maitlands were to leave the Spring House, Helen talked him into taking her to see the otters down in the marshes. It was a sentimental wish on her part; her father had often spoken of them. Something about a book with colored pictures by a man named Audubon that Helen and her father had looked at in those long days of Mr. Maitland's illness.

How could he refuse her? He knew she dreaded returning to the city. He also knew, though she hadn't told him in so many words, that her mother would bully her into marrying the first twit who proposed. He even knew he'd awakened in her a sense of romantic possibility that she might have been happier without. Full of regret but also wild excitement, he borrowed a rowboat. Helen crept out of the Spring House at sunset, on an evening when her mother had gone down to the city. She met Joshua on the dock, wearing an old calico gown. "I told them I had a headache," she said proudly. "And I got them to make me sandwiches, in case I got hungry later." She gestured with the basket she carried.

"I thought ladies didn't get hungry," he teased her. They had reached the stage of teasing.

"No, they don't. They're generally delicate." Unspoken: She was not delicate. He liked her that way. He held out a hand as she stepped down into the little boat. Did he hold it a bit longer than necessary? She felt the blood rush to her face as she permitted herself to realize what she had put in motion: not just an escapade but several solitary hours alone with Joshua. Out of sight, out of her mother's reach, very close together. She could still feel, she thought, his touch on her hand.

It was a beautiful evening, with the first cool hint of autumn.

Joshua rowed through the channels of the marsh and they saw egrets, turtles, and many insects before they found the otter burrows. They stayed for a long time, watching the otters in silence. They were side by side on the center bench, with Helen's skirt wet at the hem from the water that dripped when Joshua shipped the oars. He put an arm around her. He felt so warm and large and solid. She leaned against him. Nestled, really. With the gentlest of touches he turned her face toward his and kissed her. His beard, his lips, his tongue, his hands on her back, the rocking of the boat, his breath on her neck . . . What was this? No one had ever told her. Could it be that this enchantment was what her mother had always feared? She closed her eyes and ran a hand up into his glorious hair. He murmured her name. Time passed. They didn't notice the tide. Joshua had not noticed the moon.

But it was full. The tide went down. Sunset turned to dusk and the narrow channels in the marsh became impassable. Joshua tried pulling the dinghy but the keel stuck fast. Eventually they sat together in the stranded boat on a broad mud flat. The moon glowed as big as a plate and inched across the sky. They could hear the otters splashing and chattering across the wide maze of marsh grass.

The water finally came seeping back but it was hours before Joshua could row freely. And when they rounded the point there was a lantern on the Maitlands' dock. Joshua shipped his oars and let the boat drift. "I'll stand by you," he said. "Whatever you want me to do, count on it."

"It's going to be bad," she answered, trying not to let her teeth chatter. "I'm sorry, Joshua, I'm so sorry."

She was seated in the stern, facing him, and he reached forward to clasp her shoulders. Someone on the dock was shouting but the voice came to them as a mere thread of sound carrying across the water.

"Don't be sorry," he said. He ran a thumb gently over the little furrow between her brows. "Listen, I love you, Helen. I didn't dare, before . . ." In the moonlight he saw her eyes widen and he cupped her cheek with his hand. "I never thought—there's such a distance between us . . . But now, your mother will think the worst." He wondered briefly if she even knew what that could be, then pressed on. "I want to marry you." He leaned forward and kissed her firmly, rocking the little boat. "Won't you make me happy and say yes?"

She hesitated for an instant, breathing hard as she felt joy rocket through her. Then she laughed fiercely. "Of course I will!" she told him, and took his face in both of her hands. In the waning moonlight she could still see his features though now, she thought, she knew them better. Having touched them, kissed them. Made them hers. A thought came to her and she dropped her hands. How, after all, could it be possible? How could this marvelous man want her? "Truly?" she asked, before she could regret it. "You don't have to. No one needs to know about this." She gestured to the boat. "Mama can hush it up."

Joshua Wilcox was no gentleman according to New York standards—but how could he fail to be moved by this generous, openhearted girl? In that moment, he knew he loved her whole-heartedly.

By the time they reached the dock, Selina was almost hopping with rage. Beside her stood Helen's maid, with a blanket over her arm. Joshua handed Helen out of the boat, then tied it up neatly and stepped onto the dock himself. Selina was shrieking. He ignored her and took the blanket from the maid to wrap it around

Helen's shoulders. Briefly, she leaned back against him and he squeezed her shoulders.

"Stop," he commanded Selina in a voice that always worked on horses. Shocked, she closed her mouth. "Helen and I are going to marry."

"No, you aren't," she retorted scornfully. "I'm taking her back to her bedroom and she'll never see you again."

"By all means take her to her bedroom." He turned to the maid. "She's chilled, though. A bath would help." The maid nodded at this sensible suggestion, and without asking Selina's permission, turned to walk back up to the house. Joshua said gently to Helen, "Go with her. I'll be back tomorrow, bright and early, I promise." Then, in front of her mother, he kissed her gently on the forehead. "I'll take care of this, don't worry."

And he did. He arrived the next day in his best clothes, full of resolve though gritty-eyed from lack of sleep. He used the front door of the Spring House for the first time.

Selina had not slept well, either. She realized that she'd handled Helen's escapade clumsily by dragging the servants into it. The story would be all over Tenders Landing by noon, and would reach the city not much later. None of the well-mannered boys from her circle would marry Helen after that. So Selina and Joshua met as reluctant allies, cooperating to provide Helen with an acceptable future.

Joshua, giddy and exhilarated—marrying Helen! Who could have thought?—was taken aback by some of Selina's terms. Limited contact with his family, who were not to attend the wedding; the forced sale of his business because Helen could not marry a "wagon driver"; the requirement to live in New York and accept an allowance for Helen's comfort. Accept an allowance! When all he wanted was to take care of her himself! He protested that condition but Selina made a scornful comment about "love in a cottage" being unsuitable for her daughter, and Joshua, despite his rage, understood that she was baiting him out of her own fear and anger.

Helen, meanwhile, had wakened to a sense of exultation. Joshua! Her husband! Her wedding day! She had never dared to dream of such good fortune! She floated through the morning submitting to bathing and hair-combing and the anxious confection of a wedding dress from a simple batiste morning gown and a fichu of some priceless Brussels lace of her mother's. Her younger sister, Dora, disturbed by the maids' half-heard gossip, tiptoed into her room to ask, "Are you really marrying that Wilcox fellow?" Helen noticed there were tears on Dora's face but assumed they were tears of joy, like her own.

Joshua didn't see Helen again until she stood next to him for their wedding ceremony, wearing her white dress and a wreath of asters on her head. The only witnesses were a pair of lawyers from the city, and Selina, in deepest black. Helen blazed with happiness and Joshua felt awestruck as he slipped an old-fashioned thin gold band over her knuckle. There was no celebration afterward, but they signed a great many papers. Then they were shipped off to Europe, to Helen's great satisfaction. "It's what families like ours do with wayward children," she explained to Joshua. "Out of sight, out of mind." And as Selina whispered later to Dora, "He'll lose some of his rough edges as they travel."

Thus, they did not exactly elope, and he was not exactly a stable boy. Still, the match was not what New York expected for a girl like Helen Maitland.

But if two young people from very different worlds were to

make a go of marriage, a protracted honeymoon on neutral ground was an excellent start. In a setting where everything was new to both of them, they turned with increasing confidence to each other. Helen quickly learned that her instinctive assessment of Joshua's kindness and reliability had been accurate. She had underestimated, though, his curiosity and his eagerness to learn. He was never afraid to ask a question. He made her understand that he delighted in her point of view and relied on her cultural knowledge as they traveled. His lavish approval was an astounding novelty to her.

They shared their delight, boredom, and puzzlement at the "sights" they were expected to visit in various capitals. The Alps thrilled them. The casino at Monte Carlo appalled them. The secrets of the marriage bed (adumbrated with terrifying vagueness by Selina the night before their wedding) came as a delicious revelation to Helen and within weeks she was pregnant.

This news, promptly cabled to New York, produced a flurry of instructions and by early December the newlyweds were settled in a small rented house in London since Helen couldn't possibly risk childbirth under Continental medical care. In any event, they had tired of sightseeing. The honeymoon, in fact, was over.

After their giddy period of mutual discovery they settled down to the task of defining who they might be together, as Mr. and Mrs. Joshua Wilcox. Helen might bear his name but he would move into her world.

Money was the first issue, and until they returned to New York, it would all be hers. Wilcox's Wagon had been sold to a friend and the proceeds deposited (at the Maitland Brothers' Bank) with provision made for his mother's and sister's benefit. He only hoped the money would last until he could begin earning again. That was the sore spot for Joshua. Everything about his upbringing had taught him that a man's role was to provide for his women, and not the other way around. He was often testy for hours after cashing one of Helen's letters of credit. In addition, he had been shocked by the prices they paid for hotel rooms, meals, and first-class train tickets and he loathed the idea that he would become accustomed to these gratuitous comforts.

In addition, Joshua himself had to be refashioned, and this process nearly destroyed the new bond between husband and wife. All of his clothes—gone. Too coarse, too baggy, too worn, too crude. From the skin out he had to be outfitted with new garments and then taught how to wear them. Gentlemen didn't put their hands in their pockets. A cravat must be tied in a certain fashion and fastened with a stick pin. Gloves must be worn in the city regardless of the weather. He possessed four different hats for different occasions. Fortunately Joshua grasped the importance of appearances and furthermore enjoyed Helen's frank admiration. Nevertheless he had to submit to a certain amount of tweaking and frowning and overall critical scrutiny that infuriated him.

Helen did not take his objections lightly. Who could bear to be told that he was uncouth? Some of what Joshua needed to know could be presented simply as a set of useful skills: Sharing space with a lady, for instance, wasn't that different from sharing a stall with a skittish horse. You had to be alert and move carefully, whether sitting, standing, or opening a door. Then there were the little courtesies like offering a lady an arm to cross a street. Ladies, Joshua observed to Helen, seemed to be all but helpless. "That's merely what you're supposed to think," she answered with a smile.

Table manners, though, were a terrible challenge. It took Helen several weeks even to broach the subject, with a long preface about "fitting in" and "doing as others do" and "making people uncomfortable." Finally she had to inform her husband that he didn't know how to hold a spoon. The news didn't come as a complete surprise; Joshua was observant. But he deeply resented the finicky business of upper-class dining. What was the point of three different forks anyway? Why must he chase green peas around the plate without using a piece of bread to capture them? Calmly, Helen persisted, knowing that the effort was necessary. That moment of impulsive chivalry on the dock at Tenders Landing could only be completed by a certain amount of transformation. For better, for worse, for richer, for poorer. "Richer" and "better" went together. Besides, Helen knew, when Joshua was earning again, he would feel more like a man.

And indeed the Wilcoxes' greatest preoccupation during those London months was the all-important question of what Joshua would do for a living. Helen had been taken aback by the limits of his official education. He didn't know who Hercules was. He didn't have a word of Latin. He couldn't name a single English poet. He did know the Bible backward and forward, though that wouldn't help in business. What struck Helen was his curiosity about how cities worked. He was always watching the streets to see how traffic moved and he liked to visit the quarters where warehouses and factories lined the streets. He had sold Wilcox's Wagon outright; life with Helen meant moving to the city. But in London he began to wonder if there might not be room for another transport business in New York.

That was when the broader practical benefits of his marriage became apparent to Joshua. The upper-crust hostility to outsiders didn't exist merely to discourage social climbers; the hidden prize, it appeared, was access to people he could never have reached as an unknown wagoneer from Tenders Landing. If Joshua wanted to start a business in New York, he'd need a bank, wouldn't he? Then, Helen informed him, he should write a letter to her second cousin Peter Suydam, a vice president of the Maitland Brothers' Bank. And Selina Maitland had written that Noble Latimer was courting Dora. He was a trusts and estates lawyer, Helen said, but he would certainly know an attorney with business expertise. Joshua wrote the letters and courteous responses arrived.

As with access, so also with information. Could Mr. Suydam recommend trade publications about American cities? He did—and a colleague with interests in the field would be visiting London. Perhaps Mr. Wilcox would like to meet him? In the event the two dined together at Simpson's; Joshua absorbed a great deal of information and at the end of the meal, picked up the bill in a lordly way, as if he'd been born to the habit.

So the Wilcoxes wintered in dark, wet London and arrived at the Spring House in June with a brown-haired baby named Jemima Suydam Wilcox. They planned to conquer their world.

CHAPTER 5

PRESENTING MR. AND
MRS. WILCOX

September 1857

Of course nothing is ever as straightforward as the dreams of a pair of newlyweds. When Joshua and Helen returned to New York they moved into 130 West Twenty-Sixth Street, one of a row of brownstones just built at the northern edge of prosperous Manhattan neighborhoods, purchased for them by Selina. It boasted five stories (the topmost being servants' quarters), hot and cold running water, and gaslight on every floor. Selina had it stylishly furnished with gleaming mahogany, deep-hued upholstery, and a tasteful amount of gilding. When Joshua carried Helen over the threshold she wept with happiness.

The house, however, was the easy part, as Selina was all too happy to confide to her friends. The challenge when Helen and Joshua returned to New York was to introduce them to New York society—at least to the portion of it that was willing to be introduced. Selina's own godmother, octogenarian Felicity Sterling, refused outright: "Helen was a dear little girl," Mrs. Sterling explained, "but I really couldn't know a woman who was married to a stable boy."

"No, dear Felicity, not a stable boy," Selina answered smoothly.

"He is the owner of a transport company. Very ambitious and hard-working, from a respectable family upriver. You wouldn't meet him at my house? I'm planning a small reception for our closest friends."

"Not with his family there!" Felicity said in shock.

"No, no," Selina soothed her. "Mrs. Wilcox isn't interested in our world."

"You've never *met* her!"

"I have," Selina said proudly. "I called on her in Tenders Landing and she was most affable, but of course we won't meet again. We have so little in common."

"Well, I admire the way you're trying to put a good face on this," Felicity said. "But I'm obligated to maintain our family's standards. I feel sure my mother would never have known a—"

"Of course," Selina interrupted, rising from her chair. "But they do say the world is changing."

The reception for the newlyweds was small indeed. "Select," was how Selina preferred to describe it. Most of the Maitland family still lived in a gloomy Albany mansion, and they trooped down to New York to demonstrate solidarity but they had no real power in Manhattan. Several of Selina's old beaux came, along with Helen's godparents and the full strength of the mighty Latimer clan, whose scion, Noble, was wooing Dora. Helen and Joshua were so obviously happy with each other that every guest was charmed. At the party's end Helen embraced her mother and said, "Mama, thank you. It was a delightful party and I was so happy to see everyone who came." She didn't mention those young ladies— her friends, she had believed—so conspicuous in their absence. Nor did she ask her mother about the ladies she had called on, who did not return her call.

But a few weeks after the Wilcoxes' return to New York, Helen spent an entire afternoon at home, prepared to receive callers in her most fetching Parisian ensemble. Each time a carriage rolled past the house she looked up from the book she was only pretending to read, but not one stopped at her door. When at last the Irish maid Moira came in to light the lamps, Helen burst into tears, embarrassing both of them, and ran upstairs to change out of her elegant dress. Joshua came home for dinner to find Helen listlessly stitching away at a petit-point cushion cover while tears ran down her cheeks. Of course he had taken her into his arms and tried to comfort her, but he had a hard time comprehending what was wrong. Even when Helen had explained, the system made no sense to him. "Older ladies pay calls first on younger ones. And ladies who are more prominent call first. A young matron like me waits to be called on."

He watched her carefully. "I don't understand. You've known most of these women all your life," he said.

"Yes, that's true. But, you see, I knew them as Helen Maitland. And Mrs. Joshua Wilcox is a new person."

Joshua rolled his eyes. "When new people arrive in Tenders Landing my mother takes them a cake."

"I know our way isn't friendly," Helen answered. "But my mother always told me this was how the nice people behaved. And I always assumed I was one of them," she went on, but her voice started to wobble. "Now it seems that isn't true."

"But some of your friends must have called on you," Joshua said. He noticed that she didn't seem to have a handkerchief and handed her his. She hid her face in it for a moment, then mopped her eyes.

"Edie Chamberlain left a card before I'd come downstairs," she told him. "She didn't even wait, though Moira told her I'd be right down."

Joshua moved closer and put his arm around her. "I will never understand women," he said. "Men are never this vicious."

"What am I going to do?" Helen asked him. "I never expected to be shunned when we came back here."

"Make new friends, I suppose?" he suggested. "Have you asked Dora for advice?"

"Dora said that eventually people would get over the shock of my marrying you," Helen answered bitterly. "She wasn't terribly sympathetic. How am I supposed to pass my days? Who should I talk to? The baby?"

"What would happen if you called on some of the ladies who aren't part of your usual circle?" Joshua suggested warily. This world was so foreign to him that he couldn't be sure he was even using the right words.

"I'm going to have to, aren't I?" she said with a sigh.

So Helen made the best of the situation. She was still wounded by the sight of girlhood friends who looked right through her as if she were invisible when they passed each other on the street, but she dutifully returned calls to those women who called on her. A few of them, out of ignorance or daring, flouted New York's codes by entertaining on Sunday nights or "overdressing." Helen, however, came to feel that wearing satin before sunset was a gaffe she could overlook in a woman who was willing to be her friend. Gradually she assembled a circle of friends her mother and sister would not have received but who provided warm, humorous company and, it had to be said, a broader view of New York than Helen had been used to. Laura Montgomery, for instance, actually wrote novels (naturally published under a pseudonym), and Polly Exton was the wife of a Columbia College professor who gave tea parties in a white clapboard house up near the college campus on Forty-Ninth Street. Selina

Maitland would not have found them "presentable" but Helen was always happy to see them at her own tea table. And it had to be said that their conversation was often more wide-ranging than the gossip and chatter about fashion at her sister's house.

Getting Joshua professionally placed was more straightforward, thanks to the groundwork he had done in London. It turned out that even after his months living in what felt like luxury, he had underestimated both the Maitlands' power and their wealth. Within a week of the Wilcoxes' return to New York, Noble Latimer took Joshua to lunch at the very exclusive Union Club and enlightened him. The Maitland family feeling was that transport would be an appropriate occupation. New York City was growing and people needed to reach their places of employment. Had Joshua ever thought about setting up passenger horse-cars as well as freight transport? Joshua had not but instantly saw the point. He also grasped that the scale of business envisioned for him as Helen's husband dwarfed anything he had imagined.

There were conditions, however. The Maitlands and the Latimers and their friends had made their money in trading, banking, and the law. Helen Maitland's husband could not trudge around town with manure on his shoes. Nor could he be seen driving one of his own wagons. "Your life and Helen's—and Jemima's, too—will be easier if you just do as we all do."

"My mother and sister are just upriver. I'm not going to forget about them."

"No," Noble answered mildly, placing his knife and fork gently across his plate. "Everyone already knows where you come from. And from my point of view, that creates an opportunity." He smiled. "I have an understanding with Dora Maitland, you see. But Mrs. Maitland has reservations."

"Mrs. Maitland just enjoys creating difficulties," thought Joshua. But he merely nodded. "And do you have any other advice for me?"

"I would be happy to act for you in connection with family legal and financial matters," Noble said. Then he hesitated and Joshua sensed something new: embarrassment. "Naturally Helen's inheritance from her father is in trust. The beneficiaries are your children. Should, er, anything happen to Jemima, or to further offspring, you would not be able to touch the principal. I apologize for bringing this up but Mrs. Maitland wanted to be quite sure you understood."

Joshua stared at him and took a deep breath while Noble fidgeted with a fork. "My God," he finally said. "She really believes I married Helen for her money."

"I merely wanted to clarify . . ." Noble began but Joshua interrupted him.

"Would you please tell Mrs. Maitland that Helen's money simply complicates matters for me? I don't especially want to live in a house my mother-in-law bought and furnished, you know. But I'll work my fingers to the bone to support Helen and all of our children in the style she's used to!" Then Joshua sat back, aware that he had raised his voice, no doubt a Union Club taboo.

Noble was silent for a moment. "Naturally. It's just that Mrs. Maitland is cautious, and Helen's background brings some benefits. For instance, I may know men who can advise you on your business. Certainly I'll propose you for membership in this club, if you think that would be helpful." As Joshua's eyes widened, Noble continued, "Not yet, I suggest. But New York is a small town in some ways and you'll probably need some of these people sometime." He glanced around the room. "If nothing else, to marry your children to theirs."

"You certainly take a long view!"

"I am a lawyer," Noble reminded him. "We think in generations. Two more things: You may need a man to handle the money as the business grows. Negotiate loans, invest profits, that kind of thing. I'll keep an eye out, if you like."

"That would be helpful," Joshua agreed. "I already have my hands full just keeping everything running, and I could expand if I could stop poring over the ledgers."

"Good," Noble said. "But you may not like my last piece of advice. Change the name of the company."

"You mean it would offend my mother-in-law to see a wagon with my name on it trundling up and down Broadway?"

Noble met his eye. "Yes. That's exactly what I mean."

Joshua took Noble's counsel, calling the business Hudson Transit even before the first blue-painted wagon rumbled down the west side of Manhattan to the shed on Gansevoort Street. (The bright color, Helen's suggestion, horrified Selina when she first glimpsed it, but customers found it memorable.) The year after Dora made her debut, she and Noble were married in the parlor of Selina's house, with the modest pomp then considered appropriate. Amid the white satin and orange blossom, the Wilcoxes' timely trip to Niagara Falls was admired: Some of New York's ladies still had not come around to meeting Helen's husband. It was tactful of Helen to ensure that they wouldn't have to.

When the Civil War broke out, not long after the Latimers' wedding, social concerns receded. Joshua did not see battle, though he tried repeatedly to be reassigned from the Quartermaster Corps. Finally his commanding officer convinced him that he was more valuable to the Union procuring and training horses for remounts than he would have been with a gun in his hands. That was so obviously true that Joshua gave up his efforts to be transferred, and settled with rueful satisfaction to a task he knew he did well.

Helen knew that Joshua was safe most of the time, but that didn't diminish her anxiety about him. Like most of the women left behind in New York, she knew that she couldn't imagine her husband's wartime experience. Joshua wrote when he could but his brief notes only confirmed his health without conveying any of the flavor of his life. Fear, discomfort, and a vague generalized sadness shadowed Helen's days, busy as she was with raising her little daughters and, after 1861, baby Nicholas.

Meanwhile tall slender deskbound Noble served in the infantry with great distinction and swift promotion. Dora, knowing that Noble was on the front lines, took to tracking the war news with maps and pushpins. The sisters spent hours, together with Selina, rolling bandages and knitting gloves or vests to send to the soldiers. As the war years crept past, New Yorkers grew thinner, more haggard, and shabbier. Virtually everyone you saw on the street wore black to signify mourning, even if it was only an armband on a well-worn coat. No one went unscathed through that ordeal.

Yet after 1865, the wealthy of New York did their best to pretend the war lay behind them. Many of the men returned and took up their old occupations. Some, it was true, had been wounded and some were peculiar ever afterward. But at first the country's great upheaval appeared to be a finite episode. Only gradually did the broader consequences appear—such as continuous growth of the railroads, which had transported guns and soldiers during the war and had become essential now for moving products and people across the reunited country. Such as new factories, built to equip armies and continuing now to clothe and equip everyone. Such as new financial instruments and institutions that provided new ways to make startling sums of money. Such as thousands of new people, shaken loose from their homes across rivers and mountains, arriving in Manhattan like so many iron filings drawn to a massive magnet.

Who were they? Who did they *say* they were? Major This, Mrs. That, spinning origin stories without a particle of truth but full of energy and ambition. They watched and learned. They cut corners and glossed over details. They tried and failed and tried and succeeded and kept on trying to gain social footholds in the city. Above all, they kept on coming. For some of the most conservative New Yorkers, it was easy to lump Joshua Wilcox into this group of brash newcomers. He had simply arrived before most of them, and had the luck to marry well. That didn't mean he was socially acceptable.

Nor was his raffish business associate, Robey Gregson. During the pre-war years of Hudson Transit's existence Joshua had worked with a series of what he thought of as "numbers men" whose principal occupation seemed to be preventing him from expanding as fast as he wanted. It wasn't until 1865 that he met Robey and, shortly afterward, offered him a job.

The war hadn't even ended, though everyone knew it was just a matter of time. Joshua was stationed outside of Washington, hoping daily that he would not have to send out another draft of horses to the troops in the field. The man he dealt with in the provisions office was a swaggering dark-haired young wizard named Robey Gregson who always managed to procure what Joshua needed. At the war's end, as they waited to be mustered out, Joshua and Robey spent several languid weeks closing down the depot and trading life stories. Robey, it transpired, was twenty-two, a farm boy from upstate New York who had run away from home at sixteen and never looked back. He was largely self-educated, with a startling gift for figures. By the time Joshua took a train to New York after the depot closed, Robey had joined Hudson Transit, at least in theory. He spent two days in Manhattan roaming the streets and assessing the competition, then another two days poking around the stables. He finished with a long spell examining Joshua's ledgers.

Joshua had thought, until then, that he was managing the finances of the business pretty well. Even in his absence during the war, Hudson Transit had continued to grow under the temporary guidance of an old friend from Tenders Landing (who admittedly understood horses better than he understood the economics of city haulage). By 1865, there were six freight wagons and four passenger horse-cars busily shuttling around Manhattan, but Joshua wanted to expand both the number of vehicles and the area they covered.

He realized quickly that numbers spoke to Robey Gregson. Numbers told stories, set traps, beckoned, and warned. The transit costs for grain from the Midwest, the rent for a warehouse, the time it took to travel from Fourteenth Street to the Battery—all of these had significance Joshua knew he could never have divined. He quickly agreed to Robey's employment conditions. He wanted a salary but not to be a partner. "I'm a gambler," he explained. "It's gotten me in trouble before and it will again, because I like it. So we'll leave the ownership in your hands."

"It doesn't seem fair," Joshua protested, but Robey got his way.

Over the years he had become a steady, if unconventional, presence in the Wilcox household. Despite his ramshackle upbringing, he had read a great deal and had come to appreciate classical music with the fervor of the self-taught. Unlike Joshua, he could discuss culture from *Robinson Crusoe* to Beethoven to Shakespeare, though there were immense gaps in his knowledge that the children enjoyed exploring. ("You mean you've never heard of the Bible?" Nick once asked him, and Robey, deadpan, said, "No.") He also made gentle fun of their parents: Joshua's single-mindedness, Helen's proclivity to worry and her insistence on correct table manners.

Only gradually did he come to discern the strain placed on Helen by the discrepancy between her background and Joshua's. She occasionally referred dryly—never in the children's presence—to the New Yorkers she'd grown up among who now rejected her because she'd married outside the city's traditional elite. And once after the ladies left the dining room so the men could drink their ritual glasses of port, Joshua bitterly described Selina's antagonism and how Dora often mirrored it. In general Robey was amused when he caught a glimpse of the well-mannered conflicts among New York's social elite. But where the Wilcoxes were concerned, that kind of polite cruelty didn't seem funny. And Robey found Helen's way of refusing to acknowledge it rather gallant. Another woman in her precarious social position might have kept the raffish Robey Gregson at a distance, but this she refused to do. Once after dinner, under the influence of a little bit too much brandy, he had asked her why, expecting to be told that Joshua's friends were naturally her friends as well. Instead, Helen had answered, with a gleam of mirth, "When I was a little girl I wanted to know a pirate, and you're about as close as I'll get to fulfilling that ambition." It was a clue to something that had always puzzled Robey: What had brought Helen and Joshua together in the first place? She seemed so firmly embedded in the conventions of conservative New York society. But maybe that taste for adventure still lurked somewhere beneath Helen's apparent propriety.

CHAPTER 6

◆—◆—◆

BALLROOM MANNERS

October 1874

In the fall of 1874 a new tension ran through the Wilcox household, so striking that even easygoing Alice felt it. Papa, who had always been reliably cheerful, sometimes sat in the parlor after dinner staring into space and ignoring the pile of papers on his lap. At other times he spread out those papers on the center table and put on a pair of spectacles that made him look old. Alice once glanced at his work as she said good night to her father, and it was mostly columns of figures, many with red ink at the bottom. Meanwhile Mama frequently looked worried and lost her temper over trifles.

Alice didn't understand what had changed to produce this fraught atmosphere, but on a chilly afternoon she found Jemima curled up on the window seat in the parlor, scowling over an article about the Hudson Elevated Railroad in the newspaper.

"Goodness, you look gloomy," she commented. "This is just about the coldest spot in the house, you know."

"Yes, but the light's good for reading," Jemima answered.

Alice settled down next to her. "Do you at least have on a flannel petticoat?" She lifted her sister's hem to check.

"Of course I do," Jemima answered, without looking up from

the newspaper. "I'm reading about Papa's railway. Apparently it keeps getting bigger, and more people ride it, but it still doesn't make any money."

"I heard them talking," Alice confided in a low voice. Their mother was just upstairs on the landing, going through the linen press with Moira. "It seems Papa's driving freight wagons again," she murmured.

Jemima looked up from the newspaper at that. "Why?"

"I don't know. Mama hates it. She's afraid someone will see him."

"Well, it *would* be embarrassing," Jemima said uncomfortably.

"I know. But he told her nobody notices him. He wears a big hat and a heavy coat with a cape on the shoulders. And he claims he can think about the Elevated while he's driving, so it's like doing two jobs at once."

But Jemima could tell that Alice had something to add. There was a pinched quality in her voice that always meant she was fretting. "What is it?" she asked. "Something else about Papa?"

Alice looked down into her lap. "Do you know who Felix Castle is?"

"Of course, we saw him that day on the train, don't you remember? He helped Aunt Dora with her bag while she carried Trixie. He has that white streak in his hair."

"Well, apparently he's very improper," Alice went on. "He has a gigantic house on Madison Square with a theater in it, and opera people sing there for him."

"Oh, yes, Cousin Miles told me. He also said there's a fountain for champagne, but I don't know if he was teasing."

Alice looked puzzled. "It flows with champagne instead of water? But why?"

"Doesn't it sound elegant?" Jemima suggested.

"No," Alice said firmly. "It sounds showy. Like his coach. Did you know? It's a big yellow carriage drawn by four horses."

"Goodness!" Jemima exclaimed. "How outlandish!" But she was rather impressed.

"Yes, and last week, Nick said he saw Papa drive up Fifth Avenue with Mr. Castle. And they were going so fast that Papa's hat had fallen off and the two of them just galloped along laughing."

"Don't you wish you were a boy sometimes?" Jemima asked. "Think of what Nick can do that we can't."

"Yes, but Papa and Mr. Castle . . ."

"Behaving just like boys, by the sound of it. Do you think Mama knows?" Jemima wondered.

"Probably. She once referred to Mr. Castle as 'bad company,'" Alice said.

"Papa has fallen into bad company?" Jemima asked. "That's what she thinks?"

Alice didn't answer directly. "Mama and Papa don't seem very happy with each other just now," she ventured.

Jemima took a deep breath. "No," she agreed, and leaned against her sister. "You know how we used to hear them talking and laughing next door while we went to sleep . . ."

Alice nodded. "They're so polite to each other now, but . . . chilly." She glanced at the newspaper in her sister's lap and pointed to the article headlined: HUDSON ELEVATED TO EXPAND. "What does it say?"

"That Papa and Mr. Gregson are raising money to build tracks all the way to Sixtieth Street," Jemima answered.

"But there's nothing there! Just empty land!"

"I know. But I was just getting to a bit . . ." Jemima ran her finger down a column. "Here—they say that houses will be built

up there if people know they can take a train to work downtown."
She looked at Alice and shrugged. "No wonder Papa is tired all the
time."

"And worried." Alice sighed. She reached out to touch the
fringe on Jemima's shawl; it was an old paisley that usually lay over
the back of the crimson sofa to hide a worn spot in the velvet.
"Why don't you ask Moira to light a fire?"

"That's another thing, didn't Mama tell you? We're trying to
use less coal."

"But you're practically shivering!" Alice protested. Her sister
merely shrugged. "Well, don't let Mama see you, she'll be furious
if you catch a cold, with the first Dancing Class next week."

Jemima leaned her head back against the window and closed
her eyes. "Don't remind me," she said.

"Oh, nonsense," Alice answered. "You have to go, so you might
as well plan to enjoy it. And Grandmama says you look very striking in your gown."

"Does she?" Jemima asked, startled.

"Yes, I heard her telling Aunt Dora and she sounded a little bit
surprised, so you know it's true."

"Striking," Jemima repeated. Without knowing it, she sat a little straighter on the window seat. "Goodness! Thank you for telling me." She leaned forward and kissed Alice on the cheek. "I
wish you could come with me—but I suppose then all the boys
would want to dance with you instead."

Nevertheless, over the following few days, Jemima's thoughts
returned often to what Alice had told her. It had never occurred to
her that a girl of seventeen could be striking.

On the afternoon of the first Dancing Class, the Wilcox house
bustled with activity. Moira—who generally delegated the laundry

to a girl who came in twice a week—heated her specialized irons near the kitchen fire to ensure that each ruffle of Helen's and Jemima's petticoats was crisply starched. Dinner, naturally, took second place to primping, so soup and fruit were sent up to the bedrooms on trays. Nick retreated to the schoolroom in protest, but nobody noticed.

Nothing had been left to chance. Moira and Helen together had decided on Jemima's coiffure; her hair would be braided high on the crown of her head, emphasizing her long neck. As she stood before the long mirror in her mother's bedroom, wearing only her pantalettes, petticoats, chemise, and corset with her heeled shoes and embroidered stockings, Jemima's eyes widened. She raised her arms and touched the braids secured with tortoise shell hairpins.

"Does it feel loose?" Moira asked.

"Not at all," Jemima said. "It's just that I look grown up!"

"That you do," Helen agreed. She had already finished dressing, so as to concentrate on Jemima. "Now Moira and I will put on your skirt; put your arms up!" With the utmost care, the folds of golden-orange *peau de soie*, gathered to a small bustle at the back, were lowered over the petticoats. Moira hooked the waistband while Helen tweaked the skirt into place. Jemima twirled, the skirt billowed, and everyone smiled. Then Moira held out the sleeveless bodice with its velvet trim and narrow ruffle of lace around the square neckline. Jemima started to do up the row of hooks in front but Moira gently pushed her hands away.

"You're a grown-up lady for the evening, so let me dress you like a lady's maid," she said. When she finished she rested her hands lightly on Jemima's shoulders and kissed her on the cheek, to her own and Jemima's surprise. "You'll do us all proud," she said simply.

"What does your skirt feel like when you move?" Alice asked. "Can you feel it dragging behind you?"

Jemima took a few experimental steps, to the window and back. "Not a bit. The silk is very light." She stood in front of the mirror for a moment, turning from one side to another in an attempt to see herself from behind.

"Here," Alice said, and gave her a hand mirror. For a moment the sisters stood side by side—Alice dressed for the schoolroom in a calf-length dress and pinafore, Jemima attired for the evening like a grown-up lady.

Jemima nudged her sister's laced boot with her heeled velvet shoe. "Just think, next year *you'll* be wearing long skirts and putting your hair up," she said. "And Mama will have two grown-up daughters."

"Oh, girls, you make me feel old," Helen protested. "Moira, I think I need another hairpin right here," she said, pointing to a spot where her chignon was loose. "And, Jemima, go to my jewelry box, would you? I think Grandmama's seed pearls might look pretty with that neckline."

"Aren't you going to wear your diamond pendant?" Jemima asked as she complied. She took out the battered leather case that held the pearls. "I don't see it here, though."

She happened to be looking at her mother as she asked the question and was surprised to see a flash of emotion: Was that annoyance? Fear? Something alarming, at any rate, crossed her mother's face.

"Oh, yes, I'd forgotten, the clasp was loose and I took it to Mr. Tiffany." She removed the pearls from the case and clasped them around Jemima's neck. "Mama gave these to me when I was your age," she said. "What do you think?"

Jemima touched the necklace and smiled into the mirror. "I love them, Mama. And I like knowing you wore them. But don't you need a necklace?"

"I'm only a chaperone so nobody will notice me," Helen said, but Moira peered into the jewelry box and pointed.

"Perhaps you could wear that cameo around your neck, ma'am. I can stitch it to a bit of ribbon in no time."

"It's terribly old-fashioned," Helen objected.

"But it suits you, Mama," Jemima declared. "It's unusual."

"If you say so, dear," Helen conceded, and stood up. "We'll go downstairs and put our gloves on," she told Moira. "Joshua promised he'd come home in time to see Jemima in her finery."

"Who will drive us?" Jemima asked as they filed downstairs. In the last few months Morrison had reluctantly gone to work for Hudson Transit, a change he regarded as a demotion, but that meant he was still being paid. The Wilcox family could no longer afford their own coachman.

"Your father promised to send Morrison by eight o'clock," Helen answered. She went into the parlor to peer out the window. "But there's no one there."

"It isn't time yet," Alice said in a soothing voice. "But here are the gloves." She held them out toward her mother and sister.

"Oh, thank you, dear," Helen exclaimed. She and Jemima began the delicate task of working their hands into the tight ivory kidskin, smoothing and tugging until they reached halfway up the arm. Then Moira trotted down the stairs with Helen's large cameo brooch fastened to a length of brown moiré ribbon, which she tied around Helen's neck.

Helen turned her head to the right and to the left, watching her reflection do the opposite. "It's not too old-fashioned?" she asked.

"Not at all," Jemima declared. "It's pretty."

Just as she stepped away from Helen, the front door opened on a gust of cold air and all four women turned around.

"Well, aren't you the finest-looking mother and daughter in New York!" Joshua announced as he swept off his hat. "Morrison was still out on a delivery run, so I'm going to drive you myself!"

Helen froze. For just an instant she saw, not her husband, but one of those anonymous drivers wrapped in a dirty caped coat who piloted traffic up and down the streets of the city every day. A pair of filthy gloves stuck out of one of his pockets yet beneath his coat he was wearing a high-collared shirt and a cravat she had given him for his birthday. Complicated feelings washed through her: How sweet he was, to remember Jemima's first Dancing Class. Yet how inappropriate that he should drive them there; what if he was recognized?

At that moment they heard Nick clattering down the stairs from the schoolroom, where he had taken refuge from the intense feminine activity dominating the rest of the house. "Papa!" he exclaimed. "I saw you today! Was that Mr. Castle's carriage you were driving? My goodness, you were cutting through the traffic!"

Joshua met Helen's eyes for an instant before saying, "Yes, I had to go uptown to see the surveyors at Sixtieth Street. I was trying to get a cab and Castle stopped for me. He let me take the reins. Those horses of his are a marvel."

"Four matched grays," Nick told Helen. "And Papa was handling them perfectly. You should have seen it, everyone was staring!"

"I didn't realize Mr. Castle was a friend of yours," Helen said, but the warmth had left her voice. "Moira, I think it's time." She lifted her cloak from the hook next to the mirror and handed it to

Joshua, then stepped into the parlor so that he had to follow her. "You drove up Fifth Avenue on Felix Castle's coach?" she whispered angrily as he settled the cloak on her shoulders.

"Yes," he answered quietly, "and I'll do it again if he invites me to. I know Castle isn't the kind of man you want to know. I don't blame you . . . he told a few stories. He's led quite a life for a man his age. Do you know, he's barely thirty?"

She frowned for a moment. "That does surprise me. You are aware that house of his is right across the street from the Abbotts? Where the Dancing Class is tonight? They were horrified when he moved in. He entertains a great deal. Ostentatiously," she added. "Oh, dear, I sound just like my mother."

"Now you make me curious," Joshua told her with an impudent grin. "Maybe I'll drop in on Castle if I can get someone to hold my horses."

"You wouldn't!" she exclaimed sharply, imagining the gossip if Joshua were identified on Castle's doorstep by any of the Dancing Class ladies.

He ignored her query. "Have I told you how wonderful you look?" He hooked the cloak beneath her chin. "This is pretty," he added, touching the cameo. "Why haven't I seen it before?"

She flinched away from him. "Because I usually wear my diamond pendant with this dress." The glee drained away from his face and she felt a prickle of remorse as their brief moment of camaraderie faded. But she was so angry! Three weeks earlier, Joshua had come to her asking if she could borrow against her trust to make a payment for the Elevated. She had refused; he had cajoled. Then he had explained that he, along with the other three partners, had pledged what seemed to Helen like an outlandish sum to keep the Elevated running for another month. And if Joshua couldn't produce the money, he risked losing his stake in the company. One of his partners would take over his shares and everything he had put into the Elevated would be lost.

Ultimately, dutiful wife that she was, Helen had taken her pendant to Mr. Tiffany, along with a heavy gold chain left to her by her godmother, and a pair of old-fashioned earrings that turned out to be sapphires. She had handed over Mr. Tiffany's check to Joshua but, fueled by righteous indignation, had closed her ears to his thanks.

Ever since that night on the dock at Tenders Landing, Helen had trusted Joshua completely. He had promised to take care of her. But now, for the first time in their marriage, a distance had opened between them. To Helen and the Maitlands—as well as to many of their friends—fortunes were nursed carefully to hand down from generation to generation, and spending capital was practically sinful. But to Joshua money was a mere resource, something to be used as needed, because you could always earn more. But *could* he? His elevated railroad seemed like an increasingly quixotic notion, demanding ever more unforeseen effort and funding. What, Helen wondered, would be the end of it? And as if his financial difficulties were not alarming enough, he seemed to think it reasonable to supplant Morrison on the carriage box, without considering the repercussions if he were recognized. It was one thing to drive a sporting carriage on Fifth Avenue but masquerading as a servant was simply unheard of!

Both Jemima and Helen were silent in the carriage, each looking out her window. Helen knew Jemima was apprehensive about the Dancing Class and wished she could think of a way to encourage her daughter. It couldn't help that the atmosphere at home had been strained for the past weeks. Despite her best efforts, Helen knew she hadn't been able to hide her own worries.

If only Joshua hadn't bought the Elevated! He had delegated an employee to run Hudson Transit so that he could focus on the Elevated. While Hudson Transit was notably not growing, the Elevated had generated a continuous flow of permits, employment contracts, faulty loads of iron, and interference from city officials in the year and a half since its purchase. Sometimes Helen felt as if the railroad were a living thing, absorbing Joshua's attention and Helen's money. At a family dinner she had drawn Noble aside to ask about it. The caution with which he had answered chilled her: "The potential is great," he had said in his temperate way. "But there are a great many hurdles to navigate before he's sure of success."

Then they had been interrupted so Helen had not been able to ask Noble what she really wanted to know: What was the worst possible outcome? Helen's inheritance from her father was tied up in a trust fund for the children, thank heaven. But Helen knew that Joshua's partners, the kind of rough-and-tumble newcomers to New York she would never meet, did not care about Joshua's family. They would keep pressing for further investment, and where was the money to come from? As Joshua turned the carriage onto East Twenty-Fifth Street, Helen admitted to herself that she was afraid. But that was not a helpful thought at the moment. Before her lay a very different kind of challenge and she would meet it squarely, for Jemima's sake.

The street was clogged with carriages. Usually neighbors consulted each other to avoid entertaining on the same evening. But in this instance cooperation had been literally unthinkable because the Abbotts, one of New York's oldest and stuffiest families, emphatically did not know their neighbor across the street—Felix Castle.

Helen had grown up with Letitia Bradshaw, who married George Abbott at eighteen. Letitia had lived with him and their four children in a conventional brownstone row house for many years before Felix Castle had bought the two modest clapboard houses across the street. To the Abbotts' shock, those dwellings were demolished and an elaborate redbrick mansion had replaced them, complete with a patterned tile roof, carved limestone ornamentation, and even a small margin of lawn, divided from the sidewalk by an elaborate cast-iron fence. On this evening, light poured out of the mansion's open front door, flanked by two gilded torchères. A tall, solemn butler stood at the doorway, nodding at approaching guests.

Joshua lifted the hatch in the roof of the Wilcox carriage. "It will take a while to get through the crowd," he told them. "Do you want to walk the rest of the way?"

Helen sighed. "I suppose we'd better," she answered. The carriage drew to a halt and rocked as Joshua clambered off the box to open their door. He unfolded the steps and held out his hand to help Helen down, then Jemima. In the dim light from the streetlamp he could have been a real coachman, except for the fact that he kissed Jemima on her cheek and said, "The boys who get to dance with you will be very fortunate."

"Thank you, Papa," Jemima replied, and Helen saw in the glow from Mr. Castle's house that her face brightened.

Lifting their skirts above the sidewalk, they picked their way toward the Abbotts' house. Across the street two other women in long cloaks stepped down from a carriage and hurried up the sidewalk to the Castle house, exclaiming about the cold. One of the cloaks, Jemima noticed, was lined with what looked like scarlet silk. "Mama," she said in a low voice, "did you see . . ."

But her mother was already climbing the steps of the Abbotts' brownstone, so Jemima had to follow without finding out whether a scarlet lining was showy.

Jemima had not known what to expect of this first Dancing Class, but the moment she crossed the threshold, she understood that she'd inflated its importance. "Dancing," in her imagination, had implied a ballroom—but how could that be possible in a row house virtually identical to her own? Instead, the sliding doors between the parlor and dining room had been opened to create one long space, and most of the Abbotts' furniture had been removed except for a sofa pushed up against a wall. Spindly gold-painted chairs lined the walls while an upright piano stood in one corner as a lady in dusty-looking velvet sat on the stool, flexing her fingers. Three droopy potted palms stood in one corner; the general effect was uninspiring.

Alas, so were the boys. They clustered together in the bay window, shuffling their feet and elbowing each other. Jemima spotted a few sons of her parents' friends, almost transformed in their tail coats and white ties—but not completely. Robert Montague, who had once pulled Jemima's pigtails at church, had grown several inches since she'd seen him last—but he had not "filled out," as her grandmother would have put it. Another boy—and this one Jemima pitied—had apparently not yet reached his full height. The adjacent girls towered over him. Hubert Storm had tried ineffectively to flatten his curls with what Jemima, when she danced with him, found to be a heavily scented pomade. In short, one sweeping glance made vivid what she should have grasped all along: The boys she would learn to dance with were no more interesting than her brother. They were just older. The realization was both disappointing and a tremendous relief.

Every girl had a partner for every dance. Not only did the boys outnumber the girls but her mother and Mrs. Abbott relentlessly collared the stragglers and pressed them into service. The dancing master—a tall bald man with some kind of European accent—circulated among them all, sometimes seizing a girl to demonstrate the correct steps to her partner and then delivering her back into the boy's ritual embrace. Bit by bit, Jemima found herself becoming accustomed to the startling physical proximity of her partners. From time to time, when her steps matched those of her partner, the dancing could be momentarily exhilarating.

"But," she told Alice that night, as they brushed their hair before bed, "it certainly didn't happen often. Apparently not many boys can count musical beats. We should start training Nick now."

"That's a good idea," Alice said. "He'll have to dance with us when we come out, anyway. And what about the small talk? Did you do as I said?"

"I did!" Jemima crowed. She set down the brush and began braiding Alice's hair for the night. "I asked every single boy where he went to school and how he liked it and whether or not he had siblings or a dog. Evidently boys can talk forever about their dogs."

"And did you like any of them?" Alice asked. "Were they handsome?"

"One was," her sister answered. "There you go, my turn." She tied Alice's braid with a scrap of ribbon and handed over the hairbrush. "Arthur Onderdonck. Do you remember him? Mama said his parents used to live near Grandmama and that we played together in Washington Square sometimes. He's very good-looking."

"Describe him," Alice commanded.

"Tall," Jemima began.

"How tall? I want to picture him," Alice prompted.

"I could just see over his shoulder," Jemima said. "Dark brown hair, quite curly. Brown eyes. Ouch, wait, you didn't get all the hairpins out!" she exclaimed, and reached behind her head to find the one that had scratched her scalp. "Here you go," she said as she handed it over.

Alice lay it on the dressing table and kept brushing. "Was he a good dancer?"

Jemima caught her sister's eyes in the mirror and grinned. "Eventually. The dance was a waltz and I had to tell him there were only three beats in a measure. But once he caught on, we managed quite well."

"He must be very good-natured. Do you look forward to seeing him again?" Alice asked as she began braiding her sister's hair.

Jemima thought for a moment, then answered, "I think so. Although his friends all called him 'Donkey.'"

At that Alice burst out laughing. "Of course they do! How could they resist?" She tied off Jemima's braid. Yet Jemima hadn't been altogether candid with Alice. It was true that Arthur Onderdonck wasn't an especially good dancer. But once they were waltzing correctly he had said, "I overheard your grandmother tell my mother that you'd rather be at home with a book. Is it true?"

"Oh, absolutely!" Jemima had told him, startled. "Wouldn't you?"

"Of course," he answered, smiling at her. "But I never realized I could talk about books *while* I was dancing. I wonder if you're partial to the novels of Wilkie Collins?" And strangely enough, as they discussed the relative merits of *The Moonstone* as opposed to *The Woman in White*, Jemima found herself following Arthur's steps without a second thought.

CHAPTER 7

❖

SOCIETY AT PLAY

November 1874

M any of New York's wealthiest citizens were skittish that fall, without being able to say exactly why. Of course the great Panic of 1873 had occurred only a year earlier, forcing the Stock Exchange to close for the first time and decimating many a speculative fortune. Even New Yorkers with physical assets (acres of real estate or miles of rail) felt the pinch in their own way. One lady told her friends she had put her diamonds into a bank vault: "It doesn't seem right to wear them when the poor are suffering." At the same time such people were convinced that their social activities sustained the city's morale and its economy. If New Yorkers ceased entertaining, what would the florists do? What about Isaac Brown's livery stable, which existed to shuttle the right people to the right places? Certainly supporting the Italian Opera Company was essential. On performance nights the owners of boxes at the Academy of Music regarded the musicians in the pit with satisfaction. Without a doubt, they stood between those fiddlers and starvation.

In point of fact, it was not the eighteen wealthy box-owning families who supported the artists, but instead, the more than three thousand average New Yorkers who simply happened to enjoy opera and bought seats elsewhere in the house, where one could actually see the singers and hear the voices. Robey Gregson, improbably, was one of these. He adored being swept away by the ludicrous plots and the lush sounds, a complete escape from his daily life and one he indulged in as often as possible. He usually sat in the cheapest seats, among people wearing street clothes who knew the repertoire and sometimes even spoke the language being sung on the stage. But occasionally, when he craved elegance, he would take the trouble to change into a tailcoat and buy a seat in one of the upper tiers.

One evening in November, he was startled to hear his own name. Standing at the bar to buy a glass of champagne, he had just realized that his pockets were empty, and turned away with an apology to the bartender.

"Gregson!" said a voice. "Change your mind?" And there was Miles Latimer, whom he'd last encountered at the Hudson Elevated office several months earlier. At that point Joshua had been giddily contemplating elaborate shelters high above the street at each station and asked his young relative to draw some plans. Miles—as one might have expected, given his limited practical experience—had made exquisite drawings for handsome structures that cost three times the named budget.

"No," Robey confessed ruefully. "I forgot I was broke."

Latimer laughed. "Well, so am I, now that you mention it." He left the line and drew Robey aside. "Come up to our box. There's usually a bottle of something or other in the anteroom."

Robey hung back. He liked Latimer and would happily have drunk with him in a bar, but an opera box was different. "It's good of you," he protested. "But I can't come to your box. Mrs. Latimer wouldn't like it."

"She isn't there," Latimer countered breezily. "Dora has a head-ache and Noble only pretends to like opera, so we'll have it to ourselves," he went on, leading Robey up the stairs.

Robey was surprised by the stuffy little anteroom Latimer led him into; it held only a few upright chairs, a small table, and a dusty cabinet for bottles and glasses. Latimer reached into it and extracted a dark green bottle without a label. "This will have to do," he said, pouring a glass for Robey, who discovered it was a very old and excellent brandy. "My uncle must have left this here," Latimer said when he'd tasted it. "We're lucky it's not one of Do-ra's fruit cordials. These chairs look unreliable; let's go through." He gestured to the narrow door into the box. "You'll be shocked by how poor the view is."

Robey hesitated. He knew from Joshua that the stage boxes were the exclusive province of New York society, thought of as an extension of a family parlor. "Is this really all right?" he asked.

"Oh, yes," Miles answered casually. "We can invite any guests we please."

"You won't be sent back to France because I'm sitting here?" Robey murmured as he entered the box.

"No fear," Miles answered proudly. "I've just been taken on as an employee at the Van Ormskirk real estate office so I am now a wage-earning member of New York society."

Reassured, Robey followed Miles's lead and pulled a chair for-ward to the edge of the box. When he sat, he was startled. A good third of the stage was out of sight. Instead, he had a magnificent view of the boxes on the other side of the proscenium. In one of them an old lady promptly picked up her opera glasses to examine him. Robey hadn't learned much in the way of manners as a boy in upstate New York, but his mother had always told him it was rude to stare. "Are you sure I'm allowed to sit here?" he asked Miles. "Those ladies across the way look shocked."

"The ancient Popper sisters," Miles informed him, bowing across the stage to the two ladies, who both hid behind their fans. "Deaf as posts, both of them, but they come to the opera to keep an eye on the audience. That's what most people are doing here, anyway." Robey could have corrected him but instead looked out over the audience members gradually returning to their seats.

His eye was caught by a familiar face. A few weeks earlier, after a drive, Felix Castle had brought Joshua back to the offices on the far west side where Hudson Transit and Hudson Elevated, separate companies, shared quarters. Castle had politely let Joshua show him around but spared little attention for Hudson Transit. It was just one of several freight and passenger companies in the city; successful but nothing novel. The development of the Elevated, however, intrigued him. Robey recalled Castle's penetrating question, "Where will you find the next big capital sum?" His air of authority, combined with that streak of white hair, made him seem like a much older man but Robey knew he wasn't. And there he was, seated in the first tier of the opera house, looking very much at home.

In fact, Felix Castle *did* feel at home, in this or any other opera house. Growing up in a German settlement in Ohio, he had been surrounded by expert amateur musicians. Most members of his extended family played an instrument or two and they routinely spent evenings singing Bach chorales together. Felix didn't sing much in New York but he was competent enough on a keyboard to accompany the female singers whom he sometimes entertained in his house. Contrary to New York's gossip, these encounters were almost always chaste, because Felix valued conversational skills as much as musical ability. All too often he found that a ravishing soprano cared only about the brilliance of her high notes and, to a lesser extent, his rumored wealth. And all too rarely did a diva actually seem to enjoy gently flirtatious and cultured conversation—which was what he missed most in New York City.

But it seemed, from what little Felix saw of the city's upper crust, that sophisticated dalliance was generally in short supply. His seat in the first tier gave him an excellent view of the proscenium boxes, several of which were apparently owned by the gentlemen's clubs. The members, he had observed, would usually escort their wives to the opera but preferred to view the performance with their fellow club members.

On this particular evening he had trained his opera glasses on the Union Club box as the members returned from the interval, most of them quite a bit jollier than they had been at the end of the act. What did they gain from their attendance at the Academy of Music? Was it, as he suspected, a mere roll call of the blue bloods? And what would it be like, he wondered, to sit with them? To take for granted your position as one of the city's elect? To look down, literally, on the hoi polloi?

Felix knew he would never possess that calm conviction of superiority. But he was a decade younger than most of the fellows he did business with, and richer by far. Sooner or later, he was sure, he would be one of the important men socially as well as financially. That was the way America worked. Those clubmen might pride themselves on their ancestors but Felix knew that wealth was always going to win in this city. Even now, he thought, change was afoot. For instance, what was Robey Gregson doing in a stage box with Miles Latimer?

Felix would not have expected Gregson to be an opera lover

but perhaps that was narrow-minded. Gregson was almost certainly more cultured than his partner Joshua Wilcox, who after all his years in the city was hardly cosmopolitan. Felix liked Wilcox, of course; he was good company as well as being an excellent horseman. And he'd done well with his business, too; it took considerable imagination and ambition to turn a small-town freight wagon into an important city transit company. His wife's money had probably been a substantial factor, Felix suspected, but the vision had been Wilcox's. The same was true for this new elevated railroad—not many men would have grasped its potential or had the nerve to pick it up for the pittance Felix heard he'd paid for it.

Still, Felix thought, as the lights dimmed for the second act, raising capital would be a challenge. He'd gone driving with two of Wilcox's partners, Alonzo Clark and Bob Logan, the previous week, racing up Second Avenue all the way to the little village of Harlem. Felix had gone inside to get the beer and when he came out carrying the tankards, they were discussing Hudson Elevated. Felix spent a moment envisioning the comical meeting of ruthless, profane Bob Logan and Noble Latimer, the fourth partner in the venture, who looked like he slept in a high starched collar. Alonzo Clark was an equally unlikely business partner: He had been amassing acres of land uptown, often by razing the flimsy cottages and barns erected on them by squatters. (Though perhaps no less likely than Robey Gregson.) On that balmy afternoon by the Harlem River the men discussed raising money for a track extension: Each of the partners had committed to the substantial sum of fifty thousand dollars more than he had already invested. And who could say that would be the end of it? Nobody had ever run an elevated railroad along the streets of New York City. Nobody could really say what it would cost to build it. The risk was immense—especially for a man with a family like Joshua Wilcox. But so were the potential rewards.

At that moment Felix was brought back to the operatic proceedings because the soprano on the stage uttered a piercing shriek that was impossible to ignore. She then collapsed into the arms of the tenor and Felix enjoyed the resulting ravishing duet. But he was distracted again shortly afterward by a quiet disturbance in one of the stage boxes—the one next to where Robey Gregson sat with Miles Latimer. An imposing matron in garnet brocade was entering her box while clearly—in pantomime, out of deference to the music—scolding the equally imposing young lady who was clearly her daughter. (Gestures, emphatic flouncing down into chairs, agitated movement of her fan.)

Robey was surprised, too. He understood the theatrical value of making an entrance, but why would you want to compete with some of the most sublime music in the operatic repertoire?

He whispered to Miles Latimer, "Is your neighbor always this disruptive?"

"That is the mighty Annabelle van Ormskirk," Miles answered behind his hand. "She does as she likes."

Robey slewed his eyes to the left. Not more than eight feet away the regally upholstered matron was glaring at him and hissing in the ear of the young lady. Mama wanted to change seats, it appeared. Daughter was refusing. Robey casually turned toward the stage and muttered to Miles, "Do they always make such a fuss?"

Oh, Miles was smooth! Without turning, almost without opening his mouth, he whispered, "Mrs. Van Ormskirk is afraid you'll contaminate the fair Caroline."

"Contaminate her with what?"

"Lust, probably. That's the problem with opera. It's all about improper people." The scraping of chairs in the next box reached a climax that was almost drowned out by an orchestral crescendo.

Robey angled his own chair toward the stage with what he hoped was a careless air and pretended to be carried away by the music. Nevertheless, the back of his neck prickled. The girl was still staring; he was sure of it. He squeezed his eyes closed and tried to follow the opening notes of the tenor's subsequent aria but behind him the mother whispered emphatically.

When the tenor concluded and the audience burst into applause Robey dared to open his eyes and look around. Directly across the auditorium the Popper sisters had their opera glasses trained on him. He glanced at Miles, whose eyes followed the female chorus shuffling onto the stage below. Robey couldn't help sneaking another glance at the Van Ormskirk box, where unfortunately his eyes met those of Miss Caroline. Her face flamed and she flinched, as if she had touched tinder. Ridiculously Robey felt himself flush in turn. He nudged Miles and muttered, "I seem to be the cause of a disturbance."

Miles leaned back and whispered, "Don't worry about them. I'll make peace with the mighty Annabelle during the next interval."

But he wasn't given the opportunity. As the chorus that concluded the act came to an end, chairs scraped again and the ladies made their departure, closing the box door with quite audible emphasis just before the applause began.

Robey applauded and stood, then thanked Miles and said frankly that he preferred to return to his own seat. "It's been an education to sit here with the city's grandees," he added. "I never thought I'd lay eyes on the famous Mrs. Van Ormskirk in the flesh. But the ladies distracted me as much as I did them. And I did actually come for the music."

Miles nodded. "Maybe I'll sit in the orchestra with you sometime," he said. "I'm quite partial to the music myself."

The following evening at the Latimers' house, repercussions occurred. No sooner had the kitchen door closed behind the butler than Dora turned to Miles with a furrowed brow. "What's this I hear about your taking Robey Gregson up to the box last night?"

Miles hastily swallowed his spoonful of soup. "What *did* you hear? I ran into Robey at the bar. He joined me for the second act, then went back to his seat somewhere else."

Dora raised her eyebrows slightly. "And Annabelle had to leave early because Caroline was with her."

"Why shouldn't Caroline van Ormskirk sit with her mother in an opera box next to Robey Gregson? He's well-behaved, good-looking, well-dressed; perfectly presentable," Miles protested.

"No, he's not," Dora contradicted hotly. "Just because he works with Joshua! Goodness, Noble wouldn't try to present his clerks to me!"

"But Robey and Joshua are friends," Miles pointed out. "They've known each other for years. Helen finds Robey amusing!"

Dora sighed dramatically. "Helen isn't a good judge of society. I would think you'd recognize that."

"But doesn't society ever change, Dora?"

"Oh, of course it does," she answered crossly. "However, there are standards! New York's best families have backgrounds and history in this city."

"Like my admirable employer Hans-Albert van Ormskirk," Miles offered. "Whose money is earned by stuffing poor immigrants into shoddy tenements."

"At least they have roofs over their heads," Dora retorted. "And you're twisting what I say. I just mean that a man like Robey Gregson . . . well, where does he come from? Who are his people?"

"Don't you ever meet newcomers to the city?" Miles asked. "And like them?"

"Of course I do," Dora said with exaggerated patience. "But there's some connection already, they aren't just rich strangers who appear and expect to be welcomed." She turned to Noble for support. "Why should these people be taking our places at the opera?"

"But you weren't there!" Miles objected. "He wasn't taking anyone's place, the box was empty!"

Noble felt obliged to intervene. "To be fair, we do think of the box as an extension of our house. We own it, we furnish it, we entertain there."

"Exactly!" Dora chimed in. "Would you have brought Mr. Gregson here? Without asking me first?"

"No, of course not," Miles conceded. "But—"

"But nothing," Dora cut him off. "I know you won't do it again."

Miles knew when he was defeated and let the subject drop but at the end of dinner, when Dora left him and Noble at the table with a bottle of port, he brought the question up again.

"Is Gregson really so unacceptable?" he asked. "He's perfectly polite, and very entertaining."

"Oh, I know," Noble answered. "I've seen quite a bit of him through the Hudson Transit meetings, and under other circumstances, I'm sure Dora would appreciate his company. But she prefers people she can place. She still thinks of New York as a small town. Lots of our friends do—I heard about last night as well."

"Good God," Miles exclaimed. "From whom?"

Noble sat back and looked at his cousin. "Several people. My partner's mother apparently thinks Gregson is very handsome. I believe 'Byronic' was the word she used. And Caroline van Ormskirk has been out for several years, without attracting any suitors."

"So she would fall in love with Robey at first sight? What kind of a fool does Mrs. Van Ormskirk think she's raised?"

Noble shrugged. "Wealthy girls are always attractive to fortune hunters. Some people still see Joshua that way, so Dora's extra sensitive on the subject. And the plainer the girl, the more vulnerable she might be." His eyes met Miles's and they both nodded slightly. Poor Caroline van Ormskirk was no beauty. Noble went on, "You, on the other hand, while possibly eligible, should have your hair cut, according to Mrs. Swain."

"I was thinking it looked artistic but I suppose Mrs. Swain knows better."

"She's sure of it," Noble retorted. "To her, and to quite a few people we know, New York is still a village. They don't like change, and Robey Gregson in a box at the Academy of Music alarms them." He frowned slightly. "They may be right. If Robey Gregson, with his looks and his energy, wanted to marry some New York society girl, her parents might not be able to prevent it."

"I don't know him well," Miles answered, "but I'd wager the debutantes of New York are safe from Robey."

CHAPTER 8

·✦·

BUT THAT'S A FORTUNE

December 1874

A few weeks later, on a bitterly cold day after an early snow-storm, Joshua trotted up the steps of his house in the middle of the day. Helen, opening the door from the inside as he reached the top step, leapt back with a hand to her chest. "Joshua!" she cried out. "What's wrong?"

"Nothing," he answered. "I didn't mean to startle you. I just had something I wanted to discuss."

"It couldn't wait until this evening?" She stood in the doorway neat as a pin in a dark blue mantle, veil pulled down over her face, cheeks already pink from the cold.

"Well, no," he said, putting an arm beneath her elbow. "I need your help with something." He guided her into the hall and closed the front door. "Is there a fire in the parlor?"

"No, we don't, during the day . . . with coal so expensive . . ."

"The dining room, then. You had a fire there for lunch?" She nodded and he urged her down the hall without taking off his coat. "Here, sit," he said, pulling out a chair for her.

"Joshua, you're frightening me," she said, eyes wide. "Why are you here?"

He took off his coat and draped it over the end of the table, then pulled a chair to her side. "I have a question for you. And it's about business."

"For me? What do I have to do with Hudson Transit?"

"Not Hudson Transit, the Elevated." He sat down and took her gloved hand. "You should come with me on the Elevated sometime, Helen. You'd see how important it is. You practically fly above the traffic. And when it extends northward, construction will follow. Believe me when I say this, Helen: Mass transit is essential for New York."

"You're so sure you'll be able to do it?"

"That's why I'm here, about an investment. There's no time to waste, the iron for the columns that support the tracks has already been ordered. We want to start casting in the spring." Helen sat very still, but she felt a trickle of sweat run down her spine.

"So you've come to me for money," she said flatly.

"Yes," he answered, meeting her gaze. "This is a tremendous opportunity, Helen."

"Then talk to Noble," she answered, and got to her feet. "He may think it's appropriate. He might even put in some of Dora's money, too, if he approves. I really need to go, Joshua."

Joshua stood up and faced her. "Don't leave yet," he said. "I haven't been clear. I'm asking for a significant sum, Helen. It could change the future of our family."

She felt her eyes widen. "How much, then?"

"Fifty thousand dollars."

Helen flinched. "But you just put in thirty!"

"It's unpredictable, you know . . ." he went on.

"Joshua, I don't have that much money." She walked out into the hall and looked at herself in the big mirror as she straightened the collar of her blouse.

But of course Joshua followed her. "You do have that much, in your trust."

She turned around and stared at him. "But that's the point, it's in trust. I can't touch it. You certainly can't. The principal goes to the children."

"But you could borrow against it."

It took Helen a moment to understand. "Borrow? Fifty thousand dollars? Think of the interest! Besides, it's a huge sum!"

"Of course it is," he answered heatedly. "That's the whole point! The Hudson Elevated Railroad isn't a toy; we are talking about building an essential element of this city's transportation!"

"Then why are you, Joshua Wilcox, trying to borrow from your wife's family trust?" she asked just as heatedly, then lowered her voice. "Why isn't the Elevated borrowing from a bank?"

"Because the banks won't lend, damn it!" he shouted. "Or, if they will, the interest quoted is outlandish."

"Hush!" She took him by the arm and pulled him back into the dining room. "The servants will hear! And what if you lost it?"

"I'm not planning on losing it! I'm going to invest it in an essential capital project with enormous potential! Noble is putting in fifty. Robey has done it already. They're counting on me," Joshua told her.

Helen walked away from him toward the window and looked out blindly at the brick wall of the neighboring brownstone. "I can't discuss this further. You're asking me to risk our financial security on a . . . speculation!"

"It's not a speculation," he answered, almost shouting. "And you must know I would not do anything to endanger your welfare or that of the children. I would have thought you trusted me that much."

"Well, you should have spoken to me before you made promises to Robey and Noble and those other partners you've taken on," Helen exclaimed.

He took a deep breath, reining in his anger. "Yes," he said shortly. "I've gone about this all wrong." He put his hands on her arms. "I shouldn't have taken you by surprise. All the same, Helen, this is the chance of a lifetime. I could make a difference in this city, improve people's lives by making it easier for them to get to where they work—and make our family's fortune while I'm at it!" He led her gently to two chairs set together and drew her down beside him. "What's more, the Elevated might finally persuade people to think of me as something more than that stable boy you married."

"Oh, Joshua!" she answered, momentarily moved to sympathy. "Nobody thinks of you that way!"

"Not your mother?"

Helen sighed. "You know she's truly very fond of you," she temporized.

"Yes, but she still looks as if she's waiting for me to use the wrong fork," he said. "Or spit tobacco on her rug."

"And you think making money on the Elevated would change her mind?" Helen asked.

"Once she understands how important it is, yes. It's the kind of project your father would have backed without hesitation, you know."

Helen looked directly at him, and sighed. "I suppose so. It just seems so improbable. I need to go, I'm meeting Dora. I suppose there's a deadline?"

He nodded. "Next Friday."

"How can I make such an important decision in a week?" she asked, her anger renewed. "I'll need to speak to Noble, at least.

Maybe he can explain to me why he countenanced this . . . extravagance." He started to protest and she stood, flicking her veil down over her eyes. "I will think about what you've asked me."

"I promise you, Helen," he said, "Hudson Elevated will make Hudson Transit look like that wagon back in Tenders Landing. But what's more important to me is that it will secure our children's futures. Good heavens, Jemima could marry a poet and they'd still be able to live like the Van Ormskirks!" he added with a smile.

Ignoring his attempt at humor, she answered, "I understand that this is important to you. Perhaps Noble can make me see it differently." She met his eyes, then turned and walked briskly out of the house.

She heard her shoes tapping on the slates of the sidewalk as she headed toward Sixth Avenue. She did not actually need to meet anyone; she had nowhere to go in particular. But even on the coldest days Helen usually left the house for a brisk walk. It helped her to think, which was especially urgent now.

How could she make sense of Joshua's outlandish request? Fifty thousand dollars was a fortune. Yet how could they live comfortably together if she denied it?

Her task, her great achievement as a mother, would be to establish her children. She had always assumed that would mean finding pleasant husbands from familiar backgrounds for the girls. She'd watched her friends' children grow up and dreamed of marriages among them.

But what would her daughters' lives be like without assets like hers? Who would marry them if Joshua lost their dowries on the Elevated? What about Nick, what if *he* wanted to invest in a business, buy into a partnership, train for a profession? Money meant freedom. Her family's money had allowed her and Joshua to spend that crucial year in Europe, and come home to a comfortable, elegant house in an excellent neighborhood. Joshua was convinced that investing this huge sum in the Elevated now would go even further to secure prosperous futures for their children, but for the first time in their marriage Helen was skeptical. She was afraid Joshua's ambitions had run away with him. And even if he did succeed, would his earnings open the right doors? After all this time, Joshua still didn't grasp how Old New York worked.

Helen was right: Joshua didn't fully understand the older version of the city, because for the most part, it didn't matter to him. Let the Maitlands and their friends dwell in the past and pride themselves on their traditions and the streets named after their grandparents. Let them worry about what they called "exclusivity" and refuse to "know" people. He had plenty of friends and acquaintances with intelligence and ambition. He'd back them against the stuffy matrons any day.

Nevertheless he was nervous as he climbed the steps to his mother-in-law's house facing Washington Square early the following morning. Selina Maitland was the epitome of a stuffy matron and Joshua, though he hated to admit it, found her intimidating. But she controlled the purse strings in Helen's family. If Helen wouldn't commit to advancing him the sum he so urgently needed, he had no option but to approach his mother-in-law.

From her simple brick house to her ancient butler to her delicate inlaid furniture and even her slender person, everything about Mrs. Maitland made Joshua feel clumsy. As if he had tracked mud onto the faded Oriental rugs that had probably been brought to New York a hundred years earlier. He stood looking out the long window at her ice-encased garden when he heard her come rustling into the room.

"My dear Joshua!" she said, advancing toward him with her hand held out. He took it in his, careful as always not to squeeze it. "I'm sorry to have kept you waiting. If I had known you were coming . . ." Her voice trailed off, implying reproof.

"Yes, I apologize, Mrs. Maitland," he answered, then remembered to release her hand. "Thank you for taking the time to see me."

She merely nodded and sat down on the green brocade sofa with mahogany legs that he was always afraid would break beneath him. Then she looked up at him with blue eyes that held no warmth.

"May I sit?" he asked.

"Of course," she answered. "Oh, perhaps not there," she added as he turned to a petit-point armchair. "I believe the rocker may be sturdier."

The rocker was also farther away from Selina, so that Joshua would have had to shout halfway across the room to make himself heard. "I won't keep you more than a moment," he said firmly, and sat. The chair did not collapse beneath him, so he smiled at her.

"Is there something wrong?" she said. "I know you don't usually have time for morning calls." She managed to sound disappointed, as if she'd spent many an hour in her sunny little parlor awaiting the enlivening presence of her son-in-law.

"Wrong? With the family?" he asked. "No, all's well."

"Then . . . ?" Selina asked delicately.

He met her eyes. Mean, that was what she was. Why had he never realized it before? Probably because she was so slight and pretty and, despite her age, still girlish. He felt a moment's compunction for Helen. She would be furious when she found out what he was doing, and her mother would never let her live it down. But he could not leave this stone unturned, not when the other options were so much worse. "Yes," he said. "I apologize for taking the liberty of coming to you," he went on. "But I've encountered a business opportunity. We're planning on extending the track of the Elevated Railroad."

Selina raised her eyebrows. "Yes? I'm afraid I don't see what this has to do with me."

For a moment, he felt the freeze of panic. Then inspiration came to him; he smiled warmly at her and said, "Helen and I are naturally investing a significant sum in the expansion. And I wondered if you would like to join us."

His mother-in-law put her hand to her chest in a graceful gesture. "I? Oh, goodness, I couldn't think of it!"

"What a pity," he told her. If she could act, so could he. "Ordinarily we would be borrowing from a bank but since the Panic, they've been reluctant . . ." He could tell she was losing interest. "It's a tremendous opportunity, though. I believe the Elevated Railroad will change New York and, to be blunt"—he leaned toward her, as if sharing a secret—"those of us who are in on the ground floor stand to make fortunes, as well as making civic history."

Selina sat still. In the kitchen downstairs a stove lid clattered and Joshua saw her look out the window where that ancient butler of hers was scattering ashes on the icy sidewalk.

He would have to be blunt with her. "So would you loan me the money? Say, fifty thousand dollars?"

She looked up at him in genuine shock, blue eyes wide. "Of course not!" she exclaimed.

Silence hung in the room between them, and Joshua nodded. She'd never liked him, of course, but he'd had to ask—or rather, to offer her an opportunity. There she sat in her severe little room with her threadbare rugs and her plain silver tea set displayed on a mahogany dresser that must have been a hundred years old. It had probably been a mistake to imagine that he could ever convince Selina of the benefits of the Elevated.

"Did Helen send you?" she asked suddenly.

"Goodness, no," he protested. "Helen has no idea I'm here."

"And Noble? Surely you thought to consult Noble before embarrassing me in this way?"

"I certainly never intended to embarrass you," Joshua said. "Noble did discourage me from coming but he's a partner in the business, too. He drew on Dora's capital to buy shares. But," he went on, "Helen's trust documents are written differently. She can't touch her capital to participate in this investment—though of course she would like to." He'd never been a fluent liar before that very moment.

She stood, and he had to follow her lead. He was suddenly aware of looming over her and realized how much she had aged since his marriage to Helen. Aged, but in no way mellowed. "I suppose that seemed reasonable to you," she said. "But you cannot have imagined how unhappy it would make me to discuss money with you. I think we will just forget this, shall we?"

"We needn't speak of it again," he answered. "But I won't forget. You will come to see your decision as a mistake. Investing in the Elevated will help our city grow and create capital that will keep my children—your grandchildren—more than comfortable for many years to come."

"I suppose that seems reasonable to you," she said with indifference. Then she picked up the little silver bell from the sideboard and rang it. The housemaid opened the door instantly—Joshua supposed she had heard the entire conversation.

"Mr. Wilcox's hat and coat, please," Selina said. "Good-bye, Joshua. My love to Helen."

When Joshua got outside onto the street he seized a clump of ice from the side of the road and threw it onto the pavement, hard enough to shatter. Then he walked as fast as he could to the Fifth Avenue Hotel, where he found a hansom to take him to Felix Castle's house. He caught Felix coming down the steps, looking sleek as a seal and just as jaunty.

"This is a surprise!" he said as Joshua's cab rolled away. "Come in out of the cold. What can I do for you?"

"But you were going out," Joshua protested, suddenly reluctant. "I'll come back another time."

"Not at all," Felix replied, ushering Joshua up the shallow front steps. "I know how busy you are. Come in."

Joshua stared at the vaulted ceiling of Felix's front hall, a startling contrast to his mother-in-law's. There were paintings all over it; vines and flowers and fleshy individuals lightly draped in what looked like bedsheets, leering down at him. One seemed to be proffering a goblet while in a corner a weird half-goat creature ogled a pretty girl wearing only her very long hair. Joshua blinked and dragged his gaze down. Felix, at his side, was frowning at the paintings. "I think I'm going to have this painted over," he said. "It was jolly for a while but now, somehow, it seems a little vulgar. I asked for something with wine, women, and song. Probably the wrong idea. Come back to my office."

"No, no, I can tell I'm interrupting you," Joshua protested, spooked by the revelry looming over his head. After enduring Selina's chilly severity, the contrast was jarring.

"Nothing that can't wait." Felix headed down a long hall so Joshua had to follow him, past bits of armor displayed against red brocade. Someone had stuck a sprig of holly into the crest of a helmet. Felix ducked into a doorway and Joshua was relieved to see something he recognized: a big desk covered with papers. "There," Felix said, gesturing to a chair. "Tell me."

Joshua collapsed in relief. "Lord," he said. "I've just come from my mother-in-law and I feel like I've been hauled backward through a hedge."

"Got a tongue on her, has she?" Felix commented with sympathy.

"Not that. Polite but scornful. As if I were the dustman." He heaved a sigh. "The thing is, Castle, I need a loan to tide me over and I thought of you. This is what you do, isn't it? Short-term loans to businesses?"

"Not exactly," Felix said, bright-eyed. "But sometimes I invest in them, if they seem promising. The banks tend to be cautious."

Joshua drew a deep sigh. "They certainly are. I got my brother-in-law, Noble, to ask a few discreet questions but he came up empty. The Elevated is too risky for the Bank of New York and—"

Felix broke in, "And those fellows Logan and Clark are getting ready to nudge you out if you can't pony up."

"How do you know that?" Joshua exclaimed.

Felix tipped his chair back and smiled gently. "It's the pattern. You see it again and again; men have a good idea, get a business going, need more money, go to someone with deep pockets, and next thing they know, it's not their business anymore."

Without realizing it, Joshua had picked up Felix's paper knife and was testing the tip on his thumb. "Exactly, and I can't let that happen. We've put too much into the Elevated, Robey and I. It's our chance, you see that."

"Oh, I do. You just need to buy some time. That's what I'm good for." Felix dropped the front legs of his chair and began rummaging in his desk drawer. "There it is." He hauled a checkbook onto the leather top of his desk and flipped the pages open. "I suppose you'll use your house as collateral? You'll be needing a pretty big loan, I imagine."

Joshua froze. He suddenly felt both hot and cold at the same time. The house! "Well, I don't know," he began. "Can't I put up my shares in the Elevated instead? Only I'd hate to risk . . ."

"No, Wilcox, they won't be worth enough. Not even close. Mind you, I can only let this run for a little while," Felix was saying as he dipped a pen into a silver inkstand. "Maybe as long as six months, if you keep up the interest payments." He began to write, then looked up with a raised eyebrow. "I'll tell you what, I'll only charge you one percent a month, how's that?"

Joshua whistled as he made an instant calculation. The interest rate was almost double what a bank loan would have cost. "But I haven't told you how much I need," he temporized. His stomach felt hollow, as if he were standing at the edge of a pit, which was nonsense. People borrowed money every day (though perhaps not at such high interest). Robey, who gambled, often owed a couple thousand dollars to creditors.

"I'm waiting." Felix waggled the pen at him.

"You probably won't have enough cash on hand," Joshua answered. "Now that I think of it." He began to push his chair back.

"Actually, I do. What do you need, twenty thousand dollars?"

"Fifty," Joshua answered, and stood up. "Listen, Castle, I appreciate your willingness, but I can see—"

"No," Felix interrupted him and held a hand up. "I have it. Sit down. But you'd better get to work right away to find a longer-term source for your loan. I'm a strictly short-term lender—that's why the interest is so high. Understood?" he asked with his eyebrows raised.

"Of course," Joshua agreed. "Although . . . how short a term did you say?"

"Six months if you pay the interest promptly. And if you don't, Wilcox, I warn you I'll foreclose." His tone was matter-of-fact.

Joshua drew a deep breath. "You'd take the house?"

"Do you have something else to offer for security? And to be frank, I doubt the value of your house comes close to matching this sum. Do you want to take some time to think it over? Come back tomorrow?"

"Yes," Joshua said. Then, "No." He stood up and walked to the ornate fireplace where he came eye to eye with a painting of a half-naked woman with a snake twining its way up her arm. He blinked and turned his back on her, almost with fright. "No," he repeated. "I have to—"

Felix interrupted. "Risk it all? The gambler in you is coming out, hmm?" He resumed writing on the check before him. "Nothing wrong with a little healthy fear; it's a lot of money. You're worried about your family, aren't you? What's the worst that could happen?"

"How can you ask that?" Joshua answered, sitting back in the chair by Felix's desk. "I'd have nothing at all! No house, probably have to sell my stake in the Elevated—might as well head right back to Tenders Landing, where I started!"

"It wouldn't come to that," Felix said, blotting the check. "Somebody would take in your family. And you could probably talk Latimer into bailing you out. He seems sensible."

Joshua laughed bitterly. "You don't understand these people, Castle. I think when they turn twenty-one the men all take a sacred vow not to touch what Grandpa earned."

"Is that what it is? I've always wondered." Felix shook his head.

"But you're not one of them, Wilcox. You've made yourself what you are. And without this"—he waved the check in the air—"you'd become a minority shareholder in the Elevated. You'd lose all the work you've put into it, and you'd have to watch with your hands folded if those fellows ran it into the ground."

Silence fell between them for a moment and Joshua felt Felix's eyes on him. Then he took a deep breath. "That's right," he told Felix. "That's what it feels like to me. I just can't pass this up."

"Good. I don't think you'll regret it. I'm going to write out a brief agreement," Felix added, and began scribbling on a loose sheet of paper. "Press that bell, would you? I'll get my butler to witness it and then we'll be fair and square."

Joshua's elation at securing the money lasted almost an hour. He hadn't realized until he secured Felix's loan how desperately worried he had been. He hastened to his bank and watched the check in the clerk's hands until it was clipped together with a deposit slip and tucked into a drawer. For the rest of the day his mind returned to it again and again, with immense relief but also with an expanding sense of possibility. He was on his way! This, surely, was the step that would catapult him into the fellowship of the money men: the fellows like Clark and Logan who didn't depend on their labor to get rich but on the astute deployment of dollars, well invested. He permitted his imagination to roam briefly, and envisioned reinforced tracks for the Elevated that could carry longer trains. He saw himself retrieving Helen's jewels from Mr. Tiffany and encouraging her to replace the parlor curtains she said were shabby. He even—though he realized this was a highly unlikely outcome—envisioned his mother-in-law boasting to her stuffiest friends about his business acumen. "He's done very well for himself, and for Helen," she might say.

CHAPTER 9

◆

OUTRAGEOUS

December 1874

Joshua left the office late the next afternoon and the sun was casting long red rays along Twenty-Sixth Street when he rounded the corner toward home. A narrow path meandered through icy hillocks on either side and his fingers tingled in his pockets. The temperature was dropping again.

Yet when he opened his front door, Helen greeted him in a walking dress and a matching bonnet. She plucked her heaviest mantle off the coatrack and turned him around with a grip on his elbow as if he were Nick at age six. "Out," she said.

"But, Helen, I'm frozen," he protested.

"We'll walk quickly. I don't want every set of ears in the house to hear what I have to say to you." As she crossed the threshold she felt the icy air like a knife, but it did not deter her. Her sheer fury, she thought, would keep her warm. If Joshua was cold, let him shiver.

"What is this about?" he asked, reaching out for her arm. She pulled it away and headed down the steps toward the sidewalk.

"How can you ask that?" He was lingering at the top of the stoop and it took an immense effort not to break down and shriek at him. "You'd better close the door, it's already cold enough inside and I don't suppose we're going to be able to afford much more coal this winter." At that Joshua slammed the front door so hard that the knocker clattered. Maybe Moira would climb the stairs from the kitchen to see who was at the front door. Fine, thought Helen. Moira would know soon enough that Mr. and Mrs. Wilcox had been arguing. "Come down here and walk with me," she commanded, pointing eastward. Then, as a concession, "Please."

He made her wait a moment but complied. They turned together, forced into walking hip to hip on the narrow pathway between the piles of ice. "I suppose your mother called on you today," he said in an exasperated tone of voice. "I should have known she would."

"Of course she did!" Helen answered. She knew her voice sounded shrill but she didn't care. "She said you asked her for money, for *fifty thousand dollars*! The money I wouldn't ask her for!" She paused for a moment as they reached a pile of icy snow at the end of the block. Joshua held out a hand but she didn't want to take it, so she clambered over the snow alone. "You didn't even tell me!" she turned back to exclaim. "You went secretly to my mother without even breathing a word of your intention! Do you know how that . . ." But her voice was wobbling and she refused to cry in front of him, so she turned away and started to cross Sixth Avenue ahead of him.

"Wait, Helen," he called out in a tone of voice that was probably supposed to be soothing. "I don't want to shout at you."

"Well, *I* want to shout at *you*," she replied, but waited until he reached her side before continuing. "What makes you think Mama even has that kind of money available?"

"Your father owned a bank," he said flatly.

"You never have understood my family," she muttered. "The

money's all in trusts and it's not a huge fortune, just a respectable, comfortable . . . nest egg. And you'd already asked me for the money, then you went over my head to my mother! What were you thinking?"

"What any businessman would think!" Joshua answered angrily. "That this is a chance that won't come again! Maybe somehow I didn't make that clear to you!"

"You did make it clear, but sometimes we have to let chances go, don't we?"

"And sometimes we have to take risks," he answered. "You understand that. For heaven's sake, you married me!"

"I didn't have a choice, did I?" she flung back, too angry to regret her words yet. She started to cross Sixth Avenue and had to scurry out of the path of an oncoming hansom. Joshua, right behind her, seized her arm again.

"Careful! The light is terrible, they can't see you," he snapped.

"Oh, damn you, Joshua, you are not always right!" she shouted back at him. But she let him hustle her across the avenue and at the corner she had to take his hand again to climb over an icy mound to the sidewalk. "If you had asked me beforehand I would have told you Mama wouldn't loan you money! And Noble would have agreed! She lives on interest from her capital; what would happen to her if you lost that?" She let go of his hand and began to pick her way down to the sidewalk. "But do you know the worst thing?" she asked in a quieter voice. She could hear the ice crunching beneath his feet behind her. "You've humiliated me. All the years I've spent smoothing a path between the two of you. I never wanted you to know. I didn't want to hurt you. I've defended you and turned aside insults and . . ." He had caught up and stood beside her now. "She never did trust you," Helen said finally, staring straight ahead.

She shook her head and began striding toward Fifth Avenue, then turned back to shout, "And now, in ten minutes, you undo all my work! And prove to her that you married me for my money!" She could feel a tear trickling down her cheek beneath the veil of her hat but she couldn't brush it away without giving Joshua the pleasure of knowing he'd made her cry. She had to let it trickle down her cheek as she hurried along the icy sidewalk.

But Joshua had long legs and he caught up with her in a moment. "Nonsense," he said curtly. "You know as well as I do that's not true. Stop." He seized her arm with a rough grip. "I did not marry you for your money and your mother had nothing to do with my falling in love with you," he said. "Angry as you are, I believe you do know that."

"If you say so," she conceded. "Or maybe you were shamed into marrying me."

"Damn it!" he shouted in his turn. "I was not! I seized the opportunity and I've been grateful every day since then!"

"Well, you chose a strange way to show it," she said coldly, and walked away from him.

"Our marriage is not in question," Joshua said as he came up behind her. "I simply made a business decision, as I have been doing for decades. Most of the time, they pay off."

"And this one didn't!" she cried. "What am I supposed to do now? Day after day my mother is going to harp on this. 'Joshua is so improvident, it's such a pity he manages money so poorly . . .'"

"I'm sorry," he interrupted her.

She kept walking.

"I am. I didn't foresee that."

"She can be such a witch," Helen muttered.

"She can and she will," he agreed.

"Don't ever ask Mama for money again," she said. "Please."

"I won't. It just seemed . . ." He paused. "Like the lesser risk."

They were standing now beneath a streetlamp at the corner of Fifth Avenue and she could feel herself cock her head, like a bird hearing a mysterious sound. "Lesser," she repeated flatly.

"Lesser," he reiterated. "It's cold, Helen, can't we go back now?"

"No," she answered, though her toes were tingling from the cold. "What was the *greater* risk?"

"Can we at least keep moving, then?" he asked. He drew her to the right, along Fifth Avenue. The windows glowed in most of the houses, and they passed a basement kitchen where a tray on a table was being loaded with glasses by a set of disembodied hands.

"The greater risk," she repeated with a hollow feeling. "What was it?" What could be worse, more humiliating, less successful, than trying to borrow money from her mother?

They walked a few more steps before he answered and she began to shiver, either with fear or with cold.

"I borrowed money from Felix Castle to invest in Hudson Elevated so we can build the new track," he said in a soothing tone she recognized. It was the voice he used when something terrible had happened, like a flaming log rolling out of the fireplace onto the rug, or Nick falling off the porch at the Spring House. It was supposed to reassure her that everything would be all right. "Noble and Robey and I each had to put in fifty thousand dollars. So did Clark and Logan. Clark threatened to bring in new investors otherwise. We didn't have a choice."

"Why not find new investors?" she heard herself asking, but really she was just filling the silence.

"The more investors there are, the less we'll make at the end when we sell . . ." he was saying, but she gave up pretending to listen. Her body kept striding forward until Joshua tugged on her elbow and she realized she had stepped out into the street. She looked up and down the street, lined with big solid mansions. They looked warm. Elegant. Maybe those people could put their hands on fifty thousand dollars without hesitation. Without threatening their children's futures. She turned back toward Joshua and examined his face.

"How in the world will you manage?" she said, interrupting some statement about "growth" and "potential." "How will you pay him back? You're already practically killing yourself with work!"

"I haven't figured that out yet," he answered sharply. "But I can just pay the interest until we offer stock to the public, and then my share in the Elevated will have grown enough to repay Castle and set us up with a very tidy capital sum. Can't we go home now? It's so cold, Helen. I want to get you back inside to warm up."

It was true. Her nose was running, and she was suddenly very tired. "All right," she conceded, so they began to retrace their steps westward. "But how can you take enough out of the business to afford the interest payments?" she asked. "You've talked about nothing but cutting costs for months!"

"That's something Robey and I have to work out," he answered, but she thought he sounded uneasy.

"You mean you don't have a plan. You just borrowed fifty thousand dollars and you don't know how you'll repay it," she heard herself say. "Or even pay the interest. Now I am afraid."

"Of what?" he asked.

"Ruin," she said curtly.

"Nonsense," he scoffed. "Not while I can work!"

"But the stories! People losing their houses, moving to farms north of Harlem . . ."

"Those are just tales your mother tells," he said in dismissal. "Do you actually know anyone it has happened to?"

"No, but—"

"Helen," he interrupted her, "you know I would never do anything to hurt you and the children."

"Of course I do," she snapped. "Not intentionally. But people make mistakes all the time."

"True. And people who are afraid to make mistakes never get anywhere! Will you listen to me for a moment? Can you acknowledge that I've run successful businesses since I was not much older than Jemima?"

Helen instantly remembered Joshua's calm competence as they drove along the River Road in Tenders Landing, and had to agree.

"Good," he said with a nod. "There's no real difference with the Elevated, except in scale. The Elevated supplies something New Yorkers need, just as Hudson Transit has done."

They walked on, feet crunching. Without noticing, he slowed his steps to match her shorter stride. As they passed beneath a streetlight he cast a glance at her face. Beneath her veil, it was set. "I admit there is some risk," Joshua went on. "But Noble's cautious, and he's invested."

Helen sighed. "Noble doesn't have three children to raise," she pointed out.

"No."

"You know I just want the best for them," Helen said.

"Of course," he agreed. "Don't you think I do, too? Don't you think I'm making calculations about what kind of dowries I'd be able to settle on the girls if the Elevated is successful? Or finding the right situation for Nick?"

"Of course, but . . ."

He drew her to a halt. "Helen," he said quietly but firmly. "I know our marriage closed some doors for you. But the Elevated has the potential to make us a fortune. And every door in New York will fly open for you and the children and"—here he grinned—"even for me, if the Elevated is the success I firmly expect it to be. The Wilcox family will be welcomed everywhere. Even at the Van Ormskirks'."

She put her arm through his and resumed walking. "I really do want to believe you," she answered with a sigh.

"Well, that's a start," he answered.

CHAPTER 10

⸻ ✦ ⸻

INTRIGUING

March 1875

Changes came to the Wilcox household that winter. A few days after Joshua asked her for money, Helen made a detailed memorandum of the household accounts. "I realize this will not solve your business problems," she said, "but here are some ways we can reduce our expenses at home." She put the sheet of ledger paper down on the center table in the parlor, where he was reading the newspaper after dinner.

He looked up at her and sighed. "Come sit with me for a moment."

She shook her head. "I can't. Moira and I are trying to come up with something for Jemima to wear to the next Dancing Class. We're thinking about cutting down that pink-striped dress of mine you've never liked."

He glanced at the sheet of paper and said, "Thank you for this."

"I know that what we'll save at home isn't much," she said. "But you can put it toward paying interest to Mr. Castle." He didn't have the heart to tell her how little the household sacrifices would count against his debt.

And in addition to being ineffective, they turned out to be so uncomfortable! To use even less coal, the family lit no fires during the day while Joshua was out. The women bundled themselves in shawls and fingerless mitts. Helen often lingered in the kitchen when she went to talk to Moira—at least the stove retained some heat. She continued her usual routine of making calls, doing errands, and receiving friends, but each of these activities was constrained by the family's financial situation. Planning and shopping for meals became more time-consuming as Moira struggled to pare down the grocery bills, and Helen could only offer callers an austere assortment of biscuits with their tea. Family meals were often skimpy and unappetizing. Nick, at fourteen, was perpetually hungry and Joshua lost so much weight that his frock coat sagged about his chest.

The French mademoiselle was let go and Nick began going to boys' classes held by the rector of the nearby Church of the Holy Communion. Helen drew up schoolroom timetables for Alice and Jemima, hoping to simulate the comforting routine of Mademoiselle's lessons, but all three of them understood this was basically a meaningless gesture. Without supervision, the girls spent their days more or less as they liked. Alice played the piano, Jemima read, they helped Moira with the mending. That made Helen fretful: Ladies embroidered, they did not stitch up the holes in pillowcases. But as it happened, the linens from Helen's trousseau all seemed to be wearing out at the same time, and there was no money to replace them. Anyway the girls didn't mind. Alice was a good needlewoman and took pride in her tiny stitches. She was perfectly happy to sit with her workbasket, sewing away in the window seat of the parlor, where the morning light came in. Jemima, much less adroit with a needle, deployed her lopsided stitches where they would show the least.

Jemima was uneasy. Her father sometimes watched her mother with a plaintive expression, as if he wanted something from her that she'd already told him he couldn't have. Their voices sounded strained when they spoke to each other, too—almost as if they were strangers. Her mother seemed to breathe more deeply after her father left the house in the morning.

Jemima didn't eavesdrop, but it wasn't hard to guess that Papa had done something reprehensible in his attempt to find money for the Elevated. One morning when everyone was out of the house Jemima had opened her mother's jewelry box and seen that it was half-empty. Not only was the diamond pendant missing: so were Grandmama's pearls that she'd worn to the first Dancing Class. Stealthily, Jemima had searched her mother's drawers and even slid her hand beneath the mattress in case . . . in case her mother had taken to hiding her jewelry? Jemima couldn't quite explain it to herself.

And if all this unpleasant mystery about the Elevated were not enough to lower Jemima's spirits, the remaining Dancing Classes loomed. Admittedly, they had been tolerable so far. But as the boys became acquainted with the girls, a hierarchy of popularity had begun to emerge. Two of the girls were always the first with partners and they didn't mind boasting about it.

Arthur Onderdonck had not spoken much to Jemima since the first Dancing Class, until they had struggled through a very complicated minuet together in January. In her relief when they ended up roughly in the right place without a collision, she exclaimed to him, "Oh, well done! Thank you!" with a frank grin that warmed his heart. He *had* done well, he realized. And Miss Wilcox was quite jolly, so he hastened to her side when the final waltz was announced.

Jemima had tentatively decided that while she would not be a belle at the Dancing Classes, she could probably escape embarrassment. And Arthur Onderdonck did seem eager to seek her out, which was flattering. She hadn't failed to notice the envious sidelong glances from the other girls as he lingered at her side between dances. It was a pity that he was so quiet, though. Good nature and good looks were important, she supposed—but she was beginning to suspect that they weren't very interesting.

Jemima was mulling over these concerns on a relatively warm day in March, perched in the window seat at home. Mama's friend Sylvia Burke had sent over a box filled with unused dress trimmings. Mrs. Burke had—as Mama often said—a big heart. Be that as it may, Mrs. Burke also favored bright colors and bold patterns. On the faded crimson velveteen of the window cushion lay fringe and bobbles and ribbons, braid, cord, tassels, and several very pretty silk flowers in colors ranging from parrot green to scarlet—nothing that Jemima thought could possibly be pinned at the waist of the deep-blue silk gown she would wear to the next Dancing Class.

She had just discarded a length of crimson braid when she spotted a well-dressed man walking down the block toward her family's house. She recognized him at once as Felix Castle, the man who had helped Aunt Dora with her dog on the train platform back in the fall. Instinctively, she edged off the window seat and perched on the sofa. She would have liked to watch Mr. Castle walk past—what could he be doing on their block? But Mama was very strict about her daughters being seen gazing out the window. It looked "forward."

Yet the next thing she knew, the knocker was sounding. Moira was down in the kitchen helping Cook stuff a pair of rather small chickens for lunch. Alice was in the dining room, playing scales on the piano, and when Alice played the piano she heard nothing else. So Jemima opened the front door.

There he stood, hand still lifted as if he planned to knock again.

He was surprised, that was obvious. "Can I help you?" Jemima asked. Very politely.

He seemed startled. "Is this the Wilcox residence?"

"It is," she answered.

"Doesn't your family have a maid to answer the door?" he asked with a puzzled frown.

"Yes, but she's busy," Jemima told him. "You'd better come in, I suppose, to explain why you're here. My mother thinks it's common to linger on the stoop." She opened the door wider and, with a formal gesture of her arm, ushered him into the hall. He took off his hat and reflexively handed it to her.

She glanced at it for a moment. "Are you staying long?" she asked.

Instead of answering her question, he asked, "Haven't we met?" He looked at her attentively, Jemima thought. As if he really wanted to know.

"Well, last summer you rescued my aunt Dora's pug on the train platform," Jemima reminded him. She couldn't help smiling—it had been so clear how little he liked Trixie. "I'm Jemima Wilcox."

Recognition dawned on him, and he smiled. "Oh, of course! Do you know, that dog bit me!"

Jemima was startled into laughter. "Really? You hid it well." She gestured with the hat. "My parents are both out," she added.

He seemed surprised, she thought. "I'd hoped your father might be here. Your father *is* Joshua Wilcox?"

"Yes, of course," she answered. "But why would he be here?"

"He doesn't seem to be anywhere else," Mr. Castle answered. "I've been to the Hudson Transit office and even to the stables."

"I couldn't say for sure," Jemima told him. "But he's probably driving again. They're so shorthanded at Hudson Transit that sometimes he has to take over a shift on the wagon box. Or that's how he puts it, anyway," she added. "Shall I tell him you called?"

He didn't answer right away. For a good ten seconds he stood still, frowning slightly. Jemima realized that despite the streak of white hair, he was actually quite young. Then he shifted his gaze and caught her looking at him. Her eyes dropped to the floor and she felt a blush flood her cheeks. Gaping at a strange man in her own front hall! How unladylike!

"I don't quite know what to do," he confessed. "I have a matter of urgent business to discuss with your father but I've found him rather elusive."

She put down the hat on the built-in bench below the hall mirror. "If he doesn't know you're trying to find him, that's hardly his fault."

"True, but there's an element of timing . . ." He looked at the grandfather clock in the hall and sighed.

She didn't like his insinuation. "It's slow," Jemima informed him as he tugged on the watch chain crossing his waistcoat and snapped open the lid of a gold pocket watch.

"Yes, so I see. Might I leave him a message?"

"Oh, certainly," she answered. "I'll find you some writing paper. Would you like to take off your coat?"

"Thank you," he answered and shrugged it off, then handed it to her without thinking. "Wait, I can do that," he said. "You're not the maid."

"No, she's in the kitchen at the moment. Come into the parlor," she instructed him, and led the way into the room to the right of the staircase, from which they could still hear Alice playing double octaves of parallel scales without so much as stumbling over a note. "If you'll sit here, I'll be right back."

"Thank you," he said, "I'm afraid I'm disturbing you." She turned back at the doorway with a slight smile.

"Not at all," she answered. "Sometimes interruptions are welcome."

Then she felt her face flame as she went to her mother's desk in the cold little room by the front door. Where had those bold words come from? What would Mr. Castle think of her? But as she opened the drawers to find a pen, she shook her head. What Mr. Castle thought of her could hardly matter. He was no part of her social world—which, on reflection, seemed a pity. She'd never encountered anyone so debonair among her parents' friends. She found herself smiling; "debonair" was just the right word for him.

When she returned to the parlor he was standing in the bay window looking out onto the street. "I've always wondered about houses like this," he said.

"Goodness, why?" she answered. "They're so ordinary!"

"I suppose that's the point," he answered as he turned toward the room. "There are so many of them, repeated in rows up the street. Do you ever think of that?"

"Well, I do, actually," Jemima said in surprise. "If you walk past them at night, you can see in the windows and because they're all the same, the way people live in them seems so dramatic. They're almost like a series of small stages."

"Yes," Felix agreed. "That's exactly right. Everyday life displayed to the street, visible to the passersby."

"Not at your house, though," Jemima said, then felt a tide of heat on her cheeks as she blushed again. "I'm sorry, that was rude. But I went to a dancing class across the street from it a few months ago and—well, it's quite striking."

"Yes," he answered, and grinned at her. "That was the point."

She smiled back and eyed him for a moment, then ventured, "So you know that people talk about you?"

"Oh, of course," he answered. "I grew up in a small town. I know how they work."

"New York isn't small, though," Jemima countered.

He shrugged. "Enough so that the well-to-do people all know of each other. Isn't that true?"

She thought about that for a moment. "Yes. Do you mean that doesn't happen everywhere?"

"Not in my experience," he answered. "London is a collection of villages that often don't overlap. And Paris has different groups that don't mix at all." In the dining room next door Alice had finished her scales and launched into a Chopin waltz. "Your sister is an excellent musician," he commented. "Do you play as well?"

"No, sadly," Jemima answered. "Last year I finally persuaded Mama that music was never going to be one of my accomplishments."

"And what would you say those are?"

Jemima shook her head. "I'm afraid I don't have any. I just want to read most of the time. And though I used to long to play the harp, my mother always said we didn't have room for one."

Mr. Castle smiled. "And the repertoire is so limited," he added.

"Is it?" Jemima asked, suddenly practical. "I hadn't thought of that. Anyway, it's too late to take it up now."

"How old are you?" he asked, then quickly added, "I'm sorry, it's none of my business. But your father seems young to have grown daughters."

"I'm almost eighteen. Alice is seventeen. Papa is forty-four. How old are you? I'm sorry, I know I shouldn't ask. Mama always says I'm too outspoken."

"What's wrong with curiosity?"

She smiled slightly. "It doesn't seem to be ladylike. I should let you write your message for Papa. Will this do?" She moved a chair to the table in the center of the room. He had noticed how old-fashioned the house was. Furnished almost twenty years earlier, he supposed, when the Wilcoxes would have married, and not touched since. The gold trim on the crimson velvet curtains was pulling loose in places and the floral carpet had faded near the window.

"Of course, thank you," Felix answered. The girl put down a pen and a crystal inkwell with a slightly tarnished silver lid and moved to the tufted velvet settee, where a book lay facedown. She picked it up and he saw that within a moment, she'd forgotten about him.

Actually, she hadn't. Jemima knew how not to be noticed, and she wanted Felix Castle to stay right there, where she could study him covertly. In the months since glimpsing him with her aunt at the Grand Central Depot, she had tried to reconcile that soft-spoken gentleman with the individual she'd heard her father describe as one of the most daring drivers and most ruthless businessmen in New York. His huge showy house across the street from the Abbotts' presented another aspect that didn't seem to fit with the others: Did he not know that the most aristocratic New Yorkers didn't live that way? Or did he simply not care?

Felix looked up from the blank sheet of paper in front of him and saw the girl watching him. Her eyes flicked down to the pages of her book. There was something unusual about her: a kind of frankness he rarely encountered in women. Of course most of the women he knew were actresses or musicians. Lovely, many of them—but far too aware of their own charms. This girl seemed intelligent, unaffected, and oddly appealing.

Yet here he sat, in her family's parlor, writing a note that would have the effect of completely upending her life. Felix was certain that Joshua Wilcox was in trouble. He had missed two interest payments without so much as sending a word of excuse. He had, in fact, behaved exactly like a child hiding from the evidence of a mishap, Felix thought.

How dare he, anyway? After driving with him, Felix had thought he knew Joshua fairly well. Genuine camaraderie had arisen from barreling along the crowded streets of New York behind four horses that were barely under control. As a driver, Joshua was as brave as you could imagine. But what man put his family at risk by borrowing money and then not repaying it? Felix lifted his pen from the page where he had written, "Wilcox, I've been trying to find you . . ." What else was there to say? "It's time to pay your debt." He signed it merely, "F. Castle," then folded the sheet into thirds.

Jemima looked up as he stood. "Is that all?" she asked with a laugh. "It hardly seems worth your coming all the way across town."

"Oh, that was definitely worthwhile," he answered with a warm smile. "Is there a way to seal this? The message is meant for your father alone."

"I'll just prop it against the mirror," she told him. "Write his name on the back, and I'll tell him you called. I'm sure he'll be quite surprised."

She tucked her book beneath her arm and preceded him into the hall. "It looks like a chilly afternoon," she commented, handing him his hat. "I'll be sure Papa gets your message. Thank you for calling, Mr. Castle."

"I probably shouldn't say this," he answered gravely. "But it was a pleasure." He paused, then added, "And since you asked, I'm twenty-eight." He smiled and bowed his head toward her in a gesture that should have felt artificially formal but somehow didn't. He felt a surge of anger at Joshua Wilcox. How dare he gamble with the well-being of his family? As he descended the front steps, he tried to imagine that intriguing girl living . . . where? Would a relative take her in? He almost regretted his resolution to take over the Wilcox house, though of course business must come before any other consideration. Still, he couldn't help wondering.

The door had scarcely closed behind him when Alice stopped playing. She found Jemima in the bay window of the parlor, watching Felix Castle as he walked over to Sixth Avenue.

"Goodness!" Alice said. "Was Mr. Castle paying a morning call?"

"Hardly," Jemima answered. "He wanted to leave a note for Papa. Something about the business."

"I promise I didn't listen," Alice told her sister. "But it did sound as if you had a pleasant conversation."

"You could say so," Jemima agreed. She sank onto the window seat where the dress trimmings still lay. They looked different, somehow. As if they belonged to the era before Felix Castle.

"What did he want?" Alice asked. "Stop fidgeting with that braid, would you?" She plucked it from Jemima's hand.

"He left a note for Papa," Jemima answered. "He admired the way you play the piano."

Alice was staring at her. "Are you blushing?"

Jemima put her hand to her cheek. "No, why would I?" she asked. "Maybe it rubbed onto my hands from Mrs. Burke's dress trimmings."

Alice regarded her older sister with obvious skepticism, but only answered mildly, "If you say so."

CHAPTER 11

DISASTROUS

March 1875

Joshua had not meant to elude Castle, at least not that day. He had managed the first monthly interest payment of a ludicrous five hundred dollars by asking Helen to sacrifice her pearls, then had spent two months in secretive anxiety as they had nothing else of value to sell. As the fourth interest payment loomed, he remembered his beloved stallion Pete, comfortably stabled at the Spring House. Several horsemen in the Hudson Valley had long admired the big gray—Pete, in fact, was an asset. So while Felix had been looking for Joshua in the city, Joshua had taken a train to Tenders Landing, and in an informal auction, sold the Percheron to a farmer who would treat him well.

The image of Wilcox's intriguing daughter was still fresh in Castle's mind when a rumpled Joshua, smelling distinctly of horse, unceremoniously emptied a miscellaneous collection of bills and coins from his pockets onto the big blotter in Felix's ornate office. It wasn't enough cash to repay even a month's interest.

Joshua was too preoccupied counting his money to notice the pulse of anger that Felix swiftly controlled. Not only had Wilcox put his family at risk—he would probably blame Felix for his own improvidence, despite the clear terms of their business agreement.

He waited a moment after Joshua placed the last silver dollar in a stack and looked up hopefully. Felix shook his head slightly, then said, with a combination of exasperation and regret, "I'm sorry to displace your family, especially the young ladies. But those were the terms of the loan, Wilcox. I can give you two weeks to find lodging elsewhere." Joshua stood up abruptly and left without speaking. He was afraid of how he might answer if he dared to open his mouth.

Helen, meanwhile, had returned from her errands to hear Jemima describe an outlandishly inappropriate visit from Felix Castle, of all people, who had left a letter for Joshua! Helen couldn't restrain herself from plucking the note off the parlor mantel and noticing that Mr. Castle had used the leaky pen from her desk, which was somehow the last straw of humiliation. The pens at Mr. Castle's vulgar house probably never left blots. And why had Joshua allowed his business dealings to spill over into his family life?

Her husband didn't return home in time for dinner. Helen's emotions veered from fear to fury as she began imagining road accidents or similar mishaps involving bodily harm. The children went to bed. She waited in the parlor, pretending to darn a pair of Nick's socks and listening to every set of footsteps on the street outside. The parlor fire was dying down when the front door finally opened and a cold draft swirled around her ankles.

"Joshua?" she called, and went out into the hall. "Wherever have you been?" He hung his coat on the rack and turned to face her. Even in the gloomy hall she could tell something was wrong. He looked haggard. "What is it?" she asked, taking his elbow. "Come into the parlor, where it's almost warm. Have you had dinner?"

"No," he answered as he followed her. "But that doesn't matter. Listen, Helen, I've just come from Felix Castle's house."

"Yes, he left a note for you earlier today," she said mechanically, and plucked it off the mantel to hand to him. He took it but didn't read it. Nor did he face her directly.

"I'm sorry, I didn't know he would be so bold, or . . ." He glanced at the paper in his hand, and threw it unopened on the fire. "I know what it says." Then he took Helen's hands. She felt how cold his hands were, how hard the palms from all of his hours driving.

"Why did he come here?" she heard herself asking, even though she knew the answer.

"I haven't been able to pay him," Joshua answered simply. His eyes met hers. She nodded.

"And . . . and he will take the house," Joshua continued.

"What do you mean?" she asked, not quite taking in what he had said.

"I thought he might let us rent from him," Joshua told her. Time seemed to be slowing down. She heard, like an echo, "rent from him . . ."

"You risked the house? But . . . our home . . ." Helen suddenly felt a weakness in her knees. She looked at the sofa, so far away, and clutched at Joshua's arm, then somehow after a moment of near-darkness that arm had embraced her and she was reclining on the sofa, facing the fire. So that was fainting, that abrupt dip into nothing.

"I'm sorry," she said, sitting up and trying to sound more like herself. "I suppose I didn't eat much dinner . . ." Then she remembered. She pulled away from his arm. "No, it was the house! You were saying . . . What did you tell me?"

"Castle is foreclosing," he told her. "I'd hoped he would let us rent, but . . ."

Before she knew it she had flinched away from him. "Nonsense!" she snapped. "Felix Castle isn't in the business of being a landlord." She stood up again. There was something satisfying about looming over Joshua at that moment. "I'm just your wife. I don't know anything about business, but I know that much."

"No. You're right." He looked down at his hands for a long moment, then took a breath that seemed to revive him. He met her gaze and said quietly, "I would have done anything to prevent this, but I promise you, Helen, that the Elevated will make us rich. It will be worth all this disruption in the end."

She shook her head. "When? Next week? Next month? And where will we live in the meantime?" She clapped a hand over her mouth, aware that her fear made her shrill. The children must not hear this, she thought.

Joshua sighed. "It's been a long day, Helen. I went to Tenders Landing and sold Pete and took the proceeds to Castle in partial repayment and I don't know what will happen next."

Helen turned suddenly and walked away from him. "You sold Pete?" she echoed. "We all loved Pete. The girls learned to ride on him." She felt a tear trickle down her cheek for the loss of the big gray horse.

Joshua sighed and nodded. "Pete was valuable, and my father taught me not to be sentimental about horses. He'll be well-treated."

"And what about us?" Helen asked. "Did you think about your family at all? Or would *that* have been sentimental?" She managed to keep her voice sounding reasonable, she thought. "How will we manage Jemima's debut, do you think?" He didn't answer. "Teas? Luncheons? Those Dancing Classes Jemima's going to—a girl does usually have a dance when she comes out. Can we afford that? And next year, what about Alice?"

Joshua sat facing her in the firelight with his eyes on her face, but she wasn't sure he was listening. At any rate he had no answer for any of her questions. They had been no part of his thinking. Then Helen realized that her husband had not even answered the most fundamental question, and she sat down next to him again. "Joshua, where will we go? When Mr. Castle takes over this house, where will we live?"

He shook his head slightly, as though he'd been thinking of something else. "I thought perhaps—your mother?"

"No!" she exclaimed instantly. "You must know that's impossible! I can't live with her!"

"It won't be for long—" he began, but she interrupted.

"How do you know? What are your plans to provide a house for your family?"

"Well, you'll go to the Spring House soon," he said tentatively. "It's just a few months."

"But living with Mama! And the children! Where in the world would she put us all? And she's not kind, you know that. Or patient."

"No. I do know that," he agreed somberly.

Helen stared at the fireplace for a long moment. "I always thought you would take care of me," she said finally. "Mama never trusted you, but I did. After that first night, out on the marsh . . ." Her voice dwindled.

He took her hand and answered, "I wish you were angry."

"Oh, I am," she told him. "So angry I don't dare think of it. I knew you hadn't paid Mr. Castle since I gave you my pearls, but I just couldn't face . . ." She shook her head. "You didn't say anything," she went on in a raw voice. "I knew if you'd found a way to pay him, you would have told me. I just waited and waited." Helen wailed suddenly. "It's all wrong! This isn't what I wanted for the children; I wanted them to be lighthearted and not to worry . . ."

He leaned over and kissed her on the cheek. "I understand." He sat there, waiting for her to say something else. She stared straight ahead, looking at what was left of the fire.

"Go to bed," she said finally. "Leave me here to get used to the idea."

"I don't like leaving you alone, Helen," he protested. "I am so sorry things have turned out this way . . ."

"But there's nothing you can do now," she interrupted him. "So go to bed. I'll be up soon."

All right," he agreed. He didn't try to kiss her again, but as he stood up he touched her shoulder lightly. She heard the stairs creak as he went up and thought, "Every step we take in my mother's house will be heard." Where would their furniture go? That would be Joshua's affair, she decided, with a spurt of annoyance. He could make the arrangements. Find a warehouse, see to the packing. Oh, heavens, the blue wagons standing outside the house! Everyone would know! But everyone would know anyway, she realized. The shame of it! Her mind hurried ahead, imagining the questions, the sly glances, the murmurs. "Poor Helen Wilcox . . . That husband of hers . . . Living with her mother . . ."

Joshua had put business first. He had chosen money over loyalty to his family. But shouldn't sheltering his loved ones have come before wild financial speculation? He thought he was building a future for them. He probably still believed everything would work out all right, that the Hudson Elevated Railroad would make him rich. He'd have a coach and a stable full of fast horses. She was sure he dreamed of that future—but what of *her* future?

She *had* what she wanted, in fact: this happy house, these

cheerful children, Jemima poised to enter society. He had reached too far, wanted too much, and destroyed what held them together.

She woke the next morning to a feeling of dread and lay for an instant trying to identify the cause. Then she sat up slowly and looked around her and Joshua's bedroom, with its rose-garlanded wallpaper and suite of mahogany furniture. Her heart sank as she contemplated the upheaval of moving—and that part was merely drudgery. Boring and exacting, but not as painful as facing her mother. The very thought made it impossible to stay in bed. She flung aside the covers and dressed as quickly as possible, trying to avoid her own reflection in the dressing-table mirror because she suddenly looked so old.

When she entered the dining room Joshua shot a questioning glance her way but they couldn't discuss the house until the children went up to the schoolroom for what was now termed "study time." Jemima seemed to sense the strained atmosphere. "Papa, don't you need to get to work?" she asked. "You never have breakfast with us."

"This is a special treat for me," he answered. "I'm going to stay and drink an extra cup of coffee with your mother."

"They know something is wrong," Helen said softly, as soon as they were alone.

"How could they?" Joshua asked. "We've just found out ourselves." He nudged the cream pitcher toward Helen as she poured more coffee into her cup.

"Sometimes I think they're like a herd of horses," she answered. "You know how they all cluster in a corner of a paddock when a storm is coming? They feel something in the air. Let's go into the parlor; Moira needs to clear in here, she has a great deal to do today." And indeed the swing door pushed open from the kitchen as the maid peered in to see if they were still lingering over breakfast. Like any happy couple at the start of the day, Helen thought bitterly.

"The servants mustn't know yet," she murmured to Joshua in the hall. "We won't be able to keep them." He stared at her in surprise, and she felt a surge of irritation. "What did you think would happen? That life would just go on as usual?" she asked.

"No, of course not," he countered. "But I hadn't thought of the domestic . . ." He put his cup down on the parlor's center table. "I'm sorry. I've been so preoccupied." He shook his head as if that would somehow help bring order to his thoughts.

After a tiny pause, Helen answered, "I understand. And I will manage the servants. We'll have to let most of them go, of course. Cook may retire to the country, she's been complaining about her feet for some time now. I'm afraid we'll need to keep Moira on— my mother's servants can't be asked to take care of us as well."

Joshua sat in one of the armchairs next to the fire and sighed. "I don't suppose you want to hear another apology . . ."

"No," Helen cut him off, "I don't. I have one request, however. I want you to go to my mother. I want you to explain the situation, and above all, I want *you* to ask her if she will take us in." Her voice sounded hard, she thought. But at that moment she felt hard.

"I can't do that, Helen," Joshua protested, "your mother doesn't like me!"

"No," Helen agreed, "not particularly. But I can't . . . I don't . . ." She could feel her face start to crumple and she realized her self-control was more precarious than she had hoped. "This is the one thing I am asking of you," she said in a level voice.

"Yes, all right," he conceded with a sigh. "I'm sorry, I need to get to the office."

Helen tilted her head. "Go, then. I'm sorry I'm keeping you from your busy day." Her voice sounded harsh, but she went on without modulating it. "Please call on my mother today. This morning, by preference. I beg you, Joshua, do not make me explain this situation to my mother."

CHAPTER 12

◆

THE TALK OF THE TOWN

March 1875

Helen wasn't merely angry with Joshua; she was also fright-ened. Her husband, she knew, saw New York as an entity of bricks and mortar, geography more than community. In a way, that was why he was so intent on building the Elevated Railroad: How many men can actually change the fabric of a city? Helen's New York, on the other hand, was a weave of personalities and relationships, many dating back several generations. Her network was responsive to a touch. Rumors traveled along the web with astounding speed.

Thus the news about the Wilcoxes spread like wildfire that morning. Was it Felix's servants who began it? Was the word already out by the time Joshua told Helen? Had Felix himself dropped a hint? Somehow by early morning the grooms at Hudson Transit were anxiously discussing the future of the business as they prepared for the morning rush of the horse-cars. The big leap came midmorning, when the report crossed over from the servants' quarters to the fronts of New York houses. Delivery men shared it while handing over the fish. Cooks told parlor maids. Parlor maids whispered to ladies' maids, who murmured while lacing up their mistresses. Luncheon tables buzzed.

Helen had always known that spite ran beneath society's veneer. There were many kindly women eating chicken croquettes at linen-decked tables around Madison Square. But they weren't above listening to gossip about their friends, and other people's misfortune is difficult to resist. Thus many women indeed cooed "Poor Helen!" and speculated about the Wilcoxes' next address. But there were also—sometimes at the selfsame linen-decked tables—women who resented Helen for all kinds of reasons including the fact that she didn't know how lucky she was (or had been). Not many women possessed handsome, kindly husbands who seemed devoted to them. But "blood would always tell" was the verdict. Wilcox didn't come from one of the old families. Such a mistake, poor Helen. It had always seemed too good to be true, that marriage, especially when you remembered that Helen had not been a successful debutante. And wasn't she, admit it, a little bit aloof? Possibly bored by the life they all led? Thinking herself, perhaps, above it all? And some of her friends, it must be said—well, who were *they*, anyway? That Sylvia Burke, with her loud voice and her crude husband— didn't she wear diamonds to luncheon?

By teatime, the discussion had grown robust. The story of the Wilcox marriage was resurrected, dissected, embroidered. "Packed off to Europe . . . came back with a baby . . ." Someone had actually seen Joshua driving a Hudson Transit wagon. Really, these new men, they never would fit in. "Lost the house?" "Yes, stock speculation apparently." Not one in ten women understood the term but they tossed it around confidently. "No better than gambling," intoned one matron whose husband owned a small but precious tract of land near Wall Street and simply collected immense rent checks, when he wasn't collecting stamps.

Selina Maitland did not leave her house that day. She had

delicate health, as one might expect of a lady so small and slender. She mistrusted the changeable weather of spring; it was so easy to catch a chill when those sharp breezes blew. So much more pleasant to sit at home in a nest of little cushions and drink a cup of consommé for lunch. "And there I was," she would say later, "in perfect ignorance, cutting the pages of a book when in walked Annabelle with the news!"

It was a bad moment for Selina's butler, Gates, who loved Helen. The servants had heard the story early in the morning. Unlike Joshua, they instantly grasped the implications of the loss of the Twenty-Sixth Street house. As Gates said, "Of course they'll come here. Miss Helen can't live over the stable, even if Mr. Wilcox would." But all day they waited anxiously for one of the men of the family to bring Mrs. Maitland the news. Mr. Latimer would be best, they thought. Mrs. Maitland liked him.

Yet there was Annabelle van Ormskirk at the door in a chilly gust of wind, practically pushing Gates out of the way as she asked for Mrs. Maitland, and quite reluctant to wait in the parlor while he sent a maid upstairs to "see if Mrs. Maitland is at home." Then Mrs. Maitland trotted innocently downstairs and the parlor door closed and no one even rang for tea though the kettle was piping-hot and a tray was laid out in the pantry.

But Selina didn't believe Annabelle. In fact, at first she didn't even understand what Annabelle was driving at. "I came to see how you were, dear Selina," she began.

"Aren't you kind," Selina answered. "There's really no cause for worry, I simply didn't dare leave the house today. Just a touch of neuralgia," she added, wrist to her forehead.

"Oh, I'm sorry to hear that," Annabelle answered mechanically. "But I actually meant this business about Helen and Mr. Wilcox."

Selina's hand fell to her lap. "What business is that?"

"The house, of course!" Annabelle leaned closer and lowered her voice. "I just came from Abbie Townsend's. I'm sorry to say everyone knows."

"Everyone knows what?"

"That Joshua lost the house, of course. And to Felix Castle, of all people!" She sat back, watching for Selina's reaction.

"What are you talking about, Annabelle?"

"You mean you haven't heard?" This was almost too good to be true.

Selina sat up erect, eyes narrowed. "Of course not. I do believe you've been listening to servants' gossip!"

It was Annabelle's turn to straighten her spine. "What a terrible thing to say!"

"Tell me, then, how did you hear this story?"

"Oh, apparently it's all over town."

"Has anyone spoken to Helen? Or to Joshua? I myself haven't heard a thing. Don't you think that suggests you might be wrong?"

Annabelle was frowning. "Well . . . I hope I am wrong, then." She fidgeted with the reticule in her lap. "So the Wilcoxes are all well?"

"Yes, thank you," Selina answered. "And so are the Latimers. And your lovely daughters are thriving, I hope?"

"They are, thank you. In fact I must fly, we have fittings at the dressmaker's this afternoon," Annabelle murmured. "I'll show myself out." And she was gone before Selina could ring for Gates.

But she rang anyway, and when Gates appeared she looked at him coldly. "Mrs. Van Ormskirk was telling me some news," she said. "You know I abhor servants' gossip, but I must ask. You haven't heard anything today about any members of my family?"

"No, madam," answered Gates, his lean old face a mask.

"But you wouldn't tell me if you had, I suppose," she added.

"No, madam," he repeated. "We don't gossip downstairs, ma'am, I assure you."

"Well, I don't believe you for a moment," she said. "But of course you'd say that. I will have to go out this afternoon, as soon as possible. Would you tell Mosette? And get me a hansom."

Twenty minutes later, laced hastily into a sober dress with her hair merely twisted up under her hat, she was climbing the steps of 130 West Twenty-Sixth Street. It took far too long for the front door to open and when it did, Moira looked harassed. "Mrs. Maitland!" she exclaimed. "What a surprise!"

"Yes," Selina said. "I was passing and I thought I would drop in. Is Mrs. Wilcox at home?"

"Come in, please," Moira answered. "Come into the parlor. I'll see . . . Mrs. Wilcox has been very busy, it may be a moment before . . . shall I light the fire for you, ma'am?"

"Please do," Selina said. "And would you . . ." She unhooked her mantle and turned her back, indicating that Moira should take it.

"Certainly, ma'am. Will I bring you some tea?"

"That would be pleasant," Selina said. But before the tea tray was brought in, Helen entered the room. She looked . . . could she look frightened?

"Mama," she said cautiously, and kissed her mother on the cheek. "I'm surprised to see you here."

"Yes, I wasn't well this morning. Sit down, Moira's bringing us some tea."

"I'm awfully busy, Mama, you can imagine, there's so much to do . . ."

"Yes, dear, I know. But Annabelle van Ormskirk—I thought I

should tell you. There are terrible stories going around town about you and Joshua. I don't know how one puts a stop to these things, maybe Noble will have some advice. Probably the best thing would be to deny the rumors and simply let the stories die down. Or perhaps you and Joshua could give a dinner?"

Helen heard her mother as if from a great distance away, and what she said made no sense. "A dinner?"

"Well, you know what they're all saying. Or—do you? I suppose one always learns the rumors last when they're about oneself."

"Mama," Helen said finally, sinking into a chair. "Have you seen Joshua today?"

"No, dear, I've not been well. I haven't been out until now."

"He didn't come to see you?"

"No, my only visitor has been Annabelle. With some ridiculous rumor about your house."

Helen opened her eyes wide as she felt the tears come. "Annabelle knows?"

"*Knows?*" snapped Selina. "It's true?"

"Oh, no!" Helen wailed, and began to sob just as Moira backed into the parlor with the tea tray. There was a moment of confusion as Moira set down the tray and met Selina's eye, and for a strange instant seemed to challenge her. Then Moira lifted a lace-edged napkin off the tray and tucked it into Helen's hand before silently leaving the room.

Having begun to cry, Helen didn't know how to stop. The tears just kept coming, and soon there were sobs as well. Her mother handed over the other napkin when the first one became sodden. She even put a hand on Helen's shoulder and patted gently. "It's all right," she crooned. "Everything will be all right." She took her own handkerchief from her reticule and handed it to Helen. "Here, use this, wipe your eyes. I'm going to pour you some tea."

"I'm sorry, Mama," she said once the gulping had stopped. "So childish. But . . ." Her eyes welled up again and she shook her head.

"That's enough, dear," said her mother. "Surely Annabelle had the story wrong. It won't take long to correct the gossip."

"No," Helen answered, and blew her nose. "Annabelle did not have the story wrong." She sighed, then stood up and crossed the room to look out the window. "Joshua lost the house."

Her mother didn't hear, or didn't understand, or couldn't believe her ears. "I beg your pardon? You'll have to speak more clearly."

"Joshua. Lost. The house," Helen repeated. Then again, quite loudly, "Joshua lost the house!"

"Lost? How does one lose a house?"

"You'd have to ask him," Helen answered, and she was startled to hear the acid in her voice. "I wish you would. I wish he'd done as he promised and told you himself." She did not turn around but put her palm to the window pane.

"Sit down and explain this to me," Selina commanded. "You know I don't understand business."

But Helen stayed where she was. "Joshua borrowed money from Felix Castle. They, the Elevated Railroad men, needed to extend the track." That seemed to be all she had to say.

"But why did Joshua have to pay for it?" Selina asked, to help her along.

"Oh, you know this, Mama, he's one of the owners." Helen's shoulders slumped and her mother wanted to get up and pull them back, as she'd had to do so often when Helen was young. Don't slouch, stand up straight, balance a book on your head, move with grace—whatever happens.

Helen still didn't speak. Selina sighed and glanced at the clock on the mantel. "But where does the house come into it? And how did he get embroiled with Mr. Castle?"

"I don't know," Helen answered. "They sometimes drive together."

"Well, that at least makes sense," Selina said tartly.

"What do you mean?" Helen snapped.

"Well, dear, we know how much Joshua loves horses," Selina answered. "And one hears that Mr. Castle does, too. You needn't be so sharp with me. Come and sit down, now. I'm still completely at sea."

Helen didn't sit, though. She went to the door of the parlor instead, and opened it silently, peering out into the hall. Then she closed it carefully and leaned back against it. "Joshua needed money to invest in the Elevated. He said he spoke to you about it."

"Oh, that," Selina said, waving a hand in the air. "I couldn't make head or tail of it. Go on."

Helen continued as if her mother hadn't interrupted. "He had to find the money so he borrowed it from Mr. Castle, who charged a great deal of interest on the loan. Joshua had put up this house as security. Mr. Castle foreclosed. The house is his." She cast her eyes to the ceiling, as if she were measuring the room, and there was a note of surprise in her voice. "It's probably his right now. Joshua went over there this morning to sign some papers. We're probably sitting in Felix Castle's parlor."

"All right, dear," Selina said crisply, to brace her up. "That's enough. Stop wandering around, would you? Sit down like a lady and drink your tea." Sitting in Felix Castle's parlor! Such dramatics!

Helen complied, but as she came back into the light from the window Selina could see that she was still distracted. "And you'll rent the house from Mr. Castle? Some people do rent, you know.

Not many in our circle, of course. But I suppose there are reasons, sometimes . . ."

"No, Mama," Helen answered wearily. "We can't afford to rent. We had to cut back. I think I've mentioned this. And anyway Mr. Castle won't allow it."

"Oh, yes, what everyone calls that 'panic.' But that was over a year ago, and anyway, I think people talk too much about money," Selina murmured. "My mother always said that was vulgar."

"Yes," Helen answered, with that biting tone in her voice. "But sometimes it has to be discussed. In fact, Joshua was supposed to talk to you. This morning, after he left me. He was going to come to you from Mr. Castle's house."

"To do what?" Selina asked. "I never receive visitors before luncheon!"

"Not to *call* on you, Mama. To explain what had happened and to ask . . ." Helen stood up again in a swirl of skirts and walked over to the fireplace where she ran her fingers across the dangling lusters of a candlestick.

"Stop fidgeting," Selina scolded. "Your daughters know better than that! I'm practically dizzy watching you roam around the room. Would you come here and tell me what Joshua wanted?"

Instead, Helen sat with a thump on the love seat next to the fireplace and said in a flat voice, "Joshua wanted to know if we could come live with you."

"Well, of course not!" Selina answered in shock. "Where would I put you all?"

Where would I put you all? Helen stared at her mother. Could she really be so cold? So unfeeling? So astoundingly selfish? "Mama," she began in a quiet, meek voice, "we have nowhere to go."

"But my house is so small," her mother answered.

"We don't have a home, Mama! Can't you understand? This house"—she gestured around the room—"belongs to Felix Castle now." Her voice was getting stronger. "I'll have to ask if Joshua mortgaged the furniture as well," she added, with a spurt of malice. "Maybe Mr. Castle will sell it. Why not? It's worth nothing to him."

"Calm down, Helen," snapped her mother. "You're making a melodrama of this. It's just that there are so many of you. And I'm not strong, you know. I need peace and quiet. But of course I'll house you if need be. I am your mother, after all."

"And we need a *roof* over our heads, Mama," Helen shouted. "Because it seems you may have been right all along about Joshua! Maybe marrying him was a terrible mistake, because he has just wagered away our home without leaving us so much as a place to lay our heads at night!"

"Helen! Lower your voice! You always were prone to melodrama," her mother answered with a sigh. "I'm sure Joshua . . ."

"Forgive me," Helen interrupted. "But never in my wildest dreams did I imagine that Joshua would somehow lose our house— or that you would so much as hesitate to take us in! Would you prefer we go up to the Spring House? I suppose we could manage to stay warm somehow, if the chimneys don't catch fire. And I know you'll tell me that it will warm up eventually, we should be more comfortable by May. I don't know what we'd do about Nick's schooling, and the girls, with Jemima coming out in the fall . . ."

This time Selina broke in. "Stop! Get control of yourself, Helen. Think of the servants."

Helen's mouth crimped, as if she were holding back a wail. "Well, at least you still *have* servants. I'll have to dismiss . . ."

Then she heard the front door open and— "It must be Joshua," she thought. Maybe he would step into the parlor and tell her it had all been a mistake. She heard his tread on the squeaky piece of parquet next to the hat rack at the bottom of the stairs, and her mind emptied. What did you say to the man who had gambled away the family home?

But when the parlor door opened and Joshua came in, Helen found herself mute. She just stood up and stared, and let the tears pour down her face because there would have been no way to stop them. And even though she was furious with him, even though she wanted to scream and to hit him, when he took two long strides across the room and folded his arms around her, she leaned her head on his shoulder and sobbed as if her heart were broken.

CHAPTER 13

LADYLIKE

April 1875

After that, events moved quickly. Until the summer Nick would occupy a spare bedroom in the Latimer house on Gramercy Square. He was delirious at the prospect of escaping his sisters and entering the orbit of his glamorous cousin Miles. Noble pointed out to Selina how admirable her friends would find her generosity and family spirit by taking in the Wilcoxes. ("Especially with all of these new people arriving," he told her, "it's inspiring to see old New York's values upheld by a social leader like you.") Helen vanished into a welter of lists and snapped at everyone. Moira found lodging in Chelsea and would come in daily to work at Mrs. Maitland's as "an extra pair of hands."

Felix Castle provided an unexpected note of comedy when one of his glossy carriages drew up one morning and a liveried footman got out, holding a stiff ivory envelope that he turned over to Moira at the door. Alice and Jemima watched agog from the schoolroom windows as the footman—in knee breeches! At ten A.M.!—clambered back into the carriage. The note, addressed to Helen, regretted Felix's "need" to take possession of the house and offered her "as much time as you may require before vacating 130 West Twenty-Sixth Street." Helen smiled grimly and left the note propped on the bedroom mantel for Joshua. Even he must understand how inappropriate it was for Mr. Castle to address a letter personally to a married woman he didn't "know." And that Felix's offer was too little, too late.

But Joshua had no energy to spare for expressing emotion. Busy as he was, he could hardly leave Helen to manage this hasty departure from the house he had lost. So he diverted men from Hudson Transit to help pack and organize the contents of the house. The blue wagons stood on West Twenty-Sixth Street for several days, transporting furniture to the Hudson Transit warehouse, clothes to Washington Square, and miscellaneous belongings to the Spring House. Joshua shuttled among these locations as well as the offices of Hudson Elevated and Hudson Transit. And he reflected bitterly on the irony that he spent so much time traveling on the congested streets of New York, attempting to make urban travel more efficient. He did not share that reflection with Helen. They were sharing only a bed at that point, and not cordially.

To be fair, Helen could not help exhibiting her misery in those days. Everyone from Moira to Selina trod carefully around her, to avoid provoking outbursts of temper. When Alice protested against sending the family's piano into storage, Helen went still. "Is there anything wrong with your grandmother's instrument?" she asked with an edge.

"Well, it's just a cottage piano," Alice answered, "nowhere as good as ours."

"Then perhaps you'd like to explain to my mother how she's to fit a second instrument into her parlor." Alice flushed scarlet and stamped up the stairs, slamming the door to her bedroom and then throwing her slippers across the room. The Wilcox women had never been door-slammers until that moment and Alice was instantly ashamed. Mama had enough to worry about, so she went back downstairs to apologize with a hug. She didn't see her mother a few hours later, up in the former schoolroom, sobbing silently. Anger was so much easier to bear than grief.

As moving day approached, Helen kept trying to consider the children's feelings alongside the bewildering practicalities of selecting and packing what they would need (and what would fit) at Selina's house. It was Moira who suggested that Jemima be absent when the Wilcoxes left 130 West Twenty-Sixth Street. "You know how she broods, ma'am," Moira explained. So on a damp and chilly April morning, Moira and Jemima left the house for the last time. Though her mother had suggested a visit to the tearoom at Stewart's, Jemima had chosen instead to visit the Metropolitan Museum of Art. She didn't quite trust herself not to cry, and she didn't want anyone she knew to see her. The Metropolitan Museum—only five years old—had moved two years earlier to a building on West Fourteenth Street and was pretty sure to be empty, Jemima thought. It might even distract her from the misery that had colored the last few weeks.

The loss of the house she'd grown up in; the friction between her parents; the prospect of living with her critical grandmother; the general unsettled nature of life all made Jemima deeply uneasy—most of all because she could not imagine how this distressing situation could be resolved. Papa had lost their house to Mr. Castle. Their *home*! What could have possessed Papa to jeopardize it? How could the Elevated Railroad possibly be more important to him than taking care of his family? He had apologized to them all and assured them that their stay with their grandmother would be brief. They would all go to the Spring House as usual. Everything would be fine, he promised. But later that day

Jemima had asked when they would have their own house again, and he hadn't been able to answer.

Jemima didn't know how to think about this turn of events. How could her father have made such a mistake? What would prevent his making another one? Was Mr. Castle greedy? Was she herself to blame, somehow? She blushed every time she remembered his visit to the house, when he wrote that note. He had seemed . . . not merely civil but intriguing. (Strict honesty with herself was part of Jemima's rather strenuous moral code.) But perhaps he *was* also greedy. Why else would he want their house?

Meanwhile Mama was clearly beside herself. Two small furrows had appeared between her eyebrows and never went away. She snapped at everyone, even Moira. What's more, everyone knew that Mama and Grandmama didn't get along, so living on Washington Square would be like . . . Jemima searched for an image as she and Moira waited to cross the street on the way to the museum. She had once seen a pair of roosters in the barnyard at the Spring House, pacing around in a circle eyeing each other and making vicious gestures with their beaks. She was slightly cheered to imagine her grandmother as a chicken. She sighed and Moira squeezed her elbow. "You're a brave girl and you can stand anything for a few months," Moira told Jemima. "Then we'll all go upriver and who knows what will happen in the fall?"

That was the question, Jemima thought. Would she still come out? Would they be able to entertain? How? Where? Would she be invited to other girls' parties? Could they afford new dresses?

Drops of rain were falling as they reached the museum so they hurried inside. As civic institutions went, it was . . . poky. Jemima had seen pictures of the great European museums with their grand staircases and long galleries lined with gigantic portraits of kings.

The Metropolitan Museum of Art, despite its pompous name, was nothing more than somebody's old house! Once they entered—and Moira settled herself and her sore feet on a bench in the front hall—it was easy for Jemima to mentally allocate the first-floor galleries to their previous domestic uses: dining room, parlor, sitting room. Dingy white marble statues and glass cases containing broken mosaics stood awkwardly against the walls. Jemima spent several dutiful minutes examining the statues. She could not imagine why anybody had bothered to dig them up and ship them across the Atlantic Ocean to display in this sad, cold building.

By that point it was raining hard enough outside to force pedestrians to take cover wherever they could. Jemima heard the front door open and some wet passerby come in from outside. She couldn't bear to face a stranger so she climbed the stairs to the second floor. A grubby placard tacked to a door frame identified the paintings hung against the crimson-painted wall. Most of the people depicted wore very little clothing, which made Jemima feel colder than ever.

Dutifully, she began to circle the room counterclockwise to examine the pictures, but she had never heard of many of the half-naked characters they depicted. They mostly came from mythology, she supposed. People in myths often behaved in very improper ways.

She had expected grandeur and perhaps comfort from the Metropolitan Museum of Art. Instead she found nothing but melancholy. This had once been someone's bedroom, warm and cozy, with carpets and curtains and maybe even a sheepskin next to the fireplace. Now there was only a marble bench situated in the center of the room. She sat down on it. There was nothing else to do. She gazed around the room again, looking for something she could identify as beauty, or even warmth. She felt her eyes pricking and opened them very wide. She refused to cry.

Yet cry she did, and once she had begun, there was no stopping the tears. They dripped down her face and onto her mantle. Her handkerchief was soon soaked and she needed to blow her nose. Surreptitiously, she ran her gloved knuckle along her upper lip.

Then she froze as she heard footsteps sounding in the next room. How mortifying to be caught weeping, with pink eyes and a runny nose! Jemima squashed her handkerchief into a ball and brushed a remaining tear off her cheek. The footsteps came into the room where she sat and halted at the door, which made Jemima look up in curiosity. There, evidently as startled as she was, stood Felix Castle.

"Miss Wilcox!" he said. "What are you doing here?"

She found she had leapt to her feet. Somehow she didn't want Mr. Castle looming over her. Then she looked him in the eye and asked coldly, "How could you?"

"How could I do what?" he replied, eyeing her uneasily.

"How could you take our house? Our family is moving out today, so you can take it over! You couldn't possibly want it, and we're going to have to live with our grandmother, who doesn't even like us!"

He bristled. "I think you should take this up with your father rather than with me," he answered. "He borrowed money from me on very clear terms and didn't meet them. He was always aware of the potential consequences."

She kept her eyes on his face and didn't answer but he noticed tears on her face. Now that he looked closely, she seemed to have been crying for a while. He considered passing her his handkerchief but she was somehow intimidating. Odd, in such a young girl. "Anyway, what are you doing here?" he blurted out as the question occurred to him. He visited the museum from time to time but had never seen a young lady there.

"My mother thought I would be sad if I saw our things being taken away to ship to storage," Jemima answered. "So she sent me out and I came here with our maid." She stood and walked a few steps away from him, then turned back and said sternly, "I think the word for you is 'despicable.'"

"Now wait a moment, Miss Wilcox," he protested. "I don't suppose you know much about business—"

"Not a thing," she interrupted him. "And I certainly didn't realize it could be cruel."

Cruel! Felix felt the word with an almost physical shock. He wasn't cruel! He was firm, certainly. He took care to avoid sentiment in his transactions. But maybe he had been careless. Wilcox had come to him with a short-term opportunity at a good time, and he liked the fellow. It had felt like an agreement that would work for both of them. He crossed the room toward Jemima. "May I sit?" he asked. She nodded and sniffed. He perched on the marble bench and glanced up at her, then patted the bench with his hand, urging her to sit next to him. He plucked the clean handkerchief from his inner coat pocket and put it in her hand.

"This is a terrible state of affairs," he said, tactfully gazing toward a luscious Venus on the nearest wall while Jemima blew her nose. "I regret it deeply."

"Well, you didn't have to evict us, did you?" Jemima asked sternly. "I believe that's the correct term?"

"No, of course I didn't," he answered crossly. "But I'm not a landlord. I just handle money and I don't particularly want your house," he went on, then looked at her in horror. He'd made her cry even harder. She wasn't one of those girls who wept charmingly, either. Her eyes were getting puffy and her nose, where she kept scrubbing it, was pink. But she sat upright and met his gaze with an air of indignation.

"Well, that's too bad," she retorted, turning away to stare at a statue of a man holding a severed head. "Because we liked where we lived. I've been there my whole life." She turned back to him. "But I suppose that's how business works."

There was a cool intelligence in her gaze, Felix thought. Surely she must understand that her father was responsible for the situation? She stood and crossed the room, ending up in front of a small still life. In the center was a stemmed green glass with bumpy curls of lemon peel falling from its brim. Grapes, oysters, golden light on a plaster wall: It was a beautiful little window into a sober, comfortable world of plenty and warmth. Jemima heard Mr. Castle's footsteps on the creaky wooden floor as he came to her side, bringing with him a faint warm scent of wet wool and something spicy. "Look, you can see the reflection of a window there, in the side of the glass," he remarked. "Beautiful, isn't it?" He was standing so close that his arm brushed hers as he pointed to the picture and she found she was looking at his hand rather than the painting.

She flicked her eyes away to the picture, then nodded. "Yes. That doesn't make me feel better, though. I'm still going to have to stay with my grandmother on Washington Square. She doesn't care for what she calls 'young people.' We make too much noise." She didn't look at Mr. Castle while she said this.

"It's not my fault, exactly," he answered carefully, "but all the same I'm sorry." He glanced out the window and saw that the rain was still pouring down. "Would your chaperone downstairs—or your maid, or whatever she is—be alarmed if you went upstairs with me? There are more paintings. And you might as well see them all." Jemima agreed with him, so they climbed the stairs. Walking behind her, he found himself admiring her unconscious grace.

On the top floor they were confronted by a tall canvas featuring two nude men posed with some strategic shrubbery, and a very naked pair of babies. Mr. Castle instantly put his hand on Jemima's elbow to guide her away from it but she could feel her cheeks flaming. So very much flesh! Not far away hung a landscape, if you could call it that: a lot of flat land, a little bit of water, a lot of flat sky. Jemima glanced at Mr. Castle, who met her look with a shrug.

She said, "I've never been to a museum before, but I thought it would be grander than this." She took a few steps away from him and stood in the center of the room, turning slowly.

He watched her and understood that whatever this girl did, she would throw herself into completely. "Let's go and look at that vase, shall we?" He held out his arm and Jemima hesitated. He turned to face her. "Miss Wilcox, I know you aren't happy with me. But we seem to be trapped together here, at least until the rain stops. Could we, do you think, declare a temporary truce?"

She made him wait a few seconds more, then nodded. "Yes, of course. I'm sorry. I think I might have been sulking."

"Possibly," he said, and this time when he held out his arm, she took it, though she regretted the gesture instantly. She was forced to walk too close to him, almost as if they were dancing. Yet when they reached the next gallery and she detached herself from him, she felt oddly bereft.

What Mr. Castle had called a "vase" was actually an immense red and black urn with two handles, protected by a glass case. Figures seemed to be pacing in a procession around the widest portion.

One woman carried a spear, while a man with no clothes brandished a dagger. Jemima felt her face flame and turned to Mr. Castle. "What in the world is this?"

"It's called an amphora, and it was used to store oil in a Greek temple thousands of years ago. It's traveled a very long way."

Jemima walked to the other side of the vase where two men in breastplates were fighting with daggers. As she peered closely she could see tiny chips in the clay and she suddenly realized that it had been made by people with feelings and possibly families and troubles, and that it had survived. She frowned and moved around the case, studying what appeared to be a story. "Do you know what they're doing?" she asked as she stared at two ladies in long pleated dresses.

"No," he answered. "Perhaps they're making an offering."

She stepped back, then forward again. "It looks dull from a distance, but when you get close, the people are so lively. They look like us." She turned to him and added, "This is the kind of thing girls aren't supposed to look at. Mama wouldn't be happy."

"Well," he answered, meeting her level gaze, "maybe you won't tell her."

"I should think not," Jemima told him. "Do you have paintings in your house?" she went on. "I hear it's quite large. Oh!" She smiled for an instant, clearly remembering a choice bit of gossip. "I also hear you have a champagne fountain in your ballroom! Is it true?"

"It is," he said, smiling back. "Though I can't imagine who told you such a thing."

"Never mind that, I want to know how you clean it," she told him.

"Oh, my butler manages that," he answered and she actually laughed. "Why is that funny?"

CAROL WALLACE

"So lordly," she said, waving her hand to mime dismissal. "You can't be bothered with the housekeeping."

"Well, that is why I keep servants," Felix answered. But he noticed how the smile brought Jemima's features to life, and wondered how he could have considered her plain.

Still, when they went back downstairs he felt her mood change, and he stopped her on the landing before they reached the first floor. "Miss Wilcox, I really am very sorry that your family has had to move." He reached into his inner breast pocket and pulled out a small, slender volume. "Would you do me the favor of accepting this book? There's a poem in it about an urn like the one we saw upstairs. I think you might like it."

Without thinking, Jemima had put out her hand to accept the book before she realized it. "I can't do that!" she began to protest. But she caught sight of Moira in the hallway below, looking up curiously, and she turned away from Mr. Castle quickly. Speaking to a strange man in a public place—what was she thinking! She tucked the little volume into the pocket of her skirt and sailed down the stairs toward Moira. Afterward she liked to think she had moved swiftly, maybe even gracefully, away from Mr. Castle. She wondered if he had looked after her with . . . admiration? Warmth? Regret?

That night, as Alice brushed her hair, Jemima examined the little book by candlelight. It appeared to be poetry by a man named Keats. As she flipped through the pages she caught sight of one poem called "Ode on a Grecian Urn." She read it several times before Alice snuffed out the candle. She had not told Alice anything about meeting Mr. Castle at the museum; what would she say? He was turning them out of their house, yet at the same time she had found him civil and sympathetic. More, she found him disturbingly attractive. Felix Castle made those boys at the Dancing Classes look like mere children.

Jemima was acquainted with the rules about what kinds of gifts girls could accept from gentlemen. Books were perfectly appropriate tokens of a young man's interest in a young lady. Yet Mr. Castle's offering, naturally, had not been intended that way. He was not a particularly young man and she was not yet a young lady. If anything, Jemima would have said the book was his version of an oblique apology. Not that she was ready to forgive him, though.

All the same, she read a good many of the poems in the little volume. She admired them. Some baffled her, and these she kept revisiting, trying to wring significance from them. Probably, she thought, they had to do with romance, as so much poetry seemed to. But the mere presence of the book, concealed in a drawer beneath her handkerchiefs, made Jemima nervous. What if someone found it? Mr. Castle's name was written in the front! (Jemima had examined it rather often, searching for something she couldn't quite identify in his firm pen strokes.) A week went by, then another, and one day when Jemima entered the little bedroom she and Alice were sharing, she found her grandmother's maid Mosette putting away clean stockings in her drawer of the bureau. She imagined, in a flash, the kind of fuss that would follow if Mosette found the book. The solution came in the same flash: She would have Nick take it back to Mr. Castle.

The family united at the Latimers' house for luncheon every Sunday. Jemima managed to bring the book and transfer it to Nick's jacket as they played double solitaire after lunch. She had even tucked in a short note thanking Mr. Castle for the loan. Nick, who as a boy was allowed considerable freedom, knew exactly where Mr. Castle lived, and promised Jemima he would deliver the book within the week. Jemima was very relieved. It had been flattering, she decided, to have the full attention of a man such as Felix Castle, despise him though she did for moral reasons. But Felix Castle was the very last person in New York she should be corresponding with, and despite his kindness to her, she was happy to have the matter closed.

Only it wasn't. Mr. Castle wrote back to her, sending the missive with Nick. "I told him he couldn't put anything in the mail and sending one of those footmen of his was out of the question," Nick whispered to Jemima after dinner that evening. "I don't know why he was so set on writing to you, either," he added. "They say he entertains actresses and so on." (Neither one of them had a clue as to what "so on" might entail.)

"He was kind to me, that day we moved house. Maybe he thinks of me as a kind of little sister," Jemima hissed, though the idea made her obscurely unhappy.

"Well, anyway, he made me wait while he wrote this," Nick murmured. He slipped a folded piece of paper into Jemima's hand. Fortunately her dress had long sleeves, and the note disappeared into one of them until she found an excuse to go upstairs and read it.

It was insignificant, as illicit correspondence went. "Dear Miss Wilcox," it read, "Thank you for returning my book of poetry so promptly. I hope you took the time to read a few more poems than the sonnet on the Grecian urn. Yours respectfully, Felix Castle." Jemima liked the idea of someone writing to her "respectfully," but she put the note on her bedroom fire as soon as Alice's back was turned. She was still very angry with Mr. Castle.

Quite often in the following days she found herself addressing letters to him in her mind: "Dear Mr. Castle," she would begin, "Thanks to you, my family are at each other's throats. There isn't enough room in this house for all of us and my brother, Nick, is lodging with our uncle. I wonder how many spare bedrooms you have on Twenty-Fifth Street?" Or "Dear Mr. Castle, Those people parading around the Grecian urn seemed quite carefree. I rather envy them." The angriest imaginary letter read, "Dear Mr. Castle, I know you are not as old as you look. I don't understand how you can be so rapacious at such a young age."

Yet when Nick described Mr. Castle's house to Jemima, she listened eagerly. So many large rooms, so many servants, so much gilding! Nick's vocabulary for domestic details was limited but what he told Jemima made her curious, especially considering the prim austerity of her grandmother's house, where every cushion had its exact position and you could never get away from people. If Jemima sat at the dining room table to read, Gates would come in and try to set the table around her. If she sat in the parlor, her grandmother would instruct her to sit up straight. If she sat in the bedroom she shared with Alice, she could hear Moira and Mosette in the hall, bickering over laundry. There were times when too many bedrooms and footmen in gaudy livery sounded blissful.

CHAPTER 14

◆

SOCIAL TIES

May 1875

Fortunately, it was a mild spring. The elm trees in Washington Square Park hazed over with green and the surrounding lawns slowly followed suit. Better yet, because the park was relatively small, fenced, and surrounded largely by pleasant brick houses owned by pleasant, well-off New Yorkers, Jemima and Alice were permitted to promenade unchaperoned on the sandy paths at its northern end. This freedom was a boon to both girls. Despite Jemima's undemonstrative behavior, Alice knew she was fretting about something. They shared a bed, after all, and Jemima sometimes muttered in her sleep. For her own part, Alice felt, as she told her sister, "cooped up."

One morning the sisters were hustled out of the house (very politely) by Gates, since they were in the parlormaid's way. "I wouldn't mind," Alice muttered as they crossed brick-paved Waverly Place, "but I wanted to practice the piano while Grandmama was out this morning. She always fusses when I play scales, and says they give her a headache."

"I think *we* give her a headache, not the scales," Jemima agreed. "Though it can't be easy to have four extra people stuffed into the house she used to occupy all by herself. Have you noticed that she talks about the fall as if everything will be different come September? But I don't understand how that could happen."

"No," Alice agreed. "Unless, somehow, Papa's business is a tremendous success."

The girls' eyes met. "Papa does seem hopeful, except when he's exhausted," Jemima pointed out. After dinner he usually sat in the parlor at Selina's narrow drop-front bureau, reading documents and sighing. Sometimes he stayed up well past midnight, and he always left the house before anyone else came downstairs. The girls walked on for a few minutes, and Jemima suddenly burst out, "And with all these money problems, I don't understand how I can come out. What about grown-up gowns? And aren't we scandalous, because Papa lost the house? Will I be invited to any parties? I asked Mama and she just snapped at me and told me not to worry, but she can't entertain here. She used to talk about having a dance for me . . ."

"Couldn't she do that at the Latimers'?" Alice interrupted.

"Oh, I can't imagine Aunt Dora would agree! A luncheon, maybe. Or a tea, but not a dance." She hesitated for a moment and went on, "Do you think we're disgraced?"

Alice stared at Jemima. "*Disgraced?* You've been reading too many silly novels."

"Don't you think there are some ladies who will drop Mama now? And us, of course," Jemima asked.

"I suppose there are," Alice answered. "Does it matter? You'll be out in society. Maybe you won't be invited to every single party. But you don't seem to care for them very much."

"That doesn't mean I want to be excluded," Jemima said bitterly. "Oh, and I forgot to tell you about the last Dancing Class. It's a special combined class, for the girls my age and your year as well. At the Van Ormskirks'. *If* we're invited."

"Mrs. Van Ormskirk has to include us," Alice said calmly. "Otherwise Grandmama would make an almighty fuss."

"But why would she do such a thing? I mean organize a special class?"

"I expect it's for Maria's sake," Alice said. "'To give dear Maria a chance to acquire more social polish,' as she'd probably say."

Jemima laughed. Alice so rarely mocked anyone. "I could almost pity Mrs. Van Ormskirk, still trying to find husbands for Caroline and Louisa," said Jemima. "But having *three* unmarried daughters is truly humiliating. Caroline must be well into her twenties."

"Poor Caroline," Alice answered, shaking her head.

"Nonsense," Jemima retorted. "She's just plain mean. But Maria's the prettiest of those girls. Someone is bound to court her when she comes out. At least I won't be the only girl who's outshone by her younger sister. Assuming we even count as debutantes."

"You're being ridiculous," Alice said, and nudged Jemima with her elbow. Walking toward them was the elderly and austere Mrs. Ebenezer Harris. Both girls slowed their steps and nodded to Mrs. Harris, who acknowledged them with a frosty little jerk of her chin.

"When she lunched with Grandmama last week I heard her say we should be chaperoned on our walks," Alice murmured to her sister once they were out of earshot. "And Grandmama said we'd come to no harm because only the right kind of people lived here on the Square. Like the Onderdoncks. What a pity that Arthur had to go back to his boarding school."

"On the contrary! Mrs. Harris would probably think we were out here trying to lure him into an assignation," Jemima suggested wryly.

"Come to think of it, we're the only young people on the square these days, have you noticed?" Jemima asked as they reached the fountain at the center of the park.

"Aside from the students down at the university," Alice said. "And there's that man on the east side, who has the little boy."

"You mean the one-armed man? He's not young!" Jemima protested. "He lost his arm in the war!"

"How do you know?"

"Moira told me. His housekeeper is from Moira's part of Ireland. She says he's a widower, too."

Alice had a prodigally soft heart. "Oh, that's so sad!" she exclaimed. "Poor motherless little boy!"

"He's quite handsome, too, did you notice?" Jemima replied, eyeing her sister.

"No," Alice answered. "I was thinking of the child."

"You have that misty look, as if you were going to cry," Jemima observed.

"Well, I'm not. What's his name?"

"The little boy is called Charlie," Jemima answered. "Do you need my handkerchief?"

"No, the name of the father, of course. Stop teasing me."

"Thaddeus Britton. He was a colonel in the war but doesn't use the title anymore. He's an engineer, his office is on the square, his wife was always frail and died of consumption last fall."

"How do you know all of this?"

"While you're playing the piano, I listen to the grown-ups discuss the neighbors," Jemima explained with a smug smile. "Mrs. Delano two doors down from Grandmama keeps parrots. It's not all fascinating gossip by any means."

"What else have you heard?"

"Well . . ." Jemima's face grew sober. "I couldn't help

overhearing . . . it's one of the problems with Grandmama's house . . ." Then she trailed off.

"What?" Alice halted. Jemima took two steps beyond her and then turned around. Alice stood on the path with an obstinate expression. "What did you hear? I knew you were worried about something more than your season. I'm not moving a step further until you tell me."

Jemima looked at her sister, tall and sturdy and golden like an angel on a stained-glass window. "How is this all going to end?" she asked, hoping Alice didn't hear her voice break. "Papa seems to think his Elevated Railroad will be an immense success but what if he's wrong? What if he's spent all of his money and lost our house and the railroad fails? What would happen to us all?"

Alice shook her head and strode over to hug Jemima. "Then we'll live with Grandmama for a while longer. Goodness, you have the gloomiest imagination! Why shouldn't the Elevated be successful? Lots of people have invested in it, you know. Including Mr. Gregson and Uncle Noble. They understand business. They wouldn't have put money into the Elevated just out of friendship."

The girls' eyes met. "No, that's true," Jemima agreed, and sniffed. "I suppose they wouldn't." Alice plucked a clean handkerchief from inside her sleeve and handed it to Jemima.

"We should go back inside or Grandmama will think we've been accosted by ruffians," Alice said, and linked her arm through Jemima's.

"Maybe that one-armed Mr. Britton is a highwayman in his spare time. 'The Highwayman of Washington Square'—doesn't that sound like a story by Washington Irving?"

Alice knew that Jemima's levity was an attempt to mask her anxiety, but she was honestly less concerned than her sister about the Wilcox family's situation. Yes, Grandmama could be stern and the house was certainly overcrowded. Papa was worried, Mama was sad. But in just a few weeks the family would return to the Spring House for the summer, and they would all be much more comfortable. Perhaps Papa's business would turn around somehow and by September, he'd have enough money to rent a house of their own! He'd lost his money so quickly—didn't that mean he might replenish it just as fast? And in the meantime, Alice thought, she would be allowed to attend the last Dancing Class with Jemima. Surely that would be enjoyable.

Then at breakfast a few days later, her grandmother announced that Alice needed a dress for the Dancing Class. Before Mama had a chance to object, Grandmama said, "I will take care of this, Helen dear. You needn't even trouble yourself to come to Stewart's with us. I know how busy you are." Alice thought her mother looked startled but she acquiesced readily enough, and on the morning of the initial visit to Stewart's, merely kissed Alice at the door and said, "It's so kind of you to do this, Mama."

Alice wasn't entirely surprised when Aunt Dora met them at the lingerie counter. Or when Grandmama said, "We'll start with a new corset, dear. You're a very pretty girl but you're built like your father." So she was whisked into a fitting room and a tiny woman with a measuring tape wrote down every single possible dimension of her body from her neck to her ankles.

Next they chose the fabric for the dress, beautiful corded blue silk, and then the saleswoman produced a book of fashion plates. As her aunt and grandmother pondered various necklines and sleeve lengths, Alice stifled a yawn, and wondered what difference it would make whether the neckline was square or rounded. "Don't ladies get cold with their dresses cut so low and their arms bare?"

she asked, pointing to an image of a lady showing quite a bit of her chest.

"Oh, no, dear," answered Aunt Dora. "You have no idea how warm it gets in a ballroom. Not to mention the exertion of dancing."

"And for the trim, madam," said the saleswoman, "we have some lovely silk flowers . . ."

"Far too elaborate for a Dancing Class," judged Grandmama. "She's still just a girl."

"Of course, Mama," Aunt Dora agreed. "And given the Wilcoxes' situation . . ." She stopped suddenly, but Grandmama met her gaze and nodded.

"What do you mean?" Alice asked.

"We will discuss this later," Grandmama said smoothly, which meant the subject was permanently closed. "In any event, you girls should look neat and modest above all. What color is Jemima's gown? Is it that apricot one she's worn before?"

"Yes," Alice answered. "Moira re-draped the skirt and Mama was going to baste some ribbon to the neckline so that it looks fresh."

"That will do nicely," said Aunt Dora. "And you girls will look pretty side by side."

"You always look pretty, Alice. I'm sure you will be a success," Grandmama commented.

It was the kind of comment that made Alice uncomfortable. What exactly was it that her grandmother expected of her?

Selina had scoffed at what she termed "Annabelle's machinations" but nevertheless managed to insert herself into the roster of chaperones for the evening. She thus had access to minutely detailed gossip about the plans for the evening which would include, unusually, a buffet supper. Music would be provided by members of the Academy of Music's orchestra because the sound of a piano wouldn't be sufficiently loud in the Van Ormskirk ballroom. (Cue the raised eyebrows.) And dance cards—hitherto only distributed at grand balls in New York—had been ordered from Mr. Tiffany. "For a mere class!" Selina protested to her granddaughters as they all settled into the carriage on the evening itself. "Still, it's a good thing for you girls to be at ease with true formality. When the Prince of Wales visited New York before the war, I was one of the few women who knew how to perform a court curtsy." Jemima's elbow nudged Alice's. This was not new information. "And a dance card makes a nice memento," Selina went on. "I still have my card from the ball for the prince."

"Yes, Grandmama," Jemima said. "Will you have to find partners for all of the young ladies at the class?"

"Of course," Selina answered as the carriage pulled to a halt. "But I'm sure you two won't need any help." A servant opened the door and unfolded the steps, holding out a hand to help her down.

"How can she say that?" Jemima whispered to Alice, gathering up her skirt. "Considering what she keeps calling our 'unusual situation'?" She stepped down to the sidewalk and waited for her sister to emerge.

"Grandmama is just trying to make you feel braver," Alice answered cheerfully.

"Come along, girls," Selina commanded, and they followed her up the shallow steps into the wide marble-paved hall of the Van Ormskirks' house.

It was grand, certainly. A fireplace large enough to roast an ox occupied one entire wall, and an Oriental carpet led down a long corridor to an indefinite destination. Servants in black tailcoats and yellow vests accepted their coats and Selina led them toward the sound of violins.

Just before they reached the door of the ballroom, she turned to them. "You both look charming, girls." With these reassuring words, she sailed forward.

Jemima remembered very little of the evening afterward. There had been music, rather loud. She was separated from Alice by a wall of black backs. Then she was standing on the dance floor with a boy—was it Tobias Bennett?—when the orchestra began to play and they started off in different directions. Her partner managed to haul her in and she made a joke about being like a fish, which made him grin. They managed respectably until the end of the dance, when he returned her to the side of the ballroom where the girls stood.

Actually, she thought, the girls really *were* like fish. At the end of each dance they got tossed back into the pool of other girls and had to be selected again for each dance. The boys got to choose, naturally. Alice was surrounded by them.

Jemima stood next to a chair, and wondered if she dared sit. Her dance card was blank.

She noticed a bronze statue of a naked lady holding a bow. Most likely Diana the huntress, she thought; Mr. Castle would probably know. Was he a good dancer? She could easily imagine him dressed in impeccable evening clothes, talking to his partner while he guided her effortlessly around the dance floor.

"Here you are," said Alice, slipping through a group of boys, all of whom followed her with their eyes.

"Didn't Grandmama tell you that girls don't wander around ballrooms all alone?" Jemima said. "It looks 'fast.'"

"I didn't know any better," Alice answered with a shrug. "She can lecture me on the way home. Is your dance card full?"

"No, it is not," Jemima said, trying to keep her voice light. "Though I suppose yours is."

"Well, I think I might feel faint," Alice said, and gracefully passed a hand over her forehead.

"Really?" Jemima answered, startled. "Come, sit down." She led her sister to a gilt chair. "Can I get you a glass of punch?" She frowned. "You're never faint!"

"I'm merely light-headed," Alice told her sister in a fading voice. "Oh—Mr. Leddy!" She addressed a boy in spectacles who had materialized at her side. "Yes, this is your dance, but I'm afraid I don't feel well. Perhaps my sister, Jemima, would be willing to be your partner," she finished. It was quite clearly a command.

Couples were already grouped together on the dance floor and Jemima didn't have time to protest, so she found herself spinning around in a polka with the silent Mr. Leddy. At the end of the dance, though, he scribbled his name twice on her dance card. Then looking up at her he blushed, and said, "My mother warned me against you Wilcox girls but I think you're magnificent." Then he returned her to the row of chairs, where Selina now sat beside Alice, who fanned herself slowly.

"What did young Leddy say to you?" Selina asked, patting the chair beside her. "I'd heard he was very shy, but he seemed to enjoy . . ."

But Jemima didn't catch the rest of her grandmother's sentence, because the handsome Arthur Onderdonck, home from school for the occasion, stood before her, bowing and holding out his hand. "Hello, Mrs. Maitland. Miss Wilcox, I've been looking for you," he said. "I hope that you will favor me with this waltz."

"Of course I will," Jemima said with a smile.

"My mother's been coaching me," he said proudly as they took their place on the dance floor. "I've gotten better at listening to the music, and waltzes are the easiest. I promise your feet are safe this time." Then the music began with two slow introductory chords.

Arthur's arm held her close and she could feel, through all the layers of skirt and petticoat, his legs stepping forward as she stepped back, swaying to the beat. They made a spinning circuit of the room, then he said, in her ear, "I'm going to reverse directions now. Ready? One . . . two . . ." and on the lingering "three" he had suddenly steered her to rotate counterclockwise.

"Goodness, you've become an expert!" she exclaimed sincerely, and noticed him blushing.

"Sometimes girls get dizzy," he answered.

"Why does my grandmother call you 'dear Arthur'?"

"She's my father's godmother," he explained. "Did I see you and your sister walking in the square this week?"

"I'm sure you did. Next time you should come out and join us," Jemima urged him. "We don't know any other young people in the neighborhood."

"I would like that," he answered with what looked like a genuine smile. "You're very light on your feet, Miss Wilcox. Some of these girls need a good bit of urging along, if you know what I mean." Then somehow the dance was over and they had ended up back at the rank of chairs where the chaperones sat. After Jemima sank down next to her grandmother, Arthur bowed and disappeared to claim another girl. Jemima felt her spirits sink.

"You're quite flushed," commented Selina. "Young Mr. Onderdonck shouldn't make you girls whirl around like that, it's not becoming."

"But it's exhilarating," Jemima answered. "I wish I'd thought to bring a fan. Isn't it terribly warm in here?"

"It's the exertion," her grandmother answered. "Still, he's a nice boy."

"Why did Edgar Leddy tell me his mother doesn't like us?"

Selina suddenly turned a sharp gaze on Jemima. "He said that? Never mind. Dorcas Leddy's a very silly woman. Now let me see your dance card, dear. I'll do my best to find you a few more partners." But Alice was coming toward them, bracketed by two boys who seemed to be arguing about who would dance with her next. It would have been a more enviable situation, Jemima thought, if one of them had been even half as handsome as Arthur. "Look," Alice said to the one with freckles, "here is my sister. She's a much better dancer than I am."

Jemima shook her head at Alice but Selina stood suddenly and said, "You must be David Pelham. And Roger Norton?" Both boys suddenly stood up straighter and bowed toward her. "Jemima dear, do you have any dances left for these young men? Let me see your card."

David Pelham steered her around stiffly, counting beats in an undertone, and returned her to Selina with a bow. Roger Norton looked over her shoulder and talked past her ear about his sophomore year at Yale for the entire length of the mazurka. Then when the dance ended he asked her for another dance, and soon her card was completely filled with names. When Arthur Onderdonck returned to ask for another dance, she had to disappoint him—and he really did seem disappointed. "That's what happens when a fellow dances with the wallflowers," he said regretfully. "But I look forward to seeing you in the square one day."

CHAPTER 15

◆

RURAL PURSUITS

May–August 1875

Unfortunately the unexpected triumph of the final Dancing Class didn't solve the Wilcox family's predicament. They were still squeezed into Selina's house; Joshua was still distracted and overworked. Their finances were still constrained and as New York's season continued, Helen's spirits flagged. Maintaining even a limited social life required an exhausting level of tact. There had been a few awkward encounters between her friends and her mother's, most notably when Sylvia Burke called on Selina's "at home" day. The chilly, remote courtesy shown her by Selina's friends Mrs. Marquette and Mrs. Grinling would have been funny if it hadn't been so uncomfortable.

One morning a few days later, Helen's sister, Dora, came to visit, accompanied by the pug, Trixie. "I won't stay long," she told her sister when Gates showed her into the parlor. "Are the girls in?"

"No, they're walking in the square," Helen answered.

"Oh, good," Dora said. "Because I was thinking about you all. I'm sure Mama loves having the girls here, but I know it's a strain."

"Yes, I'm afraid it is. For all of us," Helen answered, looking up from her darning. Just six months earlier, it would have been Moira who mended Joshua's socks. "I was planning to go to the Spring House early this year."

"Oh, no," Dora disagreed. "You mustn't do that! Jemima would miss Patsy Marquette's luncheon and she should meet some of those girls—"

"Dora," Helen interrupted, "Jemima doesn't have an appropriate gown for a luncheon with 'those girls,' and I can't ask Joshua for the money to have one made. Apparently there's yet another emergency with the Elevated."

"Well, you know it would be a pleasure for me to take Jemima to Stewart's . . ."

"No," Helen answered. "You're kind, but I have my pride."

Dora sighed. "The thing is, she's an unusual girl. Reserved, I'd say. She'd probably be more comfortable next year if she knew girls like Eliza Howland and Mabel Forsyte a little better . . ."

Helen put down Joshua's sock. "I know you mean well," she said with exasperation. "And I'm grateful for your kind intentions. But Jemima is my daughter, and I will bring her out in my own way. Not yours."

"Well," Dora answered, "I do think I have a better sense than you do of New York society. But of course you'll do as you like. Come along, Trixie." She stood up and the pug, who had been sleeping at her feet, rolled onto her back with her furry little feet in the air, and refused to walk. Dora had to carry the dog out of the house like an oversize loaf of bread. It was rather inspiring to see Trixie get the better of indefatigably bossy Dora.

Helen had not actually been planning to go early to the Spring House; she had simply, out of irritation, wanted to thwart Dora's scheme for Jemima. But suddenly, leaving the city seemed appealing. She could easily turn down the few unimportant invitations she and Jemima had received and make day-long visits to New York to complete the modest shopping for Jemima's debutante wardrobe. Joshua, she thought with a tinge of bitterness, was working so hard that she barely saw him anyway.

She had expected the children to be delighted by her decision. They had always thrived at the Spring House, relishing their independence and indulging their own interests. Alice would spend every hour she could either driving or riding. Nick was thrilled at the idea of escaping the lessons he'd been enduring with a friend's tutor. Jemima, though, greeted the news with a protest. "So early? But what about Adele Renshaw's fork luncheon?" she asked her mother.

Helen looked blankly at her daughter: Jemima had never shown any interest in the mousy Adele Renshaw, and a "fork luncheon" consisted of eight girls around a table, pushing ladylike food around on fine china. It was the least elaborate and usually the dullest form of pre-debutante social occasions. "When is that? In two weeks? I can bring you back to town for it, if you like."

"Oh, well," Jemima temporized. "Maybe not." Then she asked, to Helen's further surprise, "What will happen to our correspondence? I mean letters that are sent here, to Grandmama's house?"

"It's a little too early to expect invitations for the fall," Helen answered. "Is that what you're wondering?"

"Yes, of course," Jemima answered after a tiny pause. "How will people know where we are?"

"Well, Papa will be coming back and forth. He usually brings our letters from the city. Besides, you and I will still have quite a bit of shopping to do before the fall. We may spend a night here from time to time."

"And when will we return for the season?" Jemima asked. "I'm just wondering."

"Oh, sweetheart, I don't know. That will depend on the weather, and whether you're invited to any parties early in September. And on how your wardrobe comes along."

Jemima reached out to touch a fold of her mother's dress. "And *that* will depend on what we can afford."

Helen took her daughter's hand and caught it between both of her own. "You are not to worry about money," she said. "It's my concern, and your papa's."

"I know," Jemima said, and looked soberly at her mother. "But I couldn't help seeing, in the newspaper, a story about the Elevated needing more money for its tracks."

"First, you shouldn't believe everything you read in the newspapers," Helen said. "And second, I can tell you that your papa is still confident that the Elevated will be tremendously successful. It's just taken more time than he imagined."

After a long searching glance at her mother, Jemima answered, "If you say so, Mama. But I could stay here to keep him company."

"And what would you do while he's working?" Helen asked with exasperation. "Ruin your sight by reading all day, most likely! You'll come with us, my dear, and you'll be glad when you get to the Spring House. You love being there." Later, as she thought about the conversation, Helen wondered if Jemima hadn't seemed strangely reluctant to leave town. But then, everyone knew young girls were moody.

The Wilcox family, once installed in the Spring House, relaxed. Moira rejoined the household. Helen felt she could breathe again simply because the house was so large that she could not pinpoint everyone's location by the sounds they made. Another pleasant surprise was Selina's obvious new affection for her grandchildren, borne of simple proximity. She taught Jemima piquet and the two of them played hand after hand of the old card game on the porch, competing fiercely for penny points. In addition Helen frequently found her mother in the parlor listening to Alice practice the piano, with evident pleasure.

And while Nick made no secret of his scorn for the subject, all of the women took a keen interest in Jemima's new wardrobe. A small sitting room upstairs became "the sewing room" which authorized everyone to drape fabric samples over the chairs and leave copies of *Godey's Lady's Book* open to the fashion plates. Dora was often to be found poring over the illustrations with great attention, and happily assumed the role of style arbiter, convinced that only she could make the most of Jemima's "uncommon appeal."

All the same, Jemima was moody that summer, given to snapping at her siblings and spending hours on the library sofa, staring at the pages of *Robinson Crusoe* but actually daydreaming. She often refused to join her siblings in their usual country activities of rides, walks, or croquet matches. "It's a pity," Alice remarked to her mother one day in July, as they sat together on the porch swing. "She was so sad when we had to move in with Grandmama and I thought she'd be happier out of the city. But now that we're here, she's still grumpy."

"Do you think she's worried about the season?" Helen asked.

"Maybe. But the last Dancing Class should have reassured her. I think she's fretting about Papa's business."

"Yes, well," Helen answered, with a tightening of her lips. "The Elevated is certainly a subject for concern."

"And it was hard, this spring, for Jemima to be crowded in at Grandmama's. Once she told me that she longed to sit by herself in a room for more than ten minutes at a stretch."

"She's certainly enjoying her solitude since we arrived here," Helen answered. "Do you know where she is now?"

"She said she was going down to the dock. She had a book in her hand."

"And a sunbonnet on?" Helen asked.

"Yes, Mama, of course. Anyway she'll come back soon. It's not actually a comfortable place to read."

Alice was correct: The dock didn't even offer a bench to perch on. But Jemima had chosen her location for privacy, not comfort. It was one spot at the Spring House where you could always see someone coming, which made it the best location for her to mull over her great secret.

A few weeks after she sent back the volume of Keats, Felix Castle had written her another note. It had been delivered by messenger to the Washington Square house—what a risk!—and Gates had brought it to Jemima, correctly, on a silver salver just as if she were a grown-up. Jemima felt she had accepted it with the aplomb of a woman of the world. It was a good thing Gates had left the room by the time she saw Mr. Castle's bold signature at the bottom of the page, and blushed violently.

In his note, he had copied out several stanzas by a poet named Spenser. This had startled but flattered her; adults, in Jemima's experience, did not always consider girls to be fully-fledged people, let alone individuals worth corresponding with. She knew, naturally, that Mr. Castle had no business sending her poetry—not only because he was in some sense her family's enemy, but on a more basic level, because well-bred young girls did not correspond with gentlemen. She had considered the situation for a week before composing a brief note to confess that Spenser baffled her. "Girls in New York," she wrote, "do not study verse on the whole. It seems to me that we are expected rather to study fashion plates." Her brief note of thanks said nothing about discontinuing their correspondence, though—as it should have. Nick delivered her note to Mr. Castle's house. At Sunday dinner with the Latimers a few days later, her brother had quite openly handed her a book.

"I came across this," he informed her with a wink. "Something told me you might like it." Tucked inside was another note from Mr. Castle that read simply, "Are the young ladies of New York permitted to read novels?"

This had all happened at a moment when Trixie tried to clamber into Selina's lap and knocked an embroidery hoop to the floor, causing a general uproar. Otherwise the Wilcoxes would have been astounded to see Nick expressing a literary opinion of any kind, let alone a recommendation of Fanny Burney's charming romance *Evelina*. Once the family was settled at the Spring House Jemima had read it in two delighted sittings, with part of her mind wondering why Mr. Castle had sent it to her in the first place. To please her? To share something he enjoyed? To ensure that she thought frequently of him? That, certainly, was the result.

There was no "correct" way for a young girl to respond to a gift from an entirely ineligible admirer, so after a token amount of soul-searching (wouldn't corresponding with Mr. Castle constitute a betrayal of her family?) Jemima wrote another secret note. In it she mentioned the fact that the Wilcoxes—including Nick, their occasional messenger—would be spending the summer out of town. Then she tore the first draft into shreds and rewrote the note to include the words "at the Spring House in Tenders Landing," just in case Mr. Castle should for some reason wish to pinpoint her location. Then, rather than leaving her note with other outgoing mail on the front hall table where everyone would see it, she had to cajole Alice to drive her in the pony cart to the little Tenders Landing post office, where she personally handed it to the postmistress. Deception, she reflected, required a great deal of planning.

Jemima did not expect a reply from Mr. Castle. She wouldn't have known how to explain his answer to her mother, if one had come. Above all, she was uncomfortably aware that her correspondence with Mr. Castle was disloyal as well as improper, considering his role in the Wilcox family's financial misfortune. Nevertheless, she relished thinking about him. She often found herself imagining unlikely scenarios in which the two of them were thrown together by accident (or by Fate, as she preferred to call it). For instance, he might coincidentally visit unidentified friends in Tenders Landing and, while out riding, be thrown from his horse and injured, then hobble to the nearest dwelling, which would just happen to be the Spring House where Jemima would soothe his fevered brow. Or—better yet—visiting the same unspecified friends, he might borrow a sailboat and, in a sudden squall, wash up at the Spring House dock. Prolonged exposure to the weather might bring on a sudden fever that would prevent him from leaving and Jemima would help nurse him back to health, prompting his warm gratitude . . . and other unspecified emotions. Sometimes Jemima simply remembered their conversation at the museum, which had felt so astoundingly direct. When she had sensed that he was interested in *her,* Jemima Wilcox, as an individual. As a nearly grown woman.

By mid-July, she had re-read his most recent note to her so often that the paper was wearing thin at the folds. Worse, she had come upon Moira putting away her petticoats in the very drawer where she'd hidden it. This was what had led her down to the dock on that blazing July Sunday. Apparently in all of the rambling Spring House there was no safe place to hide or discard a letter that began "My Dear Miss Wilcox" (my dear!) and ended "Cordially yours, Felix Castle." Burning it would have been the ideal solution and she'd even tiptoed down to the kitchen before dawn one day to bury it in the coals of the stove, but the fire had been allowed to go out. She could have slipped the note into one of the dusty old books on the upper shelves in the library but that didn't seem safe enough. What if Alice or, worse, her mother, suddenly decided to read *Pamela, or Virtue Rewarded* by Samuel Richardson?

So Jemima (suitably covered in her sunbonnet) had made her way down to the dock where, in plain though distant view of her mother and sister, she cut Mr. Castle's letter into tiny pieces with her sewing scissors before scattering them onto the outgoing tide. When she returned to the house, she was greatly relieved, if also regretful.

During the summers the combined Wilcox, Maitland, and Latimer families entertained often at the Spring House with much less formality than in the city. The strict urban routines of paying calls and sending invitations lapsed in favor of casual visits. Neighbors and city friends would appear without warning, and were often pressed to stay for a meal in what Selina termed "country hospitality." A rural lawyer might end up conversing with a Fifth Avenue dowager who would look right through him if they encountered each other in the city. Selina took great pride in gracefully playing hostess to people who had little in common.

Still, she had mixed feelings when, late one morning in July, she heard a wagonette crunch to a halt on the gravel drive. From her second-floor sitting room she recognized Arthur Onderdonck in the driver's seat with his mother sitting next to him. On the one hand, Selina was pleased to see Arthur. Surely his presence indicated some interest in Jemima? On the other hand, there were only two subjects in Martha Onderdonck's conversational repertoire: the deplorable changes in New York society, and the character of her handsome son. Selina hastily trotted down the back stairs to enter the library by the door to the servants' hallway.

"Jemima," she called quietly, looking around for her granddaughter, "the Onderdoncks just turned into the drive." Jemima's head popped up from the sofa, where she'd been immersed in *A Tale of Two Cities*.

The doorbell rang and they both heard Mrs. Onderdonck's confident voice announce that they had just happened to be driving by and wondered if anyone was at home. "I will ascertain," said Gates, using his most doubtful voice. "Perhaps you would like to wait on the porch?"

Jemima and her grandmother exchanged glances while Jemima clambered to her feet and tried to smooth the creases from her skirt, then the two of them straightened their shoulders and set out to do their social duty. "Where's Mama?" Jemima whispered as they left the library.

"Riding with Alice. They'll be back soon." Jemima nodded. She liked Arthur, she told herself. She hoped to dance with him often in the fall, once the season began in New York. She squared her shoulders and followed her grandmother out onto the porch, where the Onderdoncks were politely admiring the river view.

The usual questions were asked: Where have you come from, won't you stay for luncheon, isn't the weather lovely? Lemonade was brought and the clattering of china indicated that the table was being set. Arthur spoke at some length about training his English retriever. He thought Jemima might like to meet the dog and she agreed—not that she particularly liked dogs, but how else would the conversation continue? Surely Mama and Alice would return soon and then Arthur would turn to Alice's beauty like a sunflower following the sun.

He asked Jemima questions: What do you like best about being in the country? Do you enjoy riding? Do you ever go fishing? He also imparted rather a lot of information about himself: He enjoyed exploring the countryside. There were some remarkable trails in the nearby hills, affording the intrepid walker a splendid view of the river's curve. But they required a good stick and more than a bit of "scrambling." Not quite the thing for a young lady. When Arthur paused to draw breath, Jemima returned to the subject that had interested him on the dance floor a few weeks earlier. Had Arthur read any of Walter Scott's novels? She was in the middle of *Ivanhoe* and found it very absorbing. But Arthur, to her surprise, shook his head. He had decided that fiction was "a waste of time." Impractical, unlikely to "help a man get ahead." He read the newspaper. He thought business was interesting. Her father's Elevated Railroad, for instance. Arthur spoke about that until the plates were cleared. It dawned on Jemima that perhaps Arthur Onderdonck was somewhat dull.

Then she glanced across the table toward her grandmother, whose eyes looked quite glazed with boredom as she listened to a very detailed description of Mrs. Onderdonck's cutting garden and its current infestation by aphids. Perhaps dullness was a family trait. Jemima was just wondering if she could excuse herself from the table and never return when voices were heard in the hall—rather loud, jolly voices, punctuated by frequent masculine laughter. Helen appeared in the doorway, neat as a pin in her black riding habit and bracketed by Hiram and Sylvia Burke, with Alice bringing up the rear. The afternoon suddenly acquired the potential for comedy.

Selina, bound by the laws of rural hospitality, insisted that the Burkes must be served luncheon. More chairs were brought, new places were set. Cook's raised voice was heard to protest when the swing door to the kitchen opened. Mr. Burke was squeezed between Selina and Alice. He seemed puzzled by the dainty slice of chicken breast on his plate and peered around the table in search of more robust sustenance. Mrs. Onderdonck silently gazed at a spot on the tablecloth four inches in front of her plate, visibly wishing herself elsewhere because Hiram and Sylvia Burke were not at all the kind of people she wanted to know. Mrs. Burke complimented Selina on the china, setting off an eye-glazing lecture about a porcelain service for six dozen imported by a Suydam ancestor in the China trade, considered too precious to use.

Despite good-faith efforts, conversation languished.

Finally the awkward meal ended and the families moved en masse to the porch for coffee. "Why in the world did you bring the Burkes here?" whispered Selina to Helen as they left the table. "And just before luncheon!"

"I couldn't help it, Alice and I ran into them on the River Road," Helen murmured back. "Mr. Burke was so eager to see the house that I couldn't say no. I am sorry, Mama, I'm aware that you don't like them, but I'll explain to Sylvia that you won't know them back in the city. She'll understand."

Selina took a deep breath. "Martha Onderdonck is aghast. Did you know the Burkes tried to buy the house next door to them on Eighteenth Street? Outrageous!"

"It may be outrageous, Mama, but it's hardly my fault," Helen told her. "I'll take Hiram to look at the stables just as soon as he's finished his coffee. Then you can have a fainting spell."

"And leave Mrs. Onderdonck with Sylvia Burke? I'd never hear the end of it!"

"Well, how about this, Mama: Ask Alice to play the piano? They'll all remember urgent reasons to leave."

"Clever girl," Selina said, and patted Helen's arm. It was a sound scheme and it might have worked. Instead, over coffee, Hiram

Burke asked Helen in his booming voice, "And what can you tell us all about the Elevated Railroad's public stock offering?"

Silence fell, followed instantly by Selina's voice asking smoothly, "More coffee, Mr. Burke? Now tell me, do you and Mrs. Burke have a place in the country?"

"Not yet, ma'am," Hiram answered. "We just bought thirty acres on Long Island Sound, though. We'll be building something there before long. I'm wondering about that Elevated, though. Do you suppose I should buy a block of shares? I've heard rumors about a public offering."

Selina looked at him in astonishment and said, "Mr. Burke, has no one ever told you that in New York society, we do not discuss business on a social occasion?"

"Why no," he answered with a big smile. "Thank you for the tip, Mrs. Maitland." He looked over the porch to where Sylvia sat next to Jemima. "Did you hear that, Mother? I'm not supposed to talk about business in polite company! Why didn't you tell me? I would have thought the Wilcoxes would be excited about the Elevated going public, they could get very rich. Maybe do some repairs on this old place, or buy a better class of house in the city . . ."

"Hush, Hiram, before you say another word," Sylvia broke in, shaking her head. She stood up and turned to Selina. "I'm sorry I let Hiram talk me into dropping by, but I'm pleased to have met you, Mrs. Maitland. I am very fond of Helen."

Then the Burkes left, shepherded to their carriage by Helen in a stream of insincere assurance that their visit had been a very great pleasure. At the last moment, Hiram Burke poked his head out the window and instructed her, "Get Mr. Wilcox to tell you about that stock offering! It could be the making of your family!"

Helen climbed the steps to the porch and surveyed the

remainder of the party: the two Onderdoncks and her own family, looking stunned. "I find Mr. Burke's frankness quite refreshing, don't you?" she asked her mother in a bright voice.

Selina darted a glance at her daughter. "I suppose Joshua met him in the course of business?"

"Actually, Mama, Sylvia is one of my dearest friends," Helen said with a flicker of defiance. "I'm sure you've heard me mention her. She's very kind."

"How nice that must be for you," said the well-bred Mrs. Onderdonck. "She seems quite . . ."

". . . jolly," put in her son, Arthur, without glancing at his mother.

"Overdressed," snapped Mrs. Onderdonck. "It's high time we were on our way, Arthur. Thank you so much for luncheon, Mrs. Maitland, Mrs. Wilcox. I was delighted to meet your girls." She nodded toward Alice and Jemima and led Arthur away, though he turned back to catch one last glance of Jemima before climbing into their carriage.

CHAPTER 16

❖

MONEY MATTERS

August 1875

Meanwhile, Helen had another worry: She had not yet received Alice's invitation to the Dancing Classes. Of course the committee would send it to Mama's house in the city, but Joshua was under strict orders to bring her letters up to the Spring House when he came for the weekend. When he arrived the evening after the Burkes' incursion, she followed him up to their bedroom while he changed for dinner. "It's so strange," she said, leafing through the pile of envelopes he had deposited on her dressing table. "I really thought we would have received it by now."

"It's still early, isn't it?" he replied, shrugging out of his dark city coat.

"No, not at all," Helen said, watching as he slipped his pocket watch from his vest and set it on top of the bureau. The slanting rays of the evening sun caught his face for a moment and she was startled by the hollows beneath his cheekbones. He must be working too hard and not eating enough. She felt a surge of sympathy for him. "The invitations always go out in the middle of August."

"Well," he answered flatly, "Alice may not be included this year."

"But she was invited to the class at the end of the season," Helen protested. "That's as good as a promise, really. Even Annabelle wouldn't be so cruel as to take Alice off the list. What is it, Joshua?"

He sighed, and took her hand in his. "I've been kicked out of the Union Club," he said. "For not paying my dues." He met her gaze. "I went over there this week hoping to find Noble, and my name was on that little noticeboard in the front hall. I was trying to find out why and had a little dustup with Hans-Albert . . ."

She yanked her hand from his and felt her eyes go wide. "Your name was *posted*? Oh, Joshua!" She stood and walked away from him. Posted! She remembered her mother gossiping with some other ladies, years earlier, about a man who'd been posted at his club. Such humiliation!

"Yes," he admitted. "It was careless." He turned away from her and began pulling the studs out of his shirt. "I could have throttled Van Ormskirk, he was taking such pleasure in it all . . ."

"You argued with Hans-Albert? At the club?" Helen cried out. "I suppose there were other people there, too? The news must be all over town!" She took a breath and tried to control herself. All the windows along the west front of the house were open. She was sure her voice could be heard in her mother's bedroom. She crossed the room and clasped Joshua's arms above his elbows. "Gentlemen pay their debts!" she hissed. "What were you *thinking*?" Then she stepped away, because the tears had started and she could not bear for Joshua to see her crying.

"I wasn't thinking, damn it!" he shouted. "I've been trying to keep two companies running and I lost track of the fees for that stuffy old club! What the hell difference does it make?"

But by then she was beyond speech. It seemed, somehow, like the last straw. In a corner of her mind, Helen wondered where these sobs had come from: Was she overtired? Getting ill? She sat on the stool in front of the dressing table and dropped her face into her hands. *What the hell difference does it make?* Spoken like a wagon driver. Coarse, swearing at his wife. Ignoring his debts. Was this the man she'd married? She lay her head on her arms, knocking the ivory brushes onto the floor as she wept.

Then she felt his hand on her back; that large, warm, callused hand, snagging slightly on the fabric of her dress. He was kneeling on the floor next to her. "I'm sorry," he murmured. "I'm so sorry, Helen. I didn't realize how important the club was to you."

She sniffed, and he gave her his handkerchief. "No," she replied. "I don't think I did, either. But"—and here she blew her nose in a truly unladylike way—"my father and his friends all met at their clubs. So your joining the Union Club . . . I thought it showed that you fit in." She turned around to face him.

"I understand now," Joshua said. He stood up and went to the bureau, where he took another one of his handkerchiefs from the top drawer, and brought it back to Helen. "And maybe I thought I could do that; just fit in with the men like Noble, or your mother's neighbors. Maybe I thought I'd grow into that mold." He sighed, then sat on the floor leaning against her legs. "But I couldn't. No more than I can really be comfortable in that house of your mother's. But if all goes well, Helen, we won't be living with her for too much longer. We're going to absorb the Elevated into Hudson Transit and sell stock in the combined company to the public."

"To the public!" Helen echoed. "So that people . . . just anyone, not only people who know you, could buy shares?"

"Exactly," he answered. "Just as Hiram mentioned."

"And was Hiram correct about us getting . . . how did he put it . . . 'very rich'?"

"*I* never said that," Joshua protested, looking up at her.

"But that's your hope," she suggested. "And when will this happen?"

"Early in January," he told her, as the dinner gong rang downstairs.

"Oh, goodness," she muttered. "Quick, change your shirt." She unhooked her bodice and stepped out of her skirt.

For a moment the only sound in the room was the rustle of billowing fabric as they both coaxed sleeves, collars, petticoats, and lapels into position. "Wait, your hair," Joshua said, putting a hand on Helen's shoulder. He took a pin from the dressing table and thrust it into her chignon. "One more word," he murmured. He turned her gently around and held her by the shoulders. "The potential of this public offering is so huge, Helen. If it succeeds, nobody in New York will snub you ever again. We'll build a castle on Fifth Avenue that will make Annabelle van Ormskirk weep with envy. But I have been distracted, and I regret it."

"Good," she said, and kissed him on the cheek.

Noble Latimer and Joshua dined at Delmonico's just a few days later, after the impending public offering was officially announced. Noble gazed around the room and Joshua followed suit. Just Delmonico's on a summer evening, the buzz of male voices, a faint pop as champagne was uncorked. "I don't know any of these people, do you?"

"No," Joshua said after a glance.

"I used to know everyone," Noble commented. "These are men like us; well-mannered, comfortable. They look rich, don't they?"

They did. Not many were in evening clothes but every coat fit perfectly, each snowy cuff was starched, the hands on the silver knives and forks were all clean and soft. These were prosperous businessmen and Noble Latimer, who knew New Yorkers better than anyone, could not identify one of them.

"Think about it," Noble went on, while Joshua began forking up the sole on his plate. "We all know about the big-money men like Belmont and Morgan, and the big businesses they run. But for every one of those fellows, there are ten, twenty, dozens of smaller men who are becoming very well-off. And they are men who don't give a fig for the Union Club." He looked down and seemed to notice his food for the first time, then began eating.

"So maybe I don't need to, either," Joshua suggested.

Noble swallowed. "Maybe you don't. Do you enjoy club life? You don't play cards. You don't want to escape your wife." Here he smiled. "My point is that you may not be a clubman, and we may have reached a time in New York when that doesn't matter." He paused and rephrased his point. "We used to do business only with men we knew socially, but now the city's too big for that. And business is too important."

"I don't much like those Union Club fellows who sit around playing whist and talking about their grandfathers," Joshua said. "But I'd join Castle's Coaching Club. They seem like sound men who probably wouldn't give a damn that I started out as a wagon driver."

"They do tend to be coarser, the new people," Noble observed.

"That doesn't bother me. I just don't have the money for a coach."

"Oh, but you will," Noble answered calmly.

"You say that with such assurance," Joshua retorted with unusual bitterness. "Remember I'm living with my mother-in-law."

"Yes, and you own a substantial amount of stock in a transit company that will soon go public. Let me tell you, this city is on the verge of growth that will make the good years after the war look like child's play." Noble leaned back slightly and squinted as the waiter bent over to pour a bit of red wine into his glass. He sipped it, then nodded. "It will open up a little more as we drink it," he assured Joshua. "Look, I'll stop lecturing you in a moment. Don't worry about Hans-Albert and the Union Club. His opinion doesn't matter as much as he believes."

"Maybe, but I'm more concerned about his wife," Joshua confessed. "She seems to run New York social life single-handed. And she does not like Helen."

"Yes, but I'm convinced that her influence is on the wane. People don't care so much about pedigrees anymore."

Joshua brightened up. "And speaking of people without pedigrees, did you hear about Robey?" He sat back while the waiter reverently placed a plate before him and began to carve a rack of lamb.

"I heard a ludicrous tale about the death of a long-lost brother and Robey inheriting a gold mine," Noble said. "It sounded too far-fetched *not* to be true."

"Exactly right. He got on a train to head out to South Dakota and the mine is there, all right. He's going to get a manager to run it for the time being, thank goodness. I don't know what I'd do without him at this point."

"When he comes back—will *he* want to be in society?"

Joshua laughed out loud. "You mean go to parties the way you and Dora do? I can't imagine so. He's used to a little more excitement than Fifth Avenue offers."

"All right," Noble said mildly. "The thing is, he could marry someday. And his wife might want to know people like you and Helen. Ladies will appreciate Robey."

"They always have," Joshua agreed.

"And the right wife could pave the way into New York society, if he cared about it. A young widow like Margaret Culver, for instance . . ."

"I can't imagine it," Joshua protested. "Society enforces too many rules for him."

"That's where I think you're wrong," Noble said, pushing back his chair as the waiter poured the last of the burgundy and cleared his plate. The normally hushed dining room of Delmonico's had become almost noisy with chatter and laughter. "The city's changing. You know, I think one day even women will be able to dine here," he suggested.

"What? In public?" Joshua protested.

"With their husbands, of course," Noble added.

"It would take a very daring woman to be the first," Joshua observed.

"Yes, and in a year the place would be full of ladies," Noble predicted cheerfully.

CHAPTER 17

NOT QUITE OUR KIND, DEAR

September 1875

As August shaded into September and the big trunks were brought down from the box room in the Spring House, Helen's spirits sagged. For most of the summer she had managed to close her mind to her Manhattan miseries but they crept closer every day. She could feel herself shrinking into a smaller, harder, more defensive state as she contemplated returning to Washington Square. Living there with her mother in the spring had been miserable enough, but she'd had the freedom of summer to look forward to. Now there was no escape in view.

Once back in the city, Jemima and Alice joined classes with a friend's governess. Jemima suspected this was just a ploy to get them out of their grandmother's way for a few hours each day, but she was happy to be diverted by the schoolwork even if much of it did consist of filling in maps with watercolors. Alice—who didn't care for books as much as her sister—managed to broker an arrangement that allowed her to play the new grand piano at this friend's house for a few hours a week. It was just like Alice, Jemima thought, to get precisely what she wanted without exasperating the adults. Nick, meanwhile, had been enrolled in a day school for boys and found he had much less time to rove freely around the city and spent much more time at his books. Joshua worked as hard as ever, though Helen sometimes thought he seemed less worried and more excited about the potential public stock offering. She occasionally let herself daydream about how the family finances might change if the Elevated became truly successful. But not often: The return to dreary reality was too painful. After a week "getting settled" in New York her mother had embarked on the series of calls that would let her circle of friends know she had returned. Helen made excuses to avoid going with her. The polite (or overtly malicious) questions about her family's situation were just too embarrassing to face.

It was a crisp, beautiful day in mid-September when Selina returned home early in the afternoon to find Helen sitting at her tiny desk with her hands clasped on the blotter and a vacant expression on her face.

"My dear," Selina said, bustling into the room. "I've just heard the most startling thing. I wonder if you can shed any light on this."

"Oh? What is it, Mama?" Helen asked, coming back from very far away.

"Sit with me in the back parlor, would you?" Selina suggested. "I think it's a little bit warmer."

"If you like," Helen agreed. "Where did you go today? Are the Ambroses back?"

"Yes, and the Blakes and the Palmers. Whom have you called on? It's high time you got back into circulation."

Helen had no answer for her mother but a deep sigh.

"I mean it," Selina said as she seated herself on a stiff mahogany chair. "I heard disturbing news this afternoon."

"Oh?"

"Violet Dillon was chatting with Maisie Palmer when I was

shown into the room and they both turned scarlet and stared at me as if I were a ghost." Selina tweaked a fold of her skirt and looked directly at Helen. "They told me that Joshua had been forced to resign from the Union Club and that he and Hans-Albert had a fight. Is this true?"

Helen's gaze wandered to the French windows onto the back garden, where the sun poured like butter onto the stiff little box hedge. "Yes," she said flatly.

"Well, Alice won't be included in the Dancing Classes this fall," Selina announced. "That's what I heard today."

Helen stood suddenly. "That *witch*!" she exclaimed, and strode across to the windows, then back to the door. "Annabelle van Ormskirk is just a nasty, mean cat. How can she do that?"

"She'll have some excuse," Selina said. "Probably she'll invite that pudgy Amstell girl instead." She rose and shook out her skirts. "We can't change the situation because the Dancing Classes are private. But I think we should go right now and call on her. I want to hear her explain."

"Mama!" Helen exclaimed. "I'm not dressed to make a call!"

"Go put on a hat and that blue pelerine of mine to cover up your dress. I'll have Gates get us a cab. I know Wednesday is her day to receive callers and if we get there by four-thirty we can just wait out her other visitors." Selina's eyes sparkled with excitement. "Maybe Annabelle wouldn't be so unpleasant if someone stood up to her once in a while."

Only one carriage waited on Fifth Avenue in front of the Van Ormskirks' door, and Selina said with satisfaction, "Oh, good, that's Lavinia's. She won't be staying much longer, she has the Whitakers coming to dine." She turned to Helen as they climbed the broad steps to the entrance, and reached out to pinch her daughter's cheeks. "You're looking pale. Annabelle can't bite, you know."

Helen blinked. "I know, Mama. I'm just surprised that you take this so much to heart."

"Of course I do, dear! Annabelle can't insult my family. She needs to be taken down a peg," Selina said. The massive door swung open and the Van Ormskirk butler stood aside.

"Good afternoon, Roberts," Selina said as she sailed past him. "This is my daughter Mrs. Wilcox. I hope we're not too late?"

"Not at all, ma'am," the butler answered. He nodded to a tall footman standing in the hall, improbably dressed in a cocoa velvet coat trimmed with a great deal of gold braid, along with knee breeches and white stockings. "The ladies are in the salon," the footman said. "If you would follow me?"

Helen trailed behind her mother, full of misgiving, but when they reached the entrance to the salon, she saw Annabelle van Ormskirk catch sight of Selina and, for a second, look alarmed.

Of course that expression was instantly erased as the footman announced them. Her other caller was already on her feet, ready to leave, so there was a brief confusion as the four ladies greeted each other while the footman stood like a statue in the doorway. Then Annabelle turned to Selina and Helen.

"Won't you sit down? Shall I ring for fresh tea?" she said. Helen had to admire her aplomb.

Selina sank onto the edge of a brocade chair trimmed with gold fringe. "No, thank you, dear Annabelle. We won't keep you long." She looked up at Helen, who was still standing. "Sit down, dear. We're both so startled by your footman's new costume! When did you put him into livery? The poor man looks so . . . elaborate!"

Helen took an armchair that allowed her to see both her mother and Annabelle. Selina looked remarkably pretty, with a little flush of color and a glint in her blue eyes. Aggression, Helen realized, had always suited her.

"Oh, it's a fancy of Hans-Albert's," Annabelle replied. "When he visited London this summer he stayed with a family connection, Lord Bowers, and he thought the servants looked smart. Of course livery only works in a big household, but when you have a row of footmen it does make an impression, doesn't it?"

"No doubt," Selina agreed. "Listen, my dear, I thought I'd call . . . But wait— Helen, dear, you look thirsty. Do you think we could have tea, after all?"

"Of course," Annabelle answered with a stiff smile, and rang the silver bell on the table next to her chair. The liveried footman returned and Selina watched him with very visible fascination as he took the order for tea and bowed deeply.

"Yes, he's very well trained," she said rather loudly before the footman left the room. "You've always done so well with your servants, Annabelle."

"Why, thank you," Annabelle answered. Simpering, Helen thought.

"And you went with Hans-Albert to London?" Selina went on. "Or was this more of a gentleman's visit? I know Hans-Albert has so many friends there." Annabelle clasped her hands in her lap, and Helen wondered what her mother was hinting at. Hans-Albert and a flirtation with an Englishwoman, perhaps?

"Some of those English ladies are so lovely, they say," Selina went on. "I suppose it's all that cloudy weather. Good for their complexions. You might want to send Louisa over there. But she enjoyed Newport, did she? We'll have to go to Newport some summer," she addressed Helen. "Only the responsibilities of the

Spring House . . ." She raised her eyebrows at Annabelle. "It's really almost feudal, you know, when you own that much land."

Was there a way, Helen wondered, to keep score of this exchange? Could she assign points for each disguised insult?

"Yes, of course," Annabelle answered. "But we do enjoy the simple seaside life." She looked up as the footman, now wearing white gloves, bore down on them with a massive silver tray and there was a brief cessation of hostilities while tea was poured and accepted.

Once the footman had left the room, Selina resumed her attack. "And do you dress your servants in livery at the seaside? Or do they wear something like sailor costumes? That could be very practical in damp air."

Annabelle smiled again, and turned to Helen. "Did Mr. Wilcox get up to the Spring House often this summer? I understand he's been very busy with that . . . what do they call it? Elevator railroad?"

"Yes, it takes up a good deal of his time," Helen answered smoothly, trying to emulate her mother. "Tell me, how is dear Maria? Alice will want to know."

"She's well. She's looking forward to the Dancing Classes this fall, you know."

A pause fell. Helen glanced at Selina, whose social smile had gone rigid. "Of course she is," said Helen to bridge the silence. But her mother did not speak. Nobody moved. In the entire room, full of tables and chairs and velvet and flowers and curtains, everything froze.

Then Annabelle tilted her head and said with an unconvincing show of warmth, "Oh, by the way, the committee felt we weren't able to invite your Alice. I hope she didn't expect to be included.

Only your social situation . . . without your own house, you won't be entertaining. I didn't want to put you under a burden, dear Helen. Sometimes those of us who are more fortunate overlook the difficulties of a restricted budget," she finished, simpering.

Selina darted a look at Helen and interrupted Annabelle. "Oh, what a pity! Alice will be so disappointed. I know she was looking forward to the classes. But of course, you must act in Maria's best interest. Give her every chance to shine, you know."

Annabelle frowned, speechless.

"She's such a *good* girl," Selina went on.

"And I'm grateful for that every day," Annabelle flared up, finally recovering. "Beauty isn't everything."

"Oh, no," Selina agreed. "No one ever said it was. And the Dancing Classes will give Maria that extra degree of social polish that can only help once she comes out. Still, it's a great pity. I'm sorry you didn't see fit to let us know sooner, Annabelle, since she *was* invited to the class last spring."

Annabelle brightened and sat up straighter. "Well," she began. "That was months ago. When it seemed that Joshua's financial situation might recover." She smiled at Helen. "I hadn't intended to bring this up, and I'm sorry to be so blunt, but I believe it's always best."

"Oh, yes, indeed," Helen answered. She could feel the blood rushing to her face, though. How dare Annabelle!

"And then, after the episode at the club," Annabelle went on triumphantly, "I really couldn't recommend including Alice. Joshua said such things to Hans-Albert!"

"Oh, well, I'd forgotten about that," Selina answered superbly. "It seemed such a trifle at the time." She put her teacup down on the table and rose. "Dear Annabelle, we'll let you get on with your evening, I'm sure you have lots to do." Helen stood and smoothed her mother's cloak over her simple dress.

"Good afternoon, Annabelle," she said, putting as much false affection into her voice as she could. "It's been lovely to see you again." She smiled sweetly, and followed her mother into the carriage.

Selina sat back and tapped her toe on the floor in annoyance. "My goodness, that woman knows no shame at all!"

"Never mind, Mama," Helen answered. "She wouldn't have relented anyway, though I suppose she would have loved to see me beg. You did your best. Does Hans-Albert have a mistress in London?"

Selina leaned back and shook her head. "Oh, good heavens, he wouldn't dare. But he trailed around after an actress last time he was there, and they say he bought her a ruby bracelet. Annabelle got a new ring—rather vulgar, actually, a huge emerald—at around the same time. So I thought I might remind her that everyone knew." She shrugged. "It doesn't get Alice any further, though."

Helen chuckled. "I suppose not. But you were very clever about the footmen. Sailor costumes!"

Selina smiled. "Well, she's a fool to try to be so grand. Next thing we know she'll make that poor footman wear a white wig and won't he feel ridiculous! This is New York, not Europe, and even a big house on Fifth Avenue isn't a castle. But Annabelle has always had a taste for show. It's because her own parents didn't have two pennies to rub together." She looked out the window for a minute, then turned back to Helen. "She will tell everyone why Alice isn't going to the Dancing Classes."

Helen shrugged. "We can't do anything about that, can we?"

"Joshua and the club are just an excuse. She simply doesn't want all those boys falling in love with your daughters instead of hers," Selina said. "And you can't entirely blame her." She patted Helen's knee and said, "I've grown quite fond of both of your girls, dear. They are very pleasant young ladies." Which, from Selina, was high praise.

CHAPTER 18

◆

NOT THE SAME WITHOUT HER

September 1875

About a week later, a storm broke the lovely weather. Clouds moved in with a teasing little wind and the air took on moisture like a sponge. The wind grew stronger and rain began, then intensified as if it were being poured out of the sky from buckets. By nightfall the streets and sidewalks were streaming. Selina insisted that Joshua make sure all the shutters were closed, including up in the attic. Under the eaves he could hear the rain spilling over the gutters and he couldn't help imagining the uprights of the Elevated Railroad, sprouting along Ninth Avenue and pounded by the storm. They would be safe, sunk deep into the sidewalks. Yet his mind's eye kept toppling them, sending one through the windows of a nearby building, dropping another on a passing horse-car—ridiculous images. When he came down the stairs to the second floor Selina was waiting for him with a chamber candle.

"Nothing is leaking, I hope?" she asked, putting a hand on his forearm. "Thank you for indulging me, I don't know why I've been so silly."

"The wind and the rain together are very loud," he murmured. "But the house is watertight."

She squeezed his arm and answered, "Off you go, then. I'm sure it will blow itself out in the night."

He padded around the bedroom he shared with Helen, accustomed by now to the meager distance between bed and window and wardrobe. Before sliding under the covers he pushed aside the curtain and peered out at the rain that lashed the window panes in vicious bursts.

He woke hours later, slightly chilly, and heard a thump. Helen turned over and her braid lay tickling his face. He reached up to move it away. The horsehair in the mattress crunched as she sat up.

He sat up, too. "What is it?" he whispered.

"Did you hear that? Just now?"

"Upstairs, I thought, or maybe on the roof. Nothing to worry about," he told her. "Your mother reminded me before I came to bed that the house has stood here for almost fifty years."

"Such a comfort."

"She intended it that way," he answered, and they both lay down again.

Helen woke again just as the darkness started to fade. She picked up the shawl on the end of the bed and tiptoed down the stairs in her nightgown to look out the dining room windows into the gray dawn. She considered what she had to do that day and her heart sank when she realized she was supposed to lunch with her mother at Felicity Sterling's house. Selina had somehow found out that the two Sterling boys were going to the Dancing Classes. Helen suspected that her mother was plotting some subtle revenge against Annabelle.

She turned away from the window and returned upstairs so as not to shock poor Gates when he came to set the table for breakfast. Joshua was awake when she slipped back into their bedroom, rubbing his golden hair into a haystack and yawning. "Awful night," he said quietly. "Did you sleep?"

"Yes," she answered. "Though not well."

He nodded. "I wish we could have opened the window. What was that crash?"

"I've been downstairs. Nothing seems wrong."

"Probably the branch of a tree falling to the street," he suggested. "And it's still pouring, isn't it?"

A set of footsteps went past the door, accompanied by the faint clatter of china and a light tap on the door of Selina's bedroom. Joshua got out of bed and stretched.

Then the tap came on their door. "Ma'am! Mrs. Wilcox!" Helen opened the door to Selina's maid Mosette.

"Mrs. Wilcox, it's Mrs. Maitland! Come!"

She lay on the floor of the bedroom. Mosette stood at the door, hands to her mouth and tears starting in her eyes. Helen knelt and touched her mother's face but she knew already that Selina was dead. How could she not be, lying like that with her eyes wide open? Joshua crouched next to Helen, with an arm over her shoulders. Then he put his hands beneath her elbows and urged her to her feet, folding his arms around her.

She stood still, breathing into Joshua's dressing gown. Her mind was whirling. Dora, the children, a doctor, the servants, the rain, black clothes, the breakfast tray still lying on the floor. She could feel her face sag. "Can we get her back into bed?" she asked. "She would have hated to be found like this."

And so they did. Then everything else began.

There were rituals for death, of course, and Selina's family observed all of them: the blinds drawn, the door knocker shrouded, the somber service at Grace Church that was remarkably well-attended. Condolence letters streamed in, some even from ladies who had refused to "know" Helen after she married Joshua.

Of course the Wilcox women had to wear black from head to

toe, which required entirely new wardrobes for each of them. Recently bereaved ladies didn't go shopping, so Stewart's sent over a deferential salesman from the mourning department with patterns and fabric samples, followed by a seamstress to do all the measuring and, later, the pinning and adjusting. Jemima had the bright idea of reading *A Tale of Two Cities* out loud while she and Alice and her mother submitted to the dressmaking. It was better than remaining lost in their own sad thoughts. There was no escaping the black, though: From bonnets to stockings, they would wear no other color for months. Then they could add touches of white (collars, cuffs) and eventually change into half-mourning: shades of gray or lavender.

To Helen's surprise, Sylvia Burke arrived one day with a satchel that contained black gloves, black-bordered handkerchiefs, and a beautiful Chantilly lace scarf, also black. "Hiram's mother died last year," she explained, "and I didn't wear any of these things. I've got a pretty bonnet at home, too, that I'd be happy to lend you if you like. Pretty for a mourning bonnet, anyway," she added with a grimace.

"You're so kind," Helen answered. "The lace is lovely. I'll take good care of it." To her chagrin, she felt her eyes filling—kindness, in those days, disarmed her completely.

"I know you've had a difficult time lately," Sylvia said. "What with having to move, and the worry about Joshua's business . . ." Helen sniffed and Sylvia handed her one of the handkerchiefs, then patted her arm. "I never want to see those horrible things again, by the way, so don't you dare return them to me," she added. "I think they look so grim."

"It's the crape I don't like," Helen confessed, holding up a fold of her heavy lusterless skirt. "And putting the girls in black."

"Oh, you're so right about that, there's nothing sadder," Sylvia agreed. "Though it's probably very becoming to Alice. Black is so flattering for fair-haired women. How are the children bearing up?"

"They're sad, of course." She got up and went to the door of the parlor, then returned and sat down closer to Sylvia. "To be honest, Jemima worries me," she confessed. "She's gone very quiet. Almost secretive."

"Well from what you've told me, your mother wasn't always kind to her. Perhaps Jemima feels she should be sadder than she is."

Helen shook her head. "Goodness, Sylvia, that sounds very complicated. But I suppose anything is possible. Poor thing, she's gotten terribly thin, too. She slinks around like a little stray cat and I don't know how to make her feel better."

Jemima would have agreed with her mother's description, unflattering though it was. She *felt* like a little stray cat: displaced and unwanted. Selina's house without Selina in it seemed newly unwelcoming. Every corner, each angle of light gleaming through the windows, every object from the sofa to the saltcellar looked different. Nothing spoke of comfort. Every time she caught sight of herself in one of her grandmother's gilt-framed mirrors she was startled to see that girl in unrelieved black who looked so familiar yet so unhappy.

She was full of regret. She should have been kinder to her grandmother, listened to her more willingly, shown more interest in her stories. After all, Grandmama had known a world that was quickly vanishing, a slower, quieter, more orderly city. Jemima had seldom enjoyed Selina's remembrances of it, seeing them as criticism of the present. But it suddenly seemed possible that her grandmother had simply wished to share memories of the city she had known. And the tales of her own delightful debut might have been, Jemima thought, intended as encouragement. The thought that she might have misjudged Selina made her very sad.

She was also bored, though one could not complain about that. It became quickly apparent that the months of mourning for her grandmother would crawl past because there would be nothing to do. Recently bereaved ladies were apparently so overwhelmed with grief that they could only sit in their parlors in their gloomy garments and answer condolence notes. Jemima herself had received quite a few: formal little missives from her contemporaries, including one from the handsome Arthur Onderdonck. She was obligated to reply to them all, an activity she polished off in the first half hour of every day. She had read most of the books in her grandmother's house but one morning in a desperate attempt to pass time, she hauled her grandmother's Bible onto the dining room table and opened it to Genesis.

"Jemima, dear, what in the world are you doing with that?" asked her mother a few minutes later. "You'll be in Gates's way when he needs to set the table for luncheon."

"I know," Jemima agreed. "But I've never read the Bible, and I don't have anything else to do. Do you suppose it gets more exciting?" she asked her mother, leafing through a few of the pages.

Helen pulled out a chair and sat next to her daughter. "No. I had to read some of it with our governess, and the Old Testament just gets duller and duller as you go on. Is there nothing else to read in this house?"

Jemima waved a hand at the bookshelves on one side of the dining room, full of gilt-stamped leather-bound volumes. "Those are all letters from explorers."

"Oh, dear." Helen grimaced. "Well, while the weather is good I think you girls could walk in the square by yourselves."

"Alone?" Jemima asked eagerly. "I mean, separately?"

"Are you so tired of your sister?"

"No, of course not," Jemima fibbed. "But it would be such a relief to stroll around daydreaming by myself."

Her mother paused. "I suspect Mama would have disapproved." She paused, and said frankly, "But then, she was very strict."

"'I was brought up in a more refined era,'" Jemima said, imitating Selina. "I'm sorry, Mama, that was unkind of me. I know you must miss Grandmama."

"Oh, of course I do. But she always preferred the New York of her youth. She was such a belle, you know. It must be difficult when the world you knew starts to vanish. Anyway, she's gone now, and I don't see any reason why you girls shouldn't have a little bit of liberty."

One morning a month after Selina's death, Helen opened an envelope and when she saw the contents, exclaimed with irritation. "You'd think Sarah Bradley would know I can't accept any invitations," she said, dropping the stiff card onto what had been her mother's desk. "It's bad enough having to respond to the condolence notes without having to send regrets to invitations as well."

"I'll write it for you, Mama," Alice offered. "Our handwriting is similar, she'll never know it wasn't you."

"What do you actually write when you answer all those sympathy notes?" Jemima asked, looking up from her book. "Do you send the same letter to each one?"

"More or less," Helen confessed. "They all say the same thing, too: how shocked they were to hear about Mama, how charming she was, how much she will be missed. Some of them are surprising: men she danced with a few times, women who've long since moved away. She made a real impression on people." She sighed, and dabbed her eyes with the black-bordered handkerchief that was always tucked up her sleeve in those days. "I do sometimes wish, though, that she'd saved more of that charm for her family—especially for you children."

"I think she wanted us to be more like her," Alice offered, and her mother nodded.

"She truly thought that was the best way to behave," Helen said. "And that's why she always made her little . . . suggestions."

"Like standing up straight," Jemima added from the wing chair she had claimed as her own. "And smiling all the time."

"She meant well," Helen pointed out with a sigh. No one had an answer for that.

Jemima was greatly relieved to know that the family's financial troubles would be alleviated by her grandmother's death. It was confusing to feel that relief alongside the sadness, just as she was both sorry and delighted that her debut would be delayed until the following fall. She and Alice would come out together, as they had gone to their last Dancing Class together. On the one hand, all of the boys naturally admired Alice more than her; but on the other hand, Alice was generous and would share her partners.

There was, however, a secret on Jemima's rather scrupulous conscience.

As a young lady on the verge of coming out into society, she had begun to receive invitations addressed directly to her at Selina's house. These, of course, had stopped arriving as the news of her grandmother's death traveled through her social circle, but one morning she went downstairs early and found Gates sorting the letters onto each person's place at the breakfast table.

"Here you go, Miss Jemima," he said, handing her a stiff

envelope before setting a little pile of them where her mother sat. "I'll just be getting your tea."

Which was timely, because Jemima recognized the bold black script on the envelope and felt a blush stain her cheeks. She slipped the letter into her pocket and rushed through breakfast so she could return to her bedroom and read, in private, what Felix Castle could possibly have to say to her.

"My Dear Miss Wilcox," the note opened, "I have heard about your recent bereavement. I understand that you and your family have been living with Mrs. Maitland and I hope I don't offend by sending this note to you at her address. I urge you not to forget, in your grief, that you are a young lady of great courage. I send respectful condolences—Felix Castle."

Jemima was not a frequent weeper but this completely unexpected courtesy—from this particular source—brought tears to her eyes in an instant. He had thought of her! Dashing, handsome, sophisticated Felix Castle had thought of her and furthermore believed she was brave! She dropped the note on the dressing table while mopping her tears and blowing her nose, studying the note: heavy paper, engraved monogram, black ink. How very, very kind of him to write to her. The mere idea—imagining Mr. Castle sitting at an imposing desk in the study of his house, *and thinking of her*—prompted a fresh burst of emotion. She heard Alice's voice in the hall and folded the letter, then slipped it into a drawer among her stockings. She would find a better hiding place later.

That was just one of the first condolence letters to reach the Wilcox ladies. Others arrived from Tenders Landing, from Fifth Avenue, from all over Washington Square, including a very kind note—addressed to Jemima and Alice as well as Helen—from Thaddeus Britton, the war veteran on the other side of the square.

Joshua did his best to help with the business of Selina's death. He had been startled, when he married Helen, by the elaborate legal arrangements a mere marriage required. Now, of course, he understood how financial interests had to be nurtured and protected, and how the legal mind insisted on preparation for every possible outcome. Noble was a godsend in that regard. Selina's will, revised ten years earlier, seemed to exhibit his tact.

It turned out that ultimately, because Noble and Dora had no children, the entire Maitland fortune would eventually come down to Jemima and Alice and Nick. In the meantime, the Latimers and the Wilcoxes would share the income from the conservatively invested capital. The immediate effect was that the Wilcoxes would be able to rent a respectable house of their own, a prospect that Helen contemplated with enormous gratitude. Beyond that, the inheritance would provide dowries for the girls and support Nick until he chose a career. "I think I'd like to be a robber baron," he announced to general laughter when he heard this news at the solemn family meeting. Joshua listened carefully to the terms of Helen's inheritance, but in his view the capital sum was laughably small compared to what the Elevated might someday be worth. That was the difference, he thought, between the old New York and the new: between merely living on the money you'd inherited, and possessing the imagination and drive to make your own fortune. This was not an observation he shared with Helen, whose patience with him in those days was very limited.

The house on Washington Square was to be sold and the proceeds shared between the sisters. They would divide the contents as they chose. They already owned the Spring House jointly, and Noble made the point that the assets inherited from Selina would yield enough money to keep the country house open for quite a few years. "And by then," he said, "who knows what your situation will be?"

He and Joshua were in Noble's study after a family dinner. Dora and Helen, in their black dresses, sat in the parlor on either side of Dora's desk, answering condolence letters while Miles Latimer played three-handed whist with the girls.

Joshua leaned back in his chair and answered his brother-in-law. "That's the question, isn't it?" He gestured at the papers on the low table between them. "This income would have spared Helen a lot of worry just a few months ago."

"Don't think that way," Noble advised.

"Oh, I don't, not really," Joshua answered. "I would still have lost the house. The businesses were taking every penny I had at that point. Life would have been easier for Helen, though."

"The point is to make it easier for her now. There are no real difficulties here," Noble said, tapping the papers. "But I suppose you would all like to leave Washington Square quite soon?"

"Helen's not happy there," Joshua answered. "She says she can't bear all the reminders of her mother. And we're awfully crowded— Nick sleeps in Selina's sewing room, you know." An evasion, but an answer.

"Do you have any idea about where Helen would like to go?"

Joshua shook his head. "She was talking about wintering at the Spring House, but I managed to dissuade her."

"Good. She would have been lonely up there, whatever she may think now."

"I know I should be doing more for Helen," said Joshua, "but my hands are full with the stock offering. All those papers; I'd honestly prefer to be driving a freight wagon . . ." Then he blurted out, "Helen seems different somehow."

"What makes you say that?"

Joshua hesitated. "She seems to have forgotten how to talk to people." Noble didn't answer right away, so he added, "She's awfully quiet, anyway."

Noble shrugged. "I believe she and Dora are together quite a bit. And I'm sure the girls are a comfort."

"I suppose they are. But they don't talk, either. The three of them just sit in Selina's parlor in their black dresses, answering letters."

"Give them time," Noble said. "And take an afternoon to look at houses with Helen. The Elevated can spare you for a few hours."

CHAPTER 19

❖

"DEAR MR. CASTLE"

October 1875

Jemima was troubled by Felix Castle's note. Should she answer it? She had already written brief, polite responses to each brief, polite letter of condolence she had received from her contemporaries. Did she dare persuade Nick to serve as her messenger to Felix once more? Since starting his new school he had acquired a new group of friends who seemed to rove around in a pack, and she didn't trust her brother to be discreet among them. But could a note to Mr. Castle be slipped without discovery into the stack of outgoing envelopes that Gates handed every day to the postman?

Jemima promptly imagined a scenario in which Gates caught sight of Mr. Castle's address on a letter and showed it to her mother, ranting about "betrayal" and "disloyalty." And another scene in which her mother found the note and brought it to Jemima, sobbing out her own accusations. But in a different daydream, Jemima wrote a note to which Mr. Castle responded in a friendly way, prompting her own reply back to him . . . but even her lively imagination faltered here. There were no grounds for private correspondence between a young girl and a bachelor of any description—let alone the rapacious speculator who had forced her family out of their home, no matter how handsome and clever that bachelor might be.

(Jemima had long since admitted to herself that she admired Felix Castle's rakish looks.) Nevertheless, she sat at her mother's desk one day and dipped her pen in the inkwell and boldly wrote, "Dear Mr. Castle . . ." on a sheet of letter paper. She hesitated for a moment—then summoned the courage Mr. Castle had praised.

"Thank you for your kind note," she wrote. "We are all very sad about the loss of my grandmother." She heard her sister's voice on the stairs and swiftly folded the sheet of paper, but in her mind continued: "I worry that she died because we moved into her house and disturbed her peace and quiet. All the same, I remember what you said to me at the Metropolitan Museum. You seemed to understand how I felt. Perhaps you understand how I feel now . . ." As Alice passed behind her with a soft touch on the shoulder and sat down at the piano to play scales, Jemima blushed.

Jemima unfolded the note she'd begun and looked at it. She could never send this letter; it was far too intimate in nature. She went upstairs to her bedroom and took Mr. Castle's letter from the stocking drawer where she'd hidden it. She tried to remember what his voice sounded like, or what, exactly, he'd said to her at the Metropolitan Museum, but she couldn't conjure up the memories and she was suddenly desperately sad. Would she ever see him again? If so, how?

The front door opened and she heard her mother's brisk steps in the hall. Alice began playing the scales where her hands went in different directions at the same time. Jemima suddenly felt that she could not face her mother or her sister and the only escape was the attic so upward she fled, with Mr. Castle's note and her own half-written reply clutched in her hand.

She had only visited her grandmother's attic once before, helping Moira look for some old-fashioned oil lamps to bring downstairs shortly after the Wilcoxes had moved into Washington Square. It had been twilight then but now, in the light from the small oval windows, she saw that bureaus and trunks stood next to a long sofa shrouded in a dust-sheet. Jemima sat on it with a thump and regarded the letters in her hand. Surely she could find a hiding place in the attic for two sheets of paper? Next to her loomed a tall, old-fashioned chest with curly feet and elaborate brass handles. She slid off the sofa and pulled open the bottom drawer, which turned out to be full to the brim of papers. Theater programs, invitations, letters, and dance cards: Her grandmother must have saved them all, over her lifetime. Quick as a wink, Jemima tucked her own notes deep into the drawer and nudged it shut, then went back to sit on the sofa, relishing the quiet.

Her mother found her sitting there a while later. She sat next to Jemima and leaned back with a sigh. They remained in silence for a few minutes before Helen said, "I'm sorry, you probably came up here to be alone. That's always been the problem with this house."

Jemima turned her head to look at her mother's profile, leaning against the back of the sofa. "Might Alice and I have separate bedrooms when we move?"

"Possibly," her mother answered. "That depends partly on this stock offering of your father's, and partly on the price this house fetches. Which of course I'll divide with your aunt Dora."

"But we will be able to buy a house again," Jemima pressed her mother.

"Yes," Helen answered, and took Jemima's hand. "I promise. Your papa has promised, too. And you and Alice can make it happen sooner, you know."

"Of course we will," Jemima said. "What can we do?"

"Help me sort through Mama's papers and souvenirs and so on.

For instance," Helen said as she stood, "I think there's quite a trove in that highboy over there."

She crossed the attic and knelt before the drawer where Jemima had just deposited the notes from Felix Castle, and pulled it open. As Jemima watched in alarm, her mother plunged a hand deep into the papers that filled the drawer. "Look," she said, holding out a dance card. She unfolded it. "Nothing has changed. This was a party in 1840."

Jemima slid off the sofa and joined her mother. Where were the papers she had just dropped into this drawer? Somewhere among the sheaves, folded neatly, stacked, or tied with ribbons, lay Felix Castle's note addressed to her, and no one must find it! "Leave this to me, Mama," Jemima said. "Is there anything you'd want to keep?"

"No, dear," Helen answered. "But if you and Alice find any keepsakes that appeal to you . . . I know Mama danced with the Prince of Wales in the 1850s, she must have kept that dance card . . ."

"Is Alice still at home?" Jemima asked. "I might get started right away." She looked at her palms. "I'm already quite dusty."

"There's no hurry, dear," Helen told her. "I'm taking Alice over to Aunt Dora's—she's found some black gloves and hat-trimmings in her attic. Would you like to come with us?"

"No, thank you, Mama," Jemima said. "I think I'll stay right here."

"Don't get too untidy," her mother warned her. "Aunt Dora's coming back to have luncheon with us."

Jemima waited until she heard the front door close before she returned to the chest and pulled out the bottom drawer. Where had she put Mr. Castle's note? She knelt on the floor and tried to remember. Over to the left, she thought—she remembered push-ing it down into the layers of paper. There was a bundle of let-ters tied with green ribbon: Was the note under that? She thrust her hands down and brought up a stack that collapsed on the wooden floor next to her. Letters, envelopes, printed pages . . . Should anything in this drawer be kept? There were Christmas cards and thank-you notes for wedding presents, going back thirty or forty years. The circle of paper on the floor around Jemima grew and her hands became grimy. She found a copy of her grand-mother's wedding invitation and a sheaf of letters that her mother had written home from her European honeymoon, which she set aside to keep.

She heard a foot on the attic stairs and Alice appeared in an old cotton dress, apparently to help. "Goodness!" she exclaimed, when she saw the papers all over the floor. "What a mess you've made!"

"I know," Jemima answered. "Just you wait. You pull out one piece of paper and it's a marketing list, the next one is a clipping, then you find a series of notes enclosing pressed flowers from some man I've never heard of . . ." Jemima crouched to the floor and picked up the letters.

Alice shook her head. "You could spend days looking through all of these things. Are you looking for anything particular?" she asked.

"No! Just, this was Grandmama's life . . . we can't throw every-thing away." Jemima was pleased with the reason she gave, and realized she meant it. Still, she needed to find Felix's letter before Alice did. Alice bent over the trunk and reached for a little leather case that snapped open to reveal paired daguerreotypes of her grandmother and grandfather. "Oh, wasn't she lovely?" she ex-claimed, and held it out to Jemima. "This must have been soon after they got married; just look at her bonnet!"

Jemima handed it back to Alice. "I think you should keep this. You look so much like her."

Alice looked at the image of her grandmother and her eyes misted up. "Do you really think so? I always thought she was so pretty."

"And what in the world makes you think you aren't, you goose?" Jemima answered, and shuffled across the floor on her knees to rub her sister's back. "We'll miss Grandmama," she said in a soothing tone.

Alice gulped and blew her nose. "Yes, but also . . ." She gestured around the floor, at the souvenirs of the quainter, quieter age. "Her city's gone, too."

"It is," Jemima agreed. "I was always irritated when she compared her era with the present; you know, 'In my day young girls only wore pale colors.'"

"Or 'It was considered vulgar to have more than six guests for dinner,'" Alice added.

"I once heard her refer to Papa as 'somewhat crude.' She didn't know I heard, but I was so angry I wanted to shake her," Jemima answered. "But I think the city truly was more genteel when she was our age. Maybe that's why she disapproved of Papa. He never cared much about her New York. He just looks forward." She shifted away from her sister and looked into the trunk again. There it was: the letter from Felix Castle! And here, at her side, was Alice, sniffling into a handkerchief and waiting to see what came out of the trunk. Jemima hesitated just a moment too long.

"What is it?" Alice said, and got up on her knees.

"A paper cut," Jemima lied shamelessly, and put her thumb in her mouth, but it was too late. Alice had reached into the trunk and pulled out Felix Castle's note along with Jemima's own unfinished reply.

"What?" Alice said quietly as she read the notes. "What is this?" she repeated. She looked at Jemima with a blank face. "Is this really from him?"

Jemima nodded.

"Felix Castle wrote you a letter?" Alice repeated.

"It's a perfectly proper condolence note," Jemima pointed out.

"Not from *him*," Alice retorted. "Why, he practically killed Grandmama!" She scrambled to her feet and Jemima followed suit.

"He did not kill Grandmama," Jemima said as calmly as she could. "And keep your voice down or we'll have Mama in here."

"It would break her heart to know you'd been corresponding with Felix Castle, of all people!" Alice retorted, but kept her voice low.

"I *haven't* been corresponding with him!" Jemima protested, even though it was a bold-faced lie.

"How does he even know you well enough to write to you? What made him think such a thing could be proper? Or think that you would be *comforted*! Why does he call you"—Alice looked at the sheet of paper—"'a young lady of great courage'"? Alice dropped the note back into the drawer, turned away from Jemima, and headed toward the stairs. "You have behaved outrageously!"

"Stop!" Jemima commanded, and at the steely tone in her voice, Alice halted. "We'll go out to the square," Jemima went on. "We'll tell Mama we need a breath of fresh air. And I will explain everything." Alice glared at her sister but nodded.

A few minutes later, suitably hatted and cloaked, the sisters crossed brick-paved Waverly Place into Washington Square. It had just rained, and golden leaves were beginning to fall from the elms. "All right," Alice said as soon as they were out of earshot of the house, "explain."

Jemima eyed her sister. "I know it must seem wrong," she began.

"Wrong?" Alice repeated. "Of all things! You're not even out in society, yet you seem to be corresponding with not just any man, but a business acquaintance of Papa's who isn't even a gentleman and who *took our house!*" Alice turned and grasped Jemima by the elbows and shook her. "He's a villain! How could you!"

"It's not what it looks like . . ." Jemima began but Alice interrupted her.

"I certainly hope not! Because to me it seems that you're flirting with a rich, vulgar money man and you . . ." Alice began crying. "I can't even imagine how he knows your *name*! You should be ashamed of yourself!" Alice said bitterly.

"Well, I am," Jemima admitted. "A little bit. But I don't think I did anything wrong. Please let me—"

"You were disloyal to Papa!" Alice protested, her blue eyes blazing with indignation. "And who will want to marry a girl who's exchanged secret letters with someone like Felix Castle?" By this time Alice was frankly shouting and Jemima looked around the square to be sure nobody could hear. "And nobody would want to marry me, either! The scandal!"

"Will you hush!" Jemima hissed, linking her arm through Alice's. "Someone's coming out of one of those houses. And let me explain! Mr. Castle called at our house. He was looking for Papa, you remember. And then, the day we moved out of the house I went with Moira to the Metropolitan Museum. And he was there."

Alice pulled away and stared at Jemima. "He approached you at the museum?"

"I was crying," Jemima said. "He gave me his handkerchief."

"Where was Moira?"

"She was downstairs. Her feet hurt. And there wasn't another soul in the whole building anyway."

"She knows better than that. And so do you." Alice drew back then turned around and walked quickly away from Jemima, as if she couldn't stand to be in her sister's presence for another moment. Jemima stood where she was, and drew a deep breath. What a gloomy day it was in the park, with the sky a low lid of clouds and the damp from the gravel path working its way through the soles of her thin indoor slippers. She felt a pair of tears slip down her chin. It sometimes felt, these days, that she did nothing but cry, or regret something she'd done, or worry about the future. *Had* she been too receptive to Mr. Castle's unexpected kindness? Probably—but he had seemed like such a lifeline on that day. Attentive. Concerned. Understanding. Not only glamorous but also kind. She felt tears roll down her cheeks beneath the veil of her bonnet.

And yet, as she peeled off her gloves to manage the veil and the now-necessary black-bordered handkerchief, Jemima spotted Alice halfway across the park—in conversation with a man. Jemima frowned and set out toward them, across a stretch of sodden grass. Who was Alice to scold her, and then turn around and talk to a stranger? But he wasn't a strange man, of course—it was Thaddeus Britton. A gentleman, a war hero, a friend of her grandmother's. Perfectly respectable for Alice to talk to. Because Alice never did a single thing wrong, thought Jemima, lashing herself into anger. She arrived on the path next to Mr. Britton. Or Colonel? He was surprisingly young-looking.

"I'm going back indoors," Jemima announced abruptly to Alice, and sniffed. "In case you're worried that I'm going to do something else scandalous while you're out here talking to a gentleman *alone*." She turned to him and said, "We haven't been presented, but I know my sister is very concerned about the proprieties. I am Jemima Wilcox. As if you didn't know," she finished, close to tears, and blew her nose.

With remarkable poise, Mr. Britton said gravely, "Of course, Miss Wilcox. Perhaps I could escort both of you ladies. Not that you're likely to come to any harm here."

"Let Jemima go," Alice suggested. "She's overwrought. Clearing out Grandmama's house prompts so many memories. And you probably have some letters to write, too, don't you?" she added sweetly to Jemima's back.

Jemima paused and turned. "On second thought, I'd better stay to chaperone you, hadn't I? I feel sure Grandmama wouldn't have approved of your consorting with strange men in public."

"You would know—" Alice began, but Mr. Britton interrupted her.

"Miss Wilcox is right," he said, stepping between them. "Young ladies can't be too careful about their reputations, especially when they are in mourning. I will escort you both to Mrs. Maitland's house." And he spoke with such confidence that the sisters' quarrel simply dissolved into thin air.

Very early the next morning Jemima sneaked back into the attic and retrieved both Felix's letter and her own. The next chance she got, she tucked them at the very back of the parlor fire, with both regret and relief.

CHAPTER 20

❖

NEW YEAR'S DAY

January 1876

That was one of the last times when the Wilcox girls were able to take the air in Washington Square that autumn, because the weather was uncommonly harsh. Helen felt she was trudging through an endless sequence of gloomy days filled with the dull chores of bereavement. She and her daughters responded to condolence letters, tidied away Selina's possessions, and found ways to fill the hours as the weather and the conventions allowed. Nick was so restless and unmanageable that Helen located a boarding school in Westchester that would accept him in the middle of the year. He came home on weekends, much happier. Alice played endless scales on her grandmother's piano and began to learn Chopin's "Funeral March," which was even more irritating than the scales. Helen drafted Jemima—who seemed especially gloomy— to choose which of Selina's books they'd want to bring with them to a new house. If Jemima felt she needed to read each volume to arrive at a decision, Helen thought, so much the better: Reading had to provide more consolation for her than fretting or moping. Christmas, for the Wilcoxes, was very quiet.

But New Year's Day, in contrast, was festive. It had long been the tradition in old New York for prosperous families to hold open house for their friends: The ladies, wearing their best gowns, stayed at home while gentlemen roamed from house to house, exchanging greetings and sampling punch brewed to traditional recipes. Normally a family in mourning would not participate but it was Dora, surprisingly, who suggested entertaining as Selina would have. "The older gentlemen will come out of respect to her memory," Dora said to Helen. "Some of our friends would stop here as well, and this is a good way to remind everyone that you have two pretty daughters."

Helen was more than happy to agree with her.

It snowed on New Year's Eve. Six inches of fresh white dust lay over the gritty piles of ice in the gutters. At mid-morning the sun came out and Washington Square glittered beneath a blazing blue sky. Nick was sent out to help poor old Gates clear the brick walkway in front of the house. As she changed into her best black silk dress, Helen paused to look out the window onto the snow-covered square. New Year's Day had always been Selina's favorite holiday. She had been a formidable hostess, the kind who insisted on perfection in every detail of preparation, so that nothing could possibly go amiss in the presence of her guests.

Selina had driven herself, Helen realized, as much as she'd driven everyone around her. She had a strong sense of what was appropriate in any given setting, and she was determined to achieve it. But her standards had been old-fashioned. Helen had sometimes thought that her mother looked back to her own youth as a golden age, and found it difficult to acclimate to the present. "In my day . . ." she would sigh, offering a rueful critique of any innovation she disliked. New behaviors, new buildings, new fashions, had always unsettled Selina.

Would she herself feel more free in her mother's absence? Helen turned from the window and crossed to the bureau to check her hair in the mirror. Did she look older? Did she feel different? She adjusted the earrings inherited from her mother, handsome gray South Sea pearls. Yes, she did feel different. More confident, she had to admit. Her mother's criticisms had consistently compared the present to the past and found it lacking. Yet, Helen thought, the present held considerable promise. She pinched her cheeks to make them rosy, and turned away from the mirror to head downstairs. But on an impulse she looked back and smiled at herself in the mirror.

By two o'clock the sidewalks were clean, the punch was brewed, and every surface in the house gleamed in its own way, from the glitter of the wavy old glass windows to the soft luster of the olive-green damask on Selina Maitland's Duncan Phyfe settee. The pocket doors between the parlor and dining room had been slid open. Garlands of evergreens outlined the mantels and hung from the chandeliers. Helen and Dora had exchanged their black crape for moiré taffeta, gathered and pleated and bustled. They both wore, in their square necklines, their gold lockets made with Selina's hair, as did the girls. Alice, to her intense excitement, wore her hair up, since she was now a young lady. She and Jemima, in their own simpler black silk gowns, were somewhat awestruck by their own elegance.

"You look very pretty," Jemima whispered to Alice as the door knocker sounded. They had made their peace at Christmas, though secrets lingered between the sisters. Their mother and Aunt Dora stood together greeting their first visitor, old Dr. Silliman, who had flirted with Selina Maitland as a young married woman back in the 1840s. "Who do you think that fellow with the terrible wig might be?" Jemima whispered as she and Alice observed the visitors.

"Mama told me about him," Alice said. "His name is Wellington Wells. Remember, he's Mama's godfather? He has an ancestor who fought at Waterloo so Mama always referred to him as 'Uncle Welly.'"

Jemima shook her head, then caught sight of another newcomer. "Don't look now," she instructed her sister, "but our neighbor is here."

Naturally Alice's gaze went directly to the doorway where she saw, smiling at her, Thaddeus Britton. She felt a tide of heat wash over her face and smiled back.

"You're blushing," Jemima teased. "Oh, Alice! He's sitting down next to Mama! He wants to present his credentials to her!"

"Well, I know all of that anyway," Alice murmured. "He joined the army when he was eighteen, in 1864. And he lost his arm at Bentonville. He told me about how hard it was to learn to write with his left hand, when he went to Yale after the war."

Jemima stared at her sister. "I didn't realize you had spent so much time with him."

"Well," Alice said primly, "we've had a few mild days. And Mr. Britton does sometimes take the air in the middle of the morning."

Jemima regarded her sister with wide eyes. "Are you saying you've been flirting with a married man, Alice?"

"He's widowed!" Alice pointed out. "Didn't you notice his black cravat?"

"No," Jemima retorted. "I just noticed the way he watched you. But now I gather you've had a number of . . . goodness, should I call them clandestine meetings?"

"As if a meeting that happened in the center of Washington Square could be clandestine," Alice replied tartly. "You're not to tease me about Mr. Britton, Jemima. Let's go and greet Mr. Gregson, he won't know anyone else here."

She stood and the two of them slipped through the crowded parlor to the front hall, where Joshua was welcoming his business partner. "Isn't this swell?" he said to the girls, and pressed a finger deep into the fur collar of Robey's coat. "This, ladies, is how the owners of gold mines stay warm. After all, it's terribly cold in South Dakota."

"Oh, hush," Robey muttered, and hooked his arms through those of the girls. "I'm going to take you young ladies hostage to protect me from further mockery. Your mother's parlor is far more alarming than the worst saloon in Deadwood."

"But no one here is armed," Jemima pointed out mildly.

"Not with bullets," Robey answered in a mock-pathetic tone. "Just scorn."

"I'll introduce you to Mr. Britton," Alice said. "He lives on the square and Mama likes him very much." With that she led him across the parlor.

Jemima watched for a moment and her father bent to whisper in her ear. "Alice is beginning to remind me of your grandmother," he said. "She has that dauntless quality that you'd call bossy in a larger woman."

"Alice just wants everyone to feel at home—but it's difficult to know what Robey might consider homelike. And *does* Mama actually like Mr. Britton?"

Joshua turned to his daughter. "I don't think she's ever met him. Shall I send Noble your way? He'll know all about Britton."

"I just want to be sure he's good enough for Alice," Jemima replied with a little smile. "She seems to . . . well, you know how direct Alice can be."

Joshua grinned at her. "Are you envious because Alice has a beau before you?" Greatly to his surprise—because Jemima was rarely embarrassed—she blushed scarlet.

"Hardly," she answered, hoping to deflect his curiosity. "All of this flirtation and so on seems like a great deal of trouble to me."

"You say that now," Joshua warned her. "Just wait until some young man catches your fancy. I think you'll be singing a different tune then!"

"Well, it's a little soon since we're all still in mourning," Jemima remarked. "But if you meet some dashing bachelor on your rounds this evening, do bring him back to have tea with all of us."

"Don't get your hopes up," Joshua told her. "Noble says we should go to the Van Ormskirks first."

"I feel quite certain the man of my dreams wouldn't be welcome there," Jemima told him with a little smile. Joshua held her gaze for a moment: Was she serious? Was she teasing? It was often so hard to tell with Jemima. That was a quality that made most men uneasy. He made a mental note to discuss this point with Helen. Perhaps, if everything went well with the Elevated stock offering and he became rich, then Jemima's challenging gaze might not disconcert New York's bachelors.

Noble and Joshua left shortly afterward, taking a reluctant Robey with them. Gentlemen continued to arrive, and soon Selina's house echoed with the hum of male voices. Alice found herself in the dining room, pinned between two portly men who, after greeting her courteously, had begun to argue about business more or less over her head, so she extricated herself and went into the parlor, where Thaddeus Britton just happened to be standing by the garden door all alone. It was unusual, Alice knew, for a lady to accost a gentleman; the men took all the social initiative. But once

Mr. Britton's blue eyes had met hers and he had smiled, how could she not maneuver herself through the crowded room to end up at his side?

"I'm so happy to see you, Miss Alice," he said. "I don't know many of the gentlemen here besides my neighbors."

"They're mostly Grandmama's friends," she said. "They seem to run out of conversation after saying how much they miss her."

"Yes," he agreed. "Mrs. Wilcox is a wonderful hostess, though. She remembers everyone's name and asks after their families."

"That's true," Alice agreed, faintly surprised. It wasn't something she'd noticed about her mother. "But I've been wanting to ask you," she went on, "since you're an engineer . . . I've heard several gentlemen tonight talking about this famous bridge crossing over to Brooklyn. Have you seen it? Or at least, the part that's been completed?"

"Oh, yes, indeed," he told her. "It's quite a marvel. The two towers are very handsome. It will be the longest suspension bridge in the world."

"I'm afraid I don't know what that means," Alice said. She glanced around the room, then said, with some daring, "Perhaps we could sit down for a moment and you could explain it to me."

"Happily," he answered. "Unless your duties as a hostess . . ."

"But you are a guest, too," she said with a guileless smile. "Surely a hostess wishes to make her guests comfortable," she added, as she perched on the settee.

"Then I would be delighted," he answered, sitting by her.

"Though what I would really like," Alice went on, "is to hear about the late Mrs. Britton, if you cared to tell me. I understand you lost her to consumption."

"Yes," Mr. Britton said simply. "Those were difficult months for us. Elizabeth's greatest fear was that our little boy, Charlie, might catch her illness so we had to send him to relatives for some weeks. He wasn't talking yet, but when he came home he kept looking for her. He is so young, though, that I hope he will recover from the loss."

"Oh, that is so sad!" Alice exclaimed, and suddenly tears were rolling down her rosy cheeks. Her easy sympathy was perfectly genuine, and she had no inkling that her eyes blazed bluer than ever as she plied her black-bordered handkerchief. Thaddeus Britton, however, was deeply touched.

"Perhaps you might like to meet Charlie," he suggested. "I sometimes take him out into the square."

"Oh, yes," Alice agreed. "I love children. But do tell me a little bit more about Mrs. Britton," she went on. "Had you known her for a long time?"

"We were childhood sweethearts," he answered simply. "She grew up on the square and we married just a year after her debut."

"And what did she look like?" Alice asked.

"I have a miniature of her on my watch chain. Would you like to see it?"

"Of course I would," she answered. "Unless . . . with your injury . . ." She glanced at the empty sleeve of his coat.

"Not at all," he said, dexterously slipping the gold case from the watch pocket of his waistcoat and flipping it open to show her the tiny portrait painted on ivory.

"Oh, she must have been lovely," Alice declared.

From the doorway into the parlor, Jemima witnessed this exchange and, though she couldn't hear their words, imagined what was being said. She felt a pang of envy—Alice had such an easy way with people! She seemed always to know just what they would like to hear. That gift, along with her beauty, would make her irresistible once they were debutantes. Jemima caught sight of her mother glancing over at Alice sitting beside Mr. Britton with a look of approval. What could be more appropriate than Alice's kindness to him, after all? Just then Alice said something that made him laugh out loud and for a moment he lost the faint look of worry that made him seem older than his years. He was actually quite handsome, Jemima realized.

Most of the gentlemen callers stayed only briefly. Jemima was presented to dozens of them. She smiled and nodded and spoke very loudly when required. Her feet began to hurt. At one moment there were so many guests in the parlor that she could not hear the elderly gentleman next to her, though his mouth moved and he gestured. She merely smiled and nodded at him: That seemed to be a perfectly adequate response. Eventually he stood and told her she was a charming young lady, to which she smiled. Meanwhile there were tantalizing odors coming from the kitchen and she realized that she was terribly hungry.

Alice was still perched next to Mr. Britton, deep in conversation. Jemima looked around the parlor to see what her mother might think of this and spotted Helen backed up against the garden door, where a gentleman with a booming voice appeared to be lecturing her. As Jemima approached she heard the words ". . . insufficient tithes . . . repairs to the steeple . . . future of the parish."

She edged closer and touched her mother on the arm. "Excuse me," she said in a rather loud voice. "Mama, if I may, there seems to be a problem in the kitchen . . ."

"Oh, I'm so sorry, Mr. Cheney," her mother told the gentleman. "Such an interesting conversation but apparently . . ." and she slipped away. "Thank you, dear," she murmured in Jemima's ear. "He's the senior warden at Grace Church. I could tell you quite a bit about their finances, should you care to hear. I assume there's nothing wrong?"

"Not at all," Jemima replied. "But do you think Alice and Mr. Britton should be spending quite so much time together?"

Helen shot a glance at her. "Probably not," she answered. "Tongues will wag. Goodness, is that the time?" she exclaimed as she passed the tall clock. "Your father should be home soon and then we can have dinner. Gates has already taken away the punch bowl," she pointed out.

Twenty minutes later the guests had all made their way out into the night and been replaced by Noble and Joshua, both somewhat elated by punch they had drunk elsewhere. "I'm sorry to keep you all waiting," Noble said as they settled down at the dining room table. "We lost Robey somewhere along the way, but at the Van Ormskirks' he flirted heroically with one of those girls. Louisa?" he asked Jemima. "The eldest?"

"Caroline is the eldest," Jemima corrected him. "She must be twenty-two by now. Mr. Gregson flirted with her? That was brave."

"Well, since he works for Van Ormskirk now, it may be part of the job," Noble pointed out. "This looks wonderful," he commented as Gates set a plate of soup before him. "I'm famished."

"So Annabelle was civil to you?" Dora asked. "I must know, what was she wearing?"

"Yellow," Joshua answered. "That shiny material—satin? She's quite imposing, I'll say that for her."

"She was more than civil," Noble added. He looked over at Joshua, who was focused on his soup. "Will you tell the story, or shall I?" Joshua merely waved a hand and kept eating.

"Well," Noble began, "you all know that hall of Annabelle's, with the enormous fireplace?" Everyone nodded. It was reputed to be the largest fireplace in New York outside of a hotel kitchen. "We'd only been there long enough to greet our hostess and get drinks from one of those liveried footmen." He paused to swallow some soup, and added, "The poor fellow was wearing a white wig. I don't know what Annabelle is thinking."

"I'd heard about that," Dora said. "There's a rumor that she's going to make her servants grow their hair and powder it, but I can't quite believe it."

"After tonight, I'd believe anything," Joshua put in. "Honestly that fireplace was the size of a small cave and Annabelle— Mrs. Van Ormskirk to me, I know," he said as an aside to Helen, "had on one of those brooches that goes from here to there." He pointed to his sternum and his belt. "Glittery. Diamonds, I suppose."

"A *stomacher*?" Dora said. "For New Year's Day? It's unlike Annabelle to overdress to that extent. That story will make the rounds tomorrow."

"I don't think so," Noble contradicted her. "Because there's a far better story. We were just going to have a friendly chat with Hans-Albert. Mending fences, you might say, after Joshua's business at the club. This was in the hall. Louisa van Ormskirk was standing by the fireplace with some other girl and Daniel Reeves—do you remember him, Dora? His father died a couple of years ago. They drink in that family."

"Is this a story my young daughters should be hearing?" Helen put in.

"It's a story everyone in New York will know tomorrow so they might as well have it from an eyewitness," Noble answered. "Danny

Reeves had apparently consumed quite a bit of punch already, because he staggered over to the fireplace, unbuttoned his trousers, and . . . well. Young Louisa shrieked . . ."

"Noble!" Dora snapped. "This is not a proper story for the table, let alone in front of the girls!"

"That was the worst part," Joshua interjected. "You might as well let him finish it now."

". . . And Hans-Albert hurtled through the crowd," Noble continued. "You remember, Dora, those Reeves men are tall, and Hans-Albert is not. But he grabbed young Reeves and began shouting, then Joshua managed to get over there just in time to prevent Hans-Albert from trying to toss him into the fire."

"Then we removed the poor fellow," Joshua said succinctly, because Noble had gone back to the soup. "It wasn't easy, because he stopped to be sick and I guess that rug of theirs is priceless because Hans-Albert shoved him out of the way so it wouldn't damage the carpet. He was dancing around calling poor Reeves all kinds of names. 'Drunken baboon' is the only one I can repeat. And then we got him into a cab . . ."

". . . the cab that Joshua had paid to stay and wait for us," Noble interrupted again. "Which was brilliant because I certainly didn't want to share a closed conveyance with him at that point, and it was so cold that Reeves would have frozen to death on the street if we hadn't made sure he'd get home."

"Poor fool," Joshua commented, shaking his head. "What happens to a man like that?"

"He'll have to leave town," Noble said. "Good thing his uncle still runs the bank. And there's a branch in London. Eventually he'll be able to come back, but he won't be able to marry any of those Van Ormskirk girls."

"Or the Wilcox girls," Alice said stoutly. "Because we wouldn't *look* at a man like that as a potential husband."

"And did any potential husbands come visiting here while we were gone?" Joshua asked jovially, looking around the table.

"Dozens, if you count ancient widowers," Jemima answered tartly. "Oh, and Robey, of course." Everyone laughed at the notion of Robey as a potential husband.

CHAPTER 21

THE HUDSON
ELEVATED RAILROAD

January 1876

Thaddeus Britton did not see himself as a potential husband any more than the Wilcox family did. Who, after all, would marry a maimed widower with a child? When he had buried his wife, Elizabeth, he had resigned himself to a quiet life. His pleasures would be modest, he assumed: reading, the odd dinner at the Century Association, his work, his child. But that was before he met Alice Wilcox.

He had seen her walking in the square before he met her, and to see Alice was to admire her. That went without saying, but he allowed himself to linger on the matter; Alice Wilcox was a beauty. More, she was warm and cheerful. A ray of sunshine, he would tell himself, looking up from his drawing board toward the square. What a platitude! Yet that golden hair, those steady blue eyes, that warmth—he shook his head. Not for him. Not a girl like that. She would fall for some athletic young man with a brilliant future. It was a good thing the Wilcoxes would move soon, he told himself. It would be very difficult to encounter Alice in the square and retain control of his feelings.

Despite these excellent resolutions he had called on Helen the day after New Year's, almost convinced that he was merely acting the courteous neighbor. He was disappointed not to find Alice at home but believed he had concealed this. Mrs. Wilcox—who asked him to use her first name that very afternoon; surely that meant she liked him?—suggested he bring Charlie over for tea the following day, which of course he did. The house was full of women, and they clustered around Charlie as if they had never encountered a child before. They sat him in their laps and whisked him off to the kitchen to give him cake and taught him their names. Charlie trudged home across the square chanting, "Alice, Jemima, Moira, Alice, Jemima, Moira."

The next day Thad went to Stewart's to buy a child-size toboggan, and on the following day it snowed again. He had difficulty concentrating on his work. He had moved his work table to the window overlooking the park, frankly admitting to himself that he wanted to keep an eye out for Alice Wilcox. The square was full of nursemaids with children Charlie's age. Surely it would be natural for a father to take his son out in the snow? So Charlie was bundled up and placed carefully on the toboggan, and ten minutes later, as if by magic, the garden door of Selina Maitland's house opened and Alice Wilcox emerged.

She hadn't stopped to think of an excuse. She'd merely spotted Thad and Charlie from her bedroom window, stuffed her feet into fur-lined boots, and seized her mother's cloak from the hook by the door. "Well, good morning!" she said brightly to Charlie, and crouched down next to him. "Are you sledding?"

"It snowed," Charlie remarked, running a mittened hand through the white stuff.

"It certainly did," Alice replied.

"Miss Alice," Charlie enunciated clearly. Then he presented the side of his face to her and held still for a moment. Alice looked up at Thad, who pointed to his own cheek.

"He expects to be kissed," Thad whispered. "Apparently he's irresistible."

"Oh, he certainly is," she answered, and stooped down to kiss the pudgy cheek. Then she stood up. "Mr. Britton, where is your hat?" she asked. "You got your little boy all bundled up but you shouldn't be out here bareheaded!"

"I couldn't find the hat I like," he answered regretfully. "But I notice you aren't wearing one, either, so perhaps we're even."

"Well, that's true. To be honest, I haven't even put my hair up yet," she told him, pulling the braid out from beneath her cloak. "We're still writing our letters this morning, but I wanted a breath of air. I'll have to go inside in a moment."

"It's odd, isn't it?" he said, gesturing to the figures in the snow-covered square. "Sometimes this little park feels so domestic. Like a shared parlor."

"Yes!" Alice agreed. "I've thought the same thing! Grandmama always said it made New York feel like a much smaller town. Did you grow up here, Mr. Britton?"

"Yes," he answered. "In the house where I live now. Sometimes I wonder if that was a mistake. Mrs. Britton's health was frail and I wonder if the country wouldn't have been healthier."

"Oh, you mustn't think that way," she told him, reaching out to touch his arm. "You don't believe Mrs. Britton became ill because you lived here?"

He shrugged. "Sometimes the idea haunts me."

"Well, you must put it right out of your thoughts," Alice said firmly. "That would be as silly as blaming yourself for your wound."

He stared at her for an instant. No one ever mentioned his

missing arm. Their eyes just flicked past the loose sleeve of his coat and pretended he was whole.

"I'm sorry, should I not have brought it up?" Alice asked. "I hope I haven't offended you, or made you sad. It must have been terribly painful to lose it. And . . . awkward. Or inconvenient."

"Yes, it is," he agreed. "I used to be right-handed. I've had to teach myself to write and draw with my left hand. Not to mention getting dressed. Devising a way to tie my shoes took quite some time. Still, here I am. And here you are."

"Here I am," added Charlie, waving from the sled. "I want to go now." He rocked his little body back and forth to make the toboggan slide on the snow.

"Of course you do," Alice said. "Your papa will pull you right now. And I'll walk next to you. Did you go there for tea yesterday?" She pointed to her grandmother's house.

"Alice, Jemima, Moira," he crowed.

"Exactly," she agreed. "Though it seems we'll be looking for a new house soon," she addressed herself to Thad. "Because Grandmama's house will be sold."

"What a pity," he answered. "You are all such an addition to our life here." He had a very sweet smile for such a serious person, Alice thought. Perhaps someday he might smile more often.

When she went back inside her feet were almost frozen and she had to change her clothes from the skin out because the hems of her dress and petticoats were wet to the knees from the snow. She was rather absentminded for the rest of the day, thinking about Thad Britton's smile.

Fortunately all of the conversation at dinner that night focused on the great public stock offering for the Hudson Elevated Railway. Alice knew it was important. She tried hard to follow as her father explained what would happen. Shares in the company would be sold to the public, trading on the Stock Exchange like other businesses. This would allow Hudson Elevated to build new tracks. The price of building lots as far north as Fifty-Ninth Street had already doubled, her father said, because when the Elevated reached that far north, people could travel downtown to work much faster.

"And you'll get rich," Nick suggested eagerly. "All those fares; thousands, probably!"

"Possibly," his father said. "But it would take a great many nickels to make us rich."

"We don't say 'rich,' Nick," corrected Helen. "Well-off, perhaps."

"That would still require a great many nickels," Joshua said. "But I'll own quite a few shares in the business and as it grows, their value will go up and . . ." He caught Helen's eye. "We'll see. I am hopeful."

In truth, he was more than merely hopeful. Over and over in November and December, he and Noble had met with potential investors to describe the importance of an elevated railroad to the future of New York City, and the promise of its (almost) inevitable growth. The reaction had been strikingly positive; as a kind of test, Robey had offered a few of his own shares to Felix Castle, who immediately resold them and bragged about his twenty percent profit. Robey only told Joshua about this stratagem afterward, and with some trepidation. Still, the result seemed to show confidence in the Elevated.

As he sat by the parlor fire after the children had gone to bed, he mentally ticked over the elements: the backing of one of the city's most conservative banks, the commitment from *The New*

York Times to cover the story, support from the brokerage firms . . . everything that could be done had been done.

And he could not bring himself—even superstitiously—to believe that the offering would fail. The city simply needed the railroad. History showed that New York continuously pushed northward as it grew. Where houses were built, transport must be supplied, and conversely, where transport was supplied, houses would be built. Someday, buildings might cover the entire island of Manhattan, from the Battery up to the rocky northernmost finger of land that almost touched the Bronx. Yet with the elevated trains—here Joshua's imagination extended tracks to 125th Street and beyond—men would be able to swiftly travel the length of the island.

"What are you thinking about?" Helen asked, settling into her chair opposite his. "You're not worried, are you?" She reached into the basket by her chair and brought out one of his socks and a ball of yarn.

"Of course I am," he answered. "We've done everything we could but the public will decide. I know New York will need something like the Elevated sometime and I believe this is the moment. But investors may not see that yet."

Helen fitted the heel of the sock over a wooden darning egg and began to mend the sock. "What would be the worst outcome?"

Joshua sighed. "Well, we can't expand without this offering. We need a big chunk of capital to build track as far north as Sixtieth Street. If we don't get it—I suppose the Elevated would just keep going as it is. And probably some other group would build on some other route. There's been talk of a Second Avenue Elevated."

"Would it be so terrible, if the offering failed?"

"Embarrassing, certainly. But more than that, I think businesses operate on momentum. They're either growing or dying."

"You don't really think the Elevated is dying, though," Helen prompted him.

"No," he said, and stood up to set his chair next to hers. Then he took her hand. "I believe with all my heart that the Elevated will succeed, but I've been surprised before now. I'd hate you to think I'm one of those old veterans who drags combat stories into every conversation, but one thing the war taught us was to prepare for anything. Which I think we've done."

She squeezed his hand, then slipped hers out of his clasp to take up her needle. "That's all you can do, then." She set her own anxieties aside. There was enough worry in the room without them.

"Yes." He sighed.

A pause fell as Helen threaded the wool back and forth until the hole was filled. "I didn't ask you if you minded—but this yarn doesn't quite match the sock."

"The girl I married didn't know how to darn at all, I'll wager," he said. "Your mother must be spinning in her grave that I've brought you so low. 'That's what maids are for,' isn't that what she loved to say?"

"She did indeed, and if the offering succeeds . . ." A smile lit her face. "If the offering succeeds, Joshua, the first thing I'm going to do is throw away all of your socks and buy two dozen brand-new ones. And I'll throw away this darning egg, too." She shook it at him.

"Burn it," he suggested with an answering grin. "Go ahead, toss it on the fire right now."

Helen shook her head. "No. I'm more cautious than you are, dear. I'll keep it for now." A comfortable silence fell between them for a moment, then she asked, "Could you make a vast amount of money?"

"Substantial, certainly," he said.

"What would you do if you made a fortune? Not for the business but for yourself. Breed horses? Travel? Collect something?"

He snorted. "Like stamps? Of course not!"

"There must be something expensive that you've been secretly pining for," she suggested. "Racehorses? A yacht?"

There was a pause and Helen looked up from her darning to see that Joshua was quite pink in the face.

"What is it?" she asked with a frown. "You haven't already bought a yacht, I hope?"

"Lord, no," he answered. "I get seasick! Don't you remember, on our honeymoon?"

"Ohh!" Helen gasped, then laughed aloud. "I had completely forgotten! Lord, how frightened I was!"

"You were? I never knew that!"

"I'd never seen anyone look so miserable," Helen answered, looking at him sidelong. "The doctor said it was quite normal and two days later you were perfectly recovered."

"I do remember you feeding me some sort of gruel," he said. "And not liking it much."

"You were a terrible patient. You threw a spoon across the room and I was horrified!" She laughed aloud, a peal of pure merriment. "I thought for a moment, 'What have I done? Who is this man?'"

"I never felt that way about you," Joshua answered smugly. "I always knew you were the woman for me."

"Even in this last year?" she asked, looking at him soberly. "I'm afraid I've been quite shrewish from time to time."

"If you were," he answered, "which I dispute, I gave you reason for it."

She deftly knotted her yarn and slipped the sock off the wooden darning egg. She folded the mended sock together with its mate and handed them both to Joshua. "There," she said, then stood up with the darning egg in her hand. "This is a gesture of confidence in the success of the Elevated," she said, and pulled aside the fire screen to toss it onto the embers, where it flamed up right away.

"No woman could do more," Joshua answered with a chuckle.

N ot one of the directors of the Hudson Elevated Railroad had made a special plan for January 14, the day of the offering. Each man chose to cling to routine and pretend that the fate of the ten thousand newly issued shares did not concern him greatly. Except for Robey, who woke early in his fashionable "artist's studio" apartment and gazed up at the shadowy double-height ceiling. His brother Walter's gold mine had made him rich but it was the Elevated he'd worked to build, and he felt an almost parental concern for the company. Let Joshua and Noble and the others sit in their offices feigning calm: Robey had to be where the action was.

So on an unseasonably mild morning he walked downtown to the Corn Exchange Bank, where the book for subscribers to stock in the Elevated would lie open on a table beginning at eight A.M. A clerk would accept down payments of ten percent of the face value of the shares and if all went well, they'd be sold by the end of business. He was surprised to see, from a distance, a cluster of men around the entrance of the bank, and even more surprised to be buttonholed by a runner whom he knew worked for Felix Castle.

"Listen, Gregson, help a fellow out, can you?" the man said. "Do you want to make a quick profit? Castle wanted two hundred shares but I got here too late. I'll pay you a hundred and fifty dollars a share, half over par."

Robey shook his head. "They can't be gone already! Ten thousand shares were offered!"

"Gone in twenty minutes and rising as we speak," confirmed the man. "And you know Castle, he hates to pay over par. He'll be furious."

Robey didn't care a bit about Felix Castle but he was having trouble taking in this turn of events, so he crossed the street to a patch of sun where he could survey the drama outside the bank. There he settled down to watch himself—and Joshua and Noble—get richer by the minute.

The demand only grew, along with the crowd outside the bank. When a couple of policemen appeared to control the crowd, Robey slipped away. He'd learned what he was there to find out: The offering was a resounding success. And he wanted to tell Joshua.

That task was harder than Robey had expected. He'd headed first for the Hudson Transit office on Union Square, which was empty, and the Gansevoort Street horse-car stable, where half of the employees—the ones whose shift had ended, he hoped—were toasting each other with mugs of lager brought from the tavern next door. Of course they had to toast Robey, too, and his coat picked up a powerful odor of beer, but he still had to find Joshua. Which left only the Elevated building all the way downtown, just a stone's throw away from the Corn Exchange Bank, where all the fuss had started. Robey finally tracked Joshua down in the attic, sitting on a windowsill and scrubbing it from outside with a wad of newspaper. The smell of vinegar burned Robey's nostrils.

Joshua slithered through the window and tossed the paper to the floor, then lowered the sash. "Ridiculous, isn't it?" he asked Robey. "I couldn't settle to anything this morning."

"So you decided to wash the windows of a room nobody uses, in the middle of January," Robey observed.

Joshua shrugged. "It was either that or mucking out stalls over at the stables, and I like to think I'm too important for that these days."

"Oh, you are much too important," Robey announced with a grin. "All the shares were taken up by eight-thirty this morning. For the last couple of hours they've been traded in the street. When I left, they were going for three hundred dollars a share!"

Joshua felt his jaw drop. "Three times par? That's not possible."

Robey shrugged. "Read about it in the newspaper tomorrow, then. Or go home to your wife and tell her you're rich. I know what I'd do."

"The price will come down, though," Joshua stated.

"Certainly," Robey told him. "It'll rise and fall. That's what stocks do. But listen." He put his hands on Joshua's arms. "You and I have just made fortunes. Like that!" He released Joshua's arms and snapped his fingers.

Joshua stared at him wide-eyed. "So it's a success," he stated, trying to convince himself. "People want the stock."

"People," Robey answered, "are clamoring for the stock. This is it, my old friend."

Joshua shook his head and trotted down the stairs in his shirt-sleeves, then, followed by Robey, went out into the train yard as an engine pulled its two cars to a halt. Mechanics appeared from no-where with buckets of coal and water. "It's so strange to think of the shares . . ." He mimed expansion with his hands. "We started with *things*, and now we have *capital*. And it's over at the bank, growing like a living thing."

Robey answered, "I think you'd better go home before you catch your death of cold, and tell Helen. She deserves to know before anyone else."

"It's safe to let her know?" Joshua asked. "I'd hate to cause her any disappointment at this stage."

"It's safe. Off you go," Robey said.

Three-quarters of an hour later Joshua was standing in Selina's parlor embracing his wife—who was sobbing into his shirt front. He patted her back and made soothing noises. Gates came to the door of the parlor with raised eyebrows and Joshua beamed at him. A moment later gentle clattering came from the dining room.

"I thought you had lunch on a tray when you were alone. Aren't the girls with Dora today?" Joshua murmured in Helen's ear.

"Yes," she answered with a gulp. "I think Gates must be setting the table for you."

"He has a marvelous sense of occasion, doesn't he?" Joshua said. He took out his handkerchief and gently blotted her face. "Let's tidy up before sitting down, shall we? And I'm going to see about wine."

"I don't usually . . ." Helen began, but he interrupted.

"Today, Mrs. Wilcox, there will be wine at lunch. I'm sure Gates will find something we'll like. I'm going up to change my shirt. It seems to have become a bit damp," he said, looking down at his chest.

"Yes, of course," she said vaguely, sitting down on one of the spindly hall chairs. The Elevated was a huge success. Just like that. She couldn't, she found, take it in. So many months, so much worry . . . She stood up suddenly, hearing her mother's voice in her head saying, "This is a moment worth celebrating."

How did Gates perform his miracles? Joshua couldn't imagine. But when he peeked into the dining room a bottle of champagne was cooling in a silver ice bucket and the table was set for . . . Joshua counted the forks at the two place settings. Four courses. Someone was performing impromptu magic in the kitchen, transforming Helen's lonely lunch into a festival for two.

So the Wilcoxes both rose to the occasion. Helen pinned an enamel and pearl brooch to a white lace collar. Joshua put on a brocade waistcoat Helen had given him for Christmas. Gates beamed and offered his congratulations and Helen called in all the servants to drink a toast to the success of the Hudson Elevated Railroad. After lunch Joshua and Helen sat side by side in the parlor and Helen asked, "What does this mean, exactly? In practical terms?"

"It's too early to tell," Joshua answered. He put his arm around her and drew her close so she could hear his voice rumbling in his chest. "Except that the future of the Elevated is bright, and we'll see, when the share price settles down . . ." He hesitated.

"How rich you really are?" Helen supplied the words.

He nodded and she pulled away from his arm to look at him. "Joshua, are you embarrassed?" He grinned and turned a brighter shade of pink. "You are! Why?"

He shook his head. "I never truly imagined I'd be rich like this, Helen. The way they've been talking—the other investors like Noble and Logan—it's going to take some getting used to."

"Then let's not get used to it yet," Helen said, leaning back against him. "Let's just bask in the novelty. That will be enough of a change for me."

CHAPTER 22

❖

REAL MONEY

February–March 1876

Washington Square, in the winter of 1876, was a good place to become accustomed to altered circumstances precisely because nothing else changed there. As she lay in bed one morning, Helen looked out the window onto the faded blue sky of early morning above the rooftops she'd known all her life. Her principal emotion at that moment—as it had been ever since the public offering—was simple relief.

The bills would be paid. They could buy their own house. The girls would have dowries. So many of the practical issues that had caused her sleepless nights had, it seemed, simply vanished.

In their absence she could finally acknowledge the greater fear that had plagued her: that Joshua would fail. That the Elevated would be one of those ambitious projects that brought ruin in its wake. But most of all, she had feared her husband's defeat, and what it would mean for them as husband and wife. But instead, it was a success the likes of which had never been known on the Stock Exchange. She reached up and rubbed the lines between her eyebrows. Scowling was a bad habit, her mother had always told her. Maybe it was a habit she could discard.

And maybe listening for her late mother's voice was another one. All those strictures about how to behave and whom to know; hadn't Selina's small-town, pastel-hued version of New York been replaced by a larger, louder, more colorful city? One that the Elevated represented more accurately than the limits of Washington Square? A city that was more exciting. More *enjoyable*. And what in the world could be wrong with that? What if Hiram and Sylvia Burke were invited to dinner and Hiram drank a little bit too much and told a naughty story to the other gentlemen? Would the world end?

No, Helen thought, it would not.

In the bedroom next door Jemima still slept but Alice, like her mother, lay in a pleasant reverie. The family atmosphere had altered since her father's business triumph, and Alice was glad of that. However she had wakened to a fizz of excitement that had nothing to do with the Elevated Railroad and everything to do with Thaddeus Britton. His slender height. The way his brown hair fell over his brow. The faint hint of a Southern accent inherited, he'd told her, from his mother. The way he looked at her, drinking in her words. He hadn't "spoken"—let her know, explicitly, how he felt about her. But Alice understood that he yearned for her. And that the only real obstacle to their eventual marriage (for Alice was a practical young lady) would be Thad's ludicrous conviction of his own ineligibility. There was a certain melancholy quality to his gaze sometimes, and she longed to make it vanish.

Thaddeus Britton's thoughts, at that moment, were strikingly similar to Alice's, albeit leavened by the wish that his cook made better coffee. The Britton household rose early, so father and son sat at breakfast. Charlie built a mound of porridge while his father wondered when Alice would venture out into the square. He had moved his drafting table into the front room and spent a ridiculous amount of time watching the facade of the Maitland house. On most days, Alice came out to take the air. Thad almost always joined her.

He knew he shouldn't. She couldn't be more than eighteen, if that, and he was nearing thirty. She had spent no time in society meeting the eligible young men of New York. She might enjoy his company, Thad thought, in the quiet setting of Washington Square, but surely somewhere on the streets of the city was a strapping young banker with a booming voice and perfect confidence who could woo Alice and win her. He would ride to hounds, Thad thought, and he would be intolerable. Then Charlie tossed a spoonful of porridge onto the floor and Thad came back to the present.

It was quite cold and the Wilcox girls stayed inside for most of the day but as the low winter sun began to cast shadows onto the snow, Alice came into the parlor, where Jemima sat curled on the settee. Jemima had just discovered, on her grandmother's bookshelf, an enchanting novel by a writer named Jane Austen, and she had no desire to take the air—but Alice insisted. "You know Mama doesn't like us going out alone," Alice wheedled.

"That's not true. She doesn't mind at all. And if you go out, you'll only meet a neighbor. Like Mr. Britton," Jemima added, looking up from her book in a pointed way.

"I can't just wander around the square hoping he'll come out," Alice said in a coaxing voice. "And he said he'd bring Charlie. You wouldn't want that little boy to be disappointed, would you?"

Jemima sighed and put her book down. "I suppose I'm hardhearted, but Charlie's disappointment doesn't move me. I'm only doing this for you." She pulled on her cloak and boots, and followed Alice into the park just in time to meet—surprise!—Mr.

Britton coming down the steps of his house on the west side of the square. Accompanying him was Charlie, tightly encased in layers of heavy wool.

Charlie loved the snow. He kicked it into the air and bent down to mash it into clumps. He tried to run, fell, and roared until Alice picked him up and dusted him off. Jemima grew cold, and though Mr. Britton was very polite to her, he had eyes only for Alice and his son. So in a few minutes she told him that she felt a chill coming on and returned to the fireside.

An hour later Helen came home and found Jemima lost in *Mansfield Park* and startled to realize that it was almost dark. "Is Alice upstairs?" her mother asked, and Jemima's eyes widened.

"No," she answered. "What time is it?"

"Past four," Helen answered. "Where is she, then?"

"We went into the square," Jemima told her. "We met Mr. Britton and Charlie. But I was so cold that I came in."

"Oh, Jemima!" exclaimed Helen in exasperation. "You shouldn't have left them alone!"

"But with Charlie . . ."

"Jemima, it's practically nightfall, and a toddler does not count as a chaperone!" Helen hurried out of the parlor and Jemima could hear her in the hall, dressing to go out again. Jemima put down her book.

"Are you going to look for them?"

"They're sure to be at Mr. Britton's house," Helen answered in irritation. "They wouldn't have kept the child out in the cold and the dark, but Alice should have known better than to go home with them."

"Why not, Mama?"

Helen paused on her way out the door and turned around to

face Jemima. "To put it bluntly: Our family is marked by a certain amount of gossip already, what with your father's business affairs and that nonsense of the Union Club. If you and your sister are to have successful debuts there mustn't be a breath of scandal about your behavior. And at this moment, Alice is not behaving like a lady."

In theory, Alice did know that she should not be alone with Mr. Britton in his house, unchaperoned. But what was she to do when little Charlie fell and got a nosebleed? When he was roaring with fear and pain, and his father, with his noble war wound, could not easily carry him indoors? Alice had done what came naturally to her, and scooped Charlie up, murmuring comforting nonsense. Then she and Mr. Britton had taken him home, of course, and once the nursemaid had been dismissed, Charlie refused to be peeled away from Alice so she settled down in a wing chair by the fire.

"Let's take off your hat," Mr. Britton said, and knelt on the floor, but the child, comfortable now and delighted by the attention, burrowed his head into Alice's shoulder, damp hat and all.

The fire cast a warm light on Britton's sleek dark hair. Alice touched his shoulder. "You should get out of your coat," she said. "Then perhaps . . ." She nodded to Charlie. "Someone will cooperate."

"Of course," he said, and stood up easily, swinging the coat off his shoulder in a single graceful movement. He draped it over a chair near the fire then stooped to lift Charlie off Alice's lap. "And you ought to go home, Miss Wilcox, your mother will wonder where you are."

But Alice didn't want to leave. She wanted to stay in the warm parlor, lit only by the fire and an oil lamp on the desk. She wanted to study the pictures on the wall, the view out the window; what Mr. Britton saw every day. She wanted to keep Charlie on her lap, pinning her in place.

Instead she got to her feet and crossed the room toward the fire. "Let me just warm my hands for a moment," she told him. "Come, Charlie, let's rub our hands together to warm them up." She crouched by the fire screen and held her hands out to his. "These are cold little hands," she told him.

"Your hands are cold, too," he answered. "Papa, come, rub your hand against mine. And Miss Alice's. We will warm up together!"

Alice couldn't help glancing up at Thad when Charlie issued his command. He was looking directly at her. How could she help reaching up to him? When he took her hand, Charlie noticed. "Holding hands, all!" he crowed.

And of course that was the moment when the door knocker sounded, followed in a moment by Helen's voice asking for Mr. Britton. Alice stood up, Thad stepped back, Charlie looked around in puzzlement and began to cry again.

The parlor door flew open and Helen came in on a gust of cold air. "Goodness, there you are!" she said crossly to Alice. "Do you know what time it is?"

Alice looked vaguely at the clock on the mantel and shrugged her shoulders. "Charlie got cold," she said, "and we had to bring him . . ."

"Forgive me," Mr. Britton broke in. "Miss Alice was kind enough to help me with my son, and I didn't want to send her back out into the cold . . ."

"Of course," Helen answered in what Alice recognized as the cold, polite voice she used to mask real anger. "May I sit down for a moment?"

"Please do," Mr. Britton answered. "I know this is very unsuitable."

Helen settled onto the sofa, then patted the cushion next to her. "Alice," she commanded.

Charlie caught on instantly and clambered up next to Helen. Alice had to follow suit, feeling not much older than the little boy.

"Did you play in the snow?" Helen asked Charlie, who nodded. "I expect you were cold," Helen went on. "Hop down now and go to your papa."

Charlie did as he was told and Helen stood up. "Come, Alice," she said in the same tone of voice she'd used for Charlie, and Alice felt a surge of rebellion. Must she? Couldn't she linger in this snug parlor, with Charlie and his father? Wasn't it possible that they liked having her there? And didn't that matter more, for this little family, than what the busybody ladies on the square might think? All of these thoughts ran through Alice's head quick as a wink, and Helen managed not to sigh. She was the sweetest girl who ever was, until she turned mulish.

"Alice, you really must go home now," Thad said quietly but firmly, and Helen understood for the first time how he had managed to command men during the war. "Perhaps Charlie and I could call at Mrs. Maitland's house tomorrow to thank you properly." He met Helen's gaze frankly. "I assure you that I did try to persuade Miss Wilcox to let my maid walk her home."

"Oh, I have no doubt of that. I'm sure you know how important appearances are for a girl who isn't yet out in society," Helen stated.

"I'm beginning to understand," he answered with a rueful smile.

Once they were outdoors and beyond earshot Helen said firmly, "I know Mr. Britton is a romantic figure, but you are too young to be imagining yourself as the heroine of a great love story."

"I'm not," Alice protested. "But I do like him very much."

"Evidently," Helen answered, and stopped walking. She took her daughter by the elbows. "Let me be blunt—even vulgar. With your looks, your family, and the money that your father has made, when you are presented to society you will be able to take your pick from the gentlemen of New York."

"Yes, Mama," Alice broke in. "But Mr. Britton hasn't spoken to me about anything. . . . He probably thinks I'm just that nice granddaughter of Mrs. Maitland's."

"Oh, my dear girl," Helen responded, and put her arms around Alice as they stood on the icy path of the square. "I very much doubt that. But I want you to promise me that you won't do anything rash."

"Does Mr. Britton seem rash to you?" Alice asked her mother as she gently detached herself. "You and Papa may have spent the night in a rowboat but nothing like that is going to happen to me." She turned toward Selina's house but her mother was standing still with her eyes wide. "Of course we knew the story, Mama! Jemima and I have always thought it was very romantic."

Helen shook herself and moved forward. "Romantic but uncomfortable," she told her daughter.

The very next morning Thaddeus Britton chose a sober cravat and his finest frock coat, then called on Helen. He was amused to notice that she received him at her desk, wearing a plain dark dress: all business.

"I've come to apologize," he told her. "I know I was selfish in allowing Miss Alice to stay so long at my house."

"Alice is a kindhearted girl and obviously much taken by your boy," Helen answered. "But she is very young, Mr. Britton, and has no experience of society. She will come out in the fall and meet many young men. I would be extremely unhappy if her acquaintance with you interfered in that natural stage of a young girl's life."

"As would I, Mrs. Wilcox," he answered. "I won't deny that I deeply admire Miss Wilcox, for the warmth of heart as well as for her beauty. But I understand that to a loving mother, a one-armed widower with a small child might not be the ideal suitor." He watched her as she replaced her pen in the pen tray and sat back in her chair. "I can't help a lady put on her cloak," he pointed out. "I can't drive a carriage, although I do still ride in the country. I need help getting dressed." He looked down at the edge of her desk and sighed. "I think you can imagine, Mrs. Wilcox, how much all of these limitations and many more grate on me. But aside from these shortcomings, I believe I really am just like any other man. I know Elizabeth managed to love me even after I was wounded, and I certainly loved her." He added with a winning smile, "So perhaps my experience of marriage could be counted in my favor." Helen realized that he was really very handsome. "You might want to find a new house quite soon," he added. "Neighbors so often meet each other in the square once the weather gets warm."

He was right, of course, Helen knew. But she wasn't ready to move yet, because she still hadn't figured out who, with all their new money, the Wilcoxes were going to be. Somehow, by a process she couldn't quite fathom, the Elevated had become more than a railroad running above Ninth Avenue. It wasn't just a way to get downtown; it was, to use a phrase she'd heard, "an investment." People had spent their money on shares in the Elevated *as a way to make more money*. Helen had located—and frequently consulted— the page in the newspaper that listed stock prices. Each day she found that the price of the Elevated varied, but on the whole it rose. The Wilcox family, in other words, got richer.

For the first time, Helen found mourning convenient because it allowed her to hide. Several socially ambitious New York matrons would have hastened to call on the newly rich Mrs. Wilcox but her black gowns and hats and gloves still guaranteed a measure of seclusion. She and Dora were excluded from formal social events, though Dora had begun to entertain quietly at home. Helen merely lunched from time to time with friends. Sylvia Burke, in particular, provided cheerful company, colored with an outsider's wry view of New York social habits. Helen found Sylvia's independence refreshing, and wondered if she could emulate it. Maybe she could bring herself not to care what others thought of her. That certainly seemed easier now than it had been even a year earlier. Could Joshua's wealth be having such an effect on her?

Then one evening after dinner, as Joshua hung his coat in the wardrobe, he plucked a leather jewelry case from the right pocket.

Helen's eyes widened. "What is that?"

"It's your pendant," he said.

Helen snapped open the case and there, twinkling on its bed of suede, lay the diamond pendant she had surrendered to Joshua— now set at the center of a substantial necklace, which suddenly blurred as her eyes filled with tears.

"Just think of the necklace as interest," Joshua told her. "And there's this as well." From another pocket he drew a newer case. "It's a frame that turns the necklace into a tiara. Tiffany says they're all the rage in Europe."

"Oh, Joshua, as if I would ever wear a tiara!" Helen exclaimed as she examined it. But she was smiling at him.

"And there's one more thing," he said, smiling back. He pulled a smaller case from the breast pocket.

"You're like a magician!" Helen teased him. "Is there a rabbit in your hat?"

"No," he answered with a grin. "If I were clever like Robey I could make a joke about rabbits and carats but . . . Here you are." This case he snapped open himself, and Helen gasped because it contained three diamond-studded stars.

"Oh, my dear, you shouldn't have!" she protested, but her hands reached out for the case and she lifted one of the stars from its blue velvet bed.

"Yes, I should," he told her. "Decking you with diamonds is the least I can do. You can wear them in your hair or pin them to your gown. Or so I'm told."

She examined the star in the lamplight, then leaned over to look in the oval dressing-table mirror while she held it to her hair.

"Here, let me," Joshua said, nudging her to sit. "They attach to these hairpins," he explained. "Which are gold, by the way; nothing but the best for Mrs. Joshua Wilcox. And you place them just so in your coiffure." He guided the star into the knot at the back of her head.

"But I can't see it there," she objected.

"Maybe not, but I say it looks wonderful," he answered, and placed another one, then the third. He leaned forward to put the case on the dressing table and casually laid yet another case next to it. "And here are your pearls," he said, patting it. "The first thing I noticed about you was your courage," he murmured into her ear. "You were like a soldier that summer when your father was failing." She flicked a tear from her cheek as he went on, "And when you offered me your pearls to pay interest on that loan from Felix Castle. So the least I could do was get all your baubles back for you." He kissed her on the cheek.

"But the stars are so extravagant!" she protested. She picked up the hand mirror and twisted around to see the back of her head in the dressing-table looking glass.

"Depends on how you define extravagance," Joshua answered with a shrug, but he couldn't suppress his grin. "I've sold some shares already, to consolidate . . . You don't need to know it all. But here's the thing . . ." His smile faded and he spoke earnestly. "You won't need to worry about money again, and neither will the children."

She met his gaze but couldn't quite erase her frown. "What if there's another crash?" she protested. "How can you be so sure?"

"I could buy you a house tomorrow," he stated, "and furnish it, and pay the servants' salaries for five years, and barely know the difference." He sat down on the edge of the bed and held her gaze.

Her eyes grew wide. "The Elevated is that successful?"

He nodded soberly, like a child. "It is. I'm half-incredulous my-self, but even Noble says so. I can ask him to put it all down in a memorandum if you like."

Helen nodded. "Yes, that would help me." She reached behind her head and plucked the stars one by one from her hair, then smiled at him. "I don't want to put these away," she said. "I'd put them on my nightgown if I could."

"Wear them down to breakfast in the morning," he suggested with a wink.

"Goodness, Mama would haunt me for life!" she retorted. But Selina, she thought with satisfaction, had never owned jewelry as spectacular as those diamond stars.

Two days later the promised memorandum came from Noble, outlining the new state of the Wilcox family finances. He had written a characteristically cautious note, but ended by saying, "At the very least, your comfort and that of the children is now as-sured, dear Helen. And since my shares in the Elevated will even-tually revert to the girls and Nicholas, you may even need to guard against fortune hunters."

CHAPTER 23

❖

THE WORD IS "GRAND"

April 1876

Helen put Noble's missive in the top drawer of her desk where she saw it every time she reached for a sheet of black-bordered writing paper. Sometimes she took it out and read it again, even silently mouthing the words: "your comfort is assured." Several weeks passed, the snow melted, the month's housekeeping bills came due and as she paid them she thought that perhaps she could authorize her mother's cook to order the better cuts of meat. They could even afford early strawberries this year, which the girls would enjoy.

Then Joshua came home for dinner one evening and announced that he had ordered a carriage from Felix Castle's English coach maker! Helen merely stared at him, pop-eyed. She had hesitated over strawberries, and he had ordered a carriage?

He laughed at her astonishment and said, "Stop pinching pennies. Those days are over." On the following day she made an appointment to visit Noble—alone.

They met at the Latimers' house on Gramercy Square. Noble ushered Helen into the library and they settled into the two chairs flanking the fireplace.

"Where is Dora?" she asked.

"Planning a bazaar for something to do with typhoid fever," he answered. "She sent her love. Now tell me how I can help you."

"It's about the money," she blurted out. "Your note was helpful, but I still can't seem to grasp what all of this means. I'm sorry to ask this again, but . . . are we really that rich?"

Noble nodded. "Yes," he said baldly.

"Joshua ordered a carriage from England!" Helen heard her voice squeak in disbelief. "Can we afford that kind of thing?" She pulled the jewelry case from her reticule and opened it to show the diamond stars to Noble. "And these?"

Noble took the case and laughed out loud. "Oh, Helen! Dora will be green with envy!"

"I can't quite imagine myself wearing them," she said as she took the case back. She watched them sparkle even in the dimly lit library.

"Oh, nonsense! Are you afraid someone's going to come and snatch them out of your hair? Because I must tell you, even if that happened, Joshua could replace them."

"He said we could even build a house. He was going on about Fifth Avenue and suggested that Miles design something grand for us. That was the word he used: 'grand.'"

"And why does that worry you?"

"A little more than a year ago, we lost the very house we lived in!" Helen said with some heat.

"We live in remarkable times," Noble said. "I'm astonished myself at how some of these new fortunes have sprung up—because you know Joshua isn't the only man in his position. There are always years of hard work and sacrifice in the background, though. And"—he held up a finger, in his lawyerly way—"don't overlook luck. It's not possible to make real money today without taking risks, as Joshua did. They paid off, with commensurate reward."

"It won't all vanish in a puff of smoke?" she asked. As Noble shook his head, she added, "How can I believe you?"

"Bit by bit," he suggested, "you'll get used to being wealthy. And by the way, we'll need to revise your wills. The implications for the children are very substantial."

"Oh, goodness." Helen sighed. "I suppose this affects you, too, Noble."

"Yes, indeed," he answered with a rather wolfish grin. "I am pleased. Granted, my new riches don't compare to yours."

Helen turned over the jewelry case she was still holding. "I suppose our position in society is different now."

"That it is," Noble agreed. "The fellows at the club hardly talk of anything else! They're beside themselves with envy."

"And what do they think about Joshua now?" she couldn't help asking.

"Some think he should be reinstated, but others dislike him more than ever." He became more serious. "People will gossip about you. There's no avoiding that."

"We've been giving New York a great deal to discuss for several years now," Helen said with some bitterness as she pulled on her gloves.

"If I may be blunt . . ." he began.

"Oh, by all means," she encouraged him.

"Don't worry about what people think of you, Helen. Or what they think of the girls. You're all too rich to ignore now. You could rival Annabelle van Ormskirk, if it came to that." He smiled. "With a competing social circle. Some of us would find that very entertaining."

Helen laughed out loud. "What an alarming notion!" she said. "But thank you for your time, Noble."

"I have a few suggestions before you go," he said, standing up as she did.

"I came here for advice," she answered with a smile.

"Try not to let the children know just how well off they are. It won't do them any good."

"No, I'm sure it wouldn't," Helen agreed.

"Let them marry whomever they want," he went on. "You must agree with me that, in the end, Joshua was a good match for you."

"Yes," she said with a warm smile. "I would have agreed with you even before the Elevated's success, but . . . the money helps."

"One more piece of advice: Don't worry about what people think of your new circumstances."

"I'm trying not to," Helen answered. "People who don't even know me seem to have opinions about how we ought to live. And Dora—"

Noble interrupted her. "It's going to take them all some time to catch up, especially Dora. You can afford to be patient."

Helen kissed him on the cheek and said, "I'll try. Thank you again." But as he ushered her out the front door she hesitated on the stoop. "It would be helpful to know," she told him, "where we fit in. Do we have more money than, say, Felix Castle? Or the Marquettes?"

"Certainly more than the Marquettes," Noble stated. "Castle's worth fluctuates so that's hard to answer. You haven't quite reached the Van Ormskirk level, though."

"Well, that's a relief," Helen told him. "Though I couldn't say why."

"Because you wouldn't want Annabelle to dislike you even more," Noble answered with startling frankness.

"And you just told me not to worry about other people's opinions," Helen shot back. "While Annabelle practically runs New York society."

"You could take her on, Helen," he said with an eyebrow lifted. "If you cared to."

"Oh, I think not," she answered, and descended the steps. Halfway down the block she turned back and waved to him. Then she went to Tiffany's and found a handsome moonstone stick pin for his cravat and had it sent with a card to thank Noble for his advice. If she was going to be rich, she decided, she would start by giving presents.

B it by bit, the Wilcoxes adjusted. Jemima supposed that theoretically both she and Alice had just become more eligible: Jane Austen was very instructive about how money affected matchmaking. "If Papa is rich now," she asked her mother one day, "does that mean Alice and I will have large dowries?"

Helen looked sharply at Jemima and said, "Never mind about that. No nice boy would marry a girl for her money." Jemima didn't believe her mother for an instant, but in a way her question was answered. Anyway, Jemima wasn't at all sure she'd find a "nice boy" interesting. She wondered if Felix Castle cared about the money, and suspected not.

Nick probably had the most realistic sense of how the Wilcoxes' life could change, if only because he had the freedom to roam around New York by himself on his weekends home from boarding school. He visited friends in brownstones and old clapboard houses and even in a row of what were called "French flats" near Gramercy Park. It was Nick's opinion that the Wilcoxes should build a house occupying a full block up near Central Park, and that it should look something like a palace. Nick had no patience with old-fashioned discretion and "good taste." His standard for a

OUR KIND of PEOPLE

desirable residence was Mr. Castle's house with its adjoining stables, though Mr. Castle had toned down the decor over the winter.
The racy murals had all been replaced by dull "Pompeian" patterns
and the champagne fountain was to be removed. Jemima felt quite
a pang at that news.

"Why is he having it taken out?" she asked Nick, since they
were alone together in Selina's house and no one could overhear.

"He heard somewhere that it wasn't quite the thing if he wanted
to be respectable," Nick told her. "Said some young lady's family
would think he was vulgar." He looked up from the tea table, where
they were playing double solitaire. "I suppose that's you, though I
don't know why he would care." He carefully transferred a king to
an empty spot and turned up the exposed card. "You're not . . ." He
looked up at his sister. "You and Mr. Castle . . ."

"Nonsense," she said with perfect control. "I'm merely interested in him as a type."

"I just wondered," he muttered. "After acting as your messenger."

"He's like Papa, but more cultured," Jemima told him. "A self-
made man."

"Just because he likes opera . . ."

". . . and paintings and books . . . I suppose his house is practically a museum."

Nick looked up from his cards with a gleam in his eye. "I have
an idea. Let's go visit him."

Jemima sat back. "Certainly not!"

"Before the champagne fountain gets pulled out," Nick went
on, in a tone that might have been teasing. "I bet you've got some
book or other you can pretend he needs to read. I'll go with you.
Mama's let us go out together before."

Jemima shook her head. "If she or Papa found out . . ."

"But I'd be in as much trouble as you would . . ."

"And if I were seen! No," she said reluctantly, then reversed herself. "How would we get there?"

"I'll go out to Fifth Avenue and hail a cab," he said reasonably. Jemima considered. "I'm not that brave," she confessed.

"I thought you liked him."

"Oh, I do," she confessed unguardedly. "But I wouldn't risk causing a scandal just to see a champagne fountain."

Nick was silent for a moment, staring at his sister. "Oh!" he said, on a note of discovery. "You actually . . ." Words failed him. "I thought you were joking."

"I was," Jemima mustered a semblance of scorn. "If you're thinking I admire Mr. Castle, you couldn't be more mistaken."

"Because you're only interested in him as a type," Nick repeated her words to her mockingly.

"I was just teasing," Jemima said lightly.

"I don't believe you," he answered. "But your secret's safe with me," he said, just as Helen came into the parlor.

"What secret is that?" Helen asked.

"Oh, just a new idea for a dress," Jemima said airily. "For when we can leave off our mourning."

"I imagine Nick was most interested," Helen answered dryly.

When six months had passed since Selina's death, Helen and Dora both lightened their mourning. They could add white collars and cuffs to their dresses, wear fabrics and jewelry that gleamed, and, to Helen's great pleasure, Jemima and Alice could go back into colors. The first day Jemima put on a dress in a flowered print she kissed her mother at the breakfast table and said, "I feel so much more cheerful!"

"And you look it, too," Helen agreed.

Alice, sitting across the table, asked, "How much longer will you wear black, Mama?"

"Through the summer," Helen told her. "When you're mourning a parent, it's a whole year. But I'll be almost finished by the time the season starts in September."

"So you'll get some lovely new gowns?" Jemima asked. "Will they come from Paris now that Papa's so rich?"

"We don't say 'rich,'" Helen corrected her automatically. "And I don't know where I'll get them. Dora was telling me about a new dressmaker but she's fearfully expensive."

Jemima examined her mother with narrowed eyes. "You'd look pretty in chestnut brown," she announced. "And if Papa got a new carriage, the least you can do is have some dresses made. After all, you're a rich man's wife!"

"Don't ever let me hear you say that again!" Helen protested, genuinely shocked. "It's so vulgar!"

"I suppose so," Jemima replied. "I apologize. But it's hard to avoid the subject of money. We had to move here because we couldn't afford our old house, and now we'll move again because we can afford a better one. We can all have lovely wardrobes because the Elevated is successful. It seems silly to pretend that's not true."

Helen let Jemima have the last word because, as so often, Jemima was correct. But the situation was complicated. Joshua felt that his family could now live as grandly as they cared to. Helen, however, understood that in old-fashioned social circles a house was a symbol as well as a dwelling place. So she asked Miles Latimer's advice. "You understand the dilemma," she told him. "We will be entertaining for the girls' debuts. Joshua would like something quite grand. But . . ." Her voice trailed off.

Miles, seated in one of Selina's fragile little chairs in the Washington Square parlor, nodded his head and drew a sheet of paper from an inner pocket of his frock coat. "Solid but unassuming," he said to Helen. "Two of these are for sale, or you might prefer to rent. You may even want to build, eventually. Joshua might prefer something palatial. In any event, you'll need more servants. Something tells me that the Transit King won't be content for much longer with a housekeeper, a cook, and a maid."

Helen's eyes grew wide. "What did you call him?"

"Didn't you know?" Miles asked her. "One of the newspapers invented the nickname."

Helen actually shuddered, and answered, "Only in jest, I hope." She suddenly felt like her mother, shrinking away from poor taste.

Over the next few weeks, she considered domestic settings for a life she couldn't quite imagine. How grandly did the Wilcoxes expect to live? How many bedrooms would they need? Besides a parlor and a dining room, would they also require a library? Helen refused to consider one house because the servants' quarters in the attic didn't have hot and cold running water. She heard herself saying to Miles, "I don't think really good servants would stand for hip baths in the kitchen."

He merely nodded, but the sentence echoed in her head and she burst out laughing. "Listen to me! I sound like a *grande dame*!"

To her surprise, Miles took her seriously. "And why not? New York might be ready for a more forward-looking social leader."

"What do you mean by that?"

"New people, new money, new ways of doing things," Miles answered. "I've heard that Felix Castle's Sunday evening musicales are quite convivial."

"Why does 'convivial' always describe an occasion when gentlemen drink too much? Anyway, Mr. Castle doesn't know any better than to entertain on Sunday," Helen dismissed him. "I doubt he cares about breaking the Sabbath. Nor does he matter to our kind of people."

"True, but a Mrs. Felix Castle, if she cared, could launch a new kind of society. So could you."

Helen shook her head. "Noble made the same suggestion, but I have no desire to take on Annabelle's crown. I'd just like the girls to have a successful first season."

In the end, the Wilcoxes purchased a handsome new brownstone on West Fifty-Third Street. Helen hoped it would satisfy Joshua's newfound taste for luxury without appearing ostentatious. As she paced through its empty rooms after the closing, she tried to imagine them peopled. Whose calling cards would be left on a silver tray in the mahogany-paneled front hall? (Would the ladies who'd ignored her since her marriage fawn over the wife of the Transit King?) What gentlemen would push back their chairs and light cigars when the ladies left the dining room? What eager suitors would send posies to the girls, or request Joshua's permission to propose?

Felix Castle didn't make any particular effort to keep track of the Wilcoxes' new address, but it was the kind of information that naturally came his way. He had driven past that row of houses as they were constructed. They were all substantial, if a bit farther north than he'd thought Mrs. Wilcox would go. Though he might have underestimated her spirit of adventure, he realized. After all, she'd married Joshua. And raised a spirited, open-minded daughter. Whom he thought about quite frequently.

This was a new experience for Felix, and he found he didn't care for it. Female company had always been essential to him and he'd never had difficulty attracting attention from cultured, attractive women, but he didn't think about them when they were absent. Jemima Wilcox, in contrast, was constantly in his mind, like a snippet of persistent melody. No, more like a cool breeze, he decided. Direct, refreshing. Stimulating. The usual problem with women was that, eventually, they bored him. He would never have expected to be intrigued by a clever, opinionated girl from a stuffy family—let alone a girl whose father he had bested in business.

Worse yet, a girl whose family he'd evicted from their home! Felix rarely regretted business decisions. He knew he would make mistakes, everyone did. You had to forget them and move on. But foreclosing on the Wilcoxes was an error that he rued every day, because it had closed him off from Jemima.

Of course all was not lost, Felix told himself. He still drove with Joshua from time to time; they'd had a brief, frank conversation after the Elevated's public offering that seemed almost to restore their previous camaraderie. He'd even inquired about the Wilcox family in general terms, and learned that the daughters would be debutantes in the fall. Felix wasn't entirely sure what that meant but Joshua said they'd be buying lots of clothes and going to parties. "Dull parties, too," he added. Felix abandoned the idea of trying to get himself invited to any of them.

All the same, he was restless. It was a beautiful spring, and he'd always been restless in April and May. "In the spring a young man's fancy lightly turns to thoughts of love," he recited out loud one day. Quoting Tennyson! And he himself wasn't even that young, Felix thought as he tied his cravat one morning. Had the white streak in his hair become wider? He sighed, then turned his back on the mirror. It was ridiculous to be mooning over a girl he barely knew and might never see again.

Three days later he opened the door of his wine merchant's store on Sixth Avenue and walked into her path.

It was mid-morning on the first day of spring that was truly warm. Felix had unbuttoned his overcoat and stuffed his gloves in the pocket. Jemima was striding along the sidewalk, scowling at a list in her hand. Felix stepped aside as she came close and sensed his presence. Her eyes flew to his face and before she blushed, she smiled with what he later decided was delight.

"I'm sorry," he said, and took her elbow to steady her. "Did I startle you?"

She laughed. "No, I apologize. Mama is always telling me I should watch where I'm going."

"Well, where *are* you going?" he asked. "May I accompany you?"

She grinned. "To the butcher's. But I'm not sure what I'm buying. Can you read that?" She handed over the slip of paper.

"Could it be brisket?" He frowned at the paper. "This person has terrible handwriting. Does that say 'carrots'? Why are you doing your family's marketing? Where is your housekeeper?"

"Hush," Jemima said, "Mama mustn't know. But the kitchen maid overslept and I was so restless on this beautiful morning that I offered to come out. One doesn't expect to run into acquaintances so early. What are you doing?"

"The same thing," he confessed. "Though I do have a carriage around the corner." He looked her up and down, admiring her smart olive green jacket. "I'm glad to see that you're out of mourning," he said. "I know it's none of my business, but it must have been difficult to lose your grandmother."

"Thank you," she said. "And thank you for your kind letter of condolence. I did try to write back, but I was interrupted, and . . ." She shrugged.

A teenage boy carrying a crate of vegetables on his shoulder jostled Felix and he drew Jemima closer to the facade of the grocery store. "In any event, I'm happy that your father's business affairs have recovered," he said. "It must be a great relief to you."

"It is," she agreed, looking up at him. His hand was still on her elbow. "And we'll be moving to a new house quite soon. But perhaps you already know that?"

He smiled, and noticed how pink her cheeks had become. "Of course I do."

"Might you call on us? It's not for me to say, of course. But *I'd* be happy to see you . . ." Her voice trailed off but her eyes did not leave his.

"What do you think Mrs. Wilcox would say?" he asked. "I hold her in the highest esteem, but I'm a little bit afraid of her."

"Mama could hardly slam the front door in your face, if that's what you're thinking," Jemima answered. "Even if she does resent you."

"And Mr. Wilcox?"

"Oh, Papa's forgotten everything. Truthfully, running the Elevated is so complicated that he leaves everything domestic to Mama."

"I don't suppose you have much of an opportunity for private correspondence?" he asked. "Through more conventional means?"

"We will leave for the Spring House in June," Jemima told him. "I might receive letters, though, if they were sent to the local post office. In Tenders Landing," she added with slight emphasis.

"Tenders Landing," he repeated, smiling, as if committing it to memory. "And are you allowed out by yourself, up in the woods there?" he mocked her gently.

"Not the woods," she corrected him. "It's a gentleman's estate. There's talk this year of converting our meadow into a lawn, which is apparently more genteel. My aunt Dora thinks so, anyway."

"And do you enjoy being in the country?" he asked.

"Not especially," Jemima confessed. "There's not much to do.

But I expect we'll be back and forth to the city quite a bit to pre-pare for our debuts."

"You should wear deep ivory," he said, then caught himself and grinned. "Not that it's any of my business."

"Should I tell my mother you suggested it?" she teased him.

"Heaven forbid. May I walk you home?" he asked. "I could carry the brisket."

"You may come to the butcher's shop with me," Jemima con-ceded. "But the butcher's boy will deliver the order. Ladies don't carry their own packages, you know."

They turned to head down Sixth Avenue, and he said abruptly, "Is your father angry at me?"

"No," Jemima told him. "But my mother . . ." She hesitated. "Mama does blame you for Papa losing the house."

He drew her around the corner of Washington Place, out of the slanting beam of the early sun. "Do *you* blame me?"

"I did," Jemima confessed. "As you know." She shrugged. "But now, everything is so different. I don't suppose I should admit this but the money makes life much more comfortable. As I suppose you know," she added with a wry smile. "And now I really must finish my errands and go home," she told him.

"How . . ." He hesitated. "How might we meet again? I don't suppose I could take you for a drive?"

Jemima laughed out loud. "Hardly!"

"Perhaps the museum?" he suggested.

She shook her head. "They wouldn't let me go so far alone," she said. "And everyone is so busy getting ready to go to the country that Moira couldn't be spared to come with me."

"Well, that's a terrible pity," he said. "You'd best be going or they'll lock you in a tower like Rapunzel." Then he took her gloved hand and kissed it, right there on Sixth Avenue. And despite the clatter and bustle of traffic, Jemima felt for a moment that the two of them were alone, connected by his touch. When he loosed her hand she strode away, then turned back to see that he was still watching her with a warm smile. Even though she didn't know how she'd see him again, the brief encounter kept her happy all that day.

CHAPTER 24

⸻ ◆ ⸻

THE APPROPRIATE SETTING

April–May 1876

Jemima's secret flirtation with Felix Castle both delighted and alarmed her. She felt compunction that she was doing something so blatantly improper as encouraging the man who had taken her family's house—yet she found him fascinating. He was so different from her father, her brother, the fathers and brothers of her friends. There was something *extra* about him. A kind of sparkle, Jemima thought. He created excitement. Everything about Felix Castle seemed faintly exaggerated: his lapels wider, his hats taller, his compliments more florid. And, improbably, he had singled her out. He had seen her at her unloveliest and shown sympathy, then continued to take an interest in her. Even—though she barely dared think it—seemed to admire her. He had kissed her hand. Looked warmly in her eyes. Sought a way to see her again.

Jemima had always been a deep thinker so nobody in the Wilcox household noticed her preoccupation. Besides, before the family moved into their new house it had to be furnished, and this project claimed a great deal of attention. Helen and Dora, following the terms of Selina's will, had originally planned to share the contents of the Washington Square house. Then Dora heard from

Miles that the Wilcoxes' furnishings—brand-new from attic to kitchen—would be supplied by W & J Sloane. "Won't you want any of Mama's things?" she had asked Helen. "They were so precious to her. And there's so much history in them."

"I know," Helen had answered, "but our new house will be entirely up to date, and I'm looking forward to that." She thought of this exchange one morning as she set off to meet a new dressmaker. Morrison the coachman was waiting outside with the carriage. As he always had, Morrison clambered down from the box with a kindly smile and offered to wrap a blanket around Helen's knees. Except now the blanket was brand-new and bordered with two inches of smart blue braid that matched the cushions. Sylvia Burke had told Helen where to buy it.

Furnishing a house provided a certain challenge, Helen thought, but dressing your daughters for their first appearances in a potentially skeptical social milieu provided a far greater one. On the one hand, the Wilcox girls represented the aristocratic past of New York City, thanks to Helen's background. On the other hand, the astounding success of the Elevated had swept them into the category of the *nouveau riche*. Helen's task, she felt, was thus to walk the fine line of spending a great deal of money on gowns in irreproachable taste.

Fortunately, it turned out that Helen had chosen the ideal collaborator in the couturiere Madame Delany. She turned out to be a friendly middle-aged woman with a faint Irish accent who welcomed all three of the Wilcox ladies with great warmth on their first visit. While she took measurements of every dimension of each of them (from wrists to ankles and everything in between), she peppered them with questions, suggestions, and observations.

"It will be a real pleasure to dress you all, Mrs. Wilcox," she said as she rolled up her measuring tape. "We have a reasonable amount of time in hand, though I understand you'll be out of the city for the summer?"

Helen nodded. "Yes, we go to the country, but we can come back to the city from time to time for fittings," she added.

"I would like to propose three gowns for each of you, at first. I warn you, they will be very expensive." Helen, thinking about Joshua's coach maker, simply waved a dismissive hand. "Very well. We will begin with the colors. Naturally each lady will wear a color that flatters her, but they must also harmonize with each other. For example, Miss Alice could perhaps wear a pale cherry blossom pink. The predictable choice for Miss Jemima's gown would be a similarly pale blue, or perhaps yellow," Madame Delany said, placing swatches of those colors side by side on a big oak table. "But they would wash out Miss Jemima's coloring, so for her I would prefer a deeper shade of pink, in a different texture. Jacquard, perhaps." She held a bolt of peony-colored silk against Jemima's cheek. "Too bold for a debutante?" she asked Helen.

"I'm afraid so," Helen said.

"But flattering on you, Mama," suggested Jemima.

"True," Madame Delany agreed. "And then perhaps Miss Jemima in a cloudy blue." She took up a length of moiré silk. "Something like this."

The principal fabrics were only the beginning. No fashionable gown was made from just one: Skirts fell open over an underskirt in a contrasting color, or in the same color with elaborate trim such as fringe or ribbon. Bodices were gathered into trailing skirts that might be lined in a different hue. Bows, braids, pleats, ruffles, cording, lace, silk flowers . . . there was no end to the possibilities for trimmings. And that was before each of the women had chosen the style of her gown. Of course the bodices would be snug from the shoulders to the hips, in what was called the "cuirass" silhouette. (Like a piece of armor, as it happened.) Evening gowns were sleeveless and low cut, but the shape of the neckline and shoulders was debated for each woman. As debutantes, Jemima and Alice showed less skin than their mother. "We'll make a nice open neckline for you, Mrs. Wilcox," said Mrs. Delany, "to display your jewels." And naturally each dress was as elaborate from the back as from the front, for this was the age of the bustle and the train.

"How will we learn to manage our trains, Mama?" Jemima asked, but the only and unsatisfying response was, "Practice."

They were all exhausted after the first visit. Two weeks later, they returned to Madame Delany to try on the "toiles," or muslin versions of their gowns. Each woman stood for what felt like hours as a seamstress pinched and nipped or loosened and re-stitched various seams. The day they tried on the basted versions of their gowns in the actual fabrics, however, made clear that the effort had been worthwhile. They also began fittings for their second gowns, in a new selection of fabrics: this time blue, ivory, and, for Helen, deep gold brocade. By the time their first gowns were finished, all three of the Wilcoxes had become accustomed to visiting Madame Delany together every week or so, expecting to stand for hours while the seamstresses worked around them and Madame Delany dispensed a never-ending stream of encouragement and mild gossip. Those mornings were exhausting; the three of them often rode home in the carriage with their eyes closed, and fell asleep after luncheon.

But the results! The first gowns were finished after six weeks, and they were magnificent. When Helen, Jemima, and Alice entered the workroom in their pink, blue, and peony gowns, the seamstresses all applauded. Individually each of the Wilcox women looked like the best possible version of herself: confident and aware of her appeal. As a trio, however, they were breathtaking. Standing before the three-way mirror with their arms around each other's waists, they looked magnificent and felt indomitable. More even than that—alluring. So much so that Alice kissed Madame Delany with tears in her eyes. "Why were you crying?" Jemima asked her in a whisper as they changed back into their street dresses in the dressing room.

"Just because I looked so nice," Alice said simply. "And so grown up. Do you think Mama will invite Thad to our dance?"

"Oh, I expect so," Jemima answered. "Now that we live uptown he'll have to woo you like any other hopeful bachelor. You know, come to tea. Bring flowers. That will help Mama get used to him. Hold still," she added, and knelt down to straighten Alice's skirt.

"Thank you," Alice said. And, after a pause, "You don't still . . . There was nothing between you and Mr. Castle, was there?"

Jemima looked up at her sister, then scrambled to her feet. "What are you suggesting?" she asked with some alarm. Had someone seen her with Mr. Castle on Sixth Avenue?

"I just thought, for a little while, that you might be thinking rather a lot about him. He could be considered attractive, I suppose, to some ladies," Alice remarked. "But I never really believed you would encourage him."

"Are you almost ready, girls?" Helen's voice came through the dressing room door. "We need to hurry, Aunt Dora's coming for luncheon."

"Just a moment," Jemima sang out, to make her mother go away. Then, to Alice, "I'll tell you later."

The opportunities for secrets between Alice and Jemima were

limited, though. The family was plunged into chaos by the move out of Selina's house, and while Jemima kept trying to find a private moment to tell Alice about Mr. Castle, she was always interrupted. On the night before they moved, as they lay side by side in their narrow beds in the dark and Alice snuffed out her chamber candle, Jemima whispered, "Do you remember asking about Mr. Castle?"

"Oh, when I thought you were flirting with him?" Alice answered. "I'm sorry about that. I can't think why I imagined you would do such a thing."

Jemima had been on the verge of confession, but she decided that the moment would have to wait. Perhaps when her family had settled into the new house, after the season had begun, Mr. Castle wouldn't loom so large as a villain in her mother's and sister's minds. And perhaps by then, it would somehow be possible to see him again. She felt strangely confident that this would be the case.

The Wilcoxes took very little to their new house: only trunks of clothes and a few crates of sentimental items, as well as the books Jemima insisted on salvaging from her grandmother's shelves. On moving day Helen, Jemima, and Alice stepped into the carriage on Waverly Place and twenty minutes later, Gates opened the door to them at 45 West Fifty-Third Street. All of the servants were lined up in the hall, beaming.

At first everyone was giddy with sheer relief. Family members constantly startled each other upon entering rooms because the carpets were so thick and the floors did not creak. At breakfast one day Joshua suddenly looked up from the newspaper and said, "I don't hear any sound from the kitchen, does Gates know we're awake?" Then the butler materialized and pressed a catch in the carved paneling to open the door to the dumbwaiter—which had carried their breakfast silently up from the kitchen.

The comfort and elegance of the new house were disorienting. When you sat on a sofa, it didn't wobble or groan as Selina's furniture had. The cushions (plumped constantly by the parlor maid) yielded beneath you. Huge plate-glass windows glittered—presumably—behind the layers of muslin, silk, and velvet that hung in lavish festoons from brass curtain rods mighty enough to serve as medieval lances. Every single item was new. As Helen sat at her pretty little desk in her very own sitting room on the second floor, she gazed with satisfaction over the bookshelves, the pair of gilded armchairs upholstered in peacock-blue brocade, the Chinese-style mirror over the mantel—no object showed a crack, a chip, or any spot of wear.

Yet it wasn't Eden, after all. When euphoria had worn off and the Wilcoxes settled into new habits, they discovered the inevitable shortcomings of their new home: It was so far uptown that Helen could no longer walk to the Ladies' Mile to shop. They had difficulty finding a new butcher who trimmed lamb chops as Joshua liked them. It also had to be admitted that not all of the elaborate new furniture had been designed with human comfort in mind.

Dora had her doubts about the new decor as well. When she first came to the new house she made a beeline to Helen's bedroom to take off her hat, signaling that she planned a lengthy visit. She sat at the dressing table and said, "May I borrow a hairpin? I feel my hair coming down in back. Goodness, how do you ever keep track of what's in all these silver jars?"

"I don't," Helen answered. "I shake them until I find the one that rattles." She plucked a pin from the tray and inserted it into Dora's hair. "There you go."

Dora stood smoothly and gazed around the room. "It certainly is opulent," she said. "Very different from Mama's house."

"Yes," Helen answered dryly. "That was the goal." Dora was envious, that was clear. In her heart of hearts she was pleased for Helen, but she had spent her adult life patronizing her elder sister and that was a difficult habit to break.

CHAPTER 25

◆

ALL PRESENT AND
ACCOUNTED FOR

June–September 1876

Annabelle van Ormskirk's summer in Newport, Rhode Island, was utterly free from what she liked to call "the mercenary bustle of the city" and should thus have been entirely restorative. Nevertheless as she supervised the packing of her daughters' trunks to return to the city, she was aware of faint apprehension. For more than twenty years, her own breeding, the Van Ormskirk money, and what she thought of as a form of discreet discipline had ensured that at the houses of the right families, one would meet only one's peers. The approaching season, however, felt different. Annabelle was not a woman to admit to nerves but the prospect of introducing Maria to society seemed more daunting than enjoyable. It didn't help that she still had Caroline and Louisa on her hands. Caroline, at twenty-three, could no longer be considered girlish and one had to face the fact that New York's eligible bachelors had met her, danced with her, sat next to her at dinner—and refused the bait. Annabelle wasn't softhearted but somewhere pressed firmly into a remote corner of her memory were similar episodes from her own debut. She wished she could spare Caroline more of the same.

And then, Louisa had fallen under the influence of the handsome curate at Trinity Church in Newport, and acquired a terrible habit of talking about orphans on the dance floor. No wonder her partners always returned her promptly to her mother's side and vanished forever. Maria was certainly the prettiest and most vivacious Van Ormskirk daughter, but two unmarried older sisters dimmed her prospects. Skittish bachelors might wonder what was wrong with them all. In private moments—while sitting before her dressing table watching her maid remove the little pads of false hair that added height to her coiffure—Annabelle sometimes felt discouraged.

If launching her daughters were not enough of a challenge (for even in her rare moments of introspection Annabelle flinched away from consideration of daily life with Hans-Albert), there was also a strange mood afoot in society. The traditional boundaries she had always found comforting seemed less secure. In the past, aspirants had courted her acceptance and, upon rejection, vanished. But these new people seemed not even to realize that acceptance was required. Annabelle often shook her head as she thought of newly rich men like Felix Castle or Robey Gregson. And that showy Sylvia Burke had never even left a card at the Van Ormskirk house! Did they not understand that her approval was essential?

Ever since her marriage Annabelle van Ormskirk had looked forward to the opening of the New York season when, she felt, her leadership and dignity were most apparent and most appreciated. But as September slipped past and she left cards, attended receptions, managed her daughters' wardrobes, gossiped and listened and watched, Annabelle grew ever more concerned. The young men who served as marriage fodder were growing refractory, refusing dinner invitations and unbalancing the ratio of women to men. A flamboyant young matron of impeccable lineage had been spotted driving her own carriage—accompanied only by a groom!—in the Central Park. The Haviland sisters had sold their opera box at the Academy of Music to Robey Gregson, of all people. He claimed he needed it to entertain guests. Indeed, Helen Wilcox had reportedly bought a copy of a Worth gown for the opening of the opera season—and was planning to wear it in Gregson's opera box. The dress was rumored to have cost two hundred dollars but that, to Annabelle, was just an outrageous detail. The Gregson box faced the Van Ormskirk box directly. For the duration of the season, Annabelle would have to see that upstart Gregson every time she went to the opera. He was, it was reported, a keen music lover. As if music were even the point!

It certainly wasn't the point at the Wilcox house. Alice, of course, being musical, would probably appreciate the singing, Jemima thought as Mama's haughty new maid brushed her hair. But going to the opera might turn out to be just like paying calls: something the adults did, for old-fashioned reasons, that most people secretly found to be a great chore. She wondered if she envied Nick, who would stay at home happily absorbed in a Jules Verne novel.

The maid offered Jemima a hand mirror so that she could see the elaborately entwined braids at the back of her head. "Goodness!" Jemima said in surprise. "It looks lovely! I never imagined my hair could look so pretty!"

"And we have these flowers," Yvonne said. "We will place them when you are dressed. Mademoiselle Alice is where?"

"With my mother, I believe," Jemima said. "I'll go fetch her." She caught sight of herself in the long mirror on the back of the wardrobe. Even before putting on her gown, she thought, she was quite transformed. She looked . . . "distinguished" might be the word. Perhaps that was just as good as being pretty. Perhaps Felix Castle would even prefer a distinguished-looking young lady to a pretty one.

Because, Jemima had to admit to herself, he was uppermost in her mind. Surely he would be at the performance? Perhaps she'd see him—or rather, *he* would see *her*. The dress she'd chosen to wear for the evening was one Madame Delany had made from a length of antique floral brocade, ivory scattered with tiny multicolored bouquets. The gown itself had a simple square neck trimmed with a deep ruffle of lace, and a pale coral underskirt gathered in tiers. With its warm colors and its whiff of the eighteenth century, the dress transformed her. Even the taciturn Yvonne exclaimed, when she pinned three coral velvet flowers into Jemima's hair, *"Mais mademoiselle est ravissante!"*

"Ravishing"? Could it be true? Jemima turned away from the mirror and then turned back, as if she were just catching a glimpse of herself for the first time. With great caution, she conceded that she did in fact look quite striking. Even beside Alice, wearing ice blue satin and looking like everyone's idea of an angel.

"Are you ready?" Alice said. "Let's go downstairs, we don't want to be late!"

Their long, heavy cloaks lay draped on dining room chairs with their gloves, and Papa stood by the fire with the newspaper so as not to crease the tails of his evening jacket by sitting on it.

"Good grief!" he exclaimed when he caught sight of them. There was no mistaking his shock and admiration. "My girls! What . . . who would have thought? You're beautiful ladies!"

"Papa, are you *crying*?" Alice asked in astonishment.

"Of course not," he answered, but he tugged his handkerchief from his pocket and dabbed his eyes. "But I am . . . amazed."

An immense gold-framed mirror hung over the fireplace in the new dining room and Alice nudged Jemima around to face it. "It's true," she said in a matter-of-fact way. "We do make a striking pair." She kissed Jemima on the cheek and whispered in her ear, "The gentlemen will be speechless."

"Apparently so, if Papa is any example," Jemima whispered back. "Will Mr. Britton be there, do you think?"

"I expect so." Then Alice took Jemima's hand and breathed, "I hope Mr. Castle will as well." Then she smiled at her startled sister and they both turned to watch their mother enter the room.

The quality that made Madame Delany a true artist was her ability to create dresses that conveyed or elicited emotion. She knew her clients' histories—what dressmaker could afford to ignore gossip?—and grasped the dramatic importance of the city's various social occasions. So for Helen, emerging from mourning and newly wealthy, she had created an assertive masterpiece in mahogany watered silk with a contrasting deep pink satin underskirt. Helen's hair had been dressed high and the diamond stars sparkled from her chignon. Joshua gasped and dropped the newspaper.

"I don't think I've ever seen you look so pretty, Mama," Jemima said. "Actually, maybe I should say 'magnificent.' Don't you think so, Alice?"

"Mama always looks nice," Alice said, "but I think you are the one who will astound everyone."

"While you'll look like the beauty you've always been," Jemima said. "That blue should make you resemble a doll, but somehow it doesn't. Mrs. Van Ormskirk will be sick with envy. Maria's her prettiest daughter and she resembles a cocker spaniel."

"Don't be unkind," Alice protested. "She can't help her looks."

"No more than you can," Jemima agreed. "But it must be trying for her mother. And, Mama, won't Mrs. Van Ormskirk be annoyed at seeing you in Mr. Gregson's box?"

"Why should she be?" Alice asked.

"Because Mr. Gregson isn't quite the thing, and Mrs. Van Ormskirk can't make up her mind about Mama."

"Jemima!" Helen protested. "Where do you get these ideas?"

"I just listen," her daughter said coolly. "Shall we put on our gloves in the carriage? I'm sure Morrison is waiting."

All over New York gentlemen were examining their watches as their wives and daughters dabbed on perfume or watched their maids clasp the women's necklaces. Fingers were worked into new kid gloves, silk-lined capes were unfurled, gleaming top hats given a swift polish with a linen handkerchief. Outside elegant houses waited hansom cabs and a handful of private carriages like the Wilcoxes', all prepared to carry the elite of New York to the Academy of Music on Fourteenth Street.

On Gramercy Park, Dora Latimer was irritable even though she knew she looked lovely in her new lavender grosgrain gown with the famous Latimer amethysts. Once again she said to Noble, "It's going to look so odd that Helen is sitting in Mr. Gregson's box instead of ours!"

Once again Noble amiably agreed, and for good measure added, "It's nice to see you in colors again, Dora," and nudged the pug, Trixie, away from his ankles.

In the vast hall of the Van Ormskirk house Annabelle inspected her three daughters like a captain surveying a set of new recruits. Maria looked pleasant, Louisa looked bored, and . . . "What has happened to the neckline of that dress?" she addressed Caroline. "Surely it wasn't that low last year!"

Caroline's eyes opened wide. "I couldn't say, Mama."

"Mr. Van Ormskirk is in the carriage," intoned the butler, so after another suspicious glance at Caroline's bountifully exposed bosom, Annabelle surged out of the house with her girls following like a trail of ducklings.

Her irritation diminished somewhat once the family arrived at the Academy of Music. She was aware of eyes on her, admiring and respectful as she made her way through the throng. People stepped aside, often with a friendly smile, as she advanced. She nodded slightly at just a few familiar faces. Surely this was how a queen moved among her people. She dropped her shoulders and allowed her cashmere shawl to fall to her elbows, displaying her antique garnet necklace and brooch more prominently. Hans-Albert, at her side, crooked his elbow for her to hold as they climbed the first flight of stairs. "What are we seeing tonight, anyway?" he asked.

"Oh, I have no idea," Annabelle answered.

"I might watch the second act from the club box," he warned her.

"As you like. I'm sure we'll have plenty of visitors in the intervals," she replied.

Whatever his faults might be, Hans-Albert van Ormskirk had been taught the courtly manners of his own father. He set an armchair for his wife just where she liked it, at the center of the box facing squarely outward rather than angled toward the stage. He seated the girls around her, instinctively placing Maria, as the prettiest, most prominently. He himself perched on a small chair at the back, which gave him an excellent view, not of the stage but of the house. He would endure the opera because one always did, but the real drama occurred in the audience. Here was the source of unity in the Van Ormskirk marriage, as Annabelle and Hans-Albert together parsed the appearance and behavior of friends, along with their guests and their gowns. Opening night at the Academy of Music was the command performance for New York society and both of the Van Ormskirks felt proprietary.

Annabelle tapped Hans-Albert's knee with her fan. "Do you see? Tabitha Howland has had her pearls restrung in that dog collar style."

He lifted his opera glasses. "Just makes her neck look shorter."

"But now there are more rows," Annabelle pointed out. "It's quite imposing."

Silence for a moment, eyes roving over the crowd. "Who's the redhead in the club box?" she asked him.

"Redhead," he muttered, and peered through the opera glasses. "Ah. A young Englishman, Lord Evesham. Got into trouble with debts at Oxford, or maybe it was a woman. He's a connection of the Ambroses."

"Oh, look!" she murmured. "My goodness, how dare they?" She reached back and tweaked the opera glasses from Hans-Albert's hand. "I would never have expected . . ."

She stared for a moment, then handed the glasses back to him and heard his indrawn breath. "Damn, that Wilcox girl is a beauty!" he whispered.

"Hans-Albert!" she hissed, and snatched back the glasses. "Language!"

But his language was not what Annabelle objected to. Nor indeed was it his enthusiasm per se. It was the rustle, the alertness, the gentle movement like grass blown by a breeze, as eyes turned to the Gregson box.

Eyes turned, and stayed. Lorgnettes were brought into play. The redhead in the Union Club's box stopped speaking in mid-sentence. Of course Alice, with her fair coloring and perfect profile, rewarded the eyes of everyone who cared to look. But so did each one of the ladies. Helen, wearing a novel pair of tawny suede gloves, gently waved an immense fan of bronze feathers. When, Annabelle wondered, had Helen Wilcox become fashionable? And the plain daughter, Jemima, had the air of a slim young queen in that flowered dress. Behind the ladies Joshua and Robey Gregson resembled the impeccable masculine figures in a fashion plate, though, noting a flash from Mr. Gregson's wrist, Annabelle wondered if he could possibly be wearing diamond cuff links. (Actually even Robey knew better than that; they were sober black pearls.)

The men took their seats behind the ladies in large gilded armchairs and Caroline muttered to her mother, "Mama, I don't remember Mrs. Wilcox being so well-dressed."

"No," Annabelle answered, still staring. "Of course, she was in mourning last year."

Caroline went on, rather loudly, "You'd think, for the girls' first opera, they'd be sitting with the Latimers. After all, they're family." Annabelle had to whirl around and hush her and point to the neighboring box, where Miles Latimer had just emerged from the anteroom.

But Caroline was only expressing what was on everyone else's mind: Was that dark-haired, theatrical-looking man the famous Robey Gregson who'd bought the Haviland box? And look at those striking Wilcox girls, due to come out during this social season! The young men would throng to the Wilcox parties! Women assessed the ladies' stupendous gowns with simultaneous admiration and dread—just think of the cost! Would new fashions be set by these people with all that new money?

CHAPTER 26

◆

DRAMA ON THE STAGE AND OFF

September–October 1876

Of course several thousand of the individuals seated in the opera house had actually come for the musical performance, and they settled back into their seats as the orchestra began tuning its instruments.

The first act began with a heavyset baritone (probably a father) and a soprano wearing an implausible blond wig (no doubt his daughter) in a castle keep, set before a backdrop of mountains. A chorus of jolly male peasants trotted onstage to dance, laugh, and tread grapes in a massive vat. One of them stayed behind when the others exited, and fell to his knees before the girl in the wig. Alice sat frozen: She had never heard such music! Such pathos, such harmony, and those voices! Jemima, at her side, simply wondered how long it would all last. Robey glanced at Joshua, who leaned over to whisper behind a gloved hand, "Is it always like this?"

Across the auditorium Caroline van Ormskirk had shifted in her chair to monitor both the Gregson box and the stage. Mr. Gregson was listening carefully; could he possibly speak Italian? She spared a glance for the Wilcox girls, so rich, so beautifully dressed—the handsome youth on the stage would probably fall for

Alice. Gentlemen always admired pretty girls. Caroline felt a pang at the cruelty of life.

Jemima searched the audience for Felix Castle. Their box faced the stage so she couldn't turn around to look for him. But at the interval she would borrow her mother's opera glasses and scan the audience casually, as if admiring the well-dressed throng. A crash of cymbals yanked her attention back to the stage, where the girl with the yellow wig was running around and singing very loudly in a way that surely indicated passion.

Helen wasn't entirely sure about her gloves. Madame Delany said they were the very latest thing from Paris but were they truly as dressy as the usual white kid? And was she herself brave enough to be a leader of fashion? She lifted her eyes to the stage, where a troop of nuns, most improbably, were dancing around the blond-wigged girl as if she were a maypole. She turned her head to see that Robey's attention was fixed on the stage. Joshua caught her eye and winked—he must be bored to tears.

Directly across the auditorium Annabelle sat enthroned in her box like a statue. She had always, Helen had to admit, had marvelous deportment. And authority. Caroline's dress was cut quite low on the chest, however. Helen wondered that Annabelle hadn't at least provided the girl with a wrap. People would be talking.

People were talking about her as well, Helen supposed. Whenever the music ended she and the girls and Robey and Joshua would leave the box and promenade around the broad corridor behind the auditorium. There would be bowing, small talk, smiles, introductions, exclamations about how lovely women looked. This was as much a performance as the opera, and Helen had stage fright.

As the curtain fell and the applause began, Helen tried to quell her anxiety. When she passed through the velvet portiere screening the box from the anteroom, a waiter stood with a silver tray, proffering glasses of champagne. Helen took one and raised her eyebrows at Robey. "How profligate," she commented. "I thought champagne was usually reserved for the *second* interval."

"I was told that lemonade was usual but I don't care for it myself so I insisted those waiter fellows provide an alternative. Are you enjoying your first opera?" he asked Jemima.

"I'm quite overwhelmed," she told him with a smile, then took a glass of champagne. "Don't tell Mama," she whispered to him. "I'm not sure she'll approve." He watched her eyes widen as she swallowed the first sip, and she smiled with satisfaction before turning away so her mother didn't see the glass. Evidently Miss Wilcox was a force to be reckoned with.

"Shall we get some air? Would you like to go visit the Latimers?" Robey asked Helen after a few minutes' discussion of the opera. She assented so they all deposited their glasses and Helen took Robey's arm as they set off along the broad corridor. He felt her trembling, and wondered why. All he could see before them was a crowd of well-dressed men and women circulating slowly like big, lazy fish in a pond on a summer day.

He leaned close and said, "You and your daughters are the most stylish women here, you know." Then he drew back and added, with one eyebrow cocked, "And I am an excellent judge of the matter."

Her hand on his elbow relaxed and she laughed, then unfurled her fan with a snap of her left hand. "Thank you. And what can you tell me about this opera? The plot seems a little far-fetched."

So they strolled along slowly, trailed by Joshua and the girls. She nodded and smiled while Robey told her some nonsense about what was occurring onstage. Not until the Latimers bore down on them did Robey's party pause and regroup. The sisters embraced each other, Miles bowed foppishly to Jemima and Helen. Robey saw a tiny nod travel to Dora from her guest, Mrs. Marquette, upon which Dora made introductions. Stuffy Patsy Marquette chatting with Robey Gregson—who would ever have thought?

Somewhere along the corridor a muffled chime sounded to urge the audience back into their seats. Helen smiled at Dora and turned away, tucking her hand into Robey's arm again. "What should we expect from the next act?" she asked him.

"I don't know," he confessed, "but I'm hoping the nuns will come back in short skirts. I feel cheated when a production doesn't provide some feminine ankles."

"You'd better not say that in Mrs. Marquette's hearing," she murmured to him. "She maintains a high moral standard."

"That would explain why I've seen Mr. Marquette so often in saloons," he answered, then felt her hand tighten on his arm. Rounding the corridor with all the stately confidence of a steamship came Annabelle and Hans-Albert van Ormskirk, trailed by their daughters. Annabelle's step slowed. It seemed that there would be another pause for greetings and small talk, Robey thought. First Mrs. Marquette, now Mrs. Van Ormskirk—evidently the Wilcox family would be reinstated into New York society and he'd be carried along with them. That eldest Van Ormskirk girl had a lovely figure, he couldn't help thinking as the girl got closer, and nice pink cheeks. He'd always admired bright coloring in a woman. But Helen . . .

Helen wasn't stopping. Her hand pulled him onward and he felt momentarily like a horse being urged over a fence it didn't want to jump. Helen's intention was clear: She was not going to stop and greet Annabelle. Hans-Albert, as always, was about thirty seconds late in understanding the situation, and wheeled around to gaze openmouthed at Helen and Robey after they had sailed past him without acknowledgment.

Behind his back Robey heard a smothered chuckle and turned around to see Joshua grinning widely and shaking his head. When they reached the box, he seized Helen's waist and planted a kiss on her cheek. "My goodness, Helen, I'm so glad I witnessed that. You're a woman in a million."

The vast majority of the people seated in the audience at the Academy of Music that night watched eagerly as the young lovers onstage performed the usual duet of passion and parting. But for the occupants of the proscenium boxes, the true drama had just played out in the interval, and Helen witnessed the news travel from tier to tier. Hans-Albert appeared at the back of one box and whispered into the ear of a dowager in red, who dispatched her husband . . . Helen lifted her fan from her lap. Her hand was still shaking, so the feathers quivered. That would show Annabelle! She resolutely turned her eyes to the stage, where somehow the scene had changed to a graveyard and a chorus of female peasants moped musically around a giant obelisk. Many neat ankles were displayed by their short skirts. Robey would be so pleased.

Robey *was* pleased. He was also oddly thrilled. He had always thought that drama was what took place on the stage, but he had just witnessed a ritualized expression of hatred carried out in the corridor of the Academy of Music and it had its own force. For sheer nerve, Helen Wilcox could match any heroine he'd ever seen.

The second act of *La Figlia e Il Son Inamorato* was on the brief side but included a duet between the hero and heroine that Jemima found extremely moving. As the curtain came down, she caught her father stifling a yawn and urged him to his feet. "I'm sure you need to stroll around in order to wake up," she murmured in his ear.

"I was just dozing," he protested. "You're looking very pretty tonight, by the way. It's a terrible shock to see both you and Alice grown up all at once." They had reached the long corridor behind the boxes. "Do you really want to go down to the lobby?"

"Why not? We'll see some different faces, won't we?" Jemima asked. So they descended a flight of stairs and turned to stroll through the lobby, when she caught sight of a slender, dark-haired man who might have been Felix Castle. She must have made some involuntary movement because her father looked down at her. Then a gap opened in the crowd and Mr. Castle's eyes met hers.

It was the strangest thing. They were too far apart to speak. She couldn't think of any words. But he came toward them in the most natural way, as if he had come to the Academy of Music with no other purpose than to see her.

"Why, Castle!" Joshua exclaimed. "I've been wondering if you were here."

"I wouldn't miss the opening night of the opera season," Felix answered. "Won't you present me to your lovely companion?"

"Oh, of course. Jemima, this is Mr. Castle, who has caused us so much trouble in the last year or so. Castle, my elder daughter."

"Miss Wilcox," he said, and took her hand in a warm clasp she thought she could feel right through her gloves and his. "I am perfectly delighted to meet you. And to have the chance to apologize for any inconvenience you have suffered from my business dealings with your father."

He still had her hand. "Not at all," she told him. His black and white evening clothes played up the theatricality of his looks. "Perhaps you will call on us in our new house. Now that we are settled, Mama might like to know you."

He shook his head gently. "Not if she holds a grudge," he answered with a smile.

"Oh, but you look like a man of courage," she said lightly, meeting his gaze. "Mama's bark is worse than her bite."

"I wouldn't swear to that," Joshua protested.

"Never mind," Jemima said, steering the conversation like a woman of the world. Addressing Felix, she added, "I've never been to the opera before. Can you tell me what we can expect from the third act of this opera? It seems remarkably silly."

"Oh, indeed," he agreed. "And there's a truly ludicrous plot device coming up." Felix turned to Joshua. "It turns out that the heroine has been secretly corresponding with her lover while she's been imprisoned in the convent."

Joshua laughed aloud. "I never have understood how that was supposed to work. We'd better be going back up to the box," he added. "Mr. Castle actually listens to the music," he told Jemima.

"I hope to see you again," Jemima said to Felix as soon as her father turned aside. "We will be entertaining a good deal this fall."

"I don't want you to think poorly of me," he answered, "but I don't think I'm that brave." Yet she felt his hand gently encircling her wrist.

She pulled away slightly the better to see his face, aglow with an impish smile. "Nonsense," she told him. "The man who drives four horses at a gallop up Fifth Avenue?"

"Oh, a few broken limbs would be nothing compared to the wrath of a respectable matron." Then he leaned closer. "The completely justified wrath, I might add. I was too harsh about your parents' house."

"All's well that ends well," Jemima told him airily. "What a pity that Shakespeare never said anything about money curing all ills." Then, raising her voice to a conventionally social level, she eased away from him and said, "I'm happy to have made your acquaintance, Mr. Castle." As she and Joshua turned away, she said to her father, loud enough for Felix to hear, "So that's the famous Mr. Castle? He's rather striking-looking, isn't he?"

"Do you really think so?" Joshua asked her. "Awfully theatrical if you ask me."

CHAPTER 27

·❖·

WHAT WAS SHE THINKING?

October 1876

Three hours later, Helen finally sat down at her dressing table and unclasped her necklace before beginning to take down her hair. Her mind roamed back over the evening, but her bravado had begun to fade. Over and over again she saw Annabelle pausing in the corridor. Over and over she tried to discern exactly what impulse had made her sweep past.

Joshua came into the bedroom from his adjoining dressing room, pressing the studs from his stiff shirt front. "Do you need help?" he asked.

"Yes, please," she answered, and he began unhooking the back of her bodice. "Did I hear something about you presenting Jemima to Felix Castle, Joshua? Was that wise?"

"I could hardly avoid it," he said. "He came right up and asked me to. I couldn't quite play the part of the protective father and refuse. Besides, he and I have buried the hatchet. You women tend to carry a grudge much longer than any reasonable man would."

"Yes, that's true. But there's Mr. Castle's reputation, too, you know. All those opera singers . . ."

"You're out of date," Joshua told her. "He's become quite respectable lately. Anyway, enough about Felix, you looked magnificent tonight," he said. Then his eyes met hers in the dressing-table mirror. "I was proud to be your husband. But my goodness, Helen, I had no idea you were planning to take on Annabelle van Ormskirk like that."

"Neither did I," she confessed. "I don't know what came over me. I still can't quite believe that I did." She turned around to look directly up at him. "But she looked so haughty and self-satisfied that I simply could not bear it." She stood up so that he could reach the lacing at her waist, then turned to nestle into his chest. "I suppose I finally rebelled. Why should Annabelle have things her own way, after all?"

"You certainly shocked her. And I swear you knocked the breath right out of Hans-Albert."

"Didn't I? It felt wonderful, after he'd been so horrible to you. But I think I understand the Van Ormskirks a little better since you've made all that money." She turned and gestured at their bedroom. "Don't you feel it? Especially after living at Mama's? Now we live in this magnificent house and I can wear Worth. I know people are watching and talking about us, but no one pities me anymore." She drew a deep breath. "And no one can patronize me."

Joshua chuckled. "After tonight they wouldn't dare, Mrs. Wilcox."

She considered this, then pulled away from him. "You're right. Mrs. Wilcox is too important to patronize." She unhooked the back of her skirt and allowed it to collapse slowly around her ankles before stepping out of it, then laid it on the back of a tufted chaise longue by the fireplace.

"Is that what gave you the idea to ignore Annabelle?" Joshua sat down on the chaise and drew her down beside him.

"That was an impulse," she corrected him. "Let her taste some of her own medicine for a change. And here's another thing." She tugged on the skirt and it fell into her lap with the stiffened bustle lying beside her. "This dress was preposterously expensive."

"And very handsome you looked in it," he replied promptly.

"Thank you. What I meant to say is that it was worth every penny because it made me *feel* handsome. I was better dressed than Annabelle tonight."

"Not to mention better jeweled, if that's the term."

"Those were the Van Ormskirk garnets she was wearing, dear," she informed him. "They've been in New York since sixteen-something."

"That must be why they're so small and dingy."

"Should all jewelry be big and bright?" she asked.

"Isn't that the point of it?" he countered. "Don't women wear jewelry to show how rich and powerful their husbands are? Aside from the purely decorative aspect, that is."

"I suppose so," Helen answered. "I'll expect a great many flashy jewels from you in the future, then. You should hear the way Noble and the other men talk about you. As if you were immensely influential. Are you?"

He shrugged off her question. "I don't know, my dear. That's not my goal. I want to keep the Elevated growing, and *it* is important. But so is your happiness. I hope you know that."

She turned her back to him. "My principal complaint at the moment is that you aren't an especially efficient lady's maid. I can't get out of this bodice by myself." So Joshua applied the expertise of two decades' worth of marriage to the task, to Helen's satisfaction and his own.

Yet the next day, Helen's bravado had deflated somewhat. She woke with a feeling of dread and remembered the look in Annabelle van Ormskirk's steely gray eyes as Helen publicly snubbed the most powerful matron in New York. But it was followed swiftly by a sense of self-righteous satisfaction. Perhaps it was time for Mrs. Van Ormskirk to experience a taste of her own medicine!

She slid from the bedcovers and pulled a wrapper over her nightgown before padding across the hall to her new sitting room to settle down at her desk. Someone in Joshua's office had ruled a roll of paper into squares to lay out the entire social season until Christmas. It was October 11. The girls' ball was scheduled for the first Wednesday in December; eight weeks away. A box of invitations from Mr. Tiffany's store lay open, containing the stack of ivory cards that announced, in time-honored fashion:

MR. AND MRS. JOSHUA WILCOX
REQUEST THE HONOR OF

AT 45 WEST FIFTY-THIRD STREET
TO MEET
MISS JEMIMA WILCOX
MISS ALICE WILCOX

Helen had begun working her way through her list, filling in by hand the formal name of each guest: Mr. and Mrs. Noble Latimer, Mr. Thaddeus Britton, and so on. She had copied the same names onto specially ruled paper to keep track of the responses.

Oh, those responses! Her impulsive behavior the previous evening had been so satisfying. It wasn't often, Helen thought, that one could turn the tables on a bully.

But had her momentary pleasure been shortsighted?

Of course the Van Ormskirks were on the list of guests for the

CAROL WALLACE

girls' party. Of course they wouldn't attend. Nor would the girls be invited to any Van Ormskirk entertainment. Then there were Annabelle's allies: more doors closed against the Wilcoxes. With such factions drawn up in New York society, who would attend Jemima and Alice's reception? Helen dropped her head into her hands.

An hour later, she was sitting in Dora's second-floor sitting room, enduring a flood of reproof. "What were you thinking?" had been the first words out of Dora's mouth, even before the sisterly kiss on her cheek. "I heard all about it even before the end of the interval."

"I'm sure of that," Helen answered dryly, and sat on the sofa. Trixie leapt up next to her and for once, Helen pulled the pug close to her side. She buried her hands in the furry folds around Trixie's neck and went on, "I saw a great deal of bustle in the boxes as the news traveled."

"I just don't know what you intended," Dora said, shaking her head sorrowfully. "Patsy Marquette was terribly upset. She called you a 'rebel.'"

"She might be right, at that," Helen said darkly. "I was just so *angry*, Dora. Annabelle and I have known each other since we were little girls in pinafores and it's ridiculous to pretend otherwise just because she has appointed herself a social gatekeeper."

"Well, there you are!" Dora answered hotly. "Rebelling!"

"And why not?" Helen answered forcefully.

"Because you have two girls to present to society, and Annabelle can influence their success," Dora said. "I hear she already has."

Helen looked at her sister and nodded. "I suspected as much. I know it's early in the season but some of the people we've called on haven't returned our calls. And I can count five—no, six—parties that the girls haven't been invited to."

{294}

"Yes, I heard that, too," Dora answered. "And the luncheons are especially important for girls, because the mothers get to know them."

"But what, honestly, could anyone think is wrong with Jemima or Alice? They're modest and well-mannered: They'd never dream of doing something like—well, Caroline van Ormskirk's dress last night!" Helen exclaimed. "She was showing more bosom than those dancing girls on the stage!"

"So difficult for Annabelle," Dora agreed. "Bad enough that Caroline's in danger of becoming an old maid, but the brashness of her behavior . . ." Both women shook their heads and Dora added, "At least your girls would never do something like that."

"At least?" Helen repeated, suddenly alert.

"Well—I've heard rumors about Thad Britton," Dora said cautiously. "Clandestine meetings in Washington Square."

"How could anything that happens in Washington Square be *clandestine*?" Helen asked. "It is true that Alice got to know Mr. Britton but he's a perfect gentleman. He would never take advantage of a girl in mourning."

"Speaking of gentlemen," Dora said after a moment's hesitation, "did you know that Joshua presented Felix Castle to Jemima last night? Downstairs, during the second interval."

"Yes," Helen answered. "But I can't imagine we'll be hearing much from Mr. Castle. Jemima's just a nice young girl, I can't see why she would interest him."

"Well, I was surprised to hear it, certainly," Dora said. "Apparently all three of them were very friendly together, laughing and chattering. And I must tell you, Helen, your girls need to be extra careful. All that new money of Joshua's is on people's minds. You don't want people thinking you're vulgar."

"Vulgar!" Helen repeated.

"Why take the girls to Madame Delany for their gowns? Nice people don't pay her prices to dress debutantes."

"Well, I do," Helen snapped.

"And people are talking about it," Dora retorted. "Practically buying out Sloane's department store to furnish that house . . . it's just that some people think you're getting a little"—she lowered her voice to a near whisper—"*nouveau riche*. They're saying that Joshua—"

"No," Helen said sharply. "Say no more. You've been blaming Joshua for everything ever since I married him."

Dora waited an instant, then said, "I am very fond of Joshua, as I think you know. But people are talking about him. All that money . . ."

Helen shook her head. "Noble and Miles invested in the Elevated as well!"

"All the money that Joshua made with the Elevated," Dora repeated in a steely tone of voice, "seems to be going to his head. People, *nice* people, are just startled at . . ." She came to a halt. Which was unusual for Dora.

Helen drew a breath and completed the sentence. "People are surprised that we have new clothes after a year of mourning?"

"Well, just a year ago you were living with Mama because Joshua lost your house! And now you've had a windfall and Joshua's setting up a second carriage and spending money like a drunken sailor!"

Helen jumped to her feet, accidentally dislodging the pug, Trixie, who yelped in protest. "Good-bye," she said icily. "I will not hear you talk about my husband that way."

"Oh, stop," Dora snapped. "I didn't mean it literally."

"But you think it, Dora."

"I just mean that in our world, thrift is important! Modesty! Seemliness!"

"Like Annabelle's footmen in livery," suggested Helen savagely.

"Annabelle," Dora said, "is a law unto herself. I'm just concerned that you, or Joshua, may damage your daughters' chances of attracting nice, eligible young men from the better families. Being rude to Annabelle is self-indulgent. And you should insist that Joshua keep Felix Castle away from the girls, he could ruin their reputations quick as a wink. You might moderate your own expenditures a little bit, too. That *fan!*"

"What was wrong with my fan?" Helen asked, with her brows furrowed in a way Dora should have recognized.

"Well, if you want to be showy . . ."

"Heaven forbid," Helen replied, and stooped to kiss Dora's cheek. "Why can't *I* be a law unto myself?" And, feeling that was a rather good exit line, she trotted down the stairs and let herself out.

When she recounted the conversation to Joshua that evening he roared with laughter. Helen didn't at first see what was funny.

"Oh, what could your sister know about sailors?" he asked her, chuckling still. "You'll see, she'll apologize."

"But she meant it!" Helen protested.

Joshua shrugged. They were in the little room upstairs that had been designated the "smoking room" though Joshua rarely bothered to light a cigar. However it was cozy and the servants clearing away the dinner table couldn't overhear them. "She doesn't actually think I'm a drunk, either," he told Helen. "But, sweetheart, she's never been at ease with me."

"What if I called Noble a . . ." Helen searched for a term. "A stuffy, pedantic stick? That would be true, at least."

Joshua shrugged. "You girls will sort this out. You always have."

"She said we were showy. Because I spent all that money on the girls' dresses."

"Fine," Joshua answered. The conversation was beginning to bore him. "Then *be* showy. Spend even more. Spend a packet on the girls' party. I still don't understand why we're just having a reception here. That doesn't seem very exciting."

Helen sighed. "I know you don't, but that's the way it's done. We don't have a ballroom, and we can invite more people for a reception than we could for dancing."

Joshua lifted the lid of the humidor at his side, then closed it again. Helen didn't really like the odor of tobacco. "Why not have a real dance at Delmonico's? Like the Patriarchs Ball?"

"I've explained this; girls are presented at home," Helen told him.

"But why?" Joshua asked. "Aren't we basically announcing to the young men of New York, 'Here are our daughters, ready to marry now'?"

She shook her head. "Not to *all* the young men of New York, just the ones we know. And they will want to marry girls who've been brought up carefully."

"Who could suggest that our daughters weren't? Just because we held a party at Delmonico's?"

"Evidently my own sister," Helen muttered. "Oh, and you must not present Mr. Castle to Jemima again, Joshua. His reputation . . . and the way he treated you . . ."

Joshua stood up and stretched. "All in the past, my dear. Castle is well on his way to respectability. He's just been put up for the Knickerbocker Club. It's apparently a little livelier than the Union Club."

Helen just stared at him, stupefied.

"To return to our daughters," Joshua went on, "you must do as you see fit, of course. But a reception at home seems awfully dull. Unless the point is to reassure your sister that we're not going to do anything outrageous like drinking straight from the champagne bottles, just because I've made some money recently? Which Noble has as well, by the way."

"The point is to introduce them to the eligible young men of their social set," Helen answered.

"So these eligible young men might admire one of them and propose marriage," Joshua continued.

"Eventually, yes," Helen agreed.

"Well, since we've raised pleasant and attractive young women who will have very generous dowries, why can't we just let the process take care of itself?" He caught sight of a pair of business letters lying on the table next to the humidor, and Helen knew the subject was closed.

CHAPTER 28

ABOVE IT ALL

October 1876

By that point in the season, the Wilcox ladies' routine was firmly established. Each morning, a small stack of envelopes lay beside each of their plates, and each morning after the last cup of coffee had been drunk, they settled down to take care of their correspondence. Helen retired to her sitting room while the girls sat on opposite sides of a pretty inlaid table in the parlor. The first task of the day, every day, was the thank-you notes, as many as three for a single day, if they'd attended a luncheon, a dinner, and a dance. More, of course, if an admirer had sent flowers to one of the girls—that was usually Alice.

"Thank goodness it's just two this morning," Jemima said as she picked up her pen on a weekday in October. "Dear Mrs. Tolliver," she chanted as she wrote.

"Don't do that, you'll distract me, and I started with Mrs. Walton," Alice protested.

"We could just swap someday," Jemima suggested. "Write each other's notes. Nobody would ever know."

"Or I'd write all of them one day, and you the next," Alice said eagerly.

"You'd have to write your own for all of the flowers gentlemen send you, though." Jemima waved toward a vase of roses on a side table by the sofa. "I'd be happily reading *The Woman in White* and you'd still be laboring away, 'Dear Mr. Babcock, You were so kind to send me the lovely roses . . .'" she quoted.

"You'll certainly never finish if you keep talking," Alice said calmly, as she folded a note and put it in an envelope. Jemima responded with a sigh, but signed her letter and began the next one. She wondered if she could possibly write the notes for that evening's parties ahead of time. They were dining at the Blakes', which would probably be tedious because dinners sometimes extended to six courses. Then the whole party would proceed to a reception at the Latimers', and if there was a form of gathering Jemima disliked, it was the reception; so many people in their fine clothes crowded into a parlor, without any special focus! Girls clustered together, of course, and young men might approach them—"Miss Wilcox, I wonder if you have seen the fine statuary in the hall?" Waiters would pass little cups of punch. Alice would be surrounded by the collegiate set, boys home for the weekend from Yale or Princeton. Even so early in the season, Alice had earned an eager following of admirers.

That was to be expected. What did surprise Jemima was that she had her own devotees. They were mostly young clubmen in their mid-twenties who liked to believe themselves worldly. Jemima Wilcox, stylish and somewhat acerbic, made them feel sophisticated. Perhaps on this evening enough of them would attend the Latimers' reception to provide amusement, but Jemima suspected that it was usually better to anticipate boredom.

"Do you ever find these receptions tedious?" she asked Alice suddenly.

Her sister signed a note and put her pen down. "No. I'm always happy to see people and hear their news."

"Even if you just saw them the night before?"

"Oh, there's always something to talk about," Alice answered. "The host's family portraits, or a friend's new dress. You expect too much from these evenings," she added.

"I always think I'd rather be reading than making small talk with Arthur Onderdonck," Jemima conceded.

"Poor Arthur," Alice said. "He's so handsome and he thinks the world of you."

"If you say so," Jemima replied. "I'm sure he has many excellent qualities, as Grandmama used to say. But you couldn't call him a brilliant conversationalist." She picked up her pen and began writing her note, then looked up as a new idea struck her. "If I could think about coming out as just another set of chores performed in pretty clothes, I might feel less out of sorts." She rolled her pen across the blotter, watching the pattern made by the drops of ink trailing from the nib. "Do you ever wonder about Mr. Britton? And Charlie? Don't you miss Charlie?"

Alice sat back in her chair and looked directly at Jemima. "Oh, I do," she said. "I miss him terribly. But I did see Mr. Britton at Martha Magaw's reception," she added. Jemima suspected she was trying to be brave.

"Why hasn't he called here? Mama would be happy to receive him."

"I don't know," Alice answered with a plaintive note in her voice. "Could he think he's too old for me?"

"He can't be that silly," Jemima exclaimed.

"And he doesn't know many of the people in Mama's circle," Alice went on carefully. "I was so happy to see him at the Magaws'. He seemed pleased, too."

"I should think so!" Jemima replied. "He barely spoke to anyone besides you! Which surprised me, because he's so . . ." She paused for a moment. "Stuffy" didn't seem entirely kind. Instead, she went on, "He's quite courtly, isn't he? He has what Moira would call 'lovely old-fashioned manners.'"

Alice beamed at her. "That's just what I think! And I did ask Mama to invite him to our party."

"Well, of course he'll come to that," Jemima told her. "But it's not the same as living so near him, and knowing that you might see him any day."

"No," Alice answered with a sigh. And she looked so sad that Jemima got up and put her arms around her sister. "I think Mr. Britton must be very resourceful," she murmured in Alice's ear. "Look how well he manages with Charlie. You'll hear from him soon, somehow."

A week later, Helen impulsively put down her pen in the middle of writing her own thank-you notes, and went into her bedroom to put on her hat. Then she announced to her daughters, busy in the parlor, "I'm going out to do some errands. I may be late for luncheon, so don't wait for me."

"All right, Mama," Jemima answered without lifting her eyes from the newspaper she was reading.

"Are we going out this afternoon?" Alice asked.

"Yes, we'll make a few calls. And the Vincents' reception is tonight. Moira's pressing your blue dress, Alice, and I think your silver taffeta would be nice, Jemima."

"Yes, Mama," Jemima answered, finally looking up. "Have a pleasant walk. It looks like a lovely day."

Jemima was right. The weather was crisp but sunny, and Helen was grateful to be outside. She reached Sixth Avenue and strode across the fast-moving traffic as quickly as possible, with her skirt grasped in both hands. She leapt over a muddy gap in the cobblestones and then scurried to avoid a horse-car. It was probably foolish to have come out like this, when her desk was piled with correspondence, but she had felt so restless in the house. She needed some time to move around, at her own pace, among strangers. And just two avenues west of her house, she encountered an unfamiliar city. On the very block where she walked, rows of brownstones were going up like elaborate chocolate puddings freshly turned out of molds, surrounded by the untidy detritus of construction: stacks of timbers, buckets, ladders, sheds, and shovels.

In front of Helen, Broadway drove its way southward, cutting across blocks on a rakish diagonal. Its cobblestones were overlaid with the silvery tracks of horse-cars, and as she stood on the curb, a bright blue Hudson Transit car rolled past. Beside her on the sidewalk a man pushing a barrow full of empty sacks paused, then launched himself into the melee of wagons and carriages. Helen hastily followed him across the thoroughfare. The next block looked very different: Building had begun only on the south side and empty lots lay on the north where the green fringe of the Central Park dominated the gaps between houses. She heard a faint rumbling and looked up. A block farther west, high above the street crossing, ran the track of the Hudson Elevated Railroad. How could she have forgotten how near it was? As she watched, a car sliced through the sky heading northward. With that, the shape of Helen's restless escape fell into place. She would take the Elevated downtown to do her errands. Why on earth not?

On another day, in another mood, she might have hesitated, remembering her mother's endless warnings about unladylike behavior. Certainly none of her friends would have dreamed of taking the Elevated. But on that morning, Helen Wilcox was staging a personal revolt, so she marched over to Ninth Avenue, then

walked south until she spied the distinctive outline of Miles Latimer's Elevated station shelter at Fiftieth Street. She scrabbled in
her coin purse and found a five-cent piece for the fare, then climbed
the stairs.

Only a handful of passengers sat on the long benches in the
station, since the morning rush had finished. Helen noticed two
soberly dressed women, a workman carrying a bag of tools, and a
pair of young men who looked like clerks. All very respectable, she
thought with a flicker of surprise.

The noise of the engine could be heard from blocks away, or
perhaps it was the vibration of the track that made the waiting
passengers stand up and gather by the door. When the engine
shrieked to a standstill, the conductor—rather splendid in navy
serge and gold braid—opened the door of the passenger car and
collected the fares. As Helen put her coin in his palm, she glanced
at his face and thought, "I wonder if he knows who Joshua is."

Then she found a seat, the door slammed, and the train started.
It was just the same, really, as pulling out of the Tenders Landing
station, with the sense of churning wheels gradually picking up
speed—except that they were up in the air. Whisking past second-
story windows, grazing the branches of a lonely linden tree, gliding over the roofs of carriages and wagons below. Helen glanced
around the car; everyone else in it was calm. This must be a routine
experience for them. Yet they were almost flying! Facing westward, Helen gazed over the low rooftops to the Hudson River
beyond, sparkling blue in the October sun with the green hills of
New Jersey rising behind.

It was so exhilarating! Why, Helen wondered, had no one said
so? This sensation of swooping along in the air, speeding through
the city like a bird—it was utterly remarkable. She glanced at the

faces around her. The clerks chattered, the workman closed his eyes, and she could barely contain her awe.

In what seemed like a moment, the brakes sounded and the train began to slow. "Forty-Second Street!" called the conductor, and a man reading the newspaper began to fold it as midtown New York unspooled beneath his feet. Helen sat back and watched a new group of passengers enter, then the train took off again. The streets below were more congested now. On the riverbank to the west, the masts of ships began to cluster more and more closely. Below, roofs of individual houses gave way to larger and larger ones while bigger buildings began to crowd the sky. When the conductor called out "Thirty-Fourth Street" Helen knew she was not getting off the train until it had traveled to the southernmost tip of Manhattan.

Thirty-Fourth, Twenty-Third, Fourteenth Street—then the numbers stopped. The Hudson River was now just two blocks away, with a dock at the end of each cross street. Helen spotted a ferry pulling out and heading westward toward New Jersey. A huge schooner was moored at one dock and her eyes were caught by the figures of sailors swarming high in the rigging.

This was not Helen Wilcox's New York: not the genteel mercantile community of handshake deals and peaceful residential squares and family dinners around tables set with eighteenth-century silver. It was a mighty city of commerce, boiling with enterprise. She glanced around the car, which was now full, as the train approached the terminus. Not a person there, she thought, would recognize the name of Annabelle van Ormskirk. How could she ever explain to the caped woman at her side why Annabelle's disapproval weighed on her? But if she introduced herself to the conductor . . . if she said, "I am Mrs. Joshua Wilcox and my husband is a director of Hudson Elevated . . ." *That* would matter. In the eyes of most New Yorkers the Elevated Railroad was far more important than what might happen in the corridor of the Academy of Music. Joshua himself, her own husband, wielded real power in this noisy swarming hive of trade and industry.

The train pulled into the station near Bowling Green and Helen followed the other passengers down the heavy wooden stairway to the street. This was the spot Joshua had brought her to on that spring morning two and a half years earlier, she realized. The tracks descended a curving ramp into a vast fenced yard full of idle cars, and she remembered her puzzlement and apprehension when she had first seen it.

But even then, Joshua had grasped the potential of that little railroad in the sky. As Helen lingered outside the train yard, another engine pulled a passenger car up the ramp onto what she now understood was the northbound track. She wondered how often the trains ran. She wondered how many people they carried each day. Joshua had probably told her but she had not understood, or appreciated, the significance of his achievement.

At the southern end of the block, Helen saw, lay a park and in the distance beyond the scattered trees glittered the bay. She glanced around at the passersby. Following her prior visit to the Elevated, Joshua had carefully shepherded her into the Wilcox carriage to return uptown because ladies didn't visit this part of town. But what harm could she come to? Everyone hurrying past had a goal in mind. Two men dressed in white carried a ladder between them while a dark-haired woman with a shawl crossed over her chest held a small child by the hand, and nobody spared her a glance. Having come this far, Helen felt drawn to the very tip of Manhattan Island. So she crossed Battery Place, threading her way among the carriages and horse-cars, a few steps behind a burly pair of men who left a pungent odor of fish floating in the air. She reached the park and made straight for the water.

A stiff breeze blew in her face and pushed insistently at the short brim of her bonnet. Wisps of hair worked their way loose and tickled her cheeks, but exhilaration kept her standing there watching sequins of sunlight perpetually shifting on the surface of New York Harbor. She breathed deeply and relished the faint tang of salt. Then she turned her back to the water and gazed uptown to where the tall buildings began marching up Broadway. As she watched, she caught a glint of sunlight reflected off the Elevated train heading north—all the way to Sixtieth Street.

A string of hansom cabs stood waiting at the edge of the park near the old Battery. She rapped on the window of the first in the queue and asked the driver to take her to Stewart's. An idea had come to her but she was not quite ready to carry it out. For one thing, her hair was completely disheveled.

At Stewart's she made her way to the Ladies' Lounge and sat at one of the velveteen stools before the long, mirrored counter. She untied her bonnet and began smoothing her hair, tucking the strands back under control. Turning sideways to the mirror she caught sight of herself from a new angle. With her flushed cheeks she looked a little like Jemima, she thought with surprise. Lively. Younger. She set her bonnet back on her head at a becoming angle, then stood and assessed herself in the full-length mirror. Were there creases in her skirt, or spots of ash from the train? No. She was perfectly presentable, as her mother used to say. (And from Selina, that had been high praise.)

Helen needed to feel presentable, because her next stop was at the door of Delmonico's restaurant on Fifth Avenue. It wasn't yet noon; waiters bustled around the room folding napkins or nudging polished glasses into position. One of them caught sight of Helen on the threshold and hurried over.

"Madam," he began, wringing his hands, "I am so sorry, madam, but we do not permit ladies . . ."

Helen shook her head and attempted to sound imperious. "I know," she said. "I am not here for the restaurant, but I would like to see the gentleman who manages the ballroom. Would that be possible? I realize it's unusual for a lady to call here." The waiter was in such a hurry to remove Helen from the premises that he scuttled behind a screen and shortly emerged with a portly man wearing a neatly cut frock coat and a discreet cravat.

"How can I help, Madam?" he asked with a French accent.

"I would like to inquire about your ballroom," she answered. "Please forgive my arriving so informally."

He was one of those men whom life cannot surprise. "Of course, Madam. If you will permit, I will take you upstairs." He opened the door for her and they emerged onto Fifth Avenue. "The ballroom is reached by a different entrance," he informed her as they walked around the corner onto Twenty-Sixth Street. "We wish our guests to have the privacy they expect at home."

The entrance was discreet and the stairway broad—no different, really, than in any comfortable house. Two flights above the street they emerged into a handsomely wallpapered lobby where the manager pointed out the ladies' cloakroom, the gentlemen's cloakroom, and the service stairs that came up directly from the restaurant kitchen.

"Then," he announced, "we enter the ballroom itself." He opened one of a pair of mahogany-paneled doors.

Three steps into the room, Helen saw how it could all work. She and Joshua and the girls would stand to the right of the entrance to receive their guests. The musicians would play from the cleverly designed alcove along the western wall. A midnight buffet could be served in the neighboring supper room. She stood in the center of the gleaming floor and rotated, populating the room in her imagination with whirling figures, and instantly abandoned her previous visions of a sedate reception on West Fifty-Third Street. At Delmonico's, Jemima and Alice's coming-out party could be a proper ball.

The manager stood still at Helen's side. He did not know who this lady was, but he knew the city he served. She was one of the conservative ones, he thought, judging from her quiet dress and reserved demeanor. One of those Patriarch people, or part of their circle. They did not usually entertain outside their gloomy houses. Yet here she was, examining the room with that calculating expression he had seen on the faces of hostesses back in Paris. She was, he knew, considering guests and costs and also, perhaps, novelty. "Could Madam tell me what sort of entertainment she has in mind?" he asked delicately.

She turned to him. "I think I won't, just yet," she said. "But I would like to return with my husband at a time that is convenient to him." The manager nodded. He liked her hint of grandeur. A great hostess should know how to keep people at a distance.

It wasn't until late that evening, after the Vincents' achingly dull reception, that Helen found a chance to confide in Joshua. She located him in his dressing room, with his coat flung over a low crimson velvet chair as he pulled off his patent leather pumps. He grimaced and rubbed one foot. "I don't know how you ladies manage to stand for hours in those tiny shoes of yours," he complained.

"With heels, no less," Helen agreed. She hung up his coat and sat in the chair. "I wonder if you should have a valet to take care of your clothes?"

"Good Lord, no!" Joshua protested. "I don't want some fop fussing over me at the end of the evening."

"You may change your mind by the middle of the season," she told him. "There will be weeks this winter when we go out almost every night."

He shook his head as he looked at her. "I certainly hope they'll be more entertaining than tonight. Will our girls' party be like that? People just milling around and talking? What do they all find to say to each other four nights a week?"

"How pretty the debutante is. How young her mother looks. And we ladies can always fall back on our gowns as a topic of conversation. It's probably more difficult for men since they aren't supposed to discuss business," she added with a malicious little smile.

"Why didn't you warn me that bringing out the girls would be a crashing bore?"

"There will be plenty of more entertaining parties," she reassured him. "Musicales, for instance. There's always one debutante who plays the harp, because her mother thinks she looks graceful."

Joshua leaned against the chest of drawers and looked down at Helen. "You looked very pretty this evening, anyway," he said. "What did you do today?"

Helen's smile deepened. "I rode the Elevated," she announced.

"You did? Why didn't you tell me? I would have gone with you!"

"It was an impulse," she told him. "I just thought . . . oh, it was a beautiful day and I was going to do a few errands. So I set out and there was the track . . ."

"Where?" he interrupted. "What station did you use?"

"Fiftieth Street," she told him. "Why?"

"I suppose I just want to imagine my wife on the platform of an elevated train," he said with wonder. "And what did you think?"

"It's a marvel," she said simply. "I rode it all the way downtown."

He stared. "All the way?"

"It was so exciting . . ." she started to explain, then asked, "Do you remember the first time you rode an elevated train?"

He nodded. "I was terrified, to be honest. The car vibrated so badly I thought it was going to pop right off the rails."

"Well, I didn't feel that," she said. "I was just amazed." She stood up and put her arms around him. "It was thrilling. I was so proud." She lay her head against his chest for a moment. "Truly, Joshua," she went on. "I wanted to say to all the other passengers, 'My husband built this! You're flying along in the sky because of my husband!' I didn't, of course, but I thought it." She pulled away from him and met his eyes. "I'm sorry it's taken me this long to realize how magnificent the Elevated is. I'd like to go again, with you and the children. They should understand, too. We could ride it from end to end."

"Of course we will!" he answered. "I'll introduce you to all of the conductors so they won't collect a fare!"

"And then," Helen said, going back to her original point, "I went to Delmonico's. And I think you're right. We should have the girls' party there."

His eyes opened wide. "Another surprise! Does this have anything to do with the Elevated?"

"Maybe," she answered after a moment's consideration. "Yes, indirectly. I think riding on the Elevated made me feel bold. And then tonight, the Vincents' party really was dreary. I couldn't bear the idea of the girls' debut being so dull and so predictable."

"Good!" he said. "So they can have a proper dance!"

"It will be expensive," she warned him. "I'll invite quite a few more people than we could have had here. Though quite a few may not come, since I cut Annabelle. That's the risk."

He shrugged. "What's the worst that could happen? Jemima and Alice will still enjoy the party. They'll be 'out.' Annabelle will be disagreeable but that's nothing new."

Helen hesitated while she thought out her response. "I suppose you're right," she said, frowning. "Maybe there's nothing to lose." Her eyes met his. "What a strange idea."

CHAPTER 29

◆

R. S. V. P.

October–November 1876

So the very next morning, at the breakfast table, Helen announced her new plan to her daughters. "I've reconsidered your party," she told them. "What do you think of having a dance instead of a reception like Nina Vincent's?"

Both Alice and Jemima stared at her. "Isn't it awfully late to change your mind?" Alice asked.

"We'll keep the same date," Helen explained.

"But . . ." Jemima turned in her chair, sizing up the dining room. "Even with the parlor and dining room combined, there wouldn't be much room to dance."

"No, I was considering something completely different," Helen told her. "I visited Delmonico's yesterday. There's a ballroom upstairs from the restaurant, quite private. It would provide plenty of room not only for dancing, but also for a midnight supper."

"My, how grand!" Jemima teased her. "So it would be a proper ball!"

"Of course we would never call it that," Helen said with an answering smile. "We Wilcoxes don't have any notions of grandeur. Still, there's a stage for four musicians, and the food and staff are all furnished by the restaurant."

Alice spread some jam on a slice of toast, frowning. "Have other girls . . . has anyone we know had a dance there?"

"I doubt it," Helen answered. "We would have heard about it."

"So if we had our party there, that would cause gossip," Alice suggested.

"Yes," Helen agreed frankly. "It probably would. Does that worry you?"

Alice stirred her tea, frowning. "I just wonder . . . after all the talk about Papa and the house . . . wouldn't it be better to have a traditional, quiet reception? Imagine what Grandmama would have said: 'Delmonico's!'" she exclaimed disdainfully, sounding exactly like Selina.

Helen took a moment before answering. "You're right, of course. Grandmama would have been horrified. But she was a debutante forty years ago, and New York is utterly changed from those days. Of course if you dislike the idea, we can have a reception here as we'd discussed before. Why don't you girls think about it for a day or two?"

Jemima darted a glance at Alice. "Yes, Mama, we will. Does Papa know about your idea?"

"Your father," said Helen, "has made it quite clear that he will be happy to pay for and attend any kind of coming-out party you girls want. I don't need your answer today." She looked at the pretty enamel watch pinned to her bodice and said, "I have quite a few letters to write this morning. Then I believe we're lunching at Sylvia Burke's."

"Oh, good," Jemima said. "We haven't seen her lately."

"Will Mrs. Burke be invited to our party?" Alice asked, with a little frown etched between her brows.

"Yes, of course she will," Helen answered. "She has been a good friend to all of us, and is very fond of you two." She picked up the letters that had been left by her plate, and headed off to her sitting room.

Alice sighed and looked at the envelopes on the tablecloth before her. Jemima, who was using her butter knife to slit open her mail, said, "What's the matter?" Then she glanced up at Alice and saw she was crying.

Alice wept like a girl in a painting. Her nose didn't run and her eyes didn't turn pink; tears simply slid down her cheeks in silence. But Jemima knew that it took a great deal of hurt or worry to make Alice cry, so she got up and went around the table to kneel at her sister's side. "What's the matter?" she murmured. "If you don't like Delmonico's, we'll have our dance here! Mama would never want to upset you! Coming out is supposed to be exciting! It's not supposed to make you miserable."

"I know," Alice answered, mopping her cheeks with the clean handkerchief that she just happened to have up her sleeve. "It's just . . . Thad . . . what if . . . ?"

Jemima pulled a chair closer to her sister. "What is your worry? That Thad would disapprove of Delmonico's?"

"He hasn't called here," Alice said, sniffling.

"Not true," Jemima contradicted her. "He called when you were out."

"I can't call on him, though."

"No."

"And I can't see him."

"Not easily," Jemima agreed. "But of course he'll call again."

"And I'll have to talk to him with Mama there. It won't be the same."

"I suppose not," Jemima agreed, suddenly remembering the

freedom of her own *tête-à-tête* conversations with Felix Castle. "But . . . are you worried that he would disapprove of Delmonico's?"

Alice's tears flowed faster. "What if he wouldn't come? Because he can't dance?" She sniffed loudly, and resorted to her napkin to blow her nose.

"That is the most ridiculous thing I've ever heard!" Jemima said. "Thad Britton is a sensible human being and he admires you greatly. He has already called here. That's as good as announcing that he wants to keep on courting you. If you're concerned, you could suggest that Mama call on him. She could ask him about his intentions," Jemima teased her.

"Yes, all right," Alice snapped. "I'm being silly. But it's so difficult! Girls never get to know anything about what gentlemen are thinking."

"I'll be your interpreter, shall I?" Jemima offered. "Mr. Britton wants to give you a chance to meet younger men. Which is very honorable of him. But if he calls here again, I'll manage to leave the two of you alone. Would you like that?" Alice nodded, so with a new briskness—*that* problem was solved—Jemima stood up. "We need to write thank-you notes to Mrs. Sparkman and Mrs. Olin before we go to Mrs. Burke's."

Ten minutes later Jemima was seated in the parlor with a sheet of paper before her. She had written, "Dear Mrs. Sparkman," but the ink was drying on her pen. At least, she thought, Mr. Britton could call at the Wilcox house without creating a scandal. She paused. What *would* happen if Felix Castle called at West Fifty-Third Street?

She sighed, and dipped her pen in the inkwell again to write out the standard formula for a thank-you note: "such a pleasure . . .

most stimulating company . . . grateful to be included. . . ." At least Mama didn't read over her notes the way some debutantes' mothers were reputed to do. What did those suspicious mamas think their daughters were writing?

Jemima froze, pen in hand, and smiled. The Wilcox ladies' correspondence was placed on the hall table each day. Gates was responsible for gluing on the stamps but he never bothered to read the addresses. And when the invitations to their party went out— what if one were addressed to Mr. Felix Castle? Her smile broadened, then faded as she imagined his reply to the invitation arriving with her mother's letters. Well, she'd just have to write her own name on the invitation. Mr. Castle wouldn't have a clue that the protocol was incorrect, and he would send his response directly back to her. Would his bold masculine handwriting on the envelope prompt questions from her mother? Jemima considered the question briefly, then dismissed it. That was a risk she was prepared to take.

When Helen went to Tiffany's to order new invitations for Jemima and Alice's dance, the stationery counter did not have a format prepared for a private party occurring at a commercial location. Together with the clerk, she decided that the word "Dancing" in the lower right corner and "Delmonico's" with the address in the lower left would convey all of the essential information. As Helen addressed the envelopes, her mind wandered. She imagined the shock on her fellow matrons' faces when they read the invitation, and the excitement of the girls' fellow debutantes. More than mere anticipation, Helen knew, there would also be envy. The social season was far enough advanced to have produced a certain tedium. Everyone had already been to receptions, to formal dinners, to musicales, and to the small dances that could be held in a family home, but a dance at Delmonico's was unprecedented. Helen could imagine her mother's opinion, delivered with cutting clarity from beyond the grave: "The very breath of commerce at a girl's introduction to society is a shocking mistake." Nevertheless, she calmly wrote and blotted and folded and on November 8, left the stacked envelopes on the front hall table for Gates to entrust to the postman. One missive bore Jemima's handwriting, but it was not discovered.

To the dozens of recipients in New York's most elegant homes, this invitation conveyed a great deal more than the usual "what" and "where" and "when." The Wilcoxes' choice to formally present their daughters to society at what one father termed "a watering hole for stockbrokers" broke with tradition in a way that, some declared, threatened the very meaning of society. Traditionally a debutante should be guided with the utmost care from the shelter of her parents' home into the arms of an eligible husband. Her reputation could be tarnished along the way by exposure to the faintest impropriety, the sources of which were (in 1876 as ever) sex or money. Presenting a girl at home masked the fact that money was spent on the entertainment, while the ballroom at Delmonico's implied dollar bills cast around with abandon. Worse, of course, was "the atmosphere of the barroom," as one starchy dowager put it in discussing the Wilcoxes' ball—to which she had not been invited. The implication was that blushing, innocent Jemima and Alice, along with their entire cohort of maidens, would be contaminated by the lingering echo of bawdy songs performed on the first floor.

The debutantes themselves ignored the adult disapproval—or indeed, welcomed it in their modest girlish way. After several weeks of being "out," some of them were already bored senseless by quiet dinners, sedate dances, and heavily chaperoned evenings at the opera. Only the meekest shared their mothers' objections to the Wilcox invitation. In addition, a crucial cadre of debonair young men received it with surprise and delight. At least at Delmonico's, they all said to each other, there would be enough drink and rather good food.

As Helen sat at her desk in the following days and began tallying the responses, she was pleased to note a substantial number of acceptances, especially from the men. Her closest friends also replied quickly, in the affirmative. Even Patsy Marquette, she was surprised to see, said she would come. The regrets were unsurprising: The Farragut family would be out of town. One friend of Alice's had to go to Boston for a debutante tea given by her tyrannical grandmother who still held the family purse strings. Moses Dawson had died suddenly so his entire family was plunged into the seclusion of mourning.

Examining her guest list, Helen discerned a pattern; a few powerful matrons, it appeared, were delaying their responses and many timid guests were waiting to follow their lead. She tapped her pen against her thumb and calculated: Three weeks remained until she had to give the Delmonico's manager an estimate of attendance. She added up the names, and imagined the party with forty-odd guests—among them a round dozen youthful bachelors. She imagined them scattered around the Delmonico's ballroom, dancing, chatting, flirting, proceeding to the supper room. She tried and failed to envision Robey nodding politely to Miss Van de Berg, or procuring a cup of punch for Dora. Would Noble dance with Sylvia Burke? Did Hiram Burke dance at all? She told herself resolutely that it didn't matter and that the party would be a social success, with or without the stuffiest ladies.

Though Helen Wilcox did not see it that way, the party she

proposed to give was nothing less than a revolution. The most traditional wing of New York society had grown tired of itself. For
years it had looked backward for its legitimacy, and the refined
charm of its somewhat pallid entertainments had justified its control. However, once social life becomes routine, boredom floods in.
Good taste will always, after a battle, give way to luxurious novelty. Helen Wilcox just happened to be offering an alluring new
form of hospitality at the moment when some of the city's patri-
cians were ready to take a chance. After all, many wives had been
dying to get a look at Delmonico's.

But as Helen sat at her desk on that November morning, she
suspected that her most conservative acquaintances had decided
unanimously to hold their breath and see what happened. At a
musical evening on Fifth Avenue (lightly attended by young men,
Helen couldn't help noticing), several ladies seemed to avoid her.
Even Dora kissed her cheek and moved on, murmuring something
about finding Noble in the crowd. Yet to her own surprise, Helen
felt defiant rather than discouraged. She looked around the brightly
lit parlor where Rowena Dillon was settling down to play the
piano and gentlemen in tailcoats congregated near the door for
ease of escape. "No one," thought Helen, "will want to leave my
daughters' ball before the very last dance."

The next day she went back to Delmonico's and conferred with
the manager. Yes, he told her, certainly the ballroom could be divided. Foliage could be brought in to make it seem less empty. Or
perhaps Mrs. Wilcox would like small tables to be positioned
around the edges of the dance floor? Unusual, certainly. The gentlemen seemed to like them, though. And if the guests proved to
be a more "exclusive" group (his euphemism for "small"), the room
would still be comfortably full.

That evening, after a rare quiet dinner at home, Joshua asked Helen about the plans for Alice and Jemima's dance.

"I still haven't heard from a great many families," Helen told him. "I think most of them are waiting until the last moment to answer."

Joshua watched her as she finished winding the clock on the mantel in the parlor. "You don't seem terribly concerned." She looked pretty. Maybe a little plumper than she had been. It suited her. "Is that a new dress?" he asked.

"It is," she acknowledged, looking down to admire the elaborately draped skirt. "It probably cost as much as a horse. And here I am wasting it on an evening at home with my husband."

"Hardly wasted. Haven't I just admired it? And you look . . ." He searched for a word. "Blooming. Why aren't you worried about this party for the girls? It's only three weeks away."

She sat down in an armchair that looked like a piece of a church. The salesman at Sloane's had persuaded her to buy it but she was already reconsidering the Gothic flavor of the room. It seemed ludicrously gloomy. "You know, that man at Delmonico's set my mind at ease," she informed him. "If a hundred people come, it will be one kind of party. If forty come, it will be smaller and quieter, but I think the girls and their friends will enjoy themselves."

"I didn't know that was the point," Joshua teased her.

"No," she answered with a smile. "It isn't really. But it's been a dull season so far and I don't mind providing the young people with some excitement. You'll have to dance with me, by the way. And with the girls, of course."

"I'll even dance with Dora, goodness, I'd dance with Annabelle if it came to that!"

"I don't believe that will be required," Helen told him. He

looked up from his newspaper at that, and caught a rather piratical glint in her eye.

"You invited the Van Ormskirks, didn't you?"

"How could I?" she replied. "She doesn't know me, and I don't know her." She looked smug.

"Good grief, Helen," he roared with laughter. "What's come over you?"

"Money," she said simply, and tried to sit back in the tall chair. A knob dug into her spine, though, so she got up and took a small cushion from the sofa. "I'm still not quite used to it, you know. I say to the man at Delmonico's, 'I am expecting fifty guests on December 6 and we would like the Veuve Clicquot champagne,' and he says, 'Very good, ma'am.' I go to Stewart's and say, 'Send over a dozen pairs of those white kid gloves I ordered last time,' and they arrive at the house and the maid puts them in my glove drawer." She shrugged. "When people just say 'Yes, ma'am' to you all day long, you do become more confident."

Joshua watched Helen try to position the cushion behind her back and observed, "Money may not be able to procure us a comfortable chair, however. Take mine instead." He stood and went to the fireplace to poke the coal in the grate. Then, leaning with one arm on the mantel, he studied his wife. She looked back at him tranquilly.

"Yes, I think we'll have to redecorate the room from top to bottom," she told him. "The people at Sloane's did try to suggest a Moorish theme, is that something you would like?" He couldn't repress a look of blank horror and she laughed out loud. "Teasing aside," she told him, "I decided I could do without Annabelle. I'm trusting that our money will make up for our failure to follow the conventions."

"Our money and your resourcefulness," he answered. "It's occurred to me recently that Annabelle and her like—your sister among them—are fighting a rear-guard action."

Helen cocked her head. "Joshua, you're too young to start tossing military terms into polite conversation. What does that mean?"

"When a battle is lost, the losing side assigns fellows to protect the retreat. Sometimes the rear guard can do a little damage while the main body of troops gets away."

"You have just made me imagine Annabelle armed with a rifle," Helen said, "and it's very alarming."

"Well, I don't think that rifle of hers is loaded anymore," Joshua answered. "And I certainly doubt her foot soldiers are going to take her orders for much longer."

None of the Van Ormskirk servants would have agreed with Joshua's statement out loud. They, after all, were paid to take their mistress's orders. Still, the atmosphere in those marble halls on Fifth Avenue had acquired an edge of suppressed conflict. Bedroom doors slammed. The girls sulked. Annabelle flinched when Hans-Albert took her arm to escort her to the dinner table. Witnessing this, the butler met the footman's eye and neither man's face changed, but the gesture had been noted. (The Van Ormskirks were not popular employers.)

Thus Annabelle was already irritable when Caroline entered her writing room after breakfast shortly before Thanksgiving. Each morning, the girls were supposed to attend to their own correspondence or practice the piano, to learn habits of discipline. Annabelle stealthily drew a sheaf of letters over the novel lying open on her blotter.

"Well, Mama," Caroline began, dragging a chair to her mother's desk, "something must be done." She plumped herself down and Annabelle noticed yet again that Caroline certainly looked . . . strong. Her sleeves strained over her upper arms.

"Done about what?" Annabelle asked. She would have required more deference from Louisa or Maria but somehow Caroline had appointed herself as her mother's lieutenant. She frequently offered Annabelle hints about how to handle the servants or aired her opinions at the dinner table, despite her father's striking lack of interest.

"This ball of the Wilcoxes', Mama," Caroline stated. Her gray eyes met her mother's with a challenge. "We haven't been invited, I suppose."

"Of course not," Annabelle answered. "Helen made it plain to all of New York that she doesn't want to know me. Just as well. We don't want to encourage her."

"But we *do*, Mama," Caroline contradicted her. "We have to! How else am I to meet Robey Gregson?"

"Oh, nonsense, Caroline, that's enough about Mr. Gregson. You've already made a spectacle of yourself, staring at him at the opera. And don't think I didn't find out about the bodice of that dress, either!"

"Mama, I am getting to be an old maid. I'll be twenty-four very soon. I need a husband."

"I know, dear," Annabelle soothed her. "But this season, surely . . ."

"The boys are getting younger," Caroline asserted. "Much younger than me! And if any of the men my age had wanted to marry me, they would have."

Annabelle stared at her eldest daughter, who seemed to see this as an entirely practical matter. "Isn't there anyone you like? I thought for a while that George Ambrose seemed interested."

Caroline shook her head. "He just wants to talk about the chickens at that farm of his on Staten Island. He might do for Louisa, though. He has all kinds of ideas about feeding poor people. And Louisa likes chickens." Caroline stood up and strode across the carpet to the door, then back. She had always been a fidgety child. "Robey Gregson, Mama. I just need a chance to meet him!"

"And then what?" Annabelle asked. "Do you think we'd actually let you marry him? If he's even a marrying man."

"Well, then I'd know." Caroline returned to her mother's desk. "Maybe I wouldn't actually like him, either, and then I suppose I'd give up and set my sights on some young widower—they say Clementine Swain's got consumption." Her voice had turned suddenly savage. "If she's carried off and Ned Swain doesn't grieve too deeply I suppose we could be a match by the time I'm twenty-five." Then she dropped her face in her hands and wept. Like everything else about Caroline, her grief was emphatic. She sobbed and the tears trickled through her fingers. Annabelle sighed and searched through her desk drawer to find a handkerchief.

"I'm sorry, Mama," Caroline said, and blew her nose. "But I just don't see how I'll ever get married if I can't meet someone like Mr. Gregson."

Annabelle got up and put her hands on her daughter's shoulders. Bossy and narrow-minded she might be, but she did love her daughters and wish the best for them, within the limits accepted by New York society. Marriage to Robey Gregson could not possibly fall into that category. But perhaps another solution—or another man?—would appear if she took the right steps.

"All right, dear," Annabelle told Caroline. "I'll see what I can do."

Two days later, an hour before lunch, Gates toiled up the stairs at 45 West Fifty-Third Street with a silver salver to present to Helen at her desk. "Did you say I'm not at home?" she asked him.

"The lady was quite insistent," Gates replied and nodded toward the two visiting cards on the tray. Helen read them and her eyes flew to his. He nodded slightly. "They're in the hall," he whispered.

"Show them into the parlor, offer them tea, and tell them I'll be down in a moment," Helen instructed him. She stood up and slowly walked twice around the room, trying to calm herself. Then she sailed down the stairs and entered the parlor, where Annabelle and Caroline sat at either end of a massive paisley settee.

"Annabelle, what a delightful surprise. I hope you'll have some tea?" she said, and sat on the edge of a high-backed chair.

"You're very kind," Annabelle answered. "You know Caroline, of course?"

"I do indeed. And your other girls are well?"

"They are, thank you." Gates had returned to the room, practically staggering beneath the weight of a massive silver tray that Helen had never seen before. Behind him followed the latest parlor maid, with the equally imposing teakettle. "I will pour, thank you, Gates," Helen said.

"I owe you an apology, Helen," Annabelle stated as soon as the servants had left the room. "I should have called on you at the beginning of the season. This looks like a very comfortable house. I'm sure your mother would have been happy to see you settled here."

"Thank you," Helen replied. She handed a cup of tea to Annabelle and poured one for Caroline. "It is a relief to have a home of our own," she said boldly. "Milk? Sugar?"

"Not for me," Annabelle answered, and "Yes, please," Caroline said at the same time. A brief silence fell while the two mothers watched Caroline with the sugar tongs. The handles were so elaborately scrolled that Caroline seemed to have difficulty grasping them.

"You don't find the location a little bit out of the way?" Annabelle asked. "There are so few other houses up here."

"True, but Joshua and I have been able to build quite a commodious stable across Sixth Avenue, so we always have our carriages available," Helen said smoothly. "It's rather a relief not to have to rely on a livery stable anymore." She thought the veiled boast was worthy of her mother. "Has Maria been enjoying her season so far?"

"Indeed she has," Annabelle answered. Silence fell.

"And you, Caroline?" Helen asked. "It must be pleasant for all three of you girls to go about together."

Her remark caught Caroline with her cup to her mouth and those bulging gray eyes looked over it coolly. She swallowed and answered, "Naturally."

"Shall I ring for Alice and Jemima to come down?" Helen asked. "They're just taking care of their correspondence. You girls must have a great deal to talk about."

But Annabelle returned her cup to the table at her side and gathered her skirt. "Thank you, dear Helen, but we have so many errands. We just wanted to call, informally. No doubt we'll see you very soon."

Helen rose in her turn. "I'm so glad you came. Perhaps we'll see you at the opera. I believe it's *Così fan Tutte* this week."

"Ah. *Così fan Tutte*," Annabelle repeated vaguely. "Of course. I hope you'll bring your daughters to call. They and my girls have always been such friends."

"Naturally," Helen answered. As a special mark of courtesy she escorted her visitors to the door instead of ringing for Gates, though she spied him lurking in the dining room, pretending to set the table. She stood on her stoop for a moment watching the liveried Van Ormskirk footman tuck a cocoa-brown blanket around Annabelle's knees before climbing onto the box next to the coachman.

Gates emerged into the hall and as she passed him, she commented, "I believe my mother would have been very amused to see Mrs. Van Ormskirk here."

He merely nodded, but she wondered afterward if he hadn't perhaps winked at her as well. Then she returned to her sitting room on the second floor, where she found Jemima seated at her desk.

"What was Mrs. Van Ormskirk doing here?" Jemima asked. "I thought she didn't know you."

Helen looked at her astute daughter affectionately. "I believe that was an overture of friendship," she answered.

"With Caroline as the peace offering?" Jemima asked.

"I suppose so," Helen said. "Poor thing."

Jemima stood up. "So now you can invite them to our party. Does this mean everyone you invited will come?"

"A great many of them," Helen answered. She took an invitation from the box on her desk and placed it on her blotter. Then she looked up at Jemima. "I think it might be quite a success," she said, trying out the words.

"Oh, nonsense," Jemima told her, and leaned over to kiss her mother's cheek. "It will be the party of the season. You'll see."

CHAPTER 30

BELLES OF THE BALL

December 1876

Of course this was largely bravado on Jemima's part—but over the next few weeks, she came to believe that her prediction might well be accurate. There was a great deal of gossip circulating about the Wilcox party. Girls who had been indifferent to her at earlier gatherings now longed to become her friend. Boys who had danced with her once for good manners now competed to bring her cups of punch or hold her fan. "Honestly, I feel almost as popular as you," she told Alice one night as they drove home in the carriage from a musicale.

"Oh, Jemima," Helen protested, but Alice cut her off.

"No, it's true, Mama," Alice said. "The boys are afraid of Jemima because she's so clever, but everyone wants to be invited to our dance." She linked her arm through Jemima's. "They drop the most obvious hints about it. Asking if it's true that we're going to have a full orchestra or serve champagne all night long."

"Boys often ask me if you prefer one dancing partner to another," Jemima teased Alice. "I always tell them that you do but that it's a secret."

Alice trod on her foot in the dark of the carriage as she protested, "That's not true!"

"Oh, I know," Jemima said. "But sometimes they're so tactless.

A really clever boy would pretend to be fascinated with me for my own charms, not just because you're my sister."

With a rare flash of acerbic humor, Alice answered, "I'm not even sure there's such a thing as a really clever boy."

After a moment's silence Jemima added, "You're right. Look at Nick," which made Alice snicker, then Helen hushed them by pointing out that in any event, the responses to their invitations had all been positive so far, and that the dance was bound to be a great success.

Madame Delany insisted on coming to the Wilcox house with a seamstress to help Helen and the girls get ready, and on the early evening of the dance, the second floor was an intensely feminine bustle of female voices, platters of sandwiches and cups of tea and snippets of ribbon. Finally, just after eight o'clock, they were all dressed, from their long kid gloves right down to the dancing shoes that had been covered with spare fabric from their gowns. Helen had chosen a striking teal-blue taffeta crossed with bands of silver-embroidered brocade and a bustle with a short train lined in vivid green satin. At Madame Delany's suggestion Alice's dress, in a simple silhouette, had been made from yellow satin embroidered with tiny butterflies, while Jemima's green eyes were brought out by the fern-patterned silk brocade of her gown with its fringed sash. Alice frowned slightly as she eyed her V-shaped neckline in the mirror. "Do you think it looks a little bare, Mama? Should I borrow a brooch?"

"I think you look like a ray of sunshine," Jemima told her.

Moira and Madame Delany held their fur-lined velvet evening cloaks and Joshua called out from downstairs.

"If you want to reach Delmonico's before our guests, we should leave now!"

Jemima peered over the stair rail. "Aren't you elegant, Papa!"

she called down. "Goodness, Nick, you are, too!" she added as he looked up at her. "Some girls might even call you handsome."

"Didn't the florist bring your *boutonnieres*?" Helen asked as she descended the stairs.

"They're here," Joshua told her, pointing to the square boxes on the hall table. "But first . . ." He picked up two flat velvet cases. "These are for you girls," he said. Jemima caught Alice's eye, delighted.

"Papa!" she exclaimed. "What a lovely idea!" Inside the box, lying on a bed of soft suede, was a string of perfectly matched pearls.

"Mr. Tiffany had a hard time finding pearls for two necklaces at once," Joshua said proudly. "Let me put them on you girls."

"But there's another one," Alice pointed out as he clasped her necklace. "Did you get something for Mama as well?"

"Well, I did!" he exclaimed, and picked up the third case. He snapped it open and held it out to Helen. "Of course you don't have to wear this," he said, suddenly unsure. "I don't know if it goes with your gown, or . . . perhaps it's too gaudy, though Mr. Tiffany said not. . . . Oh, no, you're not crying!" And he gave her the starched handkerchief from the breast pocket of his tailcoat.

Helen lifted her eyes to his and smiled as a pair of tears trickled down her cheeks. "Only because I'm so touched," she answered, and reached out to touch the largest of the glittering clusters flashing at her from the case. She reached up and took his face between her gloved hands for a kiss. "Thank you, dear. This is so kind, and so generous . . ."

". . . and nothing more than you deserve," Joshua said as he lifted the necklace and placed it around her neck, where its ten imposing sapphires flashed among garlands of smaller diamonds.

Then he steered her toward the mirror in the front hall. "What do you think? Of course Mr. Tiffany will take it back if you aren't pleased."

"No, he won't," she answered, laying a gloved hand over the necklace and smiling at him. "These are the Wilcox sapphires now."

Then the doorbell rang and Morrison—who had not quite adjusted to his employer's new grandeur—came in on a blast of cold air announcing, "It's time to be moving along, Mr. Wilcox."

So move along they did. By nine o'clock, the Wilcox family stood at the entrance to Delmonico's ballroom. Helen took a deep breath and leaned slightly against Joshua's sturdy shoulder. "You don't feel faint, do you?" he asked her under the sound of the violins playing behind them.

"No," she answered. "Not faint." She looked past him to Jemima and Alice, glowing with excitement. "Don't the girls look lovely?"

"Of course they do," he agreed. "But not lovelier than you. Will you dance with me this evening?"

"I thought you hated dancing," she teased him.

He grinned, and touched her necklace with a gloved finger. "This isn't your only present this evening," he said. "I've taken a few dancing lessons."

"Joshua!" she exclaimed. "You haven't!" And she burst out laughing at the proud look on his face. Then she reached up and planted a kiss on his cheek, witnessed by the first guest to arrive—Selina Maitland's sour old friend Miss Van de Berg.

"You've filled out since I saw you last," she said to Jemima as she moved down the receiving line. "You've probably forgotten."

"Not at all," Jemima said promptly as she curtsied. "I remember that you were a dear friend of our grandmother's. Perhaps you didn't meet Alice that day," she went on.

"Oh, the pretty one," Miss Van de Berg said. "I suppose your papa bought you those pearls. Of course in the best families we don't buy our jewels, we inherit them." And with that she turned on her heel to enter the ballroom, prepared to disapprove of everything she saw.

Alice's eyes met Jemima's. "I'm nervous," she suddenly said.

"About what? You like parties," Jemima answered.

"What if . . ." Alice's voice trailed off and Jemima turned toward her.

"Are you thinking about Mr. Britton?"

"No," Alice said. Then, "Yes. What if he doesn't come?"

"Why wouldn't he come?" Jemima asked. "Mama received his reply."

Alice turned to Jemima and said in a low voice, "But will he dance with me? What if he doesn't really care for me? What if he can't dance because of his arm? I wouldn't want him to be embarrassed."

Jemima took a deep breath. "Sometimes, Alice, you are an utter goose. Mr. Britton is brave and resourceful and he's faced many more frightening things in life than a pretty girl on a dance floor. Look, here are the Burkes," she added, to distract Alice. In truth, she had her own apprehensions. What if Felix Castle came? But then, what if he didn't? She couldn't decide which outcome worried her more. Mrs. Burke's gown was vivid pink, trimmed with green satin ribbon, and when she hugged the girls she left a cloud of patchouli. After her came the Latimers, whose impeccably tasteful evening clothes by comparison looked almost dowdy. Soon a steady stream of guests flowed past. Friends of their parents; their own friends; Robey Gregson looking somewhat tentative but very handsome. The sound of voices from the ballroom grew louder and louder.

Finally, "I think most of our guests are here," Helen said to Joshua. "And no one will dance until we do. So in a few minutes more we'll go in, shall we?"

"Your mother said just a few more minutes," Joshua murmured to Jemima. "Then we'll open the dancing."

Jemima nodded and passed along the message, then glanced at the door. She suddenly felt a clutching sensation in her chest.

"What's the matter? You just turned pale," Alice whispered to her. "Wait—that's not Mr. Castle coming up the stairs? Mama would never have invited him!" she protested with wide eyes.

"No," Jemima muttered. "I did." She linked her arm through Alice's.

"Mr. Castle!" she could hear her mother exclaiming. Then, after a tiny pause, "We are so glad that you could be with us this evening. You know Joshua, of course," she said. "Look, Mr. Castle is here," she said brightly to her husband.

"Castle!" Joshua said in surprise. "Well, my goodness!" And then, passing him down the receiving line, "Jemima, I believe you met Mr. Castle at the opera."

"How do you do?" she asked. He was smiling down at her with a hint of mischief in his eyes.

"Miss Wilcox," he answered, taking her hand. "I'm so delighted to be here this evening." Somehow her hand was still in his. Then he leaned forward and murmured, "I recognized your handwriting instantly. Did your parents know you'd invited me?"

"No," she told him, suppressing a grin. "And I intercepted your response."

"My word!" he answered with a warm smile. "In addition to your many other charms and accomplishments, Miss Wilcox, you seem to be adept at subterfuge. May I hope you'll save a dance for me? A waltz, by preference. Or several."

"Of course I will," she told him. "But you must also dance with Alice, and my mother. To explain."

Then Felix took Alice's hand with an elegant bow. "Miss Alice, I have led your sister astray. Can you forgive me? My intentions are respectable, I promise."

Alice was stupefied. "Mr. Castle," she managed to say, "what a surprise!" At that moment Helen leaned forward to catch her daughters' eyes. Alice read the shock on her mother's face, but it was Mr. Castle who spoke up.

"Mrs. Wilcox, may I call on you and Mr. Wilcox tomorrow morning?" he asked brightly. "We have quite a lot to discuss."

"I should think so!" Helen exclaimed, but she couldn't even pretend to be angry in the face of Jemima's radiant happiness.

As Felix slipped away into the ballroom, Alice watched him move easily among the other guests. "I should have known you were keeping a secret," she told her sister. "How did you dare send that invitation?"

Jemima shrugged her bare shoulders. "I couldn't think of another way to see him. Wouldn't you have done the same?"

"I don't know," Alice answered, and then she clasped her sister's gloved arm. "Look, he's here!" she whispered. And all of her worries about Thad Britton faded away. He was even handsomer than she had remembered, tall and lean and graceful. He unfurled his cloak with a sweeping gesture and handed it to an attendant. Alice watched him greet her mother and her father with an easy smile. His silky brown hair had been freshly cut, and he wore a pink rosebud in his buttonhole. When he took her hand, his warm smile made her knees feel weak.

"I hope you'll save a dance for me," he told her. "Believe it or not, I waltz rather well."

Alice, with her eyes raised to his, was momentarily speechless, but Jemima answered for her. "Of course *I* believe it," she said, "And I do hope you plan to dance with both of us."

"Of course, and with Mrs. Wilcox as well," he answered, smiling. "I want to ensure her good opinion of me."

Alice felt the heat of a blush on her cheeks, but she managed to say, "That won't be difficult."

Mr. Britton seemed to be the last guest to arrive. Helen peeked into the ballroom, where the guests were gathered, black evening coats mingling with glorious gowns in every possible color. She caught the eye of the manager, and nodded. Then she returned to where her family was clustered at the entrance.

"All right girls, it's time," she told them briskly. "Your father and I will begin the dancing. Nick, you and Jemima will follow. Alice, your uncle Noble is waiting for you. Then everyone will join in." She paused, looking at her lovely daughters for a moment. "I wish your grandmother were here to see you," she said. "She would have been so proud." The strains of a Strauss waltz began and Joshua stepped to her side.

Nick and Noble seized the girls and swept them out onto the dance floor. For a long moment, only the three couples whirled around the polished parquet, then other couples began to join them until the dance floor was full of radiant color and movement.

"So this is it, then?" Joshua said into Helen's ear. "The girls are out now?"

"This is the great moment," Helen told him.

Just then, the waltz wound down. The dancers stopped spinning, the gentlemen bowed to their partners and escorted the ladies to the gold chairs lining the floor. For a few moments ladies fanned themselves and checked their dance cards, then their next partners claimed each of them with an elegant bow.

Helen had chosen to forego the mazurka, a strenuous folk-dance that involved a great deal of stamping and whirling. Instead she slipped into the dining room to check on the arrangements for the supper. The guests at most dances were offered dainty sandwiches or tartlets and tiny squares of cake, but Helen saw no reason why the gentlemen should go hungry, so she had ordered sliced filets of beef and turkey breasts as well as scalloped potatoes and other vegetables, to be followed by various mousses and jellies. She was examining the handsome table settings when, to her astonishment, Felix Castle came into the room and approached her.

"Mrs. Wilcox," he said, "I'm so glad I caught you alone. Can you spare me a moment?"

"Why should I?" she asked with a surge of anger. "I am not aware that I invited you to this party."

"No," he agreed. "But Jemima did."

Helen stared at him, astonished. "How . . ." But after a moment's thought she realized it didn't matter. "I've been outmaneuvered, haven't I?" she asked him.

He nodded sympathetically. "I'm afraid so. The truth is, we've been conducting what I believe is known as a clandestine flirtation."

Helen stood gazing at him for a long moment while she struggled to take in his words. He was extremely handsome, she realized. "Just explain how you met, would you?"

"I went to your house in search of Joshua. I am very sorry about hounding him to pay his debts, Mrs. Wilcox, but perhaps you'll understand . . ."

"Never mind that," she said. "You went to our house, and I suppose Jemima answered the door."

"Just so. Something about the maid being busy elsewhere. We had a brief conversation. Then on the day your family moved, I happened to be at the Metropolitan Museum." He was still watching her, both sympathetic and amused. "She is a very compelling young woman, Mrs. Wilcox, and I think about her all the time. I hope eventually to make her my wife."

"But she's just coming out," Helen protested.

"*Eventually*," he repeated. "I'm asking for your approval."

"Does she know this?"

At that, he smiled gaily, and Helen realized how young he actually was. "I've made no secret of my interest in her," he said. "But I doubt she knows that I'd marry her tomorrow if I could."

"A suitor usually speaks to a girl's father," Helen pointed out. "Were you afraid to address Joshua with your request?"

"Not in the least," he answered. "But I wouldn't speak to Jemima without *your* approval, Mrs. Wilcox. And I'll do whatever you ask in order to win it."

Helen stood for a moment facing Felix Castle. "Nothing I know about you suggests that you would make a good husband," she told him. "So much nonsense about loud parties and improper women."

"Youthful follies," he answered, "often exaggerated. Please believe that all I want is to make Jemima happy. And I trust that she will indicate how I should do that." He smiled slightly and added, "She is rather direct, and I find that refreshing. If you don't mind my mentioning it, I know that your and Joshua's courtship was unconventional. Don't you think that Jemima might share your sense of adventure? Can you honestly imagine her being happy with that handsome blockhead Arthur Onderdonck, for instance?"

Helen couldn't help smiling. "That's what Joshua calls him, too." In the ballroom, the violins were playing the frenzied finale of the mazurka and she conceded, "I won't stand in your way, Mr. Castle. Jemima has always known her own mind. Let's go back to the ballroom. Perhaps she has a dance for you."

Naturally, Jemima did, having scribbled something illegible

next to two dances so that she could hold them for him. When she explained her ruse, Felix laughed out loud and kissed her hand. The first of them was a waltz, and as they took their first steps, he said into her ear, "I have won over your mother."

"Already?" she exclaimed. "She loathes you!"

"Not anymore," he said smugly. "I told her I want to marry you." She stared at him and missed a step, but he steadied her. "I'm not proposing here and now," he went on. "I want to woo you properly. What's your favorite flower?"

"I've never thought about it," Jemima told him. "Surprise me," she suggested.

"I will," he agreed promptly. "You're very light on your feet, Miss Wilcox. Has anyone ever told you that?"

"No," she answered, laughing. "Because I've only danced with boys until now and inexperienced boys, at that. You're a wonderful partner, Mr. Castle. You must have had a great deal of practice."

"Yes, but it all depends on the lady," he told her, looking into her eyes and pulling her just a bit closer.

Meanwhile across the room, Thad Britton had presented himself at Alice's side as the waltz began. "May I?" he asked, and then his arm was around her back and their feet moved together in the steps of the waltz.

He held her very close. Her right hand fell naturally to her skirt, which she lifted a few inches from the floor. She felt light and confident and utterly natural as he murmured in her ear, "I have been waiting very eagerly for this moment, Miss Alice."

"Couldn't you just call me Alice?"

"If you will call me Thad," he said. "We seem to be foregoing all of the usual formalities."

"Yes," she agreed, as he steered her into a spin. "Mama would say I was very forward." Her eyes met his and his hand moved slightly on her back.

"Charlie has missed you terribly," he said. "He keeps asking when you're coming back."

"I haven't been invited," she teased him. "But I wish you would bring Charlie to visit at our new house." There was a lock of hair falling against his cheek that she longed to tuck behind his ear.

"I wish we could dance forever," he murmured. "What would happen if I called on you without Charlie?"

"That would be delightful, too," Alice answered. "Perhaps I could play the piano for you."

"I would like that very much," he answered. "Do you suppose your parents would object?"

"To your calling on us?"

"To my courting you," he told her with a shy smile. "After all, I am older than you, a widower with a child, and maimed. While you are the loveliest debutante of your year, and, forgive me for mentioning it, an heiress."

"Nonsense," Alice said emphatically. "Besides, everyone knows the story of my parents' marriage. And look at them now."

Indeed, Joshua and Helen were at the center of the dance floor, whirling around as if they did it every day. Joshua said something into Helen's ear and she answered with a peal of laughter—possibly not ladylike but certainly joyful.

Looking back in later years, New York society saw the Wilcoxes' party as a turning point, the night when stuffy old New York began capitulating to the new people with their new money and their drive to belong. Yes, Hiram Burke's voice grew loud by the end of the evening. Yes, Jemima Wilcox plucked a glass of champagne from a passing tray without even consulting her mother. On the other hand, Nick Wilcox, although the youngest male there, heroically danced with matron after matron to his mother's astonishment and eternal gratitude.

Were some of the guests boisterous that evening? Yes, they were. There was more strong drink consumed than at the usual coming-out party. The music was livelier, the musicians more numerous. The young men—so often dragged unwilling onto the dance floor—responded eagerly to liquor and music, and swung the debutantes around the floor with gusto. There were no wallflowers.

It wasn't just novelty that affected the guests that evening: It was also exhilaration, possibly prompted by Delmonico's large dance floor, perhaps by the lavishness of the refreshments, certainly by the high spirits of the Wilcox girls. Greatly daring, Helen had included a cotillion in the evening's schedule, just before the supper. A dapper little man in impeccable tails chivvied the dancers into lines and led them through a sequence of formal figures that Joshua likened to square dancing—only, of course, more refined. When the cotillion ended and the dancers bowed to each other, the spectators burst into spontaneous applause. It was that kind of party. Well before midnight, everyone knew that *this* was the place to be on that evening in New York City.

Annabelle van Ormskirk, in a show of protest, had worn a three-year-old gown and a sad little demi-parure of seed pearls that, she informed everyone, had belonged to her great-grandmother. "And you know," she would add, touching the necklace, "we must wear our heirloom pearls, or they dry out and die." She spent much of the evening trying to disparage the location, the decorations, and the lavishness of the refreshments. "In my day," she told Noble, "a genteel tea party sufficed to introduce a young lady to society."

With a frankness unleashed by several glasses of champagne, he retorted, "Yes, and a dance like this is far more entertaining." Then, abandoning all caution, he went on, "How else could Caroline meet Robey Gregson? They seem to be getting along famously." Her eyes widened as she scanned the room and spied Caroline whirling in Robey's arms, looking blissfully happy. She straightened her spine, ready to protest, but at that moment Nick Wilcox approached and swept her off onto the dance floor before she could even protest. When he bowed to her at the end she managed to say, "Thank you, Nicholas, I enjoyed that very much," while Hans-Albert, standing nearby, eyed Nick with stupefaction.

Helen had engaged the musicians to play until twelve-thirty but sometime after midnight, her daughters crossed the dance floor together at the end of a spirited polka. They were both slightly flushed from the dance and a lock of Alice's hair had escaped from its pins to lie against her neck with a fetching effect.

"Mama," Jemima began, "must the band stop playing? Everyone is having such a lovely time!"

"I might ask them to stay on," Helen answered, trying not to smile. "But first you must confirm whether what Felix Castle told me is true. Have you been carrying on a clandestine flirtation? You were the most upset of all of us when he claimed the house!"

"Oh, yes, we've maintained a secret correspondence ever since then," Jemima told her mother flippantly, and kissed her on the cheek. "I have no sense of propriety at all. What's more, Alice has been flirting scandalously with a widower all evening," she went on, putting her arm around her sister's waist. "It's a wonder all these respectable people have stayed this long, Mama."

At that moment Joshua approached them from the edge of the dance floor. "Well, look, if it isn't the Wilcox women!" he called out, and Helen thought he had probably had too much champagne.

"Listen, I told the band they should stay for another hour," he told her. "No one wants to leave. People keep telling me they had no idea a debutante's dance could be so much fun." He lowered his voice slightly. "Lord, did you see Nick dancing with Annabelle? Why in the world?"

"Robey bet me I wouldn't," Nick announced, looming up behind his father's shoulder. "Ten dollars." He took out a gold piece and flipped it in the air, but missed the catch so it clattered to the floor, where he trapped it with his dancing pump.

"Nicholas Wilcox!" Helen exclaimed. "I've never seen anything so vulgar in my life! Please don't ever do that again in my presence!"

"Or if you do," Jemima said sweetly, "at least catch the coin. It's more debonair that way."

Nick stooped to retrieve the coin and slipped it into his waist-coat pocket. "I just need to practice more," he excused himself.

"No, you don't," Helen answered. "Just think what my mother would say!"

"'In my day . . .'" Alice began, but Jemima cut her off.

"Yes," she agreed. "But I'd say it's our day now, wouldn't you?"

ACKNOWLEDGMENTS

So many thanks go to so many people, beginning with my dear husband, Rick Hamlin, whose support has never wavered, no matter how far-fetched my ambitions seemed to me. My sister Eve asked some essential questions about the text at a crucial point, prompting a helpful change of focus. Writing this book would have been much harder without Stacy Schiff's tireless and witty encouragement.

I'm also deeply grateful to Emma Sweeney for several incisive early readings, and Margaret Sutherland Brown of Folio Literary Management for persistent encouragement and guidance.

The team at Putnam has been wise, brisk, energetic, and unflaggingly cheerful. Hats off to Helen Richard O'Hare, Ashley Di Dio for her swift and clear management of editorial matters, Claire Sullivan, Ivan Held, Sally Kim, Meredith Dros, Maija Baldauf, Tiffany Estreicher, Lorie Pagnozzi for creating a book design so evocative of the 1870s, Anthony Romondo, Christopher Lin for the beautiful and intriguing cover, Brennin Cummings, Cassie Sublette, Ashley Hewlett, Ellie Schaffer, Alexis Welby, and Ashley McClay.

Tara Singh Carlson's guidance made *Our Kind of People* better than I could have imagined. Throughout the editorial process she balanced enthusiasm with expertise and notable efficiency. I am so very grateful.

OUR KIND *of* PEOPLE

CAROL WALLACE

Discussion Guide

A Conversation with Carol Wallace

BOOK
ENDS

PUTNAM

DISCUSSION GUIDE

1. What did you think of Helen and Joshua's relationship throughout the novel as they encountered both riches and ruin? Discuss the different aspects you either admired or disliked.

2. Did you find some parallels between the Wilcox family and your own? If so, what?

3. What was your favorite custom during the process of the Wilcox girls' coming out into society? Were there any you disliked?

4. In many ways, Selina represents the old ways of New York City society, antiquated customs that Helen and her daughters sometimes come into conflict with. Are there any customs or traditions from the previous generation that you find yourself moving away from? If so, why and how?

5. Do you feel you are more like Jemima or Alice, and why?

6. Discuss the issues of social and economic class in *Our Kind of People*. How do you think these same matters are similar to or different from today's issues?

7. There is nothing more important than the Wilcox family bond in *Our Kind of People*. As the patriarch, do you think Joshua ultimately did the right thing for his family? Why or why not?

8. Which was your favorite scene in the novel, and why?

9. Were you surprised by the ending?

10. What do you feel lies ahead for the Wilcox family beyond the page? Where do you see each character ultimately ending up?

A CONVERSATION WITH CAROL WALLACE

What inspired you to write *Our Kind of People*? Did this writing process differ in any way from your previous experience writing both fiction and nonfiction?

I honestly don't remember what got me started on this book, except that I wanted to write something that I'd enjoy reading. It was a long process, involving several years and many drafts and a great deal of patience, especially on the part of my editor, Tara Singh Carlson. I normally write fast. But it took me ages to figure out exactly who was at the heart of this story. At one point, for instance, the book included a substantial section involving Robey's love life. An early reader whose judgment I value inquired why I'd given Robey so much space when he was a secondary character. I might have been so upset that I threw something that was on my desk. Possibly a keyboard. Which may or may not have survived the episode.

In fact, I probably cut almost as much material as remains. There was a *lot* about the business development of the Elevated, which I can only say was a rabbit hole I occupied for a while. And in early drafts, Alice was the elder daughter, until I realized it would be more interesting to have the introverted Jemima be the pioneer in entering society. I'm pretty sure I even had a backstory about Selina's debut all written out (it was very Edith Wharton-esque) but that didn't survive for very long.

Our Kind of People takes place at such a turning point, both innovatively and culturally, in American history. How did you perform the historical research required for this story?

I have always had a soft spot for the late nineteenth century, maybe because I grew up in a Victorian house. I love the literature of the period, and one of the more successful books I've written (coauthored in this case) was *To Marry an English Lord*, which is about American heiresses marrying English aristocrats during that period. So when it came time to research *Our Kind of People*, I knew my way around the New York social scene of the 1870s. The best part, though, was that this book is set late enough that mass production of images was pretty well established. For instance, the opera scenes in the book are set in the New York Academy of Music, which was torn down in the 1920s, but there are many images of its interior online that I could refer to when writing the scenes.

It also helps that I've lived in New York for a long time, and over the years I've profited from cultural experiences that played to my interests. For instance, the Museum of the City of New York has a collection of glorious turn-of-the-century dresses and accessories. Helen's big fan, the one she carries to the opera late in the book, is based on a fan in their collection that I saw in the 1980s and never forgot!

Quite a few reminders of Old New York are still plainly visible. The north side of Washington Square in Greenwich Village, for instance, is lined with beautiful houses like Selina's. And while the Hudson Elevated Railroad is fictional, several portions of our mass-transit trains do run on aboveground tracks, and I take them often. One of my first apartments in New York was on the third floor of a brownstone that certainly gave its shape to the Wilcox house—especially the mirror and hat stand in the front hall. And the Merchants' House Museum on East 4th Street inspired the décor of the newlywed Wilcoxes' home.

Are any of these captivating characters based on real people, or inspired by anyone in particular?

Annabelle van Ormskirk is not exactly based on the famous

society doyenne Caroline Astor, but anytime you have a wealthy wife throwing her considerable weight around the New York social scene in the late nineteenth century, Mrs. Astor does come to mind. It is also a fact that the Astor money came from real estate, and that Mrs. Astor's social power relied more on her bossiness and determination than on her charm. Sounds familiar, doesn't she?

There are so many scandalous and gasp-worthy moments. What was your favorite scene in the novel, and why?

I especially relished writing the scene in Chapter 17 where Selina drags Helen over to the Van Ormskirks' to confront Annabelle. There's something so delicious about those ladies pretending to be polite while attacking each other with every (verbal) weapon at their disposal.

Whether it be romantic, familial, or social, there are various complex relationships throughout the novel. Which dynamic was your favorite to write, and why?

I'd have to say that all of Selina's relationships were fun to think about because as a character she's just a bundle of contradictions. She's so pretty and delicate and feminine, but she has an iron will. And while she rides roughshod over poor Helen, she does truly have her daughter's best interests at heart. The problem is that she simply cannot imagine herself into anyone else's situation, so she believes that what would work for her would also be good for Helen. Some of Selina's confidence comes from never having adapted to the way New York has changed in her lifetime. Or maybe she hasn't adapted because she has no emotional imagination. And then, just when you are ready to write her off as selfish and cold, she reveals her great love for her family. She was quite unpredictable, even to me.

Although this is a Gilded Age historical novel, are there particular rules of cutthroat high society that you feel still apply today? What do you feel harkens most to our modern-day rituals?

What a terrific question! I'm always surprised at the extent to which certain manners and rituals of nineteenth-century society have endured. If you've ever received an engraved invitation to a formal event like a wedding from one of the stationers like Cartier or Tiffany, you're seeing exactly what might have been sent to Helen Wilcox. I certainly grew up answering those invitations in the traditional way: "Miss Carol Wallace/ accepts with pleasure/ the kind invitation of/ etc." Tuxedos haven't changed much in a hundred years. White tie hasn't changed. Tables are set in a way that Annabelle van Ormskirk would have recognized (though she would probably have thought our meals rather skimpy). And don't get me started on the thank-you notes!

Who was your favorite Wilcox family member to write, and why?

I'd have to split that choice between Helen and Jemima. I'm a mother, so I relished writing about the domestic and child-rearing part of Helen's life. It's so clear that she would do anything to ensure Jemima's and Alice's and Nick's success. But it's also clear that her understanding of the social world corresponds more to the world she knew at their age than to what they face. It's a natural dynamic in a family, isn't it? The younger generation is always willing to push limits that their parents took for granted. And Helen's anxious; I often picture her with a little furrow between her brows, as if she's scanning any room for the smallest thing that might go wrong. That's why I so enjoyed her behavior at the opera late in the book. She throws caution to the wind in a surprising way.

As for Jemima, don't authors always love their bookish characters? Don't we assign them our own self-doubts, our own worries about how we appear to other people? I'm not saying that Jemima is my alter ego, but I could always find my way into her thoughts, and that wasn't necessarily true of every other character.

Is there something you'd like readers to take away from the Wilcox family's story?

Another wonderful question! This isn't something I was thinking about while I wrote, but in the end I think what we can learn from the Wilcoxes is that there are often going to be conflicting interests in a family. Sometimes things aren't going to go our way: We have to move for a spouse's job, we can't go to the school we prefer, we have to share bedrooms with siblings we can't stand. I'd like to think that the Wilcoxes' couple of bumpy years show us the value of flexibility and taking the long view. Which, alas, is so often easier said than done!

Without giving anything away, did you always know how the story would end?

I wanted a satisfying ending, to be sure. But it was a while before I understood what exactly that would look like. In a way, though, the larger challenge for a writer—larger than wrapping things up—is to figure out how your characters are going to be challenged in the course of the narrative. That's what really shows us what they're made of. So each of them has to go through a trying experience that resolves, but perhaps not in the way they'd imagined.

What's next for you?

Writing *Our Kind of People* was so much fun that I didn't want to stop, so I've been poking around 1880s New York. I'm hoping I can build a book around two real-life figures, Collis Huntington, a married railroad baron from California, and his eventual second wife, Arabella. The title I'm working with is *She Calls Herself a Widow*. Which Arabella actually did, when she first came to New York from Richmond, Virginia, with her son, Archer. She lived very grandly, supported by Collis and ignored by New York society. Sounds like fun, doesn't it?

ABOUT THE AUTHOR

Carol Wallace has written more than twenty books, including *The New York Times* bestseller *To Marry an English Lord*, which was an inspiration for *Downton Abbey*. She is also the author of a historical novel, *Leaving Van Gogh*, and a co-author of *The Official Preppy Handbook*. Wallace holds degrees from Princeton University and Columbia University, and is the great-great-granddaughter of Lew Wallace, author of the novel *Ben-Hur: A Tale of the Christ*, which was first published in 1880. She currently lives in New York, New York.

Visit Carol Wallace Online
CarolWallaceBooks.com
CarolWallaceBooks
Carol_Wallace
Carol_Wallace